The Fulbourn Pitch & Sickle

Book Five

THE DIABOLUS CHRONICLES

D K GIRL

The Fulbourn© 2022 by Danielle K Girl

Cover Art by Deranged Doctor Design

Edited by Inspired Ink Editing

ISBN: **978-0-6453274-6-5**

All rights reserved.

This is a work of fiction.

CHAPTER 1

S ilas lurked outside his own bedroom door like a ne'er-do-well. He had been banished from the room for days. His *own* bloody room. He was beyond frustrated with the situation, but he knew better than to argue with a sickly daemon. And Pitch was certainly unwell.

Silas pressed an ear to the door, listening in on the conversation taking place inside. In truth, it was less conversation, more battle of wills and wits.

'If you just hold steady, Tobias, this will be over in a moment.' Jane was her usual measured self, calm as a summer breeze. 'You are making this far more difficult than it ought to be.'

Silas winced. Her reasoning would not go down well at all. His fingers tightened around the mahonia blooms he'd just picked from the garden. Soon enough, the crash of something fragile against the floorboards arrived.

'You gib-faced, vazey, hedge-creeping bitch,' Pitch decried, and proceeded to let loose with a string of quite terrible ways he was going to show Jane how difficult he could be if she did not cease and desist with making his existence a misery.

Silas had not discerned exactly what the air elemental was doing to the daemon. There was far too much yelling to make out the details, but he knew it was supposed to make Pitch's life *less* of a misery. The treatment

1

he was undergoing was designed to rid the prince's body of the lingering dregs of Gu.

For a time after their escape from Gidleigh House and the greensward, it seemed as though the daemon would suffer no ill effects of his poisoning, something Lady Satine was mightily impressed with. By her account, the prince should be dead, or so close to it they might as well measure him for his coffin. Neither was the case, which evidently she was pleased with.

As was Silas.

'Destroying a vase is not going to speed up this process.' Jane was prim. 'What if that was Silas's favourite you just ruined?'

'The man adores headstones,' Pitch scoffed. 'He will not give a shit if he's missing an ugly piece of porcelain from his bedroom dresser.'

'He may care that the flowers in that vase are now strewn about his room. You've noticed, no doubt, that he is partial to anything from the garden.'

'Of course I've bloody noticed. But he brought those flowers days ago. They are as good as dead now. And he brought them to *me*. So they are mine to do with what I like. And I *like* to see them strewn about on the floor.'

Silas glanced at the new arrangement he held. He knew the floral offerings to be silly, really. But he hadn't known what else to do. Several hours after Lucifer's unsettling visit Pitch had declared himself unwell. The prince had slunk off to Silas's room, declaring he intended to sleep off a sudden headache and churning stomach. Alone. When Silas checked in on him a few hours later, he'd found Pitch buried beneath the blankets and pillows till he was all but hidden save for a few lengths of gold-streaked hair peeking through the covers. His light brown shade was altering each time he used the flame, and there were far more gold highlights at the fore now. The prince had been fast asleep, and Silas had slept on the couch rather than disturb him. One night had since extended to three, and an upset stomach to violent regurgitation.

'Goodness, you talk a load of rubbish, don't you?' Jane now was most derisive. 'I can see on your face you are quite horrified at what you've done.'

'You need spectacles, then. I don't give a damn about those fucking flowers.'

'You are a terrible liar. How surprising, I thought you were a master.'

Pitch muttered but the words were lost to Silas.

Jane was right that the daemon lied about not caring for the flowers. When Silas had brought him the first bouquet of golden spiked mahonia three days ago, Pitch had gone all shades of fetching pink as he watched Silas arrange them in the vase at his bedside.

'You were out there in the cold, gathering these for me?'

Silas had been taken aback by the sheer disbelief in the prince's tone.

'I was. There aren't so many as I'd hoped – slim pickings at this time of year, of course – but they are quite pretty, don't you think?'

Pitch had stared at the simple bouquet with a look Silas could not unravel. When he'd not replied, Silas moved to pick up the vase.

'They aren't making you feel more wretched, are they? I can take them away.'

'No.' Pitch had lunged to stay Silas's hand. 'Leave them...please.'

The heat of the daemon's skin had warmed Silas through, and he had seated himself gingerly on the edge of the bed. 'Is there anything I can do for you? Some chamomile tea, perhaps? Some cake?'

The prince, propped up on one elbow, drained and bleary-eyed but no less beguiling, had shaken his head. 'I couldn't eat. Satty said Mr Ahari believes he's found something that will rid me of what remains of the poison, but that old bastard is taking his time bringing it to me.'

'That's good news though, isn't it? You'll soon be feeling well again.'

Pitch nodded, making a vague sound of agreement. He was watching Silas closely, or rather, Silas's mouth. 'Being ill is inconvenient. I don't like being kept from things.' He wet his lips with a delicate swipe of his tongue and edged closer, making the air between them thinner. Silas's pulse had begun to race. 'Do you suppose...that it might be...helpful to...' Pitch had paused, and the air had crackled. At least, that is how it had seemed to Silas, who had been awash with indecision. He'd longed to press in, to offer the kiss he thought was being asked for, but what if he was terribly wrong? The daemon prince was fragile as a butterfly's wings with all that had been done to him...and what was now expected of him.

So Silas had held back, waiting for Pitch to lead the way.

The daemon had slipped his hand behind the ankou's neck, urging him closer, vanishing any ambiguity. With a hushed sigh, Silas had leaned down.

Only to be slapped back.

'Gods, get out! Get out!' The daemon had rolled away, lunging for the chamber pot beneath the bed, and been very, vigorously ill.

That gut-churning path had continued for him ever since. Reaching for the pot once or twice an hour, according to Jane, and Tyvain, who had only dared go in the once and not again, for fear the daemon would make good on his promise to tip the severe black liquid he was vomiting all over her.

Silas had not been allowed anywhere near the sickroom...his own bedroom...ever since.

Now here he stood, flowers in hand, listening in like the voyeur Pitch accused him of being.

'Oh fuck,' the unhappy prince cried. 'Are you not done with tormenting me, you daft elemental cow?'

'Do stop carrying on. So long as the akaname are still feeding, it means you have Gu left in your blood. Wouldn't you rather it all be gone, or do you think it quite fetching to be doubled over and hurling your guts out?'

'Piss off.'

'Good gods, sit still, will you?' Jane admonished. 'They keep sliding off. You need to let them get their pincers into you.'

Silas set his hand on the door handle, his guilt growing. If he had heeded Pitch's warning about Balthazar Crane, they would never have stopped at Gidleigh House. And there would be no need for the daemon to have *pincers* set upon him at all.

'Right, well that's all of them. None left after this, so we best hope they finish the job,' Jane said. 'Mr Ahari says you are to leave them on as long as you can endure.'

Rightfully so, Pitch thought little of that and voiced his displeasure in no uncertain, rather bawdy terms. Silas was so preoccupied with how painful this supposed treatment was that he heard no sign of Jane ready-ing to leave until the door handle turned beneath his grasp.

He took a hurried step back, as though he were the sort of man who could slink into the shadows.

The door opened and Jane appeared. The oddest thing occurred. A melody played in Silas's mind. One he could read as though it were sheet music before him. The way an educated man might read the newspaper. *Elemental. Air.*

Of course, he'd already been told what type of natural Jane was, but now Silas *knew* it.

Silas could not see the hues, the auras, that surrounded naturals, for the most part. He'd glimpsed the aura on the traitorous ankou, Balthazar Crane, and the melody denoting his presence had played along, sure enough. But that day it had been the bandalore singing the ankou's truth. Not today. The scythe was in a mother-of-pearl inlaid jewellery box on the mantel downstairs.

The greensward had, it seemed, done more than shake loose distant, ancient memories.

'Did I startle you, Silas?' Jane smiled. 'If you were seeking to hide, it can be difficult to do from one like me.' She touched her nose. 'Especially when you have those lovely specimens with you.' Jane nodded her head at the flowers in Silas's grasp.

He hid them behind his back. 'How is he?'

She wore her long hair tied back in a single bind, and a dress of loose chequered linen. 'Aside from cantankerous, whiny, and generally in a mood?' she said. 'He is handling it reasonably well. He's not being ill so often and says the cramps are not as bad now. It looks promising.' She patted the small metal box she carried, a biscuit tin for shortbread normally. 'Can't say the same for the akaname though. They don't last long after they have a full belly of the stuff. But they aren't known as filth-lickers for nothing. Their propensity for a diet of fouler things seems to be getting the job done. Mr Ahari made a good call with rec-ommending them.'

Silas nodded, peering over her shoulder. He could just make out the foot of the bed, and a lumpy shape beneath the covers that might be

Pitch's feet. Heat emanated from the room, as likely from the daemon himself as the small crackling fire in the hearth.

'Would you like to go in?' Jane stepped aside.

'He doesn't want me there.'

'Go away, Silas.' Pitch was muffled.

'See?'

'He's an idiot.' Jane shrugged. 'And you are here anyway.'

'I said no, Silas.' The daemon was firm. Definitely cantankerous.

A displaced wind moved against Silas's back, sending his hair into his eyes. The force of the sudden breeze pushed him forward, sending him across the threshold of his room.

'There you go.' Jane was most cheery. 'I'll be back to check on you in a little while.'

The door shut behind Silas with a decisive clunk.

Pitch lay on his stomach, with the pillow over his head and the blankets piled over his lower body, covering it entirely. He was shirtless, a state that usually would have pleased Silas very much, but not so this day. Pitch's back was peppered with creatures that resembled leeches. The shapes were similar, but the colouring very different. These specimens were mottled shades of oranges and reds and browns, like slug-shaped autumn leaves. And they were at least double the size of any leech Silas had had the misfortune to find in his boots. Where they sat, Pitch's skin was the purple and yellow of fresh and old bruises.

'Gods, you are still here, aren't you, Silas?'

'I am.'

'Clearly, you *have* gone deaf since I last saw you, then,' Pitch huffed from beneath his pillow.

'Do the akaname pain you?'

'Of course they pain me, Silas. They have teeth like razors.' Pitch pulled his head from beneath the pillow. The movement set the creature nearest his right shoulder blade curling in on itself, and the daemon hissed like an angry serpent. 'Fuck.'

'Are they helping at all?' Silas asked, clutching his silly flowers. It struck him that no melody had erupted on seeing the prince. No musical declaration *Here lies a daemon*. There was every chance Silas's new skill was as temperamental as his memory.

'I suppose they are not making it worse.'

Silas decided to rely on Jane's assertion that Pitch *was* improving. 'Are these creatures from Arcadia?'

Pitch snorted. 'Gods, no. Lucifer refused to deliver me an antidote. I was not dying, which he was no doubt disappointed about, and he didn't wish to make another journey so soon for fear of drawing attention. So I am to suffer through, as a woman does through her morning sickness.'

His irritation caused him to move a little too much, and his groan had Silas hurrying to the bedside.

'Try to stop moving about.' He dropped the flowers onto the bedside table, next to the remnants of the shattered vase which Jane had piled there. There was a damp patch on the fawn-coloured rug.

'And *you* try to stop bloody fussing, Silas. Equally impossible tasks I'd say.' Pitch kept his face turned towards the window. 'I want you to go away.'

'The problem is I don't wish to go. So here we are, at an impasse.' Jane had been right to push him. Silas should have shouldered his way in here before now, no matter the daemon's tantrum. 'I really don't care less if you throw up on me.'

'Well, I bloody do,' Pitch said, a little too emphatically, twitching in pain. 'This is not about you.'

'It is very much about me actually.' Silas stooped to pick up a shard of pottery that Jane had missed. 'I fail to see why I must be banished. From my own room at that.'

'You know why.' So low Silas barely caught it.

'Because you seem to think it a terrible thing if I see you in any distress, but that is exactly when I am most concerned with seeing you.'

'Gods, you are ridiculous.'

'Not so much as you.'

That made Pitch laugh, which was not really a good thing at all. It caused him to jolt. The akaname must have bitten in harder, for he released a furious yell.

'Enoch's fucking taint!' The cursing went on for some time.

'Easy now, stay still.' Silas forgot his own rule about touching the daemon unless requested and laid his hand on Pitch's bare shoulder. The prince's ribs flared with a deep inhale. 'I'm sorry...for what you are having to –'

'Stop apologising,' Pitch said, soft but curt. 'If I have to move to slap you, I won't be pleased.'

'Nor will I.'

Pitch's body shuddered with another stifled laugh. 'Fuck. You are not helping at all.'

'Perhaps I *should* go, and leave you be.'

'You're here now.' He was short. 'So you may as well be useful. You could do that...rubbing thing you do to me.'

Silas's brow lifted. 'Rubbing?' His mind went a tad feral. 'You'd like me to...rub you?'

'My dear fellow, where are your thoughts taking you?'

'Nowhere,' Silas croaked.

'And Jane thinks *me* a terrible liar.' A gentle chuckle came from the daemon. 'When I can roll over without heaving, you can show me exactly where you have a preference for rubbing me, but for now I was hoping you might just tend to my back. Like you did in the carriage, and when that man with his witch bottles vexed me.'

Silas nodded, face ablaze. 'Of course. I wasn't sure if it annoyed your or pleased you, to be honest.'

'It does both.' Pitch was more teasing than unkind.

'Oh.'

'But I don't hate it either way.'

'I suppose that's as good a compliment as I'll hear.'

'Yes, so do get on with it.'

With a smile, and a trembling hand, Silas ran his fingertips over Pitch's shoulder and down along one of the prongs on the pitchfork tattoo that had given the daemon his nickname.

He stayed well clear of the akaname as he went. There were not so many of them as to make it difficult, five of the creatures latched on to pale skin, their bruising marks fanning around them. Neither they nor the daemon moved as Silas traced his way over the hint of muscle and bone, keeping well clear of the section where he knew the halo's scars to be. Pitch sighed every now and then but was otherwise silent.

Silas's pulse thudded along as he worked, his chest tight with contentment. Bloody hell, the prince was heavenly to touch. Velvet skinned with the jut of hard muscle hinting right beneath, an exquisite mix of soft and hard that he wanted to drink in.

He had meant what he said to Pitch about having no expectations, that he would give the daemon all the distance he required as he recovered from what had happened to him at Gidleigh House. But how utterly wonderful it was to be allowed this close again. The nights on the couch had been lonely. And his worries great.

The task assigned to the daemon prince was a lofty one. Destroying a cursed halo sounded like anything but a walk in the park.

Silas would be by Pitch's side, of course. A dozen Lalassu's could not have stopped him, but he feared he may not be able to lessen the load upon the prince's shoulders as well as he hoped. Silas may be Nephilim at his core, but he had much to learn...to remember...about what advantage that could give him.

'Will you do something for me, Sickle?' The daemon was drowsy, as close to content as he'd sounded in a while.

Anything, was what Silas wished to say. *Anything at all.* But it was far too soppy. He'd be laughed out of the room, and rightly so. 'That depends what it is you ask for,' he replied, drifting his fingertips down near the rise of Pitch's arse beneath the sheet. Christ, it was difficult not to linger there too long.

The prince turned his head, looking at Silas. It took effort not to inhale too sharply. Certainly the daemon was pale, and his lips were stained blue by the foul Gu that had drenched them many times, but his gaze was precise, focused, and breathtaking.

'When you're done...and there is no hurry...take the watch with you when you leave.' He gestured at Silas's wardrobe. 'I put it in the pocket of one of your coats so as to keep it away...but it still bothers me.'

'Bothers you? How so?'

'Will you just keep it for me? Keep it at a distance?'

There was a note there in his tone, one that warned Silas about asking any more. 'I will.'

Pitch glanced at the table, where the tiny pile of rubble and fresh flowers lay. 'I shouldn't have done that.' He tilted his head so that his hair flopped forward, covering his eyes. 'I'm sorry I broke the vase.'

'I wasn't particularly fond of it.'

'It was hideous.'

'I'll not challenge that.' Silas smiled, and the daemon relaxed beneath his fingertips. He traced a path between two of the akaname, slipping his finger over the nub of Pitch's spine, crossing the dark line of the amuletum. 'Will you tell me why you wish me to keep the watch? Surely it is important that you have it safe with you?'

Pitch sighed. 'Promise me you won't get all bothered and fearful if I tell you why?'

Silas struggled not to show just how bothered and fearful he'd become immediately. 'Pitch, what is it?'

'Gods, there it is. You have your wide-eyed-with-horror face on. You do adore that one.'

'Tobias.'

'Since when do you ever call me Tobias? I don't like it at all.'

'Tell me what is wrong.' Silas was stern.

'A small thing really,' Pitch said. 'Why did you stop rubbing my back? I didn't tell you to stop.'

'I wasn't waiting on your orders, Your Highness.' Silas felt the daemon tense. 'Sorry. I didn't intend to...damn it, Pitch tell me about the watch, now.'

The prince waited a few moments in imperious silence, and then, 'Having it too near...hurts. The watch seems to stir the markings of the halo. It is...not pleasant. And as you are capable of carrying death's blade with no trouble, I figure you can carry Seraphiel's token too.'

'How badly does it hurt you?' Silas was not sure he'd believe the answer but he'd ask.

'Badly enough. But there's every chance it won't be quite so annoying when the Gu is out of my body entirely. Perhaps I'm just more sensitive to such things at the moment.' Pitch turned his head, huffing. 'I knew I shouldn't have told you. Now I have to see that face of yours all bent out of shape.'

Silas shifted his jaw, as though that might rid his features of concern. 'I'm grateful you told me, and yes I'm worried, of course I am, but I agree. Let's wait and see how you feel once the akaname are done with. I will happily carry the watch for you until then.'

The watch that bade them to search for Edward Charters.

Pitch's illness had been a distraction from Silas's other great worry: the whereabouts of Charlie. Yesterday, he'd nearly cried with relief when Tyvain told him the lad had been spotted at a pub near the Charters' residence in Mayfair just last week. Silas's heart had lifted at the news and then sunk just as readily when the trail ran cold. The soothsayer was out now searching. Jane too, when she wasn't tending Pitch.

Lady Satine had denied Silas's repeated request to join them. 'We must be discreet,' she had said. 'The maleficent sorcerers have you firmly in their sights, Silas. And it would do Charlie no favours for them to know that you are so desperate to find him. If you would step into a magick circle to help a stranger, what wouldn't you do for a dear friend? Your kindness is rather your weakness too.'

He knew she spoke some sense, but it made it no less easy to wait behind.

'We will find them, Silas.' Pitch slid his hand over the covers to find Silas's knee. 'Charlie and the lieutenant both.'

Silas nodded, trying to shake off his deep concern. 'I'm sure we will. What do you suppose you need to find Edward for? Have you had any time to think on it?'

'Oh, it will be something trivial, I'm sure. He's only human, after all. Likely I need something he can give me, or show me. Perhaps Seraphiel hid instructions on how I'm supposed to destroy this fucking halo somewhere in the Charters' family library, and I'll have papercuts from here to Arcadia when I finally head off on this moronic quest.'

'Well, I can't help you with the reading, but I can turn a decent page –'

Pitch's smile began to slide along his lips, only to turn sharply down. 'Fuck, chamber pot, where is it?' He came alive, wriggling his way over to the other side of the bed, hissing bitter curses in between wretches. The akaname on his back all curled in like snails balling themselves up against a predator. Silas hurtled to his feet, snatching up the pot which was actually beneath the bedside table, and raced around the bed, boots crunching on another stray piece of vase. He only just managed to position the porcelain beneath Pitch's head as the first wave came. The prince's slender body jerked with spasms as the Gu made its sudden appearance, with it a sour stench.

Pitch coughed something about the ankou leaving the fucking room. But Silas ignored every barely distinguishable word. He'd not be chased away again.

He stayed on, holding back the daemon's hair until all was said and, very messily, done.

CHAPTER 2

The akaname, or filth-lickers, as Mr Ahari named them, had been purchased from a black market stall down Croydon way. A market, according to Tyvain, that was run by naturals of some ill-repute and with a reputation for selling poor-quality stock with a propensity for causing accidents and ills. Their conversation had Silas in a fluster by its end, but Jane was adamant that Mr Ahari knew exactly what he was doing.

The air elemental, thankfully, was right.

It took near on a hundred of the unfortunate creatures to make it so, but Pitch was much improved by midday. And by the time Jane was finished taking her lunch, she had declared the treatment done with. She stopped in to remove the last of the akaname from their tethered places upon Pitch's back, and despite the grunted demands by the daemon to do so, Silas refused to leave the room. He'd stood by as Pitch gritted his teeth as tiny fangs were coaxed from his skin. The akaname had rounded mouths, leaving small pinwheels of punctured skin behind. The bruises looked awful with their mottled colouring but would disappear before long.

Pitch slept for hours after Jane was done, only stirring when the afternoon considered giving way to evening. On waking, he seemed bright and restless enough that Silas suggested a short walk around the grounds. The afternoon was mild, the fresh air would do the prince good, and Silas himself was quite desperate to be outside. Nearer to the graveyard for a spell, if he could encourage the daemon that far.

When Silas suggested the walk, Pitch rolled his eyes and declared that in Arcadia this sort of carrying on would see his valet Forneus, the skriker's namesake, lose two of his seven eyes for insubordination.

In the end, it was the promise of strawberry tarts that drew the daemon from his sickbed, but it took another half hour of infuriating coaxing and goading to have Pitch dressed well enough for a stroll. The blasted fellow could not decide on which coat to wear, so in the end Silas thrust a purple velvet number at him, told him he looked beautiful in it as he did most things, and ushered the preening prince downstairs.

For himself the choice was simple. Silas threw on his newly laundered and repaired-once-more royal-blue Inverness coat and headed for the front door. Pitch took his time, making much of his limp because it suited him to do so today.

'I think actually my hip is too worrisome to bother,' he announced, just shy of the door.

Silas had to take a breath before he spoke. 'I could find you a cane, I'm sure.'

'If you wish to be beaten with it, certainly.'

'You are likely stiff for having been immobile so long. All the more reason a walk is just what you need.' Silas was determined to get at least one daemonic foot outside, even though his ears might bleed soon from so much complaining.

He opened the door, and a jolly little tune played itself to him as Silas's newfound musicality returned. Quirky, spirited notes revealed the supernatural nature of the chap he had been hoping to find outside his door.

Elemental. Earth.

Gilmore, grumpy and very gruff but marvellous in the kitchen, stood with balled hands on his hips, glaring up at them both. His peaked cap of berry red was quite fetching, setting off the pale colouring of his hair nicely.

'Perfect timing,' Silas said. 'Have you brought the tarts, Gilmore?'

'You're about to put ya giant foot in them.' The gnome jerked his chin. Silas peered down to find a small wicker basket on the doormat.

'Thank you ever so much.' Silas swept up the basket and stepped out onto the porch, making room for the prince to join him.

'Gods, gnome,' Pitch said. 'What's on your head? Did someone drop a tub of strawberry jam on you?'

Gilmore snatched his cap away, revealing a head of pale hair that looked like it had never put a strand out of place in its life. His deep-set eyes were filled with a quiet contempt.

Silas was not so happy himself as he turned to the daemon. 'Really? You are going to be churlish with the gentleman who has just made you his strawberry tarts, which I recall you saying once were without equal?'

Pitch had the decency to look admonished. 'Fine.' He waved an airy hand. 'Thank you, gnome. Much obliged. But that doesn't change the fact that your cap looks foolish.'

'Not as damn foolish as your face,' Gilmore retorted. 'Pity you didn't turn yourself inside out with all that gagging.'

'Even wearing my own entrails for jewellery I'd still be more pleasant to look upon than you.'

'Christ.' Silas picked up the basket, in no mood for the pair of them. 'I'm going to go for a walk, and I'm taking these. If you want to come along, Pitch, do. If not, I truly do not care. You can stay here and trade juvenile insults.' He tipped his head at the gnome. 'Thank you for these, Gilmore. I appreciate your haste with preparing them. Good afternoon, gentlemen.'

'Afternoon, Mr Mercer.' Gilmore smirked, casting a snide glance towards Pitch. 'Guess even your ankou has his limits with you, then.'

'I'm not his bloody ankou,' Silas muttered.

He strode away and followed his nose towards the dank, heavenly scent of the graveyard that was drifting in on the easterly breeze. A place where he might find some momentary peace. Pitch's issues with the Gu were resolved, but that was not to say all worries were extinguished. Far from it. Charlie's whereabouts plagued Silas. He'd not slept well in days and was at times empty-headed with fatigue.

Lost in his thoughts, Silas was almost across the green before he re-alised how quickly he was walking. Far too brisk a pace if Pitch had followed.

Which, to his surprise, he had. He lumbered along in an awkward jog that fell to a casual walk the moment Silas turned to look.

'What?' Pitch said. 'You are holding the tarts for ransom. I shall have to endure your company.'

Silas kept the smile from his face until he turned about and the dae-mon could not see.

#

The late-afternoon air was more bracing than Silas expected. As they sauntered into the garden, his nose was dripping and his ungloved hands ached from the cold. But there was pleasing colour in Pitch's cheeks, especially since he'd eaten several of Gilmore's tarts. Edward's watch had been left behind, resting alongside the bandalore in the jewellery box on the mantel, so he was not plagued by that discomfort at least.

But that did not seem to have made him any more congenial.

'I understand your obsession for being outdoors now,' the prince declared, licking at his pastry-flecked fingers. 'We are surrounded by dead things. You must feel right at home.'

'Well, it may appear all is dead, but it's not the case. Look here. These little buds on the shrubbery here? This is a Christmas rose. This will be a blanket of white before long.'

'Yes, because it will be damned well snowing. Gods, snow is tiresome.'

As though the garden were offended, Pitch tripped upon an exposed root. He would have gone flying if not for Silas's quick, steadying hand.

'I'm quite all right. No need for that.' Pitch adjusted his velvet tailcoat, despite the rich purple fabric sitting perfectly well. 'Pass me another tart, will you?'

'No. Not yet. It would be foolish for you to gorge yourself.' Silas pointed to a bush with bare branches and creamy-white blooms with yellow stamen. 'Winter honeysuckle. Lovely, isn't it?'

'Hardly the word I'd use.'

Pitch was not going to receive another tart for some time.

'I think it's beautiful.'

'It's not terribly ugly, I suppose.' Pitch snapped a bloom free. He twirled it between his fingers, and quite out of the blue, he said, 'If we hear nothing from the hag by dinnertime, I'm going to take matters into my own hands. I will go myself to search for your little friend and Mr Charters, whether Satty permits it or not. I must. It is as simple as that.'

Silas thought Lady Satine allowing such a plan unlikely, considering all they had told her of the Morrigan's exploits at the greensward, but his heart lightened to imagine it.

It was Pitch who had informed the Lady of what the sorcerers were calling themselves. He had learned the name from the Alp daemon. Pitch said very little else to the Lady about what happened between him and Onoskolis. Silas would guard that secret forevermore, if that was what the prince wanted.

Pitch touched at the flower's stark-white petals.

'Whatever plan you have in mind to find them,' Silas said, 'I'm going with you, of course. If Charlie has been harmed in any way...' He couldn't finish that train of thought. 'Tyvain should never have sent him off on such a foolish task.'

'Now, now, Sickle. I'm sure your little friend is quite well. Mr Charters is hardly one for dangerous pursuits. He's dreadfully sensible...most of the time. Perhaps Charlie has chosen to disappear.'

'Absolutely not.' He shook his head, his fingers curling about a flower-laden branch of honeysuckle. 'You saw for yourself how keen he was to remain with Old Bess at Harvington Hall. He wouldn't simply disappear.' If only he could speak to Pitch of the connection he had with Charlie's family line, the ancient blood that somehow bound them to Silas and the bandalore. But he could not speak of such things without revealing too much of his Nephilim origins. And the prince had far too many concerns weighing him down as it was.

'Fine,' Pitch said. 'Then maybe it is Tyvain's carrier pigeons that are to blame. That is how the messages from your lad were coming, was it not?'

'Yes. I believe so.' Silas nodded, clinging to the idea that Charlie was likely fine but the bird carrying his message was not. Caught by a farmyard cat perhaps, or in the sights of a hunter's gun.

'But, Silas, I have to admit, I do not care much about the whereabouts of your lover –' The prince raised his hand at Silas's attempts to protest. 'Well, you fucked, did you not?'

'Once only –'

'Apparently that was more than enough for you to develop an unseemly softness for the lad.'

Silas blinked. Pitch's words were spiked with a strange accusation. 'I care for Charlie's welfare,' he said. 'Yes, of course. And this is not an easy world for him.'

Pitch fluttered his fingers as though the conversation bored him. He tended to act this way whenever Charlie was mentioned, and yet it was often he who brought up the lad to begin with. 'Whatever the case may be,' he said. 'He is not who is important here. Edward is, according to the watch my dear old papa shoved at me. If there is ever to be an end to all this, I need to find him.'

'*We* need to find him,' Silas said, pointedly. 'I'm terribly worried about Charlie, but I fear for the lieutenant as well. He was such a troubled man when I saw him last. The angel's possession had left him in a terrible state.' Silas actually bit his tongue. 'I did not mean to be so –'

Pitch traced a finger over the petals. 'Truthful? Edward is a wreck, and I made it far worse by continuing to see him. That is the way of it.'

'No, that is not the way of it at all.' Silas shook his head, angry all at once. 'How were you to know? You had troubles of your own. If it brought you some comfort to...to go to Edward' – Silas swallowed – 'then you should not feel guilty for that. He is unsteady because of Seraphiel. The angel toyed with both your lives. I was there when Lucifer said it, I heard it clearly. Seraphiel used you, and he stole the life of a man you...had some care for. That angel made you a prisoner in that bloody Sanctuary it seems, and now you are to run about cleaning up a mess he made thousands of years ago. Christ, if I had the chance to meet him, I'd...well, I'd...' His heated words lost a little of their steam when he saw Pitch's bemused smile. 'What?'

'Slap his wrist and tell him what a naughty boy he was? You are quite a dolt but a fetching one at that.' The prince raised the blooms to his nose, the petals glancing at his cheeks. 'Can I tell you something though, Silas?'

'Of course.'

Pitch cleared his throat. 'If I ever reach this Blood Lake, wherever it may be, for Satty seems content to let me wonder...' He paused, shaking his head, verdant gaze distant. 'I fear she and Lucifer, and Seraphiel, are expecting a miracle from me when I can only deliver ruin. It is lunacy, sheer and utter lunacy, to believe I am a deliverer of any kind.'

'One step at a time,' Silas said. 'And I will take each one of them with you.'

Pitch lowered the blooms, the air between them white as warm breath met frigid air. 'You are quite set on staying with me?'

'I am.'

'It won't be a lark to the seaside, you know.'

'I'm aware.'

'Fine.' Pitch's gaze traced the collar of Silas's coat. 'But I should tell you that if you manage to get yourself killed...again...for the sake of my foolish little quest, I shall be most pissed off at you.'

Silas's ribs thrummed with his quickened heartbeat. 'Well, if *you* dare saddle up Sanu and seek to ride off to handle things on your own, there will also be consequences.' That had Pitch's gaze lifting to him, and Silas hurried on so he would not do anything foolish, like kiss him. 'I know you consider it. But if you try to run off without me, don't think for a moment I will not hunt you down, pull you off your horse, and throw your royal arse over my knee because I...' Bloody hell, where was he going with this? He busied himself with the flowers, wondering if there was a badger hole he could crawl into.

'Do go on, tell me how you shall punish me.' Pitch's lips twitched. 'Would you spank me? With your hand? Or with a paddle, perhaps?'

'Stop it.' Silas battled to stop the images that came to mind.

'Tell me, I truly would like to know.'

'I don't...well, I'm not certain. I fear I've not given my threat true consideration.' But bloody hell he was considering it now.

Pitch dissolved into a bright fit of laughter, the sound chasing away the ever-growing chill. Silas shook his head but struggled not to smile.

He took another tart from the basket, the treat managing to still retain the oven's warmth.

'It's really not that funny.' Silas shoved the pastry at the prince. 'Here, stick this in your mouth, and do shut up.'

Pitch did half of what he was told, biting into the tart but still chuckling. They continued their stroll, heading towards the gate that allowed a view of the graveyard. The heady waft was thickening with the darkening evening, brushing at Silas's skin like fine cobwebs.

He breathed in deeply.

'You truly relish the graves, don't you?' the daemon said around a pink mouthful.

'I truly do.' And he'd not apologise for it.

'I've known men with stranger fetishes.'

'I'm sure you have.'

The vines that had concealed the gate when he'd first discovered the exit were now trimmed to fall neatly around the archway. The ivy, an evergreen, was a pleasant dash of colour in the winter-sore garden. He stared out across the open space to where Highgate Cemetery lay, with its blocks and pillars of stone, its crypts and mausoleums. As much as the place called to him, soothed him, he did have some unwelcome memories of it.

Of the open grave that had swallowed him whole when he'd sought to evade the harpies.

Silas shivered, gooseflesh tracing his arms.

'I told you you needed your jacket under that coat,' Pitch said, scrutinising the piece of golden pastry he held.

'I'm not cold. I'm just remembering the harpies.'

'Here or the greensward? They can't get enough of you it seems.'

'Both, really.'

Pitch was in the mood for saying things out of the blue today. 'I'm sorry I did not get to you sooner, Silas, when they had you in that greensward.'

'What?' The sincerity in the daemon's voice pained him. 'Pitch...honestly, you must not think –'

'I'll think what I want. And what I think is that I will not let them hurt you again that way. Now go and stare longingly at your graveyard and give me another damned tart.'

Silas would rather stare at other lovely things. He held out the basket. 'Can I say then that I am sorry, too.'

'You usually do –'

'That I did not search harder for you that day.'

Pitch snatched at the basket. 'Don't be ridiculous. You weren't to know. You had no reason to think I was being anything other than the prick I am. I'm sure you just assumed I had abandoned you to take my pleasures elsewhere.' He tried to take hold of the wicker handle, but Silas covered his hand, squeezing gently.

'And because I was being petty and petulant, I let that assumption blind me. It was a mistake I shall always regret. And is not one I shall make again. I promise you.'

The basket was all that separated them. Pitch was watching him, gold hinting beneath the emerald in his eyes as though his flame stirred. The silence was thick with something indefinable. The daemon's lips parted as though he were about to speak. He leaned forward, and Silas wondered if the kiss that had been so violently interrupted by Pitch's illness was finally to be realised.

But the fading afternoon's light glanced against beating wings, drawing Pitch's attention.

'Shit,' Silas muttered low beneath his breath.

A tawny owl landed upon the stone seat near the gate, grand talons clacking against the hard surface, enormous dark eyes wide and unblinking, fixing on Pitch as it landed. It held a mouse in its curved beak, the critter clearly no longer living.

And the bird was not alone.

Another shape descended, wings spread wide. Another owl, though this one was mostly white as fresh-fallen snow, with a little dappling upon the wings, and much larger than the first. It had not yet landed when Silas heard the first notes. A serpentine tune reminding him of wind whistling through treetops. He found himself thinking of moonlit nights, the scent of cedar, and rain on moss-carpeted soil.

Djinn. Snowy owl shifter.

At least one part of the melody's naming was obvious enough.

The creature flapped its wide wings, stirring a wind towards them that had Pitch pushing errant strands of hair from his face and muttering unhappily.

'Always so dramatic.'

There was a rustling, like a wheat crop caught in a breeze, followed by a flurry of white, as though the owl had suddenly come apart, feathers threatening to scatter in all directions. But the sudden blur of white settled like a blizzard easing, and there in the place of the owl stood a willowy, very naked man. His skin held an odd tinge of grey, as though there were storm clouds beneath the surface. Between his legs there was the barest hint of a cock, nothing of balls, and instead of pubic hair, he had downy feathers. His hair was long, falling nearly to his waist, and hanging in heavy locks that resembled an actual bird's nest, twigs and feathers and hair intertwined.

'Ankou...daemon.' The djinn's voice was raspy as a parrot's. His eyes had not shifted to resemble anything remotely humanlike, far too round and far too big to be anything but disconcerting. And his lips were dark grey as though rubbed with ash.

'Marcus.' Pitch slipped the wicker basket from Silas's suddenly slackened grasp. 'I thought you must have been hibernating, it's been a while.'

'Owls don't hibernate.'

'Well, you're not an average owl though, are you?'

'I have been in Devon.' Marcus's head turned, or rather swivelled, to face the other owl, which still stared at Pitch. 'The tawny wishes to thank you.'

'For what?'

'Saving his son. At the witch-bottle house. You released him from a cage.'

That comment pulled Silas from his mannerless stare. He recalled the owl in the cage very well. And this bird might not be so pleased to know his son had witnessed Silas sticking his tongue down the daemon's throat and his hands down his pants.

The tawny owl spread its wings and glided to land at Pitch's feet, where it dropped the mouse before him.

'He thanks you,' Marcus said.

Pitch wrinkled his nose. 'Oh...all right, then.'

'You need to accept the gift.'

'Yes, yes, I accept it.'

'You need to pick it up.'

'That's not going to happen.'

The djinn managed to look angered without narrowing his enormous eyes. Silas decided to put a quick end to things. He went to one knee before the tawny owl and scooped up the still-warm body of the mouse.

'This is a generous gift.' He bowed his head. 'We are glad to hear your son is well, and very happy we could set him free.'

He glanced up at Pitch. The prince was giving him a quizzical look. 'You do grovel well, don't you?'

'It is a generous gift. This is a decent meal he has parted with.' Silas curled his fingers about the dead mouse. It did not irk him to do so. In fact, it felt entirely natural to hold the dead critter.

The tawny owl swung its head to look up at the djinn. It released a call, soft hoots that varied in length.

'The tawny is pleased,' Marcus said. Silas wondered if the djinn was cold, for it was a very cool evening and the shape-shifting gentleman was *very* unclothed. 'He wants me to tell you that although the daemon's flames were very pretty and he was right to burn that house, the ankou is far nicer and should not waste his time playing with the daemon's –'

'No, no.' Silas's skin burnt to a crisp. 'I will stop you right there.'

'Marcus, why are you here?' Pitch said. 'I doubt Satty sent you just to deliver a mouse's corpse and judge where Silas should bestow a hand job.'

Marcus shook his head, and his knotted, matted hair rubbed his chest. 'The Lady has sent me to summon you to Holly Lodge. She wishes to see you. Now.'

'You really could have started with that.' Pitch's irritation prickled. 'Instead of the mouse, you daft fu–'

'Thank you, Marcus,' Silas said. 'Please tell the Lady we will be there at once.'

CHAPTER 3

I t was not a long nor a particularly strenuous walk up the hill to where Holly Lodge perched, but as the journey went on, Pitch's limp grew more obvious. He refused to take Silas's arm and was breathing heavily by the time they finally reached the Lodge's impressive portico. The imposing columns that supported the structure were spread wide, right out over the driveway, allowing coach passengers to avoid foul weather as they alighted. Silas had waited, impatiently, in a coach right here for Tobias Astaroth before they had begun the train journey that would take them to Black Annis.

He offered his arm to the daemon to aid him up the short flight of stairs to the double doors.

'I can manage a few steps.' Pitch waved him off. 'Let's get this over with.'

Silas was not insulted by the curt tone. He too was nervous. But he decided Lady Satine would have come to them directly if anything dire had happened to Charlie...or Edward. Tyvain, at the very least, would have screamed the bloody village down if the news were terrible. She didn't like to show it, but she too had a fondness for the lad.

The double doors swung wide, though no butler was evident behind them. They entered into a surprisingly plain foyer. Silas had been expecting far more elaborate trims and intricate tiling than the contrasting black and white upon the floor and the bare, dull brown walls.

'Down here, gentlemen. Quickly if you don't mind.'

Lady Satine's voice came from a ways down the hallway. The passage-way had no floor runners, and the pine floor was in need of a restain, with patches of the teak colouring worn away in places. A paltry number of gaslights, flickering behind rather dirty panes of glass, lit the way. There was a sense of emptiness to the place. Silas glanced back to make sure he'd not drawn too far ahead.

'I'm coming,' the daemon grumbled.

'Move along, will ya?'

Tyvain's voice guided Silas into a room that was again startling for how plain it was. The parlour was quite bright with natural light and the air not so stale as in the hall, but there was little in the way of furniture, or at least furniture that was being used. There were a great many items hidden under white sheets; a large shape Silas suspected was a piano rested over towards a set of lovely French windows that were as in need of a clean as the sconces; a hulking sheet-draped form against the back wall was a buffet perhaps; and towards the centre of the room, a lumpy muddle was likely a set of chairs and a small table.

There were no paintings here either, and no fire in the hearth, but the room was pleasantly temperate.

Silas took two steps into the room and was rocked back on his feet by the heavy scent of the sea, of salt and brine and ocean life. A melody played, the whistling notes of the wind as it punished the waves into a frothy frenzy.

Silas's focus was drawn to the Lady Satine, the music taking him there. She lounged upon a chaise at the centre of the room. The sudden smack of ocean scents faded, but her melody rose. Great and tremendous as a tsunami, her tune was astonishingly loud, a grand orchestra of notes, soaring, magnificent for the most part, with an undercurrent of whimsy and delicacy but plagued with irksome off-notes that pained him to hear.

Djinn. Shifter...

There was more, he knew, but the melody lost its way. Silas frowned. The tune of the other djinn he'd met had been clean, precise. Untrou-bled. Not so here. The very notes themselves seemed uncertain of how to play.

Leviathan.

The high squeal of a violin at its limit, stretching on, breaking. Silas winced, touching at his ear.

'Something wrong, Silas?' Pitch's voice sliced through the unpleasant tune, cutting it free. Bringing blessed silence.

'No, no. I'm fine.'

'Afternoon, gentlemen.' Lady Satine wore the same physical guise as when Silas had seen her with Lucifer: rich brown skin, unmissable violet eyes, and a shock of curly white-grey hair. Her gown, the sepia of a river after heavy rain, spilled around her. She lay along the length of the chaise, her bare toes peeking from beneath the gown's folds.

'Afternoon.' Silas greeted her with a dry throat, feeling strangely unsteady. He tugged at his earlobe, still hearing the echo of the Lady's enormous song. He knew her to be djinn, but what else did it take to be Lady of the Lake?

Silas found a welcome reprieve when regarding Tyvain. There had been talk once of her having a minute amount of djinn blood, but evidently it was so small as not to trigger Silas's newfound detection. He'd keep that to himself, he decided. The soothsayer would not take the news well that he heard nothing at all with her.

'Took ya time. Not so speedy on ya feet these days, are ya, daemon?'

Tyvain's auburn hair was pinned back in a severe style that lifted at the edges of her eyes. She was clad in a prim and proper gown of sensible navy blue, with a high neck and a row of pearl buttons that ran all the way down to her waist, complete with delicate lace gloves. Never had an outfit suited a person less.

'Oh, I am really not in the mood for you, hag.' Pitch had barely made it into the room, but now looked set to turn about and leave right away.

Silas stepped in, blocking his exit. 'Don't pay her any mind, Pitch,' he said quietly. 'I'm sure she is just placing her worries for Charlie on you.' He prayed, to no one in particular, that it was worry and nothing worse than that. 'Come now.' He spotted the only other uncovered chair in the room, a wide armchair of a well-worn leather that had faded in some places and cracked in others. 'Take a seat.'

He touched a light hand to Pitch's elbow, fully expecting a slap in return, but the daemon allowed himself to be guided. Silas quickly turned the chair about so that it was facing the chaise instead of the barren hearth and the soothsayer with her oddly unreadable expression. A tightness held Silas's ribs. *Let this be good news and not bad.*

'Well, we are here. What's this summons for, then?' Pitch said.

If Silas was not mistaken, the daemon made a small grunt of discomfort as he lowered himself into the seat.

'You seem much better, Tobias.' Lady Satine toyed with one of the tight spirals of her peppered hair.

'I'm as well as I'll be, I suspect. Now can we get on with things? What do you have to say to us, Satty?'

'It is not me but Tyvain who shall do the speaking.'

Pitch glared at the soothsayer. 'Get on with it, then.'

'Did ya know there is such a word as please? Ya little shit.' Tyvain waved a lace-gloved hand at the prince. Silas wondered if she knew exactly who it was she was treating with such disdain. He highly doubted it. No one would be that reckless with their safety.

'Did you find them, Tyvain?' Silas hoped he did not sound as desperate as he felt. 'Is Charlie all right? The lieutenant?'

'Nah. That's the thing, ya see.' Tyvain's gaze fell to her hands, where she rubbed at the too-delicate seams of her gloves. 'Last I 'eard from Charlie, 'e was thinkin' of strikin' up a conversation with Charters at some pub near Berkeley Square. Now I can't find the lad, and it's like Edward Charters vanished plain off the face of the map. Friends don't know nothin' of note, save for 'im being unwell, which no one seems surprised about.'

'Berkeley Square?' Pitch said. 'That's near his residence. I'm presuming your superlative detective skills involved knocking on his door?'

'Of course.' The soothsayer scowled. 'I tried to get in ta see 'is mother. It's just 'er and some sour-faced butler livin' there. But I couldn't get a foot past that old bastard, Thomas. Made the mistake of sayin' I was from the Order. Thought they might be 'ankerin' for a seance like the rest of society is. That went down like a feckin' charm full of shite. Might as well 'ave said I was a whore come lookin' for me payment. Thought about mentionin' you, Astaroth.' She jerked a thumb towards Pitch. 'But that didn't seem like a grand idea. Just thinkin' about it 'ad me bloatin' up like I'd eaten a rotten egg. Then I realised why that was. You and the lieutenant was flirtin' all season. Had London society buzzin' and puttin' bets on 'ow soon it would be before you got your dick in Mr Charters's arse.'

'Good god,' Silas coughed. 'Tyvain –'

'All's I'm sayin' is there's 'istory between 'em. The sort the lieutenant's ma wouldn't like 'earin'. Nor that fella Thomas neither.'

Silas studied his hands, trying very hard to keep the image of Edward and Pitch at the Moon Inn from his mind.

'Probably the most sensible thing you've done in years, hag, not mentioning me, I mean.' Pitch crossed his legs, smoothing at his thigh. 'Thomas is not overly fond of me since he copped an eyeful of Edward and I in the study, with my tongue between his master's arse cheeks. But I say that will teach the old cunt not to spy on others.'

Lady Satine's chuckle was throaty, while Tyvain's disdain mingled with amusement, but Silas had heard more than enough.

He folded his arms and paced away from the daemon, scowling. 'As delightful as this trip down memory lane is, I fear the point of this conversation is far less amusing. Tyvain, what your gut is telling you, in summary, is that you don't believe Edward is at home convalescing, and you still have no idea where Charlie is?'

Pitch was watching him. Silas felt the graze of emerald upon him, but he could not look at the daemon. He feared if he did so, Pitch might see how talk of his dalliances with Edward had stung. And such petty jealousies were embarrassing and ill-timed.

'That's what I'm sayin'.' Tyvain sighed. 'I tried a few other of me own contacts. A scullery maid in Baron Faversham's place, who I thought might 'ave 'eard some whispers. But I got nothin'. With winter 'ere, some are sayin' 'e's likely gone to the Continent. Others said 'e's run off with a new paramour so as to get away from 'is mother, who 'e don't much like. But a week ago 'e was out and about. Not lookin' fit as a fiddle mind. Word is 'e's been moping about for a while, but 'e was still keepin' in touch with 'is circle of friends often enough. Until suddenly 'e ain't, and I ain't got no carrier pigeon comin' back to me from Charlie. We need to get into that 'ouse to 'ave a proper look around, I say.' She shrugged. 'Maybe the lad got 'imself locked in a cellar or somethin' pokin' about...and all this worry is for nothin'.'

'There'd be no need for worry at all if you had not sent him on such a dangerous errand.' Silas's anger warmed him.

'Weren't meant to be dangerous, in me defence,' Tyvain returned. 'Besides, the lad's capable of undertakin' a dangerous errand, Mercer. 'E was by 'imself on the roads a long while before you met up in those woods.'

'But he should be safer now,' Silas said markedly. 'I asked you and Old Bess to keep him close. To keep him safe.'

Tyvain had the decency not to protest. 'Yeah...I know ya did. I don't feel good about this, all right? I'm so sick to me gut, I don't know what is worry and what is a bloody sign.'

'You and your gut can stand down, hag. Silas?' Pitch waited until Silas turned around to look at him. 'We will find them. I promise you that.' Silas gave him a grateful nod. 'We need to do more than sneak around their house, though. Just because Edward's not to be seen here in London doesn't mean he's disappeared. Mr Charters's family has houses all over the country, and *all* have cellars perfect for a lad to get locked in while he's sneaking around. Now it is true that Mr Charters *has* been unwell for some time.' Pitch's resolute manner faltered. 'He's prone to a dark mood. It's likely he has just spirited himself off to one of the country houses, or is indeed on the Continent.'

'And not a one of his friends knows about it?' Silas remained uncertain.

Pitch did not look convinced of his own theory. 'Perhaps?' he said. 'Maybe he wished to be alone. What we need to do is speak with Edward's mother.'

'Well she ain't sayin' nothin' to nobody.' Tyvain scratched at her neck, dragging down the high collar to reach the spot.

'Nobody like you.' The daemon ran his finger along one of the cracks in the leather seat, his brow furrowed.

'What are you thinking, Tobias?' These were the first words Lady Satine had uttered in some time.

'What day is it?' Pitch asked. 'Tell me it's not Tuesday.'

'It's not Tuesday,' Lady Satine replied. 'It is Sunday evening.'

Pitch's smile was a pretty swing of full lips. 'Marvellous. I seem to recall that Mrs Charters was partial to a soirée on a Tuesday night. She has an insatiable appetite for baccarat. It is invitation only.'

Tyvain snorted. 'Sorry to break it to you, sweetheart, but Tobias Astaroth ain't got no chance of gettin' an invite to that place.' The soothsayer cracked her knuckles, ruining the veneer of refinement her stiff clothing gave her.

'Of course.' Pitch was smug. 'But the woman that Mr Charters was courting briefly this summer will be welcomed with open arms.'

Lady Satine sat up, her skirts bunched about her, one sleeve slipping from her shoulder. Her hair was mussed at the back by the cushions. For someone Silas suspected was altogether far more powerful than he imagined, she looked a right mess. 'What are you up to, Tobias?'

Pitch shrugged. 'Mr Charters and I were very near to being affianced at the beginning of summer.'

That gave Silas cause to stop his pacing. 'I beg your pardon?'

Pitch laughed, no doubt relishing the confusion in the room. 'Mrs Charters is very aware that Edward has always had a preference for a pretty boy and is not so fond of a skirt. It causes her no end of grief, what with the need for heirs and all that, but it made for lovely sport for a while there. For a short time, I became Miss Margaret Cargill, just to mess with her sensibilities. A lovely American visitor to British shores for the summer, and a member of an astonishingly rich family. An heiress, no less. And one who thought Edward a dream. Mrs Charters nearly blew her wig off when he first introduced me. A rich and suitable child-bearer.' His gaze slid to Silas. The ankou did his level best to keep his expression smooth. 'It was a way to amuse myself, pass the time. They were all falling over themselves to impress me, which brought me no end of pleasure, and Edward was free to indulge his predilection for a cock whilst I could wear corsets to my heart's content. It didn't work out for us, of course. I got bored with being gawked at like a prize bird in a cage. So I returned Miss Cargill to American shores, just a few weeks after the affair began.'

'I do recall that phase of yours.' Lady Satine's laugh was brittle. 'You had my seamstress thinking I'd gone mad for corsets, the tighter the better, and preferably near to works of art.' She cupped her hands beneath her breasts and wriggled them about in a manner that had Silas glancing away. 'But it has always astonished me why you prefer to wear these confounded things. I truly don't know what I was thinking when I made this form. It's an inconvenient sex at times.'

'Well, you are not so prone to coming apart as I am,' Pitch said. 'You'd understand then why I adore a decent lacing up.'

Silas glanced at him, hearing the dry, tangled note of self-loathing in the words. He tried to catch Pitch's eye, but the daemon would not look at him.

'So you reckon this Cargill woman can get an invite to this party, then?' Tyvain said.

'Certainly,' Pitch said smoothly. 'We should request one immediately, advise her that I'm in town and would like to attend. If he is just ill, Mrs Charters will soon have Edward on his feet if she thinks he's in with another chance to turn his seed into an heir.'

Silas looked to the Lady Satine, hoping he'd see her shaking her head and casting out the idea as foolish. But instead she pursed her bottom lip and nodded slowly.

'Come now,' Silas said. 'It's all very well to put on a dress and some rouge to deceive the purebreds, but do we not have greater things to concern us? The Morrigan for one. Should we not be worried about Pitch's natural state being noticed?'

The natural state Silas's new musicality had apparently not noticed enough to declare.

'We can deal with that,' Lady Satine replied. 'There is an elixir I've concocted, capable of concealing a natural's aura, though the results do vary. For me it was a day, perhaps a day and a half, but it worked much better for Sybilla when she tried it. Four days I think she was concealed. Trouble is it loses efficacy with each use until it does not work at all. I've not found the time or inclination to fix that.'

'Lucky Cinderella only needs to go to one ball, then,' Tyvain declared.

'I'll take anything, so long as it doesn't make me throw up.' Pitch rubbed at his chest. 'I've had far too much of that of late.'

The Lady shook her head. 'Nothing like that. But I do have concerns about how effective it will be for one of your...shall we say, unique calibre?'

'Oh by the feckin' saints.' Tyvain scratched at her armpit. The dress did not agree with her at all. ''E's vain enough as it is. Don't give 'im any more reason to feckin' prance about like one of them princes from the House of Windsor.'

Silas studied his nails very closely. At least he knew for certain Tyvain had no clue who Pitch truly was. He doubted even the bold and very brassy soothsayer would be so boorish if she knew the truth.

She also did not know when to shut up. Tyvain jerked her head at Pitch. 'I can't see those auras you lot talk about, but I've 'eard yours looks like a shit stain.'

'That's enough, Tyvain.' Lady Satine got to her feet, stretching her arms overhead. 'You are hardly in a position to cast aspersions. If you'd told someone, anyone at all, about your premonition regarding Mr Charters, we'd not need this meeting to begin with.'

'Figured I'd find 'im first, see if 'e was actually important later.' Tyvain sulked into her chair. 'Didn't seem ta make sense 'e was truly worth a damn, so I assumed me signs were all fecked up as usual. Thought I'd save ya all lookin' at me like I'm shit on a wheel like you usually do when I tell ya me guts are swirlin'.'

'Because it's normally the beans you ate the night before and nothing more,' the Lady said. 'You must admit, your strike-to-win ratio is rather high for the strike. I do sometimes wonder if you are truly your mother's daughter. But at least there is a plan now. We shall see where this leads.'

'And where do I figure in this plan?' Silas demanded. 'I am going with him, surely?'

'No.' Lady Satine and Pitch were in unison.

'You stand out a feckin' mile, you daft cock.' Tyvain lifted her chin to fiddle with the tiny pearl button right up under her chin. 'You could 'ide your aura all you like, and chances are they'd still know the giant from the Order 'ad arrived.'

Silas despised her choice of words. 'My lady, you yourself said he's likely become even more of a target after...' He faltered, glancing at Pitch, who was far too interested in the rich purple velvet of his sleeve. 'Well, you are a master of disguise, are you not? Perhaps *you* should go?'

'I'm quite busy on Tuesday nights, and I do recall just telling you that the elixir no longer works on me,' Lady Satine said smoothly. 'We'll hire a purebred driver and carriage, but Isaac shall travel with him. There will be eyes in every fire in every hearth in the house –'

'Would that not be noticeable...' Silas said, 'to those who know how to look?'

The Lady shook her head. 'Highly unlikely. The elementals are changeable and unpredictable, like the elements they command. Trying to catch a glimpse of Isaac in a flicker of flame would be like trying to make out the patterns on a hummingbird's wings as it flaps them.'

'Unlikely is not impossible. I don't like this plan at all.' Silas balled his fists. 'I should go too. I can wait in the carriage –'

'You are not going, Silas.' Lady Satine fixed him with a glare, and he shrank from his own protest like she'd doused him with cold water.

'If you are as dreadful at cards as you are at billiards, my dear Silas,' Pitch said, 'then it is better for the Order's coffers that you stay away.'

Silas was in too much of a mood to even dignify that with a response.

'Now we should start thinking about what Tobias will wear,' Lady Satine declared. 'I must deal with your eyes as well. They can't stay that shade. We'll have you take the elixir early so as to ensure it is working. Be warned, it's cold as ice and not very pleasant in the ear canal.'

Silas had been summarily dismissed. Like he was nothing more than a servant whose services were no longer required. He had no wish to be here a moment longer than need be. He turned and headed for the door, well aware that all eyes had shifted to him the moment he moved.

'Mr Mercer?' Lady Satine called. 'Is everything all right? We'll be serving dinner in a short while.'

'Thank you but I'm not very hungry.' He strode out of the room and made his way back towards the front door.

A sublime sound, a chorus in perfect unison, bloomed in his head. An ethereal tune that spoke of strength and fortitude, and a world of things beyond his understanding.

Angel. Valkyrie.

Sybilla entered, flicking the hood of her cloak from her head. Her short, tight stark-white curls seemed to glow in the gaslight. 'Silas, it's good to see you in one piece.'

His mood lifted to see the familiar face. 'A pleasure to be in one. I didn't realise you were around.'

Now he knew the angels at least, were not beyond his detection. Only the daemons apparently.

'I wasn't.' Sybilla discarded her cloak. She tossed it towards the wall beneath the stairs. A panel in the wood swung open revealing a cavity with a neat line of hooks. The cloak flew of its own accord to settle upon the one nearest the door. 'I've just returned from up Shrewsbury way. Gods, what I won't do for a decent bath right now.'

She flicked her fingers, and the panel closed. Silas had never really stopped to wonder if the Valkyrie held any divine magick of her own. But of course she did. Pitch had said it was the gift of all angels. With only a select few, like Samyaza and Azazel, powerful enough to cultivate that magick in unique ways.

'And did you have any luck finding the tosher on your travels?' Silas was uncomfortable with remembering why Sybilla had set off to begin with. He had learned about the tosher in Shrewsbury paying good money for fresh dead through some rather unfortunate means. Silas had flown into a rage when he'd discovered a gravedigger in Bishop's Castle digging up corpses, and the poor man had parted with the details in fear of his life. It was not Silas's proudest moment.

'I found our tosher, yes.' Sybilla nodded, though did not look too pleased. 'It was Old Bill Toggins. They dragged him out of a well about three days before I got there. He'd been buried not a day before I arrived.' She sighed. 'Locals weren't saying much, too bloody scared, I'd wager. But I shared a few wines with a very chatty night flower one evening, and she'd been on her back for Old Bill a couple of times since he came into the money. He'd told her someone at Birmingham Medical School was paying the coin for corpses. Had a name too, but when I followed it up, no one had heard of the man. The secretary was most put out when she understood what I was investigating, and said I'd be better off sticking my nose in over Oxford or Cambridge way. Seemed to think there had been talk of coin being paid for body snatching for years at those universities.'

Silas lifted his shoulders, trying to shrug off the sickening feeling that came with hearing of the desecration of graves. 'And did you find anything?'

'I headed straight for London when I heard what had happened to you and Tobias.' She touched his arm. 'I am sorry I was not closer by, Silas. I hear you have endured a terrible time of it. You and Tobias both. Are you all right?'

'It's not pleasant to know that others wish you well and truly dead. And Pitch...what they did...' He pressed his lips, taking a moment to stifle the rage that came with thinking of it. It was not his tale to tell. 'We survived, but it was awful. And I've gained a few extra worries certainly...'

'Here stands one of those worries, I'm afraid.'

Silas started. He'd not heard Pitch come up the hall behind him. The daemon leaned against the wall just a few paces away, arms folded, head tilted so that his hair fell in fetching gold-tinged waves across his cheek.

'Well that is hardly a surprise.' Sybilla's smile was genuine. She pulled off her gloves, finger by finger. 'I suspect you rather enjoy troubling our fair ankou, don't you, Tobias?'

'It is not so amusing as I expected,' Pitch said quietly. 'Will you come and have dinner, Silas? Your rumbling stomach will keep me awake all night otherwise.'

Silas felt Sybilla's gaze shift between them, making assumptions. But she'd be wrong. They weren't sharing a bed, not even the same floor of the cottage when it came to sleeping arrangements. There was Pitch's illness of course, but Silas was also waiting for sign from the daemon he was ready for such intimacy once more. Now the prince's suggestive comment had him awash with hope. He stood, rather pathetically trans-fixed by the jade-touched gaze that was levelled at him.

'The soup perhaps,' he said.

'Excellent.' Pitch sidled up and, after a very brief hesitation, looped his arm through Silas's, hooking him in close. 'Will you take me to dinner?'

'Just be sure you can afford to pay that bill, Silas.' Sybilla winked at him, pushing past to make her way down the corridor. Her leather trousers creaked as she walked.

'No need to make such theatre of it,' Silas mumbled. 'It's just a meal.'

Pitch patted his arm. 'And Tuesday is just a soirée, where my talent for the theatrical will be most useful. I shall be beautiful, and tongues will be loosened, and I will learn the whereabouts of our missing pair. Then I shall bore you senseless with all the gossip when I return. Be prepared to be woken in the early hours and made to listen to all the scandals.'

Silas chuckled. Damn, it was infuriating how often this creature made him laugh when he should be scowling. 'So long as you bring good news, I dare say I would even listen to you sing.'

'In that case, my sweet Silas, I'll find your little friend if it is the very last thing I do.'

CHAPTER 4

P itch admired the view in the floor-length mirror, turning this way and that to take in the flow of taffeta he wore. A row of diamante buttons ran up the front of his bodice, where a lace-ruffled collar sat high, concealing the bump at his throat. Raven-black ringlets bobbed against the tops of his shoulders, and subtle amber eyes stared back at him. His usual viridian was hidden, courtesy of some stinging eye drops Satty had produced along with her foul-smelling aura-concealing elixir.

The cloud-grey taffeta swished about him, and the diamond-and-sapphire earrings clipped to his ears dangled and swayed, their facets catching the light. His corseted waist was narrowed down to a curve that bordered on insensible. Jane had used all her considerable strength to pull in the laces, and Pitch's ribs, nearly to the breaking point. Breathing was definitely an issue. He'd have to keep his inhales short and sweet, but not too quick or he'd be liable to faint. He refused to allow Jane to loosen the lacing. He did not tell her of the contentment that came with being strapped up to within an inch of his life. She would not understand what it was to feel so secure, held tight, and less fearful of breaking apart as mad inner turmoil sought release.

She added a dash more colour to his lips before she stepped back to set away the assortment of toiletries she held, her own azure gown spreading like a pond around her. 'Right, you are done. A little perfume, and your gloves.' She indicated the lengths of white satin that were draped over the edge of the vanity as she dabbed her finger over the top of an open bottle of Fleurs de Bulgarie. 'By Royal Appointment. If it's good enough for the Queen, it's good enough for you, I say.'

Jane pressed her damp fingertip behind Pitch's ears and under his chin. He offered up his wrists, barely accessible due to the tightness of the fabric. The sleeves were full length and tight all the way up to mid upper arm, where they exploded into a superb bulge of taffeta. He couldn't deny it; the dress Jane had chosen was perfection. And he a work of art beneath it. He rubbed at his left ear, his hearing still a bit muffled after the Lady had put the drops of elixir in an hour or so ago. The immediate effect had been total deafness for that eardrum, which was unpleasant but bearable when Satty had declared the elixir a success. He could not see it himself. A natural could not see their own hue, but he was assured there was not a trace of his supposedly rain-washed and twisted aura about him. Satty likened the elixir to bottled camouflage. The djinn were creatures born of the animalistic power of nature, and nowhere else but in the wild were there more splendid displays of camouflage to be seen: from the chameleon to the mountain hare changing its colours for the winter.

'Careful though,' she'd warned as he shook his head, trying to dislodge the uncomfortable sense of movement in his ear canal as the elixir filled it. 'The eye tint will hold till tomorrow at least, but I'm not confident about the elixir for you. I think it best you are back as soon as possible. By midnight if you can.'

Pitch smoothed his skirts, finding it hard to look away from the sultry raven-haired beauty that stared back at him in the mirror.

'Gods, you are vanity on legs, aren't you?' Jane said.

'Well, look at me.' Pitch gestured to the vision. 'Tell me that is not a beautiful example of humanity.'

Jane rolled her eyes, but she nodded. 'You do look quite fetching, I can't deny it. But I know what lies beneath, and I have no interest in going there again, I'm afraid.'

'Nor do I, my dear elemental.' Pitch adjusted the lace that spilled over the edge of the high collar. 'I'm rather partial to balls presently.'

'I'm sure you are.'

Jane laughed, not in the least bit insulted, and he liked her all the more for it. He'd never say so, but she was not terrible company to be around. Silas certainly enjoyed her presence. A weight seemed to lift from the ankou when she was around, and that smile on his face when Jane had first come to the cottage on their return? Pure joy. Not irritating to see, in the least.

Not at all.

Jane fussed about in one of the many drawers in her bureau, searching for something. She loosed a little cry as she withdrew a tiny bottle. The glass was the colour of amber with a neat silver stopper. 'I was looking for another pin for your hair, but you might like this even more. Rose oil. In case you and Silas have run your supply dry.' Her grin was wry, but Pitch's own smile struggled to stay aloft.

Gods, Jane would choke on disbelief to know that he, a veritable whore when he so chose, was sleeping alone. And by choice. Silas had kept a subtle distance, undemanding of any repeat of their intimacy in the carriage, asking nothing from a pathetically fragile prince. Pitch had woken several times now in a sheer panic, mistaking his tangled sheets for an Alp daemon and the ceiling rose for magickal runes. His cries would bring Silas at a run, the ankou taking long, patient minutes to convince Pitch that he was not being held down and controlled. That he was safe and would not be forced where he did not wish to go.

The nightmares that used to hold visions of Seraphiel were now full of horns and knives and pinned-down fear.

Pitch continued working the gloves on. 'The oil might prove a boon this evening, should I need to go to greater lengths to get the information I need.'

Let the illusion hold. Let them all think he was just as he'd been before Gidleigh House. He'd not told Lady Satine of the full extent of the Alp's assault, and did not intend to change that. Silas alone held the secret with him, and so long as the ankou never dared look on him with pity, Pitch could bear it.

Jane gave him a puzzled look. 'Oh. I thought...never mind. Here you are, then.'

While Pitch finished pulling on the second glove, Jane tucked the rose oil into a cleverly sewn pocket that was hidden among the folds of the smoke-grey skirt.

'I've not seen Silas around,' Pitch said, casual and careless. The silly dolt had been in a temper ever since he'd learned he was not allowed to attend the soirée. 'Is he off picking me a corsage?'

Considering it had been dark for several hours, it seemed unlikely, even for the garden-obsessed ankou, to be out. When he'd told Silas he was off to Jane's for the dressing, the oaf had waved him off with an absent farewell and wished him a successful evening before picking up his book and burying his nose in the pages. When Pitch had pointed out the fact that Silas could not read, he'd blustered about there only being one way to learn and that was by doing. Pitch was not sure that was how learning to read worked. But he'd been gifted with the aptitude for it when he'd created his human form, so who was he to say?

Jane glanced up at him as she tidied up her dresser. 'I believe he went to the Lodge with Phillipa to see what the ghost thought of his ideas to refit Lady Howard's carriage. He's quite keen to use it, I understand.'

'Oh. I see.' Pitch interlaced his satin-covered fingers. It hardly mattered that the ankou wasn't going to see him off. But really, could he not have spared a minute for a goodbye? Offered up a good luck kiss or something menial like that?

'We are done here, are we not?' Pitch pressed his palms into the severe curve of his waist. The room was overly warm. The least the air elemental could have done was stir a cool breeze.

'You're ready, yes.'

Pitch followed after the elemental as she breezed, quite actually, from the room. Her azure gown showed off the stunning contrast of her warm brown skin against a white lace trim.

Pitch's shoes were sensible. Jane had given him a pair of lace-up boots in soft black leather, but even wearing those, it was a task to move down the stairs after her, his hip stiff and unhelpful.

They were almost at the foyer when the door swung open. The one dismal candle that Jane had lit – the elemental refused gaslight, gods knew why – fluttered and barely managed to stay alive.

''E gone yet?' Tyvain caught sight of Pitch and gaped like she'd just seen one of Silas's lost souls. 'Jesus feckin' wept. You look...you look...' The soothsayer, for once in her life, was lost for words.

'Stunning, beautiful, gorgeous,' Pitch added helpfully.

'All of 'em, but ya know it. Get on, will ya? We've wasted enough time as it is. Isaac is across the street waitin' for ya.'

Tyvain led the way, out through the main gate to where a purebred driver waited with a dark bay and black brougham. The fellow would remember nothing of where he had picked up his passenger nor where he delivered them at the end of the evening. He didn't even look at the vision of loveliness alighting his carriage now. Pitch squeezed himself through the narrow doorway, muttering about the rudeness.

Isaac was seated with his back to the driver, in all his surly glory, more so because he'd been made to wear a suit of charcoal grey rather than his layers of nondescript black. The whites of his eyes seemed to blaze against the darkness of his skin in the dimness of the cabin. His aura, usually a trim of clementine, was gone. He ran his gaze up and down Pitch's made-up length and, without a word of greeting, turned to stare out the window.

'Hello to you too, Isaac,' Pitch said, sweet as can be. He was fairly certain he heard the unhappy elemental growl.

'Carry on, driver,' Isaac called, and they were underway.

CHAPTER 5

Just on twenty minutes later, Pitch walked up the front steps of the Charters' residence, a grand and well-situated house just off Berkeley Square in Mayfair. All the gaslights were blazing. Mrs Charters had been most proud, according to Edward, at having them installed and was likely to be the reason why British Gas would run dry before the end of the decade. A piano was being played somewhere indoors, and the heat from the interior ran up against the evening chill like a bull squaring off against a matador.

There, just inside the foyer, stiff and proper and with a portlier belly than Pitch recalled, stood the butler, Thomas.

Pitch smiled his most alluring smile, the one that teased just a glimpse of teeth between blossom-pink lips. The butler regarded the new arrival, his gaze delivered down the length of his rather bulbous nose. Pitch could see no hint of recognition.

'Hello, dear Thomas. It has been some time.' Pitch's voice was soft and feminine, edged with an American twang. He added some breathlessness to the mix. 'You may not remember me.'

He saw the moment recognition dawned, a subtle tug at the butler's eyelids, the merest hint of a twitch of his lip that might be a smile.

'Miss Cargill. How wonderful to see you again.' Thomas stood aside to allow him entry. 'Have you been long back in London?'

'Not at all. We came off the boat only a few days ago. I was so excited to learn that these wonderful evenings were still occurring. I simply had to fit it into my schedule.'

'Mrs Charters will be very pleased to see you,' Thomas said. 'You are here alone?'

There was a whisper of disapproval there, whether due to the lack of chaperone or husband, Pitch was unsure, but he was no virginal young thing that required escorting. No doubt there would be much gossip about the American's unmarried state, at such a ripe old age. Pitch didn't look a day over twenty-five, but he'd be marked for spinsterhood.

'I wonder, Miss Cargill, are you aware that Lieutenant Charters shall not be in attendance this evening?'

Pitch pouted his disappointment. 'Tell me that isn't so, Thomas. It has been so long since I've seen him, though we do write on occasion. I hope he is not unwell again? I do know he struggles with his health.' It took focus to keep his words smooth.

Thomas cleared his throat. 'I'm afraid, ma'am, that the colder weather does not agree with him. He decided a sojourn to the Continent was in order.' The butler was many things, but a decent liar was not one of them. He shifted back and forth on feet normally stuck fast to the tiles.

Pitch fluttered his fingers against his chest, where bandages and folded rags beneath the taffeta gave the impression of breasts. 'How wonderful for him. Spain? Italy perhaps? What wonders the waters of the Mediterranean can do.'

'I'm not sure it is for me to say. Perhaps Mrs Charters will see fit to tell you where he is convalescing.'

Pitch would wager every one of the jewels that dripped from his ears that the butler knew exactly where Edward was. Thomas had been with the family a very long time. Since Edward was a boy. This dreary, stern man was as close to a father as the lieutenant managed. And what a pity that was, for Edward deserved far better.

'Of course, I'm so looking forward to seeing her.' Pitch tilted his head in a way he knew to be beguiling. His smile was demure and oh-so ladylike, and Thomas beamed beneath it.

He was a crotchety old bastard but no less a man. And men weren't so hard to manipulate, even without incubus charms. Especially those men keen to see their master produce offspring and thereby ensure continuing employment. The butler knew firsthand where Edward's preferences lay, of course. As most certainly Mrs Charters did. But so long as Edward brought home something with tits that could suckle, it hardly mattered whether they were a mousy schoolteacher or a sparkling heiress.

Pitch's smile threatened to slip, but he was well-versed in keeping up appearances.

'Enjoy your evening, madam.'

'Oh, I do intend to.'

Thomas nodded and swept his hand towards the foyer, giving Pitch a sharp nod and moving away to tend to the next carriage as it arrived.

Pitch glanced at himself in the grand gilded mirror that dominated the foyer, making a few adjustments to ensure his breasts were set as they should be and that the ringlets framed his face in the most fetching way before he headed on.

The foyer itself was a wide, echoing affair of pristine white tiles which surrounded a central inlay of indigo and cream and black, a natural motif of flowers that Silas would have stopped short at seeing, no doubt.

Pitch tugged at his earring, chasing away thoughts of the ankou, focusing on the task at hand.

He exchanged names and niceties with the Honourable Ronald Piggleton, once likely a handsome man but now taxed by age's fine scribbles. He introduced his auburn-haired wife, Mrs Piggleton, whose smile was locked to her lips. She appeared ready to burst out laughing at the slightest humorous moment. The pair were energetic in the way of those who had indulged in a glass or two of Vin Mariani, with its heaped spoonfuls of cure-all cocaine. Pitch had gone a long while without a touch of snow on his gums or up his nose. Tonight may well be the night for it. Why the blazes not? He could not shake the disquiet that came with thinking about finding Edward. The sense of finality he felt when he did so.

There would be a change, he was sure. An end to the life he had here, for what that life was worth. A pity. He'd just begun to enjoy some parts of being a Horseman. One in particular took his fancy, but he'd not even bothered to wave him off at the gates. Pitch pushed aside his annoyance and swept into the hub of the evening's activities in the drawing room.

The room was clad in wallpaper of cloying shades of orange and blue, an eyesore Pitch had always abhorred. Usually the room was overstuffed with couches and armchairs of all designs, but most of them had been removed to accommodate for an assortment of card tables, two large, round mahogany tables at the centre, with seating for six at each, with smaller setups at the perimeter of the room, nestled in between display cabinets that held all manner of items: everything from dried flower arrangements beneath glass domes, to delicate sculptures of ballerinas and shepherdesses with their crooks. Mrs Charters thought herself a collector. Pitch had always thought her more of a hoarder who had no idea of what a pain it must be for the household staff to keep dust away from all her knickknacks.

All the seats at the tables were full, players deep into their glasses and hands. They sat beneath hanging paraffin lamps on pulleys, lowered so that the light was most concentrated on their cards. From the next room, a smaller sitting room if he recalled, came the vigorous thumps of piano keys, someone singing along rather loudly with the music. The louder the better for Mrs Charters, who tended to drown her sorrows in parties and idle chitchat. The wealthy widow did not enjoy focusing too much time on her woes, which included her son. Edward was a disappointment to her. He was not robust like his father, capable of making a valet quiver as he bellowed unhappiness about the creases on his trousers. Edward's father had been a bit of an arsehole by all accounts but was dead by the time his son was ten. It was Edward's mother who had pushed him towards the military, an attempt to toughen him up, apparently. Gods knew how soft he must have been before, for Edward was still, in Pitch's mind, like butter sat too close to the stove.

A footman offered a tray of bubbling glasses, and Pitch took one readily, gulping down half the contents before he remembered he was in a skirt and such greediness would see him judged badly. The Honourable Ronald's gaze undressed him as Mrs Piggleton asked as to how Margaret knew Edward.

'Mr Charters and I spent time together in the summer,' Pitch explained. 'Rather a lot.'

'Lucky bloody chap.' Ronald might as well have dribbled. Mrs Piggleton giggled, eyeing her man in such a way that it was clear she rather enjoyed seeing him hot and bothered over another woman.

'I'm terribly disappointed he's not here this evening.' Pitch took another sip. Gods, he'd missed champagne. The very different warmth it put in his belly, how quickly his head buzzed with it. 'I've heard he's on the Continent?'

'Is he just?' Ronald disappointed Pitch with his reply. 'Well, I dare say he'll be kicking himself to learn he missed seeing you.'

'You are lovely.' Mrs Piggleton's lips seemed to be fighting her control, wiggling about. 'What part of America did you say you were from?'

'Oh, I call many parts home. Would you excuse me?'

The couple's shoulders sagged almost in unison.

'Perhaps we can play a round later?' Mrs Piggleton asked.

Pitch brushed his fingers over her arm. 'Absolutely. And after that perhaps some cards too?'

His sly smile nearly killed the poor woman, who was in danger of dying from the fit of giggles that consumed her. Half the room peered their way.

Pitch sauntered off, leaving the salivating couple in his wake and doing his utmost to make his hips sway nicely. The stiffness in his muscles ruined it a little, but he thought he did quite well, even without the bloody cane. Silas could take that suggestion and shove it up his very lovely arse, Pitch decided.

He was fully aware of all the eyes upon him. The room was filled with purebreds, so far as he could see, the good lighting showing clearly the shadows that clung to their heels. He acknowledged the greetings and nods that came his way. A chap he did not recall at all certainly remembered Miss Margaret Cargill. Red-cheeked, his monocle lifting one thin brow, he spent a moment too long with his lips upon the back of Pitch's hand, decrying what a shame it was not to have seen her for so long. His companions, a trio of serious-faced older men, crowded around for their turn at flattery. Pitch was uneasy at being so pressed

46

in upon. There was a distinct disadvantage to being the loveliest in the room. Worse still, these men were of no use to him. They too thought Edward to be away. Taking the sun in Africa, according to the chap with a crooked nose.

'Good thing too,' he said. 'Poor chap's been mixing with the wrong type of company. Dreadful business, all that. How he passed over you, my dear, in favour of hanging about with Feversham and his vile crowd, none of us can understand.'

'Now, now,' Mr Monocle said. 'The lady certainly doesn't need to hear any of that.'

Pitch put on a suitably demure expression, lowering his head and managing to bring a blush to his cheeks. But inwardly he fumed. Could they all not stand back just a little? If Silas were here, he would have sent them scattering, knowing in that interminable way of his when his dae-mon was unhappy. Pitch gripped his glass tighter. Oh, for the gods' sake. Since when did he need a damned dead man to send unwelcome suitors running? If he wished, Pitch could have this entire room fornicating on the tables, using the champagne bottles in scandalous ways.

Settling his shoulders, Pitch asked, 'I wonder if you might know where Mrs Charters is? I haven't seen her yet, and I'm longing to say hello.'

'In conversation upstairs with Mr Fothergill. Some paperwork to be signed, I understand.' Mr Monocle's hands twitched, sensing that his beloved Miss Cargill was about to abandon him. Astute man, he was.

'Mr Fothergill?'

'Her business man. Been handling the family's affairs for years, since just after Graham Charters died.'

'Handling a good deal else, I'd wager.' The crooked-nose gentleman guffawed, his breath reeking of gin. 'Nothing like a fresh wealthy widow to whet a man's appetite.'

His companions feigned horror at such indelicate talk in front of a lady. Odd, Pitch thought, how they were so careful with their language around fragile females but did not think twice about hemming her in like a prize cow at a sales yard. Pitch ground his teeth behind his smile. He was fairly certain one of the men's hands had found its way to the back of his dress and dug in, looking for a pair of ripe peaches.

'There's some unsavoury talk going around, that's true. But I don't believe a word of it,' Mr Monocle insisted. 'Fothergill's kept things in order with the factory, and the estates. Edward would do well to take lessons from him.'

'Ed's too busy playing with rakes and listening to the fairies... Odd boy, that.'

Pitch smiled, joining the laughter with a delicate titter and blushing where necessary. This Mr Fothergill may prove useful. And if he and Edward's mother were together, now was the perfect time for a stroll upstairs.

'Gentlemen, it's been lovely, but I must be moving on now. We'll speak again, I'm sure.' Pitch spied an approaching footman with a fresh tray of champagne-filled glasses. 'Excuse me.'

He pushed from the dinner-suited cage with a sharp inhale, feeling a fool for allowing the press of bodies to unsettle him. He'd been in orgies with more people, buried under bodies, held down with a cock in both orifices and a lady's mouth on his pillar, and not been troubled in the slightest.

Curse the Alp for making a fool of him even here.

Pitch waggled his empty glass at the waiter. 'Might I trouble you for another?'

The lad nodded eagerly. He had lovely amber eyes, full lips, and teeth that were very cutely bucked, but he was far too slight. Pitch had a taste for a larger man now, bearded and uncommonly thoughtful.

He snatched the glass off the tray and downed a very unladylike mouthful. Perhaps if he had curbed his taste for such a man sooner, he'd not have been so vulnerable to those infernal Gidleigh House éclairs.

He took another substantial swig, appreciative of the footman's turn of the head that afforded him some privacy in his gluttony, and doubly thankful that the lad did not wander away, waiting until Pitch downed the empty glass and took another.

'Good boy.' Pitch winked from behind his raised glass. That did send the man scurrying, his neck blooming red.

Gods, Pitch had missed champagne and all this pointless frivolity and flirtation, the laughing at nothing. The gossip and lies and general vapidness of society was really quite wonderful. Far better than angelic quests and maniacal sorcerers. He was as nearly invisible here as he would ever be. Tobias Astaroth was buried beneath taffeta and Prince Vassago beneath Satty's elixir.

He was...dare he even think it...quite free.

Well, as near to free as this was, compelled to wear a disguise and sneak about in an old lover's house at the behest of a bloody piece of jewellery gifted to him by a dead angel.

Pitch swallowed down his irritation with another mouthful of bubbles. Mrs Charters and Mr Fothergill were likely to be upstairs in the study, where all the business was done. He'd go through to the sitting room and take the smaller staircase at the rear of the house.

It took a little while to travel even that short distance, for every few steps there was a pause to offer up a how-do-you-do to a variety of people. A few he recognised from about town. He was fairly certain the brunette with jewels the size of plums in her hair was the same one who had watched on, one bright spring evening, as Pitch was sucked off by her husband in their marital bed. An earl, if he recalled. Pleasant evening that one. Very satisfying assortment of mint chocolate after dinner.

Pitch took a sip from his champagne and found it empty again. He was scowling at it when the buck-toothed footman appeared, filled tray at the ready.

'Madam.' He was breathing a little harder than tray-carrying warranted.

'Goodness, what impeccable timing you have, my dear.' Pitch beamed, and the lad lit up like the blazing fire in the hearth. Isaac must be intolerably bored with watching all this, which was one small highlight of the evening out.

An exuberant older woman with wide-blown pupils and a faint shadow of hair upon her top lip pushed herself in between the footman and Pitch. The servant, appearing a little glum, took his leave.

'Oh my, you're as lovely as I recall, Miss Cargill. I'm Daphne...Daphne North...I don't know if you recall? Lovely, lovely to see you again. What a night that was, eh? We'd all had rather a lot of wine when we last met.' And a good deal else, Pitch would wager, which may account for why he had absolutely no recollection of this woman. 'And can I just say what a delightful couple you and Mr Charters made. I'll not hold back in saying, I was most disappointed we did not see an engagement between you two.' Her eyes were glassy, her jaw working hard, and she stood far too close. 'Such a pity the lieutenant can't be with us, isn't it?'

'Terrible pity. I haven't heard yet where he's gone off to.'

'I'm hearing he's sunning himself in India.'

'Really?'

She nodded, so hard she was in danger of losing her pearl earrings. Her drink sloshed over the sides of her glass as she lifted it too quickly to her lips. Daphne giggled at the damp spots she'd made on her satin bodice. Once, Pitch might have decided her a worthwhile target for an enchantment. Already half-gone, it would be an easy slide into the bedroom. But instead he just found her irritating and was ready to shove her aside if it looked like she'd stain his dress with her carelessness. The crowd was bothering him, the air a fraction too stifling, and he was surprised to realise he did not wish to be here at all. But be here he must, for a while longer at least. Clearly, he needed more than the champagne to make it endurable.

Perhaps this woman could be useful after all.

'I say, might you know of where I could find something more...' He indicated his glass. 'More stimulating than this, shall we say?' Pitch wiped a crooked finger slowly beneath his nose, hoping she was not too inebriated to read the signal.

Wide pupils widening further, the woman nodded heartily. 'Oh my dear, of course. Come, come. I've some in my purse. Let us go to the powder room.'

Daphne linked her arm through Pitch's and led them through into the sitting room. It was almost as busy as the parlour, but thankfully with this woman at the helm there was very little pause in their journey. Evidently, she was very eager to share her tincture. She kept him on a firm path, dragging him along as his hip slowed him, moving too quickly for anyone to think of interrupting them.

They were a step shy of reaching the open doorway that led out into the hallway when someone passed by in the corridor. Pitch nearly tripped over his own feet. Not because he was partly invalid, but because the man he'd seen was very familiar.

'Everything all right?' The woman patted his gloved hand.

'Yes, yes, of course. Just a little tired.' Down to the very bone at times.

'Well, we shall soon fix that.' His guide grinned. 'Can't have you leaving the party too soon. I've a nephew arriving shortly who you really must meet. He is a delight, and terribly good company.'

Of course he was. Pitch might have been more irritated discovering the woman's friendliness reeked of ulterior motives were he not trying to decide if he should disappear back into the parlour or call out to the man who was striding down the hall, the oil on his bald head shining beneath the gaslights.

'There, there, my dear.' The woman patted his hand a second time, and Pitch considered stepping very hard on her toes. 'You must have seen Orientals in the United States, surely? Aren't they just dreadfully exotic and wonderful? Not as wonderful as my nephew, mind.'

Sweet gods. He was scowling deeply before he remembered he was a godsdamned lady.

'They are precious, aren't they?' He smoothed his features. 'But it's not that. He seems familiar, that's all.'

'Oh, should we call out to him? Here, I'll do it.' Daphne had best have the world's most sublime cocaine because she was testing his patience truly. 'Yoohoo! You there...stop where you are.'

The man did as he was ordered, but not with any happiness. He grunted and turned on his heels, clearly annoyed at having his journey interrupted.

That pockmarked face, flat cheeks, and all-too-familiar scowl could belong to none other than Kaneko, The Atlas's insufferable bartender.

Pitch's breath caught. Lady Satine's elixir was about to be much tested.

'How can I help you?' Kaneko demanded, hands clasped behind his back.

A good thing Kaneko's skills in The Atlas kitchen were above reproach because he was abysmal when it came to being pleasant company. He barely glanced at Daphne's companion, and when he did, seemed utterly disinterested in the vision of loveliness that Pitch was. Barely spared him a blink. Mildly insulting, but pleasing. Pitch knew the hues of his aura were rather unique, patchwork and drained as they were. If they had been visible to the tsukumogami, he doubted Kaneko would have shown no sign of seeing it.

Pitch *was* fucking invisible. He could barely stifle his grin.

'Dear me, no need to be so rude,' Daphne declared.

'I'm not a servant, if that's what you are thinking.' Kaneko turned side on, readying to leave. 'Just delivering canapes for the lady of the house, and I'm late back to where I need to be. So, good evening to you, ladies.' He managed to roll the word like gristle between his teeth.

'Wait, it's just that –'

Pitch stayed Daphne with a light touch. 'Never mind. It's not who I thought. Let the man go.'

But the man was already going. Kaneko was not waiting for any permission. Pitch watched him stalk away. He had a faint recollection of hearing that Kaneko's services were in demand outside of The Atlas. He'd probably catered more than a few of the parties Pitch had attended over the past year, but as the tsukumogami was a master of savoury treats and not sweet, Pitch had little reason to pay his skills any mind.

'Goodness, he wasn't interested in a chat, was he?' Daphne said.

'Just as well.' Pitch touched at his curls. 'I'm rather keen to take what you offered.' He tried for a conspiratorial grin. 'Shall we have that tincture now?'

Daphne returned his smile tenfold. 'Oh yes, let's do. Superb mix this one. Wonderful stuff. You'll not know yourself afterwards.'

Pitch could only hope.

CHAPTER 6

S ilas scowled and pushed up his sleeves. The paintbrush he held dripped with black lacquer and the stench was making his head spin.

I think you missed a section over there.

It was the third time Phillipa had pointed out such an oversight.

'Good grief, why don't you do this, then?' He flicked the brush with irritation, sending droplets flying.

Because I'm dead, Mr Silas, sir. As you know, the lost soul replied with no trace of irritation. *And these hands aren't so good with precise work. I can push things off shelves, mind. Maybe even lift a candlestick if I really put my mind to it, but painting a carriage is quite beyond me. I'm not too proud to admit it. You are doing a very fine job though, otherwise.*

Silas gritted his teeth. He'd come here to the carriage house at the Lodge, seeking Phillipa's company, as he could not decide where to place himself while he waited on Pitch's return. After Jane had made up the daemon to within an inch of his life, she and Sybilla had headed out for a dinner meeting with a chap from St George's University of London, following a lead regarding body snatching. Tyvain was not the sort of calming company Silas sought, any more than Gilmore.

He'd considered heading over to Holly Lodge and speaking with Lady Satine about what he had learned of himself at the greensward, but he was unsettled enough as it was. What with Lucifer's arrival and cursed halos to contend with. Not to mention Pitch being off without him, following the whim of the pendant watch.

Christ, it turned Silas cold to think of what was expected of the daemon. Lucifer claimed Seraphiel had made a monster of him. Well, so far as Silas was concerned, it was Lucifer and the bloody angel who were monstrous. Demanding so much of Pitch, and offering nothing in return.

Silas jabbed his brush at the door panel he was working on, repairing the damage done where the removal of the macabre dressing of bones had scratched off the paintwork. The task should have rested with someone with far greater skill but when Phillipa had lamented the damage, Silas had grabbed at the opportunity to do something other than pace.

He'll be all right. I'm sure.

'Who?' Silas stabbed the brush at a spot that he'd been over a dozen times already.

Now, now, Mr Silas, sir. No need to be like that. You have been like a badger caught in a trap since that pretty fellow of yours walked out the gates looking like a dream.

The paintbrush suffered another thrust against the wood. 'He is not my fellow.' Bloody hell, it had moved on from *his* daemon, to his fellow.

Whatever he is, he's no stranger to you.

'Of course not.' Talk of a stranger wouldn't make his pulse madden as it did now. 'We ride as Horsemen, we are partnered. And yes, I am concerned. Of course I am. You know as well as anyone what horrors lurk out there.'

That I do. Phillipa's sinking mood was palpable, and regret touched at Silas. She'd suffered a great loss, and he was being petty over a word.

'You are very safe here, Phillipa.'

I know. And I thank you for it. The lost soul sighed, and the horrid gaping wound at her chest contracted. *Your fellow will be fine, I'm sure. He doesn't seem the type to be easily bested. Good gracious me, didn't he look a vision when he left here? I'd never in a hundred years have imagined a man lay beneath that dress.*

Silas kept quiet. He was not sure he could speak of seeing Pitch wrapped up in a gown and made up with rouge and raven-black hair without making a bloody fool of himself. He'd been furious, of course, that he'd not been allowed to travel with the daemon, but beneath the anger and worry had been other stirrings entirely. He'd not dared to get too close; he'd not even gone to say goodbye. The bloody tent-pole in his trousers made that impossible, for one. Silas could picture very well the man who lay beneath those layers, wrapped like a scandalous gift.

'There you are, Silas.'

The brush slipped at the unexpected voice, smearing black lacquer onto a section of the window.

'Lady Satine. Is everything all right?' Silas rose to his feet.

'Tobias is fine.' She regarded him with gentle violet eyes. 'He's had no trouble getting in to the residence, so all is well there. Now we just wait.'

Silas exhaled. 'Indeed.'

'I wondered if we might have a word?' Lady Satine tilted her head. She was a handsome woman in the appearance she had made for herself. This was her true form, her *human* form at least, when she was not borrowing bodies to deliver a message: superb olive-toned skin and a head of remarkable salt-and-pepper curls. She held a resolute air, a firmness to her that spoke of strength rather than sternness, much like Sybilla.

'Of course.' Silas darted a look up at Phillipa, who sat on the carriage roof, feet dangling.

Oh, I get it. Leaving, right now. I'll be in the Morrison crypt in the cemetery if you need me. Mrs Morrison is an absolute riot.

'I'm sure,' Silas said. 'But don't go wandering too far. And be watchful. Tell me at once if you hear any talk of the Blight...the gloaming, you may hear it called.'

Yes, yes, Mr Silas. There's no news of it here in the city so far though. Now don't go fretting over me. You're doing enough of that already over him. A few pints is what you need, I'd say. Phillipa gave him a cheery wave, fading away until Silas was blinking at thin air.

'What did your ghostly friend have to say, Silas? You look like you've just sipped on foul milk.'

Silas glanced at her. 'I thought you could hear Phillipa?'

She had done so when they were in the carriage on the way back from the greensward.

'Not always. It seems when they are most riled and anxious, I am privy to some snippets. But I dare say your friend is calmer now than when we last met.'

'She is.' Silas nodded. 'The Morrisons are keeping her distracted enough from her sorrow.'

'Good. Good.' Lady Satine settled her honey-coloured shawl about her shoulders. She wore a simple cotton gown but the single lonely gaslight installed in the carriage house distorted its true colour, making it appear somewhere between off-white and subtle yellow. 'Now I just need to do one more thing before we chat...'

She threw up her hands and sparkling droplets flew from her grasp, as though she'd held fistfuls of rain. With the move came the waft of the open sea, the same that had struck Silas when the melody named the Lady Satine a djinn. A leviathan.

The spray rose upwards and the droplets grew larger, their consistency more akin to quicksilver. As they began their descent they spread outwards, arching to form a dome encompassing Silas, the carriage, the Lady herself, and a good portion of the interior of the carriage house. The droplets, large as sovereigns and evenly spaced, hung as though held precisely by hidden wires.

'There. Can never be too careful,' she said, dusting off her hands. 'But we can speak freely now with the shroud in place. I've been hoping to speak further with you about your experience at the greensward. I know you've been very distracted by the daemon's illness.'

Silas studied his paintbrush. 'Pitch did have me greatly concerned.' The truth but not the whole truth. He'd been avoiding speaking about that horrid day and was quite sure the Lady knew it.

'I know you both endured a terrible time there.' Lady Satine strolled over to where a stack of hay bales made for a makeshift lounge. 'I know of the pond they tried to drown you in, Lalassu saw the remnants of it well enough, but what of Tobias?'

Silas's knuckles whitened with his grip on the brush. 'What of him? You know they kept him in a sigil-infested room and poisoned him with Gu.'

'I do. But I wanted to be certain I knew all there was to know.'

Silas swallowed, his throat dry. It was not his place to tell the whole story.

Lady Satine plucked a piece of straw and twiddled it between her fingers. 'I sense a delicacy in the prince that worries me. How badly did they hurt him, Silas?'

Setting down the brush, Silas considered his words. 'Well enough.'

'And could they weaken him that way again?'

'No.' Silas was razor sharp. 'They will never do that to him again.' He could not shake his sense of guilt. Not only had it been he who had insisted on going to Gidleigh House, but Silas had then been the weakness the Alp could exploit in the daemon. 'The Morrigan sought to break him and they failed. He destroyed every inch of the prison they made for us. He saved me, and I am grateful for it, but the toll on him was enormous, I fear. Every moment of that rescue pained him.'

'And I dare say more pain is to come.' The lady exhaled heartily. 'As it will for all of us who seek to take on Blood Lake.'

He'd hardly expected reassurance all would be fine, but still...some hope would have been nice.

'A fool's errand.' Silas swiped hard at the stains on his fingers. 'Was that not how Lucifer described any attempt to destroy the halo?'

'He did and he may be right.'

'Then why the bloody hell are we chancing it?'

'Because there *is* a chance to take. Even Lucifer, stubborn as he is, knows it to be true. He'd not have brought the watch here otherwise. Gods, after two thousand years there might yet be a way to end Samyaza's legacy for good.' Lady Satine straightened, eyes shining with a lighter hue of violet. 'Imagine it, Silas...a world with no Blight to plague it. A world that no longer harbours a secret capable of tilting the Severance War in Elyssiam's favour.'

'The halo is truly that powerful, even without Samyaza to wield it?'

'It is a part of him. A remnant of the Seraph's strength.' The Lady took another piece of straw, adding it to the weave she made. 'With Azazel's expertise in cultivation, Samyaza's power could see the Exarch rebirth the Nephilim...or create new monsters in their place. That damned bloody war he has fought with Enoch for untold years has been on a knife's edge for centuries. This world may prove the tipping point if Azazel finally learns that Blood Lake is more than a graveyard.'

The frigid air did not reach them through the droplet barrier, but Silas felt the ice burrow into his bones nonetheless.

'And you truly think Pitch has a hope of destroying the halo?' he said quietly.

She contemplated her weaving. 'Since the death of Seraphiel there has been a change in the balance of things in this world. For the past two years the lake has been the most restless I've ever known. When Lucifer dumped the prince on my doorstep near-on a year ago, Vassago had already spent a year in the abaddon. The king delivered a wretched creature, but told me very little about him. Barely weeks after Vassago's arrival, the sightings of teratisms began to rise. Slowly at first, but strengthening to the point where it was necessary to summon you, the Pale Horseman, once more. At first I thought the stirrings of the Blight due to the angel's death, somehow, too. Seraphiel created one of the three seals on Blood Lake, after all. It stood to reason his demise would have resonance. But then Lucifer deigned to tell me more of Vassago's connection with Seraphiel, about how the angel's last wish had been to see the prince survive. It seemed plain to me that the strife in this world had a connection to our friend Tobias. That the halo might be sensing a threat to its existence. But the King of Daemonkind was harder to convince. There had been much talk in Arcadia, apparently, of Seraphiel's state of mind; whispers of growing madness, of the Seraphim Michael seeking to overthrown him due to his erratic behaviour. Lucifer and Seraphiel were close. I think the daemon had seen an angel's madness close up, and he presumed Prince Vassago a part of it. But even Lucifer himself could not pretend blindness to what was happening here; the shift in the Blight, a rise in purebreds wielding maleficium, the likes of which we'd not seen since the early days, before Sybilla was gifted to me to put an end to those born with divine magick.' She inhaled with a quick, shuddered breath. 'Do I think Tobias capable of destroying the halo? Perhaps. Do I want him to try? Definitely.' She closed her eyes, clutching the straw to her chest. Silas watched her, his pulse quickened by her words. 'Gods, we could be free at long last, Silas. The legacy I was shackled with when the djinn became guardians of Blood Lake, would be over with. And you could finally rest, *finally* pass over, as all souls must do. *Should* do. Surely a part of you must long for rest after all this time?' She looked at him so earnestly...so hopefully, it seemed churlish not to nod and agree wholeheartedly. But he stayed still. Satine shook her head, setting her tight curls bobbing. 'You still cannot remember the passing of so many years, can you? I thought memory had returned to you after the greensward.'

Silas folded his arms, pressing sticky fingers against his ribs. 'Memory of dying, yes. Many times. But there was nothing of my life nor of being called to ride for you.'

'Well, you never recall your living years. That's not so strange. But I had hoped you might recognise me a little by now.'

'We have known each other from the beginning?'

'To be honest, I don't really *know* you, Silas. You've never been open to revealing much about yourself. Conversations didn't exactly go on all night by the fire when we met. I'd be lucky to get two words out of you. It seemed that being a servant of the goddess of death meant being deathly dull. When I've tolled the bell for you in the past—'

'Bell?'

The Lady's glance was laden with many things, frustration among them. 'Yes. You must have heard the blasted thing when you woke in your coffin? Damned near sent me deaf when the goddess rang through your arrival.' She leaned back against the stacked bales. 'When I have need of my Horseman, of you, I ring the bell and place it on an unmarked headstone over an empty grave. Mr Ahari does the digging, thankfully. I think this time there was only a simple cross at the head of your plot. The stonemason was busy, but we could hardly wait. Still, it worked just as well, for the bell tolled again when the goddess had you in place. We dug up the grave and there you were.'

That day of waking in his coffin seemed one of many lifetimes ago. But Silas *did* recall the tinkling of a bell, the only sound at first until the steady thump of digging had begun.

'Bloody hell...' He cringed. 'I sound like a turkey being baked for a Sunday lunch. I'm surprised Mr Ahari didn't stick a fork in me to make sure I was done.'

Lady Satine snorted and let the circlet she'd woven drop into her lap. 'Goodness, you are much improved on your past reiterations. I mean you look very similar each time...like you are the brother of the man that came before you, but in personality, this time you are night and day to the rest.' She waved her hand at him, like he were a piece of art for perusing. 'Oh, yes, this is far more likeable. Gods you were boring, what with all your *I must dispatch the teratism and return to my grave, Satine.*'

'I said that?' Silas tried to wrap his mind around this bizarre conversation. One that felt as though it involved an utter stranger.

'Not in so many words, because you didn't really use many. Very serious chap for the most part. Dedicated to the task at hand. You were rather like a very handsome automaton, once such a thing existed for me to compare you to. You kept to yourself, did your work, and were gone. I have to say, as concerning as your extreme lack of memory is and how painful it's been to watch you bumble about, I think I may actually miss you this time when you leave. You are so very...well, you are the most human I've ever known you.' The Lady crossed her legs beneath her, resettling her skirts on her makeshift throne of hay. She drew another piece of straw and picked up her circlet of golden dry stems. A light drizzle was falling beyond the wide-open doors of the carriage house, though Silas could not hear any hint of it through the shroud's sparkling barrier.

His head ached. 'Forgive me, but this is all very—'

'Ah-huh.' Satine pointed at him with the unwoven straw. 'See that...that right there...delightful. Humble and polite to a fault, modest...gentle and prone to worrying too much. I wonder if you were more like this to begin with? In the very beginning I mean.'

'When I first lived?'

Silas only knew a terror-struck young man drowning in a loch. He'd not stopped to wonder what else he'd been.

'Yes.' Satine embellished her circlet with little loops, casual as you like, as though they were not discussing the endless years they had both lived.

'Mr Ahari and I have many theories about why you are such a blank slate this time.'

'Do you intend to share them with me?'

Somewhere beyond the Lady's veil of quicksilver, an owl hooted, drawing him to thoughts of Marcus in the garden...and the tawny owl's son at the witch-bottle house. Silas peered beyond the shimmering layer, wondering how Pitch fared, disliking the distance between them.

'Most of the ideas are nonsense.' Lady Satine was clearly in the mood for conversation. 'I assured Mr Ahari you are definitely *not* an automaton and nor do I believe you have a touch of decay dementia.' The lady held up her braiding to survey the work. She pursed her lips, angling the untidy weave of straw back and forth. 'My theory is that the sand in your hourglass runs thin. You have served the goddess far longer than any other ankou, thanks, I'm sure, to the Nephilim blood that once ran in your veins. But you've always retained your humanity, even when it was hidden beneath dullness and duty. And your humanness has never been more evident than with this reanimation. All purebreds grow old and die. It is the way of things. And I believe the time soon approaches when the goddess will take back her scythe. My theory is, Mr Mercer, that you are dying.'

Silas blinked. 'Well, to be fair, I die on a very regular basis. And re-member far too much of it. Even down to the very first sacrifice.'

He found himself not so shocked at the Lady's words as he might have expected. As though this truth already lay somewhere in the quagmire of his many memories. He knew he was not immortal.

'Sacrificed,' the Lady said, 'because your mother had fallen prey to Samyaza's wiles and they feared the angel's blood in your veins would turn you monstrous, like so many other bastards of the Watcher King had done. I know the tale, it was one of the few you ever deemed to tell me. I think you were rather pissed off at the stupidity of humankind. Believing the death of a frightened young man would appease a furious god. You were never a monster, nor have you become one.'

'Wait, just a moment.' Silas bristled. 'If you've known so much about me all along, why have you said nothing all this time? You could have told me who—'

'Being told is not the same as remembering.' Lady Satine moved from seated to on her feet in the actual blink of an eye. 'And you were foggy to begin with the last time you rode, but it all fixed itself eventually. I thought, given time, it would do the same now.'

Silas stared at her. 'A word here or there would have been appreciated. I've had a horrendous time, what with being so lost and empty-headed.'

'I may have let you stumble about too long, I'll grant you that. But you were still a master of your scythe, still capable of carrying out your task. Now, don't speak to me of being left in the dark, for I'm well familiar with it. Lucifer and I have known each other a long while. He came here often in the early days to see to things, but I had not seen him for a long time when he turned up with a sickly Dominion prince, demanding to be directed to Seraphiel's Sanctuary so he could conceal Vassago there. I told him he was asking entirely the wrong person. It was not as if I'd ever been invited around to the angel's place for tea. I think I saw Seraphiel thrice, in all the time I've been beholden to Blood Lake. How the hell would I know where his lair was? And if he'd not deemed to tell Lucifer of it before he died, that was hardly my fault. So the Village had to suffice.'

'Then, you don't know what the angel might have done with Pitch at the Sanctuary?' Silas asked.

'I understand there was fucking involved, Lucifer was not happy about that. Jealousy doesn't look good on a king, I have to say.'

With a wince, Silas shook his head. 'No, I mean you spoke as though you understood Seraphiel's designs on Pitch, when Lucifer delivered the watch.'

'I understood designs existed, but that was all. I doubt even Lucifer knows the ins-and-outs, that's why he's so cantankerous about it all.'

'Did you know that Seraphiel possessed Edward's body, when he had Pitch at the Sanctuary?'

The Lady's gaze snapped to him, her fingers tightening over the straw circlet. 'The angel used the lieutenant?'

'Yes.' Silas had the sinking feeling he'd said something he should not, for it seemed very odd for Pitch not to have mentioned such a detail to the Lady.

She tapped her heel against the hay thick floor, turning to look out beyond the carriage house doors. 'I was not aware, no. Whenever I met the Seraphim he was in a guise of his creation, he was not hitching a ride, as it were.' She sighed, and relaxed her grip on the weaving. 'Tobias deigned not to tell me such details. He's angry at me still, for many things...for treating him like a prisoner mostly, while I waited for word from Lucifer. And for having Sybilla tie his tongue. I suppose his dislike is not unwarranted. If he wishes to keep his secrets, then so be it. At the end of the day, this is his quest, not mine.'

She turned to look at him. Silas had the unsettling sense of a great chasm lurking in the depths of her pupils. He was not afraid of her, per se, but very much aware he saw only a glimpse of all the Lady Satine truly was in the woman before him.

'I share this trial with him.' He shoved damp palms against his trouser legs, rubbing at the lacquer that refused to budge. 'I don't care how many days I have left, so long as there are enough for him.'

She bent to pick up her discarded straw crown and studied it a moment before she spoke. 'You are loyal to the prince, and you clearly care for him a great deal.' Silas would not deny it. 'That is not a terrible thing. But be careful it does not distract you from the task ahead. Guide him, Silas. See the prince to where he *must* go.'

Wherever that was remained to be seen. Silas was much more certain of where he should be right *now*.

'I will guide him, Satine. Not because you say so, or because Lucifer thrusts an order upon us to heed a trinket's will. I do it because I promised Pitch he would not face this alone.' Silas gestured to the dome of gleaming silver dots around them. 'I would ask you to take down your shroud. I am going to the soirée, it is where I should be. I've no wish to openly defy you—'

'But you will, if I hinder you.' The Lady settled her circlet of straw upon her head, where the makeshift crown sat crooked amongst her curls. 'It seems you're not so far removed from your past reanimations after all.' Her smile was relaxed, the tension of earlier gone. 'Your strength of will was always considerable and your blunt determination infuriating. Both have survived well, whatever else may be gone. I think your combination of death's servant and smitten purebred is precisely what's needed here.'

'Smitten? I am hardly—'

'Hush your pointless denial. Just know it was never my place nor intention to dictate Vassago's journey, or yours. Lord Enoch put his mark upon me for a higher purpose, when the Mother of Djinn gave me up to Arcadia and its angels. I have a job enough to do without holding your hands all the while, but I see now that there is no need for coddling, anyway. The prince has a much better hand to hold in yours. Your bond is quite unexpected, I must say. And allows me to dare imagine that perhaps, this is not a fool's errand after all.'

She raised her hand, clicked her fingers, and the droplets sprayed outwards, falling away from Silas and the Lady, so neither were touched by a drop. The quicksilver veil vanished before it touched the ground.

Silas was free to go.

He made his way at once towards the open doors. 'I shall need your elixir.'

'See Jane for that, and your clothes. But, Silas, I cannot shrink you down. Your aura shall be hidden, but what of the rest of you?'

He waved off the question, eager to be on his way. 'I have something in mind for altering my appearance. And besides, I don't intend to go into the household. I just wish to be there when Pitch is done and I can see him safely home. Will you tell Isaac I am coming?'

'I will.'

Silas gave her a nod, his mind on how quickly he could dress and leave. 'Then we are done here. Thank you, Satine. For all you have shared with me today.'

'Good luck to you, Mr Mercer.'

'And to you, Lady of the Lake.'

CHAPTER 7

Pitch headed upstairs, taking the steps two at a time as Daphne's tincture kicked in, giving him a jolt of pleasing vigour. His grin was plastered to his face, and his cheeks were already aching a little. It was potent stuff, and mixed with the champagne, fuck. He'd need to dance the entire night away before he could even begin to consider sleeping.

He gathered his skirts about him, enjoying the feel of taffeta in his hands. As ludicrous as all the layers were, he could get used to wearing them. Pitch's stretched grin widened. He pictured himself announcing to Silas that he would be wearing ballgowns from now on. The ankou would go pink as a baby in a hot tub, he was sure. He'd see that delightful heavy-lidded look the ankou always wore after Pitch had his tongue down his throat and hand on his cock. He giggled in the still corridor and brushed his hand against the stirring hardness between his legs.

Maybe he should just forget all about the bloody lieutenant and go back to the Village right now. Hide back under those covers and take Silas with him this time.

Someone stepped from a room further up the corridor, and Pitch was drawn out of his musings. Mrs Charters appeared lost in her own thoughts, cooling herself with a black lace fan. She wore her favoured off-the-shoulder-style gown embellished with far more bows and trim than was becoming and a shade of pink that bordered on too bright to be sensible. Mrs Charters was a handsome woman. Pitch had always thought she would seem far more at home in the military services than Edward ever had been. There was a natural sternness to her, a weight to her presence that was added to by a heavy-set face and robust build.

'Mrs Charters,' he called, swaying a little too much. 'How wonderful to see you.'

She stopped short, head snapping up to take him in. There was some distance still between them, but Pitch was fairly certain there was no joy on her face at seeing him. He shouldn't be surprised he supposed. In the end, Miss Cargill had been a vast disappointment, for she had fled and left Edward unmarried.

'Oh...Miss Cargill, you made it. I'm sorry I wasn't there to greet you. I've been waylaid, I'm afraid.' Mrs Charters glanced over her shoulder. Despite the drifting music, he could hear her sigh from where he stood. 'Gracious, it has been a long while. What brings you to London?'

In the past, Mrs Charters could not have invited Pitch, in Miss Cargill's guise, into the house fast enough nor plied him with enough tea and biscuits to keep him there while she extolled all the virtues of her son to the woman she thought might have designs on becoming his wife. It had been so trite and amusing at the time to play with her. Edward had been stiff and awkward to begin with but had eventually found amusement in the charade too, enjoying the spoils when he unlaced Tobias later in the evening. But the frivolity faded as quickly as the lieutenant's health and Pitch's enjoyment.

'I am here for the month to celebrate Christmas with some dear friends.' Was he speaking too loudly? Hard to tell with the way his pulse beat in his ears. He fought to tie down an errant smile. The tincture was rather too rousing. 'I recalled your excellent Tuesday soirées and hoped they might still be on.'

Mrs Charters moved at a slow pace, fussing too much over a section of her pink skirt. She was in no hurry to draw close. 'Have you travelled with your husband?'

Did this woman think of nothing else but marriage? Pitch's drug and champagne-addled tongue nearly gave her a piece of his mind.

'No, no,' he said demurely. 'I'm unwed.'

There was a small, unsteady flicker of interest at that, but then her shoulders slumped, and she went back to bothering at her skirts. 'I see. My dear, if you are here to see Mr Charters, I'm afraid I must disappoint you –'

'I heard he is on the Continent, actually. I'm sorry to have missed him.'

The woman's hand halted its brushing of chiffon. 'Yes, yes. The Continent. He'll be there a long while.' Her face was pinched, her manner at once tight and unhappy. 'That's right.'

'I myself am travelling to visit my aunt in Rome early in the new year,' Pitch said. 'I wonder if I could pay him a call. Might I know where he is?'

'No.' Spoken with bite, and far too quickly. 'I mean, he asked me not to say.'

'Really? Not even to me?' Pitch put forth his most charming smile, tilting his head and softening his gaze in a manner that had given him what he wanted a hundred times over. 'I have thought of him so very often since we parted this summer.'

Mrs Charters stood but a foot away and had not raised her hand in greeting. She looked up, and her anguish was terribly evident before she hid it away. 'I do so wish it had turned out differently between you, believe me when I say it.' Pitch had no doubt, for Miss Cargill, at least in theory, had all the right body parts in all the right places. 'But Edward is...he's not...this is terribly hard, but my son is...'

A tinkling of understanding chimed for Pitch. 'I know he has not been well,' he said. 'Not just in his body but his mind.' Edward's mother looked mortified at the statement but held her tongue. 'He was greatly troubled, and I did what I could for him, but I fear I could have done more.'

Guilt made the words stick fast, and his ire towards Seraphiel rose another notch. He did not know what had led the angel to choose Edward as his vessel. A lover of Pitch's from a few years past, when the prince wore a different face and name to Tobias Astaroth while he indulged his incubus needs? The angel could have created his own form, as Pitch did, rather than possess a purebred who was likely to buckle beneath the weight of such a powerful invader. The decision had always struck Pitch as curious, especially considering Seraphiel did not take Edward's body beyond the Sanctuary walls whenever he and the daemon were there. Perhaps it was meant to distract Pitch from who was actually being so rough with him in the bedchamber, where pleasure crossed the border into pain on a regular basis.

'If there is anything at all I can do,' Pitch said, 'please tell me. Perhaps I can pay him a visit to give him some cheer? I miss him so.'

'You are very kind, my dear. I always thought so.' Mrs Charter surprised him by reaching to take his hand. The woman trembled, and her eyes seemed to glisten in the faintly green gaslight shed by sconces along the wall. 'He has been keeping some dreadful company... There was a young man, an unsavoury fellow he associated with who I cannot help but think is in part to blame for...' She bit at her lip and patted Pitch's hand. He wanted to slap her. 'Never mind all that. You are just what Edward needed, I know it, but he could not be told.'

'Perhaps I could persuade him.' Pitch laid a gloved hand over the older woman's, tapping his foot restlessly beneath his skirts. Mrs Charters shook her head, her hair so stiffly held with pins it did not shift.

'I'm afraid it is not possible to see him.' She edged closer, glancing back the way she had come. 'It would be unseemly for a lovely young lady such as yourself to visit such a place.'

Pitch fought back a shudder. Gods. He suspected he knew exactly why the lieutenant had disappeared without a trace. 'Oh my goodness, you have me truly worried now. He is not on the Continent, then?'

Mrs Charter's grip on Pitch's hand bordered on painful. 'I'm afraid not.' She dashed her free hand at her eyes. 'I won't burden you with this. You are here for enjoyment, not unpleasant details.'

But Pitch was far from done. He lowered his voice to a whisper. 'I assure you, you have my utmost discretion in this matter. Mr Charters is still dear to me. I simply must know. Has he been taken to an asylum?'

Edward's mother sucked in her breath and lowered her head. 'Miss Cargill, I cannot say.'

And yet, she may as well have just affirmed it with a shout. Fuck. They had sent Edward to a madhouse. If the poor bastard were not already barely holding on to his sanity after being pulled from pillar to post by a damned arrogant angel and an intolerably selfish daemon, he would surely come undone in one of those places.

'I have a cousin,' Pitch launched into a lie, 'who needed some care, across in Ireland. Tyvain is not of sound mind in the slightest, terrible thing, very sad, but we did what needed to be done. We did what any caring family would do...what you have done for Edward.' He must remember to tell Tyvain he'd made her a madwoman. The soothsayer would be delighted.

'Oh my dear, how awful for you. Isn't it just dreadful? The shame of it.' The glistening in Mrs Charter's dull brown eyes, nothing like Edward's light grey hue, was obvious now. Any moment a tear would be shed, tears she was spending on herself and not her son. Pitch balled his fist amongst the folds of his gown.

'I know how it is not to be able to speak to anyonef. Let me be your shoulder.' And he would grow some thorns on that shoulder to pierce her cheeks. Gods, Edward deserved *none* of this. 'Sometimes one just needs to air their grievances to feel better about things.'

Mrs Charters clung tight. 'I don't know what I've done to deserve such a son,' she sniffed. 'I care for him, of course I do, as any mother would. But he...' She shook her head. 'Well, if he had not been so foolish as to decline your company, we might have both been able to make a more admirable man of him.'

Pitch crept ever so close to realising that slap. 'Where have you sent him?'

Mrs Charters sighed and at last released her hold on Pitch's arm. 'Luckily, I've been spared the gruesome details. It is being taken care of by Mr Fothergill. He was my late husband's man of business. I trust him implicitly. He ensured me Edward was taken somewhere he'll be well cared for and has, in fact, just informed me that he seems to have settled in well.'

Pitch wiped at where her fingers had laid. 'Of course, I totally understand.' He barely got the words past his grinding teeth. Fuck, he should not have indulged so much with the tincture. His insides were wobbling like jelly.

'Shall we go downstairs, then?' Mrs Charters asked. 'My guests will have missed me by now. I'm being a terrible hostess.' And a more terrible mother. Though he only guessed at that, for Pitch had none of his own for comparison.

'Actually, I was just hoping to freshen up a little. If I recall correctly, there is a water closet in the bedroom at the end of this hall?' At the very most inopportune time, a memory struck him. One of asking such directions at Gidleigh House. He flushed to think of it, the heat unpleasant and stifling.

'Yes, second last on the right.' Mrs Charters nodded. 'Do come and find me when you are ready, won't you?'

With Mrs Charters disappearing down the stairs, Pitch made his way along the corridor, skirts hushing as he moved. He refused to be bothered by how much the dimly lit passageway also reminded him of Gidleigh House. By the gods he was not about to be cowed by those memories. Onoskolis could be as damned as Seraphiel. He paused outside the closed room he'd seen Edward's mother exit and leaned close to the mahogany door. A shuffling came from within, a rustle of papers, a clearing of a throat, which was followed by a nauseating snort as they vacated their nose as well. Pitch's foot tapped its incessant rhythm, and he wished he had brought another glass of champagne with him. His mouth was dry. He touched at his bodice, made sure all was in order, set his best look of innocence upon his superbly made-up face, and opened the door.

CHAPTER 8

Pitch caught Mr Fothergill by surprise. The Charters' financier was bent over an open drawer on a green-topped pedestal desk, a bulky thing that dominated the room. The fireplace was unlit, shutting Isaac's eyes to what might go on in here. Lucky perhaps, for Pitch intended to use enchantment to get this over with. He'd no doubt have heard the cursing in the carriage from here if Isaac had to watch him play with cock.

Fothergill was a striking man, even with his rather wild head of light brown hair that seemed unable to decide what direction to point. His pronounced square jaw gave him the look of a stern army captain. Fothergill jerked upright as Pitch swanned into the room, papers slipping from his grasp and fluttering to the desk.

'My goodness, madam, you startled me.'

'Pardon me, I'm so sorry.' Pitch played at being startled. 'I've quite gone and headed into the wrong room.' He laughed, high and merry, touching fingertips between his make-do breasts.

Mr Fothergill's shrewd eyes followed the path of Pitch's hand unabashedly. 'No mind, no mind at all.' The man gathered his paperwork, tapping it into an ordered pile atop the desk before he slid the pages into a drawer, locking it with a tiny key.

He sauntered out from behind the desk, bumping against a corner as he went. There was a distinct sweet air in the room. Pitch would wager the man had been downing more than a sherry or two as he worked at seeing Edward vanished from society.

'I was actually looking for somewhere to freshen up,' Pitch continued with his airy helplessness. 'I'm terribly sorry to have bothered you.'

Mr Fothergill's stovepipe pants showed off all the bulges and curves the man had to offer. His tailoring was admirable, Pitch had to admit. His double-breasted tailcoat was a green so deep as to be almost black, with a subtle trim of silver that was quite fetching.

'My dear, if I may be so bold, you are entirely perfect as you are. Nothing whatsoever needs freshening.' His smile had something of the wolf in it, far too many teeth by half. Pitch considering trying to wipe that smile away by declaring that freshening up simply meant he needed to take a piss, uttering words that should never cross a lady's lips. His own drunken smile rose at imagining it.

'You are a vision, my dear,' the wolf declared.

'You are far too kind...Mr...?'

'Oh, my apologies, I've been rather neglectful.' He stopped in front of Pitch, and the waft of sherry moved with him. His cheeks were far redder than the stuffy but not overly warm room accounted for, and he was glassy-eyed. Mr Fothergill extended his hand. He had extremely slim fingers, and rather too long. 'Whom do I have the delightful pleasure of meeting here?'

'Miss Margaret Cargill.'

'And you are from somewhere far beyond the Cliffs of Dover, I dare say.' He pressed his lips to the back of Pitch's gloved hand and remained there too long to be proper.

'I am indeed. The United States, as I'm sure you have guessed.'

'Well, I'm ever so glad you left them and found your way into this room.' He probably thought his tilted smile was charming. 'Perhaps we could linger here a while, away from the madding crowds as it were, so I might speak with you more easily.'

Pitch's laughter was suitably coy as he put up a weak protest. 'I'm not sure that would be proper, are you?'

One of Mr Fothergill's teeth was a shade darker than the others and a tad crooked, like a tottering soldier.

'You are quite safe with me, Miss Cargill. I would be appalled to think you believe otherwise.' Mr Fothergill's eyes widened with false alarm as he pressed a hand to his belly in a suitable display of horror.

'Of course not.' Pitch fluttered and preened. He caught the edge of his lip between his teeth and ran his fingertips over the place on his glove where the man had kissed him. Sending all the signals that said although Miss Cargill might appear proper and respectable, she was not averse to straying. This was just like the many of the days, since Lucifer had dumped him here, and before, when Pitch had no cares in the world but besting his own record for purebreds bedded in one night. He'd revelled in the mindlessness of it, the lure of the base nature of desire. But here his pulse was too quick for comfort.

The tincture, he was sure.

'We could indulge in a quiet sherry, perhaps?' Mr Fothergill read all the signals loud and clear. He shifted on his unsteady feet, tugging at his vest as though it were suddenly too tight for him.

'Oh, you have found my weakness, I'm afraid. Sherry is my very favourite.' Pitch abhorred the stuff, which was odd considering how sweet it was. He spied a half-filled decanter, its stopper sitting by its side and a glass with the dregs of a previous drink sitting nearby. The drinks cabinet sat between two windows that looked down onto a back alley running past the house. There was a courtyard between the house and the alley, an entrance for deliveries and servants. Mr Fothergill watched him, like Dickens's Tiny Tim eyeing the turkey.

'I shall pour us those drinks, then.' He might as well have licked his lips.

Pitch would barely need to flex an enchantment to have this man at his mercy. Normally, that would have given him a thrill. A tryst where the other party needed little convincing of what they desired. But in place of a tightness in his belly, a heat down low, there was just a plain knot. Cold and tight and irritating.

By the gods, this was hardly the time for reticence.

It was not as though he needed to bend and spread for the man. Fothergill's tongue was already loose and wet enough thanks to the sherry. At most the unpleasant chap may require a little handwork, likely a kiss or two would do it. No need for Jane's rose oil here.

The knot made itself known, twisting tighter.

Pitch growled inwardly, admonishing himself. One little incident with a saggy-titted Alp and he was all jittery and dry-mouthed.

It wouldn't do.

He swayed his hips as he joined Fothergill by the wicker-and-pine drinks cabinet. The lecherous fellow's eyes barely travelled above Pitch's hips until he was near enough he could reach for the offered glass of sherry.

Gods, the man was generous with his pours.

Likely the sherry would not mix well with the champagne of earlier, but needs must. Pitch took a long draw of the sickly liquid, far longer than any lady would have done, but he had always thought the restraints of womanhood ridiculous and faintly cruel.

As the sherry slid down his throat, the enchantment rose from him like steam leaving the skin after a hot bath.

Fothergill hummed into his mouthful, the incubus touch reaching him almost at once. He smacked his lips, running the back of his hand across his mouth, and set down his glass with a thud, the sherry sloshing over the rim. The man, no gentleman at all, moved fast as a snake, and just as unwelcomed, to grab Pitch's wrist, who barely managed not to punch him in the face.

'My dear,' Fothergill slurred, drunk on liquor and enchantment both. 'I have to say, you are exquisite. How is it that we've not met before? How do you know the family?'

'Through Edward, actually. There was a time last summer when I thought perhaps I might become Mrs Charters.'

A strange growl came from the man. 'What a waste that would have been.' His free hand slid around Pitch's waist, and he urged the daemon closer. Well, it was less an urge than an insistence, and Pitch was not in the mood for being dragged about. He took a step back and did not hide the fact he was strong enough to do so. The journey was short though, his skirt kissing at the desk, the backs of his legs doing the same a moment later.

Fothergill's eyes narrowed. His grin was sly and slippery and not terribly nice. He was enjoying seeing his quarry cornered. 'Come now, no need to play coy here. I see clearly that you want this, as I do. Let us not waste too much time with false protests.'

To be fair, the enchantment would have the man believing his desires were returned, so it was not as dreadful a statement as it sounded. But Pitch was beginning to think he'd been too heavy-handed with this chap.

Fothergill's desires held a tinge of darkness to them. Many purebreds' did, and under the right conditions they could be intoxicating. But they were not to Pitch's taste today. The sooner this was done with, the better.

He allowed Fothergill to kiss his neck. Far too much tongue was involved, but he was distracted by the clock on the mantel, its embellished hands declaring it was half past the hour of seven.

It wasn't late yet. If he got this over with now and headed back to the Village at once, Silas would likely still be awake and could help him out of these layers. Or perhaps the ankou was too busy for that. He'd evidently been too occupied to say goodbye.

A sharp curl of anger ignited, with the help of the tincture and the sherry and the arsehole who had placed his hands on Pitch's hips and was sliding his lips along Pitch's jaw. A kiss was dangerously close, wanted or not.

He suspected Fothergill would prefer not.

'You have quite taken my breath away.' Pitch giggled, and tilted his head back. He pressed a fingertip to Fothergill's lips, urging the man back, and when there was some give, he wiggled free of where he was pinned against the desk. Fothergill was not impressed, making a disgruntled sound as Pitch swished his way to stand at the furthest window. 'Are you certain no one will disturb us?'

He stared down into the courtyard. It was empty save for a small pile of horse shit off to one side, yet to be cleaned up by the stablehands.

'I am quite certain. I told Mrs Charters I would be a while yet with some paperwork. A lie, I'll admit. I'm not one for cards. This is far more to my liking.' The hunger was evident in Fothergill's tone. Pitch had stoked this fire; now he'd best use it to his advantage.

He hummed, a noncommittal sound Fothergill would undoubtedly take as confirmation that rough flirtation was to Miss Cargill's liking too.

'This is certainly much more interesting than any of the parties I attended with Edward,' Pitch said, watching the shadows that leaned into the alleyway. He half expected someone to walk by, with one of the dark patches seemingly shaped as though it had a head and arms. 'A sweet man, but rather dull and terribly troubled.' It did not come easily, to speak of the lieutenant so disparagingly. 'I am not at all surprised to hear you've arranged for him to be shipped off to an asylum.'

Fothergill's laugh was coarse. 'Where did you hear such nonsense? He's gone to the Continent.' He came to stand behind Pitch at the window, and his hands found the daemon's waist once more, slipping to lie over Pitch's belly. Shrugging off the sense of being far too surrounded by the man, Pitch laid his hands over Fothergill's. The tincture still had his pulse at a race, or perhaps that came from how tightly he was being held. Fothergill moved about, angling himself around the swell of Pitch's dress. The jut of his prick rubbed at the side of the daemon's hip. It took a measure of self-control not to send the man flying out the bloody window.

'Come now,' Pitch said, a little roughly. 'You are about to have me over this desk. I suspect we can share a little honesty between us.'

The man groaned and buried his face into the curve of Pitch's shoulder. 'You look like a princess and have the lips of a whore. Good god, what have I done to deserve this?' He peppered kisses around the narrow glimpse of bare flesh at the top of Pitch's high collar.

'Absolutely nothing,' Pitch muttered.

'What was that, my dear?' The dab of a wet tongue found the back of Pitch's ear.

'Keep going.'

'With pleasure.'

The man's hips began to move, light thrusts against Pitch's back. He kept his eyes fixed on the view. Not long now, and the location of the asylum would be his, and he could summon Isaac and return to the Village, where he would sink into the deepest tub the Lady could provide. He adored this dress, but with this leech's handprints all over it now, he was not so keen to keep it on.

'Where have you sent him?'

A sound of annoyance came from the mouth nibbling at his jawbone. 'That doesn't seem important right now.'

Pitch's laughter was sugar and spice and all things very nice.

In the alleyway, a shadow stretched long, shifting from wide and squat to narrower, as though someone approached from somewhere further along but was still hidden behind the wooden fence which separated the courtyard from the alley.

'I suppose not,' Pitch said. 'Do you suppose he's in a straitjacket? Chained to his bed perhaps?' He made sure to let his shiver be felt, the note of glee behind his words to be heard.

Fothergill's breathing grew heavier. 'If I didn't know any better, Miss Cargill' – his hold tightened – 'I'd say the idea rather excites you.'

That was Pitch's intention. To appeal to the man's beastlier nature. But he had misstepped. Not for the man but for himself. It was too soon to speak so flippantly of being restrained.

'Would you think me terrible' – Pitch had to pause to cough the words forth – 'if I said it did rather?'

'I'd think you only more glorious.'

'Well, then tell me...what is it like, where Edward is?' He sucked in his breath, biting at his lip. 'Is it frighteningly awful?'

Mr Fothergill's grin was savage, ravenous. 'Dr Severs was all for Hanwell Asylum when I put word out we needed matters dealt with. But the chap changed his mind at the last minute. Fulbourn, he said. That is the place. Cambridgeshire, so not so terribly far away if by some miracle his mother wished to see him, but far enough he can be put out of mind. Cheaper, as well. Haven't been there myself, but they say it's near to bursting at the seams with lunatics. I suppose they would *have* to chain them to keep control of things.'

Pitch dutifully made himself heavy-lidded, swooning on hearing such a lurid tale. 'Oh my, how ghastly,' he gasped.

Fothergill slid around to stand in front of him, and just as he got in the way of the view outside, Pitch thought he glimpsed a body moving by, a member of the household staff perhaps, or a police officer making the rounds. They seemed a large enough fellow. He had the strangest urge to wave at them. Gain their attention and...and bloody what? Have them come and beat off the man *he* was seducing?

Gods damn it. He was tired of this room, and this prick. Both the man himself and his appendage.

He'd purposely chosen a line of conversation that would reduce Fothergill to a near-mindless mush willing to say anything at all so long as it got him beneath Pitch's skirts, and it had worked perfectly well. An incubus at his best, manipulating the fellow superbly. Why then did Pitch feel so unbearably hot, the corset painfully tight? Why was he damned well trembling?

Curse that fucking tincture.

No more champagne. Until next week at least. Pitch's gaze drifted over the man's shoulder, searching the alleyway again. Looking for sign he was not alone. He frowned at the strange thought.

Fothergill cupped his chin, seeking Pitch's full attention. He breathed in short pants, his pupils blown wide. 'Shall I tie *you* down, my dear? Would you like that?'

A wave of bitter, foul memory crashed through Pitch's skull.

Fuck.

No.

He would not like that in the least.

He moved to say so, to finish this charade, but Fothergill caught him unawares, shoving him so hard he was instantly off balance and came crashing down onto the desk. The back of his head cracked against the wood, and his vision burst with white stars. He stared up at the ceiling, where cracks in the plaster work looked, for one dazed moment, to be like faint sigils. His entire body went rigid, as though every joint had fused.

No, no, no! He shouted it inwardly.

He *knew* those lines were merely the cracks they appeared. There was no magick here, no Alp daemon toying with him. But sense was cowering beneath cold, consuming panic.

'Get off me.' Someone very, very far away was saying it. Were they his words? 'Get off me.'

Dazed, and with his own mind disabling him, he barely struggled against Fothergill as he shoved in between Pitch's legs, grabbing at taffeta, bullying his way in where he was very much not wanted. One swing, one paltry burning palm and he could have this cretin on his arse. Off of him. Pitch rolled his aching head side to side, avoiding the open mouth sinking towards him.

Pitch blinked, not sure if he was breathing or not. His pulse thumped in his ears. The shadow over him loomed larger, distorted. Pressure came to his chest. An unbearable weight.

For a terrible moment, he thought he glimpsed her again. Onoskolis grinning at him, taking him over, stealing his control. Laughing as she took what was not hers to have.

'Get off me.' His protest melted into nothing.

Heat swept over him, and it felt as though it burned away the dress, the corset, the ridiculous trappings of humanity. He was bare, splayed out, at the mercy of the shape that moved above him.

Not again. He could not bear this again.

Pitch tried to wriggle free of what nailed him to the table, like that poor sod Jesus to his cross.

He shook so hard his teeth rattled. Fuck his head hurt.

His mouth was working, pleas were leaving him, cries of protest that had the strength sucked from them the moment his lips parted.

The weight upon his chest moved. Slid down his ribs, and found the softness of his belly. And he knew, just *knew*, what came next. And it would hurt. Like nothing he'd ever known.

'Stop,' he croaked.

The shape over him swayed, emanating light that grew brighter and brighter. It would do no good to close his eyes, he knew, for the light could be stopped by nothing. The source was incandescent.

Not Fothergill; he was dull as coal. Not Onoskolis; she was a dead daemon walking.

No this light came from someone Pitch knew well. Someone who he remembered had, long ago, leaned over him and whispered fire into his ear.

'Hush now.' Not a daemon, but an angel. And his assault was as heavy as the weight of the world. But he was not seeking to fuck Pitch dry. That was not what it was. It never had been.

Fingertips pressed at his belly. Their touch would burn. He *knew* it would burn. And gods the pain would be supreme, pushing him from consciousness again and again.

A voice whispered over him. A language echoing with the depth of centuries, hissing like rain on hot coals, rising like a chorus of the gods. Pitch had heard the language of the Seraphim often enough to recognise it when it fell over him.

He'd heard Seraphiel cultivating magick more than once, too.

The language took on a baser, coarser sound when the Seraphim were casting their divine magick.

Fucking gods.

The angel had not sought a daemon prince to fuck at all, nor even to teach him how better to control his flame.

Keeping you on your back was his way of keeping you where he needed. Lucifer's words. And they made dreadful sense now.

Seraphiel, one of Arcadia's greatest cultivators, had been casting divine magick upon him.

More than once.

Many more times.

He is no daemon, Onoskolis had screamed, Pitch's blood on her tongue.

He made you a monster.

Lucifer's spiteful accusation was not spite at all.

He'd meant it.

Pitch's fury swelled. And the wildness stirred. The wildness that had always been a part of him but ever more fucking uncontrollable of late.

It was pulling at its leash now. Heat crept up from his core. If he did not wish to burn Edward's godsdamned house down, he must end this now.

Pitch sank his fingers into Fothergill's shoulders. The room was crystal clear. A prince's eyes wide open.

He raised his knee, took his aim, and slammed it into the man's pillared cock.

CHAPTER 9

F othergill buckled forward, collapsing on Pitch, his scream getting lost in folds of storm-grey fabric. Pitch grabbed a handful of the man's jacket, readying to send him hurtling away.

A sudden tingling swept through the halo's scar upon his back.

The discomforting crawl of something writhed beneath his skin. Fainter than he'd known it, but there nonetheless. The very same irritation he felt the moment Lucifer handed him Edward's long-lost gift.

Pitch recognised the touch of the pendant watch before he did the person who must be carrying it.

A pair of broad hands grabbed at Fothergill's shoulders, and the man squealed as he was dragged from atop Pitch.

'Did he hurt you?'

Pitch stared up at the great figure of a man who stood there, practically dangling Fothergill from one hand.

'What the bloody hell...?' Pitch breathed.

'Are you all right?' Silas was clean-shaven, which was astonishing enough, but he also now sported a decidedly greyer head of hair, shorter in length too, with sharp lines clipped about his ears and baring the back of his neck. His ankou aura, a hypnotic swing of silver-grey light, was absent, but still the man was larger than life itself.

'Your face,' Pitch said, rather nonsensically. The absence of the ankou's beard should be the last thing worrying him right now, but Pitch couldn't stop staring, unable to decide if it was wonderful or somehow the saddest thing he'd ever seen. Gods, maybe he'd hit his head harder than he thought. He'd gone from furious rage to dreamy contemplation in an instant.

Silas's expression shifted just as quickly from angered to anxious. 'What is it?' he said. 'Have you been injured?'

'I'm fine.' Pitch sat up, gingerly, not so sure his head agreed with him. The ache at the back of his skull made him cringe, his recollections like tumours clinging there.

'Set me down, this instant, you hooligan.' Mr Fothergill was being held by a man who could mess up his face with just his pinkie finger, yet he still found a way to be a pompous git. 'How dare you –'

'I'd suggest you shut your mouth,' Silas snarled. And it *was* a snarl. One which Mr Fothergill paid full attention to. 'Before I demand the police are brought into this matter.'

'Police?' Fothergill struggled to extricate himself from Silas's grip, but the ankou was not yet ready to let go of the man's collar. So he was going nowhere, raised onto his tiptoes as Silas held him high.

'You were attempting to assault my sister.'

Pitch blinked. Sister? After all they had done in Lady Howard's coach, in the hall, that was what Silas reached for?

'I did no such thing,' Mr Fothergill blustered. 'How dare you, man. Miss Cargill, I beseech you to set this to rights.'

But Pitch had no more time for the Charters' money man. He was well and truly done with Mr Fothergill. But Silas was another matter. Pitch was having trouble taking his eyes off him. He slipped off the table and found himself wobbly on his feet as he bent to straighten his skirts.

'There was a terrible misunderstanding,' he said, voice rusty. 'In relation to Mr Fothergill's interpretation of the word no. I'd like to go home now, if you don't mind, Mr Cargill.' Pitch kept his eyes lowered but peeked at Silas through his lashes. The ankou had come charging in like a horseless knight, here to save his damsel.

How silly. How bloody rousing.

But what the blazes was he doing here? Did Silas not think the daemon capable of handling this on his own? Had Lady Satine agreed and sent the ankou running? Silas's presence was unnecessary, of course. Pitch was fine. And he would deal with the recollections of Seraphiel at a later time too. Everything was *fine*.

He just wished to be out of this house.

'Of course, my dear,' Silas said. 'We shall go at once.'

'Now see here,' Mr Fothergill blustered. 'I'll have you know, you have entirely the wrong –'

'I'm not going to ask you to shut your mouth again, sir.' Silas's voice filled every nook and cranny in the fireless room. 'I shall do it for you the next time, and you will not enjoy it.'

Pitch's lips twitched. Dear gods, who was this bare-faced man, and what had he done with Silas Mercer? Pitch touched at his hair and made his way towards the door.

'Please apologise to Mrs Charters for my sudden departure, won't you, Mr Fothergill,' he called over his shoulder. 'Tell her I was taken ill, too much champagne I think. I shall call on her later in the week.'

He glanced back to see Silas standing over the cowering man. The ankou was quite beautifully terrifying when he so chose. 'We shall take our leave now, sir.' Silas stabbed his finger into Fothergill's chest. 'You can count yourself lucky that my sister's honour is more valuable to me than seeing your sorry face behind bars. But if I should hear a word of slander against her, I shall know you are the culprit and I will find you. Do you understand? Not a word of this is breathed to anyone, or you will learn very painfully what lengths I'll go to, to protect those dear to me.'

The ankou's words stayed Pitch's hand where it clasped the door handle. He was not sure he'd ever been *dear* to anyone. Expect perhaps Edward, but the lieutenant had been led by his cock as well as any other man and had no idea what a piece of work Tobias Astaroth truly was.

Silas, on the other hand, knew it all. And yet he was still spouting words as warm as treacle.

Pitch turned to wait for the ankou.

Fothergill's face was chalk white against the darkness of his clothing. He shook visibly, nodding like the madman he'd made Edward out to be. Silas turned his back on him, and Fothergill staggered to the drink's cabinet, grabbing at the decanter and managing to slosh half the bottle onto the cabinet, the other half in his glass.

Silas hurried to reach Pitch, and the scratching at the daemon's back intensified as the watch came with him. But discomfort be damned if it meant having the ankou close.

Silas saw the daemon watching him. He smiled. And it was like a knife cutting loose the remaining knots that held Pitch within.

'Do you have what you need?' Silas spoke softly.

'I do.'

'Good. No need to spend another moment here, then.' He placed his hand over Pitch's, which was grasping so tightly at the door handle that his bones ached. Silas guided the door open. The sounds of revelry downstairs drifted up to them. Laughter and loud voices, clinking crystal and abandon. Cigar smoke flecked the air, and the tempo of the music suggested dancing might be in order for some of the guests. Gods, how wonderful it would be to spend the night dancing and drinking.

Pitch didn't realise he was just standing there, staring longingly towards the top of the main stairs until he felt Silas's hand on his shoulder. He jumped.

'It's just me.' The ankou removed his hand and stepped back.

He would have done so because he thought it the right thing to do, to give the daemon breathing room. But it wasn't right. It wasn't what Pitch wanted. Silas should come closer, he should touch him. Maybe then it would be easier to forget angels and their hands of fire.

Pitch coughed and fussed with the creases that had formed in his skirt. 'I know it's you. I recognise the oaf beside me, even though your face seems to have gone bald.'

Silas chuckled, rubbing at his chin, and led them down the hall away from the stairs. Pitch didn't know where he was being led, but he would follow the ankou without question.

'What do you think?' Silas said.

'Of what?' Pitch drew his gaze from where it had been drinking in the ankou's new profile. He was having to work hard not to limp, but that didn't bother him for once.

'The shave.'

Pitch thought he would like to kiss every inch of the smoothed skin and trace his finger over the tiny mole that had been revealed low on Silas's jawline.

'Well.' He shrugged. 'It makes you look less like a wild hermit I suppose. The grey hair gives you a sophistication you lacked before too.'

There was that smile again. Gods. The tincture must still be playing havoc, and the floor must be decidedly uneven in this particular spot, because Pitch stumbled.

'Let us leave this place.' Silas leaned towards him as he spoke so his words were for Pitch's ears alone. 'I may have bribed a housemaid to show me the quickest route to this floor. It will make the best route of escape too.'

Silas turned to a wall panel as though he were about to attempt to walk through the wood. Before Pitch could ask what he was doing, he pressed at the wall. There was a click, and the panel swung out into the hall, revealing a servants' entrance. They made their way down a candlelit staircase, Pitch in fear of tumbling down, as his skirts made it impossible to see where the next narrow, uneven step was. Silas reached the bottom first, only asking five times if Pitch needed any assistance.

'It is not my first time in a skirt,' the daemon hissed. 'And I've used a staircase or two.'

The stairwell at Harvington Hall came to mind, where Pitch had tried to rut his confusion away in a ménage à trois. What a disappointing affair that had been. The soothsayer had made it worse by appearing in the heat of things, asking about the lieutenant.

Pitch glanced at Silas. A flutter of guilt mingled with the incessant scratching of the pendant watch. The ankou had rescued him there too. Lying with him to draw him from a mournful abyss. And what had Pitch done in return? He'd abandoned Silas. Because Pitch was a lily-livered piece of shit who had been too selfish to just admit the union had overwhelmed him. He'd been utterly desperate for what Silas offered: shelter, safety, careful handling. And the Berserker Prince did not do *desperate* well.

The last step caught him unawares. Pitch thought he was stepping onto the floorboards, only to find his heel clipping one more raised piece of wood. 'Shit.'

He barely stumbled. Silas saw to it, getting an arm around Pitch's waist at the same time the daemon realised he was falling.

'Before you protest, I know you are fine.' Silas's mouth was close to Pitch's ear. 'But a good brother would hardly hold back when his sister was in need. I have to keep up appearances.'

Oh, Pitch was going to have words, many words, about Silas's decision to make them brother and sister. It was very unsettling.

They travelled along what Silas insisted was the path he'd taken, but after they struck a dead end in a room with furniture covered in sheets, he admitted he might have been in too much haste to pay attention to the way he went. They came across a black-suited footman with his rattling tray of empty glasses, who agreed to take them to the kitchen after Pitch put on a teary display, weeping about the family emergency that needed Miss Margaret Cargill's immediate attention.

Silas had asked the footman if any new servants had been employed of late. A cheery fellow with freckles and blue eyes? He'd promptly deflated when the answer was no. The journey would have been quicker were Silas not dragging his heels, peering into each room, as though Charlie might be hidden beneath a table somewhere.

Arriving at the kitchen, and an exit, at last, Silas slipped the lad a coin in exchange for his assistance, the ankou apparently adept now at bribery. The footman left them rather hurriedly as a bell tinkled somewhere in the house.

'Charlie is not here,' Pitch hissed. 'But I know where to find them –'

'How do you know they are together?' Silas's brows knitted.

'I don't, for certain, but I'd wager a decent pile of notes on it. The lad is tenacious, is he not?' Pitch hoped to put a stop to the ankou's downward spiral of concern, deciding it wasn't fetching. 'Stubborn and moderately brave?'

'Moderately?' Silas's worry was replaced by indignation. 'He is courageous beyond measure.'

'Very well. Then we assume he's stuck to his task like a burr on a dog's arse, and we'll find them together.'

The kitchen was oddly empty, with an enormous kettle beginning to steam on the oven top and a spacious pine table patched white with dusting flour. A mound of dough sat waiting for the roller beside it to begin its work. Someone's cloak had been cast over the unused chopping block. The room had the air of being hastily abandoned.

They crossed to the door which led out into the rear courtyard. And saw immediately where everyone had gone.

There was a fire in the stables.

Nothing too grand, the cheery flames dancing about in one of the feed troughs. Hardly about to burn the house down, with all the servants in attendance flapping about like frightened gulls. Some threw buckets of water, another slapped at the fire with a rag. Stablehands were taking frightened horses from their stalls.

'Oh bloody hell.' Silas opened the door and looked for all the world like he was about to roll up his sleeves and join in the dousing.

'Walk on, Silas,' Pitch ordered. He grabbed the discarded cloak, slinging it over his shoulders and linking his arm through the ankou's. He dragged Silas along. The fire seemed rather suspect, very convenient for an escape, and Pitch was not about to waste the opportunity.

'But we should help,' Silas said.

'No, we should keep going.' He hurried the reluctant oaf along, into the shadows that clung to the far side of the courtyard, distant enough from the fire to keep them relatively hidden. The chaotic scene did the rest of the job for them. They were in the alleyway within a few moments, and if anyone had spotted them, they were too busy to do much about it. Horses whinnied behind them, calling out to one another as the smoke from the small fire stained the air.

'About time. They beat at that fire much longer, they'd start to know it weren't natural. This way, quickly.' Isaac stepped from behind several stacked crates, the coachman barely lighter than the shadows that had concealed him. If he'd been wearing his usual funeral shroud layers, they might have missed him entirely, but he had had to play along with the charade as well and wore a coat of soot-smudge grey, with a stark-white waistcoat beneath. 'You took your damn time, Mercer. Now get along with you. The carriage is up the end.' He jerked a thumb over his shoulder. 'Move it.'

The curt command brought Pitch to a standstill. Silas gave him a questioning look.

'Is everything all right?'

The ankou was a fine sight, with his shaved skin and finely arranged hair. And Pitch was all types of wonderful in his gown. There was still a touch of tincture and champagne buzzing in his veins. What a waste it would be to retreat to the dull confines of the Village right now.

'We have time,' he muttered. Lady Satine had said to be back by midnight, before there was chance of the elixir failing and turning him back into a daemonic pumpkin. But even she had admitted that was overly cautious. The elixir had worked for the Lady once for three days. And the first time it was used was always the strongest. 'We have more time than this. I don't want to go back.'

He'd not meant to sound so plaintive. Silas turned to face him, blocking Isaac's view.

'You don't want to go back?' A gentle frown gathered on the ankou's brow.

'She said it would be fine until midnight at least,' Pitch whispered. 'There's time for a stroll, surely? Perhaps an aperitif and a decent coq au vin in the West End?'

A dance would be a delight.

He and Silas were invisible. As close to human as the pair of them could be. Why not relish it? Edward wasn't going anywhere.

Silas brushed at one of Pitch's raven curls. 'Do you think that's wise?' He spoke so carefully it stung.

'I think it's possible...and that is more important to me right now. Just a short while...' He would not beg, but by the gods if the ankou didn't agree, a tantrum was to be had. 'An hour or two. That's all.'

Silas was thoughtful before he nodded.

Isaac let out a groan that bordered on a growl. 'That's not part of the plan.'

'Plans do change.' Silas looped his arm around Pitch's shoulders. 'And there's no harm in a stroll, is there?'

'How the bloody hell would I know?' Isaac retorted. 'It's not for me to say.'

'Exactly,' Pitch said. 'So scurry on home, there's a good lad. Tell the Lady we were very good boys and did what we were told. Now we are going to have some time to ourselves.'

Isaac ground the cobbles with his bootheels and stalked off, muttering all types of unpleasant things.

Pitch leaned into Silas, pressing his ear to his broad chest. A night out in London was hardly new to him. A commonplace outing. Yet he thrilled with a very *uncommon* sense of excitement at the thought of just he and the ankou, larking about as though all that concerned them was finding a place to take a drink.

'All right, then.' Silas's voice was a soothing rumble beneath Pitch's ear. 'Where would you like to go, Miss Cargill? Shall we dine? I could definitely eat.'

'I'd like to just walk...and see where our feet take us. Do you mind?'

'That sounds a very perfect idea.' Silas offered his arm. 'Madam?'

'Sir.' Pitch grinned.

He dropped a short curtsy, nestled his hand in the crux of the ankou's elbow, and they were on their way.

CHAPTER 10

S ilas pointed out a thin puddle upon the pavement. 'Careful now.'
He unhooked their arms and stepped in front of Pitch, performing
what he hoped was a very graceful move. He didn't trip or splash his heels
in the wetness he was trying to help the daemon avoid, so he figured that
was a job well enough done.

'I am saved from that dastardly puddle, how noble of you.' Pitch's
cheeks hollowed as he sucked back a smile.

'Fine,' Silas puffed. 'Walk along in wet petticoats. I truly don't care.'

'You are most uncaring, it is plain to see.'

Silas rolled his eyes, proffering his arm. Pitch slipped his hand back
into the crux of the ankou's elbow, settling comfortably.

They walked along quietly whilst the city murmured and rattled
around them with the passing of carriages and calls of chestnut sellers
in the distance. Silas left the prince with his thoughts. He'd press Pitch
soon enough to learn where it was that Edward had gone, and in turn
hopefully Charlie – good god, Silas was hopeful – but right now the daemon, though pensive, was uncommonly relaxed. Even his bothersome
hip appeared to have relented, and his limp was far less noticeable.

'Perhaps I shouldn't have brought the watch. I know it vexes you, but
you left it in my keeping and I felt unhappy about leaving it behind,
even though it was likely more sensible.' Silas could not be certain that
it wasn't the watch itself demanding to be carried along, for he'd felt

physically unwell at the thought of leaving it on the mantel in his cottage. 'Is it less harassing at least? I had Gilmore find me a lead box. I didn't tell him what for, and he grumbled about it of course, but I wonder if it helps to have it contained?'

Pitch's gaze slid up to find him. 'Somewhat. Yes.' His altered eyes were the shade of honey in sunlight. A striking hue but a poor cousin to the daemon's natural verdant. 'Thoughtful of you, Mr Mercer.'

'Who's that? Never heard of the man.' Silas smiled, warm beneath the daemon's close study. 'You have definitely had too many champagnes, my dear sister.'

Pitch's laughter was delicate. He bumped his hip against Silas's thigh. 'What appalling stock we must come from to do the things we do to each other and be related.'

'I thought the story was,' Silas said, 'that you were at the soirée to reapply for the position as Edward's wife.' Silas tugged at his collar, the darn thing a size too small all of a sudden. 'I thought having another husband appear may be problematic. Besides, I was hardly in the right frame of mind to think clearly, when I that man...' Silas paused. 'Well, he was not being gentlemanly at all.'

'No. He was not. But he's hardly the first of his kind I've met, and certainly was no issue to deal with. I had the matter in hand.' Pitch paused. 'He was just a man.'

Though they were pressed against one another, Silas wanted to draw him in even nearer so Onoskolis could not shift into any gap between them.

'You are right,' Silas said. 'I overreacted.'

Pitch pressed his hand to his belly, quiet for a worryingly long moment. 'Was that you out in the alleyway? Lurking like some ne'er-do-well?'

'It was.' Silas nodded. 'I gave the kitchenhand a bloody great shock when I came bursting in, I can tell you. Christ, that second floor has the most ridiculous number of doors. I opened every damned one before I found ...' Silas shook his head. The prince was right. He'd gone wildly overboard. 'Isaac cornered me in the alley. He'd seen me loitering and came to investigate. When he told me there was no fire set in the room where you were...well, he could not stop me. I told him to cause a distraction. I had no idea if he'd listen. We were lucky to get away with it. I could have made a right mess of things. I'm so –'

'Say it and I shall punch you as no decent lady should.' Pitch nodded a good evening to a passing couple. He squeezed Silas's arm. 'Our dear Mr Fothergill may reconsider the next time he thinks it reasonable to crack a woman's head against a table again.'

'Jesus Christ, Pitch...he cracked your –'

'Forget that. Did you see his face when you grabbed him?'

Silas's tension eased at the daemon's evident amusement. 'I thought he was going to shit his britches, to be honest.' He laughed. 'Am I truly that terrifying?'

'When protecting those you pretend dear to you, very much so.'

Silas ran his fingers over the satin concealing Pitch's hand and decided on honesty. 'It was pretence that you were my sister, but nothing else was a charade. If you still think I do not care for you by now, then I worry the hit to your head was more damaging than you are letting on.'

Pitch screwed up his superbly perfect nose. To Silas it seemed as though the daemon was confused by his words. As though Pitch truly did not see the ankou had an affection for him.

Bloody hell. This creature was infuriating, even when he was not seeking to be.

'I do think I need some more champagne,' Pitch declared. 'What say you?'

'I could be persuaded,' Silas returned. 'Do you have anywhere in mind?'

'Let's head towards Piccadilly. It will be a delightful calamity at this time of the evening.'

'All right then.'

Their light-hearted stroll was as much a deception as their appearance. They were playing at being something they were not, and it was bloody fantastic. It was a cool but not unpleasant evening, a preciously calm night before winter descended in full force. Silas grinned into the night air, bobbing his head when other people meandered by. A long-legged chap approached, draped in a dramatic embroidered grey coat, his movements in the quickened way of the nervous. Silas was startled by his delicate tune, one of flitting high notes and a beating sun, hot sand and gritty wind.

Djinn. Gazelle shifter.

As interesting as it was to imagine this chap growing hooves and horns, Silas stiffened. Was this the moment they discovered the elixir had worn from them? But the chap only glanced their way, showing no sign either of them were of any interest at all. He was more bothered with reaffixing his rather eccentric boilerman cap.

'Would you prefer to spend your evening with that fellow?' Pitch said. 'You are staring.'

'No, no, but he was djinn, was he not? He didn't notice us at all.'

Cocking his head, Pitch regarded Silas. 'You saw his nature?'

'I heard it.' He fluttered his fingers near his head. 'It's strange...a melody comes to me and I understand what it means.'

'Since when?'

Silas hesitated. 'I heard it a little when we met that other ankou.' He'd not name him ever again. 'I saw his aura too, and thought it perhaps just because he was one of my kind. But it's happening with all naturals now. It only started a few days ago in earnest. Jane was the first I heard a melody for.' He shook his head. 'I had no idea so many naturals were living amongst humanity in such a way.'

'I dare say you *did* have an idea once upon a time. When your brain hadn't turned to mush.' Pitch watched him. 'What about me? What do I sound like?'

'Nothing...there is nothing. I mean, I'm sure it will come,' Silas said quickly. 'I think you are right about my brain being mushy still. My faculties are not yet what they should be.' Likely ever would be if the Lady's guesses about him were correct. He'd not let those morbid thoughts ruin this evening though. 'But the good news is that chap did not notice us. The elixir is concealing us still.'

Pitch lifted his hand and brushed fingertips against Silas's cheek. 'As are our disguises. You are grey and shaved off your beard...to follow me.'

'I am and I did.' They had come to a standstill, right in the middle of the pavement. Silas was vaguely aware that there were some people approaching. 'I'm not sure you like the beard gone?'

'I can't decide.' He tilted his head, still touching Silas's cheek. 'Without it...it is less you.'

'Then I shall grow it back.' With the merest hesitation, he turned his head and brushed a kiss against Pitch's wrist. He'd been longing to do that awhile.

'I suppose that might be best,' Pitch whispered. 'But perhaps it is actually more comfortable this way.'

A pair of men in top hats and fine coats stepped around them. One cast Silas a wink, seeing nothing more than a man and his lady having a brazen, intimate moment.

'More comfortable?' Silas frowned.

The prince pushed himself up onto his toes, bringing himself as close as he could to the ankou's level. 'For me.'

His lips parted. Silas leaned in to meet him at once. He exhaled against Pitch's mouth and their lips met. They moved against one another so easily, so hungrily. Silas's appetite for this closeness made it hard to breathe. He cupped his free hand to the back of Pitch's head, bringing the daemon gently closer, causing him to whimper and his tongue to dance against Silas's more urgently. The delightful bittersweet tang of Pitch's mouth mingled with a hint of champagne. A breeze toyed with the daemon's wig, stirring the ringlets of ink, reminding Silas that they were standing out in the open with all of London passing them by as they kissed. The thrill of it was beyond words, his belly, and his cock, were tight and heavy with the knowledge.

The prince was first to pull back, and they caught their breath in unison. 'Now, Mr Cargill, we are supposed to be avoiding attention.'

'Then it's best you do not kiss me like that.' Silas was gruff.

'I shall never do it again.' Pitch swept his skirts back. With a tug at Silas's arm, he set them walking once more.

'That is entirely *not* what I was suggesting.'

'Chestnuts!' Pitch suddenly pulled himself free, pointing across the road. 'We need two bags this instant. Do you have any coin on you?'

As a matter of fact, he did. Jane had been forward thinking that way, pressing a leather purse into his hand at the very last moment. 'Just in case the soirée is terribly dull,' she had said with a smirk.

It calmed him to imagine she thought they may do exactly as they were now: taking fleeting advantage of a manufactured freedom. And had the Lady Satine not told him she had no intention of dictating either Silas's journey or the prince's?

Pitch dashed off, skirts and cloak lifting to show a glimpse of stocking-clad ankle, which was far more alluring than it ought to be. Silas focused instead on not getting run down by a growler as it thundered past. By the time Silas joined him, Pitch was already holding two paper bags brimming with hot chestnuts.

'Two pence.' The vendor was missing a front tooth, the request hissing through the gap. He held out his hand, waiting as Silas fumbled about for the coins. Pitch was moaning around a mouthful of chestnuts, which admittedly smelled glorious, a hint of honey upon them if Silas wasn't mistaken.

They continued on, Silas having to pry the second bag from Pitch's grasp. The daemon let them go with very clear reluctance.

'We can buy more, don't be greedy.' Silas tried to sound stern, which was difficult with the ridiculous noises the prince was making as he indulged.

'An asylum.' Pitch spoke through a mouthful.

'Pardon?'

'He is in an asylum. His family have had him committed.' Pitch toyed with the chestnuts at the bottom of his bag.

'Edward?' Silas swallowed. 'Good god, the poor man. Which one?'

'The Fulbourn, in Cambridgeshire. Not so very far.' The daemon played at lightness, as though it hardly bothered him that the lieutenant had been treated so badly. But Silas read Pitch well enough now.

'And you think Charlie has followed him there?'

'What do you think, Silas? The lad is better known to you than me.' The subtlest of pauses. 'Do you think he would have followed when they bundled Edward off?'

Silas nodded slowly, the brush of something like hope finding him. 'Yes, yes, he would. He is tenacious, just as you said. And Edward's disappearance was sudden, wasn't it? Perhaps Charlie had no chance to send word.' It did not account for why no news had come from the lad since then, but Silas would take this for what it was: an explanation that did not have Charlie running away...or worse...lying facedown in an East End gutter somewhere.

Pitch rolled a chestnut between his fingers. 'I should have told you as soon as I knew. I didn't, and I'm sorry for that.' He darted a sideways glance at Silas, who waited for him to go on. 'I don't know why I didn't.' He popped the last of the chestnuts into his mouth and scrunched up the bag so tightly he'd be sure to stain his gloves with the oily residue left behind. 'That's a lie. Part of it was that I didn't want you to know, for you've seen Edward's state of mind and understand exactly why he is a candidate for such a place.'

It was tempting to embrace him, there and then, but it was not, Silas decided, what was needed.

'Oh I understand all right,' he said with a rough clearing of his throat. 'And the sooner you get it into your thick skull that you are not to blame for it, the less I shall be annoyed by your insistence on shouldering the blame for Edward's delicate constitution.' He definitely had Pitch's attention. The daemon had one superb eyebrow raised, his mouth circled with surprise. 'I'm loath to say it, but perhaps he's in the best place he can be. The doctors may be able to ease his troubles.'

That seemed to interest Pitch. 'Do you truly think so?'

Silas doubted it, very much, but the daemon looked so achingly hopeful. 'It's possible.' He mused over another thought. 'So what happens now? Will the Lady have us go to the asylum, or will Edward be brought to the Village?'

'Why does the Lady get to decide on that?' he snapped. 'This is my confounded fucking quest, is it not? The decision should be mine.'

Silas considered his reply. This was not the first time Pitch had voiced his displeasure at being ordered about. And Silas did not blame him for it. 'What would *you* do, then?'

'I would abandon the fucking quest altogether and go dancing and drinking until I could not remember any of my names. You would come with me of course, and we'd get riotously drunk, and you'd kiss me like you just did another hundred times over. And not just on my lips either.' Pitch heaved a weighted sigh. 'But we should go to Cambridge...now.'

'Pardon? Go now?' Silas was stuck further back in the conversation, the part where he'd be visiting Pitch's body with his lips.

'Why not? It is the perfect time. No one knows who we are.' He swept his hand towards the road. 'I've just seen a leipreachan fae look right through us to ogle the chestnut cart.' He sniffed. 'No accounting for taste of course, but there we are. We are invisible, Silas. We could catch a train and be there in a couple of hours.' He brightened with his idea, and Silas could not bring himself to extinguish that spark. 'I'll find my way into the asylum, present the watch to Edward if need be, we'll find out what it is he knows or has...and we shall be done with this malarkey.'

'Do you think it's that simple? You just need to speak with him?'

'It must be. He's human, and not one in a fine state either. What else is he capable of? He's hardly going to sail me across Blood Lake.' Pitch shook his head, a scowl marring his features. 'Maybe he has another trinket for me...or he has the blasted front-door key to Seraphiel's fucking Sanctuary, who knows. But if at the very worst we do need to get him out, how would that trouble us? We've faced far more formidable opponents than a lunatic asylum's chief physician, have we not?'

Silas nodded, slowly though, to give himself time to work out an objection that would not see Pitch storming off in a huff. Anyway, he was not so sure he *wished* to object. Much of what the daemon said made sense. And it would mean finding out if Charlie was with the lieutenant now, instead of more delay with running back to Holly Village and waiting for others to decide the course of action. From what Lady Satine had told him about the ankou he'd been, bluntly determined and strong of will, his former reanimated selves would not have thought twice about heading off right now.

'We have faced far worse indeed,' he replied. 'But the elixir is uncertain... And what if the Morrigan should find us whilst we are about on our own?'

'You just said yourself the elixir is plainly still working. And the Morrigan are looking for an ankou and a daemon. We are not them...we are free, Silas.' Pitch was earnest, clutching at the crumpled empty bag. He stepped up close, his skirts covering Silas's feet, the taffeta finding its way between his legs. 'We could be there and back before Satty does her morning piss tomorrow.'

Silas inhaled, his head a battle front of pros and cons. 'I thought you were keen to enjoy your evening with more trivial things?' Which he was not averse to at all. He'd been enjoying their game.

'I don't want to find him, Silas.' Pitch ground his teeth into the words. He turned about and continued along the pavement. Silas kept close. 'You once threatened to spank me senseless – the worst attempt at a threat I've ever heard – if I tried to ride off and handle this on my own. But I was not thinking of running *towards* the threat, only away. Far away. I was not fooling when I said I'd abandon this quest at once if the decision was mine.' He paused, tracing white satin against the metal of a streetlight. 'I don't want to find Edward, Silas, because I know once I do...I'll understand what has been done to me and what will become of me, and what is expected of me. And I have no right to protest any of it because I should not be drawing breath at all. So I was letting myself indulge in this little delaying fantasy, with warm chestnuts in my hand and your tongue in my mouth. But the truth is the decision to run or stay or play is not mine. We have masters who must be obeyed, you and I both. And they do not give a shit if I'm enjoying being on your arm and wearing my pretty frock and having you look at me the way you do. So we should abandon it now, before they rip it from us. From me. I need to go to Cambridge. This must be done with.' He frowned, gave a slight shake of his head. 'Does that make any sense at all? Or am I still high and sounding like a fool? I feel I may be veering towards foolery.'

Pitch was in truth a little bleary-eyed, his jaw working too hard at grinding nothing, but he did not sound a fool. Silas felt the undercurrent of the prince's desperation and his fears, very keenly. Bloody hell, was there no chance he could bundle him up, grab the nearest hansom, and demand the driver take them to the very darkest corner of the Isles?

'You do not sound foolish at all.' He touched Pitch's back, knowing just where the daemon preferred, though the corset formed a barrier against offering much real comfort. 'We are both set on a path we must follow, but yours is particularly rough. You have every right to protest how it has been handled and I want you to know that what you want does matter, very much, to me.' He adjusted the drape of Pitch's cloak, tugging the two folds so the rising breeze could not sneak beneath.

'You're fussing,' the prince mumbled, though did not slap him away.

'You bring out my inner fusspot, what can I say?' To Silas's delight, he drew a muffled laugh from the daemon.

'I understand entirely if you prefer to return to the Village,' Pitch said. 'I know you are a careful man and might –'

'We both know I'm not going anywhere but where you go, so let's not waste time with all that.' As Silas turned towards the road, he thought he saw Pitch's shoulders slacken.

He lifted his hand, waving down a hansom cab. A prancing bay tossed its head as the driver pulled up alongside them. 'Where to?' a squat-faced man called from behind his thick muffler.

Silas took a quick, firming breath, aware this was likely not the wisest choice he'd ever made but feeling a small thrill because of it.

'We need to catch a train to Cambridge. Do you suppose they are still running?'

'Suppose they are.' He sniffed deeply. 'Been some trouble on that line today, so they are all running late. If you're lucky, you might still catch the last one.'

Silas held out his hand to Pitch. 'Shall we?'

'We shall.' The daemon slid his fingers across Silas's palm and held tight. 'And if *you* are very lucky, we shall have a cabin to ourselves.'

CHAPTER 11

They reached Liverpool Street Station before the departure of the last train. It had been delayed by forty-five minutes, so there was luck there. *And* they were lucky enough to secure two of the last remaining seats on the busy train.

But that was where their luck ended.

Pitch's notion of fooling about in the carriage with the ankou, taking as much pleasure as he could before a dreary trip to the asylum and beyond, was cruelly dashed. Not only would they not have their own cabin, they would not be seated together. There had been only one seat in each class available. Pitch would take the first-class seat, of course. He was a lady, gods damn it, and it was hardly proper to have him squeezed in amongst the common folk on uncomfortable wooden seating. The ankou sensibly did not try to challenge that decision. Silas would take the second-class seat.

'Would it help you endure the discomfort,' Pitch said as they wove their way through the buzzing crowd, 'if I said there would be a superlative hand job waiting for you at the other end?'

Silas's eyes bulged. 'Truly, you must stop that.'

The ankou glanced about, ensuring no one had heard the exchange between Mr and Mrs Bellingham. Pitch had insisted on the new marital arrangement. He was not partial to incest. They had chosen a new moniker purposely, too. He and Silas were a striking pair, even with their guises, and tongues may wag. No need for any word to reach the Charters that the Cargills were headed straight to the asylum they weren't supposed to know about. London could be a small town at times. Especially when wealthy families were involved.

'Stop the hand jobs? I've hardly started giving them to you.'

Silas grimaced, shifting his hips. 'I beg you, please don't say such brazen things when I'm not in the right environment to walk around with a maypole in my trousers.'

'Hardly my problem you cannot control yourself.'

'Bloody hell, you are dreadful.'

It was adorable really, how hard the ankou tried to stay stern while his smile fought to rise.

Pitch sipped on some peppermint water Silas had bought for him, giving him something else to do with his jaw rather than grind it. He was grateful that Daphne's tincture was fast losing its punch. Cocaine was wonderful and all, but not without its downsides.

There was still a comfortable fifteen minutes until departure. The jostling of the passing traffic was beginning to piss Pitch off. Twice someone had trod on the hem of his gown, and twice he'd let them know how displeased he was, using language Silas assured him was not befitting of Mrs Bellingham.

They reached the gate, where the ticket collector was having a hearty conversation with a trio of young lads who had clearly been enjoying London's public houses. Pitch envied them their inebriated state. He'd begun to think again of what he'd recalled in Fothergill's office: an angel, obsessed with righting his wrongs, uncaring whether it fucked up a daemon's life entirely.

Perhaps a bottle of champagne on the journey would soothe him. It was two hours to Cambridge. A daemon could get well and truly sloshed in that time.

'Gracious, what is the problem? My feet shall crack if I don't get these shoes off in an instant,' said the prim and proper women ahead of them in the line. She wore a ludicrously large feathered hat, which bobbed very close to Silas's nose. But the ankou didn't move away. In fact he seemed rather fixated on the downy lilac feathers dangling before him.

Pitch tilted his head as the line came to a standstill, curious about the lost look in the ankou's eyes.

'Mr Bellingham?' Pitch said. 'Everything all right?'

When Silas had agreed to this hurried, clandestine journey, Pitch had nearly whooped with the relief. He could have managed the asylum on his own of course. He'd been a commander of legions once upon a time, but it was far more preferable this way. His growing dependence on the ankou's nearness was a problem, but he'd deal with that later. When they had what they needed from Edward.

Silas still watched the feathers fluttering before him, his eyes shifting back and forth, as though studying something much larger.

Pitch took full advantage of his dress's power, which allowed him to rub at the ankou's arm without causing a fuss. 'My dear?'

Silas pulled his focus from the woman ahead to the false one at his side. 'Sorry?'

'You are a world away.'

'I was rather.' Silas watched Pitch's hand brushing his arm. 'I told you about the woman in...the vision I saw...in what I believe was my' – he lowered his voice – 'last death?'

'Mmm-hmm.' They were both prone to unwelcome visions.

'She wore a shade of purple just like that, so it took me back.' He gave his head a little shake. 'I just keep wondering...about the place where I die. A loch, did I tell you?'

Pitch shook his head but stayed quiet so Silas might go on. The ankou always appeared so hesitant to speak of what he'd seen when the Morrigan had held him at the bottom of the pond.

'So it is Scotland, and there is a modest castle there too in later years, and a jetty with a boatshed. But I didn't tell you there is someone else there...' Silas ran his teeth over his lip. 'A man...a boy sometimes...an age in-between on other occasions. He's there every time, and he tries to help me.' His smile was grim. 'Always. He never succeeds of course.'

The line started to move. The unhappy lavender-clad woman tutted and began to complain again about how slowly it was moving.

'Go on,' Pitch urged. He had the sense that the ankou was weighing up saying any more. 'What is it you want to tell me?'

'I'm not sure.' Silas was curiously laconic.

'If you should tell me, or if you *want* to tell me?'

Silas flashed him a startled look. 'A bit of both, I suppose. I mean it is hardly important anyway. Not with all that is going on.'

'Then distract me with this unimportant information from *all that is going on.*' He was not yet sure if he would tell Silas what he'd realised when the Charters' financier had smacked him near senseless against the desk. The ankou would only worry, and that would do nothing but give him more facial lines.

Now that the ticket collector was done with his pickled passengers, the line was moving quickly. In very little time, they'd be moving to separate carriages, and he doubted Silas would speak of this again once he'd had time to think on it. Whatever he was considering telling Pitch, it had him bothered.

'The boy always has cornflower-blue eyes,' Silas said quickly. He snapped his mouth closed, as though he'd imparted far more riveting information than that.

'Oh...well, that's...nice, I suppose.' And then the penny dropped. 'Like your lad?'

Silas nodded, his bottom lip now prisoner to the bite of his teeth. Pitch frowned. 'Like your lad...or it *is* your lad you see each time? Gods, don't tell me he is reanimated too?' Why that irritated him so much was a mystery. So the ankou and Charlie had shared hundreds of years between them and likely had a deep relationship, so damned what?

'No. No, it's not like that. It is Charlie's ancestors I've seen. They are there to...' He glanced over his shoulder, where a chap holding a small suitcase had moved up close. The ankou was getting much better at glaring. The man moved back quickly, his bowler hat in danger of toppling off his head. 'They have the bandalore when I am living a normal life. They guard it, I think. And are there to send it back with me, when I go to the grave.'

Pitch wrinkled his nose. 'Why can't you have it when you are living?'

'I'm not sure.' Silas pressed at his pocket, where Pitch knew the bandalore lay. The scythe had had a good rest of late. At least one player in this game had. 'It is an instrument of death. Perhaps it's not mine to keep when I am living.'

'Charlie is dull but certainly not the undead. Why can he have it?'

Silas had no answer for that or was too distracted with finding where in his coat he'd placed the tickets. There were only a few more passengers ahead of them now before they reached the ticket collector.

'Did Charlie bring the bandalore to you then?' Pitch asked. 'I thought the time you'd met in Wyre Forest was the first?' Had he sounded too snippy then?

'It was the first. I don't know who brought it to the Village. I assumed it Lady Satine, but I know now that is not how it works. It was not hers to give.'

'Well, it is all a delicious mystery, then.' Pitch eyed the carriages, looking to see how far along he'd have to travel to reach first class. 'Do you know what began this connection with Charlie's family?'

Silas, at that moment, tripped over himself or perhaps the feather-hatted lady's short train. 'No, no. No, I'm not sure.'

Well, well. The ankou had lied about that. Silas was a miserable liar. His face splotched with red patches, all the more evident without his beard. But there was no time to question him on the lie. The ankou handed over their tickets and went inordinately red again when Pitch demanded a goodbye kiss from his husband in front of the ticket collector, as they were to be parted and he could not *bear* it. Choking on his laughter, Pitch waved as he headed off towards the front of the train.

'That one there,' he called, seeing the ankou hesitate when he realised he could not read the numbers on the carriages and had no clue where to go.

The walk up to the first-class carriages took some time, Pitch drifting through the steam that slunk out from between the wheels and driving rods like a low mist.

He found his seat, essentially a dust rose upholstered armchair, halfway down the cabin. The gentleman opposite appeared too eager for a chat, so before he could utter a word, Pitch seated himself and hid a delicate yawn behind his hand. He settled in, unclasping his cloak, spreading his skirts around him, and wiggling about until the corset did not pinch at his belly. He closed his eyes as the stationmaster's whistle pierced the air. Just a short nap, then he'd order that bottle, maybe a dessert.

\#

The sharp rap of knuckles on glass woke him.

'Mrs Bellingham, wake up,' a muffled voice cried.

It was Silas banging on the window. Standing on the platform. The Cambridge Station platform. They'd arrived. And Pitch had slept through the entire journey.

'Fuck.' He leaped to his feet, turning about to find the gentleman opposite staring at him open-mouthed. 'What?' Pitch touched at his face, trying to blink himself awake quickly. He'd slept deeply. 'Is there something on my face?'

'It is what came out of your mouth that concerns me, madam,' he sniffed, and turned away, shaking at his paper like it were a wet dishrag.

'Oh, for fuck's sake,' Pitch muttered, pinning his cloak back into place as he limped as fast as he was able down the length of the carriage.

Silas was there at the door and very nearly had to catch Pitch as he tangled himself in his skirts and made the most appallingly inelegant departure from the train. The novelty of a dress was wearing very thin.

'I thought you were about to end up in Norwich.' Silas grinned. 'They wouldn't let me on to wake you. You were quite dead to the world.'

The prickling at Pitch's back returned with the nearness of the pendant watch. The sensation still made his skin crawl despite Silas's quaint effort with the lead box. And though he'd assured the ankou it was more tolerable, the watch made a liar of him. At least though the heat at Pitch's core seemed as sleepy as he.

'Gods, I don't think I moved for a couple of hours. One of my arse cheeks is numb.' He rubbed at the offender, receiving a few looks in return.

'I envy you. There was no such respite in second class. A poor woman had a teary babe, who has apparently been most unwell. Very unsettled, wailed at the top of her lungs for half the journey. Poor woman was beside herself, and everyone was being rather unkind. In the end, I offered to hold the child, and quite astonishingly, she fell asleep in my arms for a good hour or so.' Silas rounded his shoulder before he proffered his elbow to Pitch. 'I've a rotten ache in my arm though.'

Pitch slipped into place beside the ankou, stifling a yawn. 'Children are dreadful for the constitution. I'd have demanded it be set down at the next station.'

Silas grinned before tilting his head down closer to Pitch. 'It was the most curious thing...' His pause was dramatic, as were his furtive glances to ensure they were not being eavesdropped upon. How he decided that was the case, Pitch had no idea. It seemed half the train had alighted, and half the town was seeking to board. They were fighting through a swarm. 'The child was fae,' Silas whispered at last. 'But the mother certainly not.'

'A changeling perhaps. Surprisingly common. The child didn't show any sign of seeing your true nature, did it?'

'Tilly was her name. And she had little to say, save for *mumma* and *no*.' Silas edged himself forward to stop a distracted man who was trying to light his pipe from running into Pitch. 'A dryad...that's what the melody called her anyway...fae, dryad. But I've no clue of the specifics.'

'Hmm, well a dryad changeling is a rarer thing but a sign of the times perhaps. They are tree fae. Forest dwellers mostly, though I've known a few to linger in Hyde Park. I played cards once with a chap who had taken up residence in St James's Park. They liked to watch the queen, evidently. Anyway, the humans tend to make sport of destroying their habitats. The dryads are all up in arms about it of course.' He shrugged. 'Maybe this fae's folks decided it a case of better the devil you know. Place it with the humans before it had nowhere else to live.'

'Her name's Tilly, and she's not an it.'

'She might be, have you asked?'

Silas waggled his head, all frowny and irritated. Adorable, really. 'But if she's a changeling, does that mean the woman's true babe was stolen by faeries? That's the tale, isn't it? I have no idea why I recall that and not other things.' A bit more adorable shaking of his head followed. 'Anyway, it is dreadful.'

'The only thing that's dreadful about it is that the purebred got another babe in return. Freedom was so close for her.' Pitch shuddered. But then sighed at the worry lines creasing Silas's face. 'There is not necessarily a stolen human child, you soft-hearted fool. The fae child might have been abandoned, or the woman may have entered into an agreement to raise the child here in the human world. The fae do so love a deal. Believe me, there's more than one way to make a changeling.'

'I suppose that's a consolation.'

'If you say so.'

Cambridge Station was not a showy structure: a single main platform with one track either side; and a station building that held a ticket office, a few seats, and not much else of note. Tired travellers grumbled about the late hour. Some were desperately unhappy that the pubs had closed some time ago, and Pitch did not blame them. It must be nearing midnight, if not already past the hour that Satty had told him he should be home. Like he was a dutiful child who might actually listen to her.

He exhaled, delighting in being a very naughty boy. *Mother would be furious.* If he was lucky. This surreptitious trip to Cambridge satisfied his need to rebel, in some small form, against the stifling shackles of his life. It was a teensy bit foolish to go off without a word. But he and Silas had been sent out alone many times before this. And if the Morrigan had harboured any interest in the lieutenant after Pitch left him naked and tender at the Moon Inn, they had had more than enough time to show it.

'I asked about the Fulbourn.' Silas buttoned his coat against the icy evening. 'It turns out it is not in town but rather just outside it, twenty minutes ride at most. Visitors are allowed entry from about ten in the morning.'

Pitch rubbed at the dust of sleep that had gathered around the edges of his eyes. 'I hope you were discreet.'

'Very much so. I inquired with the mother of the child, and she was far too distracted by her infant to recall a single word. I doubt she even heard me say my name –'

'Mr Bellingham, Mr Bellingham!' A woman waved at them. She was dressed in a precisely cut blue gown with a fur stole around her shoulders. The child that balanced on her hip wore a tiny replica of her mother's dress. She was a young fae, just as Silas had correctly surmised with his newfound lack of stupidity in these matters. The babe was several years old perhaps. Pitch neither knew nor cared to know how to assess such things. It had hair white as fresh snow, and it was small and had unusual eyes, mostly olive green but with a very defined ring of amber around the pupils. And they were set on Silas.

'I'm so glad I caught you.' The woman glanced at Pitch, and her eyes widened. 'Mrs Bellingham, gracious me, you are a vision just as your husband said. I have to say, you have caught quite the special man in this one. I'm Nancy Erwood, by the way. Miss...Nancy Erwood.' Her gaze lingered on Pitch, searching, he suspected, for hint of his reaction to her title. One no reputable woman with a child should hold.

'Lovely to meet you, Miss Erwood.'

Her smile came alive, pushing up full cheeks towards eyes of a brown so deep they'd appear black if the lighting was any dimmer. She tilted her head at Silas. 'He was a true marvel. There are very few who would have been so patient and helped me as he did. I was beside myself when Tilly wouldn't settle. She's been unwell, you see...' A shadow flickered across her face. 'But she took such a shine to your husband. I've not seen her react to a stranger that way before...and I'm afraid he got lumped with cradling her for half the journey, as she insisted on clambering into his lap. I don't know what your secret is, Mr Bellingham, but I am in your debt. Tilly hasn't slept that soundly in months.' The child's gaze swept between Silas and Pitch, one hand playing with the pink ribbon that tied up its hair. 'Do you have anywhere to stay this evening? I assume you are not heading out to the Fulbourn at this hour to see your cousin, Mrs Bellingham?' Pitch slid a glance at Silas, who steadfastly avoided his gaze, waggling his fingers at the dribbling child instead. 'I'm terribly sorry...it must be ever so awful to have someone you love so unwell. I heard your trip was decided at the very last minute. Were you able to book accommodations? I should have asked before now, I'm sorry. I am just so bloody tired.' Her eyes widened, fixing on Pitch. 'Oh, I apologise for my –'

'Your bloody language?' he returned. 'It's damned awful.'

Miss Erwood's laughter came from deep beneath very full breasts that gave her jacket a decent test. 'Oh, you are a wonderful pair. I'd offer you rooms at my establishment, but the Crimson Bow is not considered proper by many. I wouldn't like to put you in an awkward position.'

Pitch's ears perked. 'I'm partial to an awkward position, I assure you.' Gods, let it be terribly so. For practical as well as fanciful purposes, of course. Lodging at a house of ill-repute would render them far more invisible than if they were to stay at a fancy hotel. Pitch swept in and clasped her arm. 'How improper are we talking?'

He did not hold back his eagerness. Miss Erwood seemed amused by his enthusiasm. Silas, though, was too busy poking the tip of his finger into a tiny cupped palm, playing some silly game with the cooing child, who had nothing better to say than *more, more.*

'Well,' Miss Erwood said slowly. 'The entertainment we offer is not to all tastes. Some might call it vulgar, but I think it's rather beautiful. I reside upstairs with Tilly.' A notable pause. 'And my good friend, Adamaris.'

'Vulgar and beautiful sounds positively wonderful.'

He thought himself an able judge of character. With so much of his time spent bringing forth the purebreds' deepest desires, he tended to see through their layers well. And he liked this woman. She was irreverent, unconventional, and not averse to dirtying her mouth. She was raising the child as her own and doing so without a ring on her finger. Whether she'd borne a child of her own before the switch was done or had simply taken in an orphaned mewling babe, he did not know, but either way she tilted her nose at society's expectation of her.

'Does it have dancing?' he pressed. He'd not yet given up on his idea of twirling Silas about a dance floor, willing ankou or not.

'There is definitely champagne...and dancing, yes.'

Nancy was still hesitant. Unsure she was reading his signals right, most likely. But he adored her little club already, whether it be a brothel or gambling den or the last of the molly houses, he did not care.

'But perhaps the dancing is not the kind you and your husband would –'

'Shall we see tits?' Pitch's whisper was stage-worthy. 'Or better yet, a phallus or two?'

110

'Pitch!' Silas hovered his hands over the child's ears. 'Dear god, mind your manners.'

But Miss Erwood had a broad smile for Mrs Bellingham now. 'I see I have misjudged you,' she said. 'There is a strong possibility you shall see some of each. I think you would like the Crimson Bow very much, and I dare say it would like you.'

'I dare say.' Pitch winked.

Nancy laughed, and the child on her hip slapped its small, meaty hands together. The fae's intent gaze darted from Pitch to Silas in quick succession. A little *too* intently for Pitch's liking, with the lingering worry of the demise of the elixir. But the child still pissed in its bloomers, it was hardly about to pose a threat. The ankou made the most ridiculous face at the little one and poked out his tongue. The resulting juvenile peals of laughter scratched at Pitch's ears.

He stared at Silas, who was beaming at having been responsible for such a racket. How many drinks had the blasted fellow had on that train journey? He must be sozzled out of his mind to find the child's squeals so pleasing.

'If you would like to come and see for yourself,' Miss Erwood was saying, 'the offer stands if you'd like to stay, but I will not be insulted if you decide otherwise. I am happy to call a few hotels for you. At the very least, if you're not too tired, come and have some drinks on the house as a thank you.'

'What say you, Mrs Bellingham?' Silas smiled. 'Are we too tired?'

Gods, the ankou looked happy, beaming like that at his unwomanly wife. He radiated an odd contentment and just looking at him warmed Pitch between the legs, making him stiff beneath the skirts.

Well, fuck the quest a moment longer, then. Let the silly fantasy return.

'Tired?' he said. 'Not in the least, my dear.'

CHAPTER 12

The Crimson Bow was actually a small theatre. And its rather bland exterior and simple unobtrusive signage belied a sumptuous interior which had Silas marvelling. The journey from station to premises had been brief, no more than a quarter of an hour, heading southwest out of the centre of the city to where the only traffic was their own carriage. Nancy told them that the university used the Bow for rehearsals while the ADC Theatre was being renovated and enlarged. It had been an opportunity too good to overlook when the freehold was offered up, just last year.

Carrying the sleeping Tilly in his arms, Silas stepped through the black-lacquered doors and into a foyer trimmed floor to ceiling with lush reds and golds. Lengths of fabric draped the walls and framed an assortment of gilded mirrors and paintings, women and men in elaborate costumes. One artwork of particular note was a woman wearing a papier mâché horse head, complete with a mane and a lush tail spilling from her lacy bloomers. The dull thump of music came from another room.

'Oh, I do like this place.' Pitch squeezed Silas's arm.

'Of course you do.'

Rounded burgundy pots filled each corner, bursting with meticulously cared-for palms and ferns. The moment Silas laid eyes on the greenery, he relaxed. Not that he held any fear about accepting Miss Erwood's generous offer, but to find such welcome surrounds, a suggestion that there was someone else here who enjoyed a decent plant as much as he did, endeared him to the place at once. Pitch could have his costumes; Silas was very happy with his palms.

The air held the unmistakable tinges of wood smoke and liquor. Pitch stared around with unabashed delight.

'Oh fuck, I can taste the whisky already,' he sighed.

'Pitch,' Silas whispered, nodding his head at the fae child in his arms. Tilly's mother had stopped outside to speak with some departing guests, all of whom had been ludicrously drunk.

'It can't understand words, Silas,' Pitch scoffed. 'Now put it down, it's not yours, and though I have many talents, I cannot give you one. Nor do I wish to.' He waved his fingers in front of his nose. 'Smelly bloody things, they are.'

Silas laughed and played along. 'Terribly offensive, yes.' An odd melancholy tinged the lightness of his words. He was never to know that look Tilly gave to her mother. Of child to parent. And he could not even recall if in his human life he had yearned for such a thing.

'Sorry about that, my dears.' Miss Erwood bustled back in, gathering the sleeping Tilly from Silas with a grateful smile. The child did not stir at all. 'Now, how about those drinks. I'll get her off to bed first of course. If you just head through those doors –'

The mentioned doors swept open, parting to reveal a woman with an astonishing head of brilliant orange hair, twisted and piled on her head in a maniacal fashion and woven through with lengths of pearls and all kinds of sparkly things. She was heavy-set, generous helpings of flesh thickening her bared arms, her breasts two great pillows of stark white spilling over a black-and-white-striped bodice. Her choker held a unique cameo: a naked woman twisting in the rhythm of a silent dance.

'Nance! Baby girl. You're back at last. I've missed your sorely.' She swept up to Miss Erwood, and it was very evident that this friendship extended deeper than society preferred. Silas was pleased to see that Miss Erwood did not hold back for their benefit, planting a firm kiss upon the woman's heavily rouged lips.

'And I you, Ada.' She brushed a crooked finger across Adamaris's chin, unspoken affection passing between them. 'Now I must get Tilly to bed.'

'Oh wait, let me get my fix of her.' Adamaris pressed her nose into the child's white hair and breathed in deep. 'Too quiet without her, without you both. I'm going with you next time you see the specialist. I've been near to bursting all afternoon to hear what was said.'

'I'm sorry, we were running so late for the train that I could not call. I shall tell you every word of course, but do not fret. There are no significant changes to worry us.' Nancy rubbed her partner's arm. 'Now, may I introduce some splendid guests that are here at my behest.' She gestured towards Silas. 'Mr Bellingham was an absolute knight in shining armour on the train. Tilly slept on him and dribbled, no doubt, for a good hour.'

'He was able to get her to sleep?' Ada's shock lit her face.

Nancy nodded fervently. 'And she did not move an inch for near on an hour in his arms. Mr Bellingham's an angel in disguise, I dare say. I've offered the Bellinghams our spare room this evening. They've made an unexpected trip up and have not yet booked anywhere to stay. I promised them drinks because Mr Bell–'

'Arthur, please.' Silas dispensed with formality, but not with deception. 'And my companion is...Thaddeus.' Silas was too busy wondering why he'd selected such a cumbersome name to realise his error.

'Thaddeus, eh?' Ada's drawn-on black brow lifted as she stared at Pitch, who in turn was giving Silas a look that could have turned the potted palms brown and crinkled.

'Yes,' he said dryly. 'That is indeed my name. I've been found out.'

'Oh yes, of course,' Nancy gasped. 'This makes perfect sense now. I knew there was something about the two of you. How wonderful. Gentlemen, I assure you, you are *very* welcome here.'

'You could not have found a better place.' Ada's rouge smeared one of her teeth, evident now her smile was so wide. 'Come on through, you've made it in time for the last show.'

'I'll just get Tilly settled and be back to join you as soon as I can.' Nancy blew Ada a kiss and stepped through a smaller door hidden behind a length of shining gold fabric.

'I'll have your absinthe ready and waiting, my love,' Ada called. 'Come, come, gentlemen.'

Ada went ahead, pushing the doors with a flourish. The hubbub of a crowd met them in a dimly lit room dank with the smoke of cigars and cigarettes and something richer: the heat of bodies, not unpleasant, but ripe enough to make Silas's eyes flutter.

'Thaddeus, really?' Pitch muttered, coming in to link his arm through Silas's. 'I'd prefer Percy if you must know.'

'Percy?' Silas laughed, not without some relief to know the daemon wasn't angry he'd spoiled the ruse. 'That's awful.'

'How dare you, sir. Percy's mother and father thought it most fitting.'

The Crimson Bow was not laid out like a standard theatre. All the rows of seats had been removed, for one. Small sets of tables and chairs took their places, each with a candle burning upon it and a gold tablecloth hanging down to the floor. Most were taken; the room was certainly not lacking for occupants. And so far as Silas could see and hear, they were all purebreds. And all intoxicated, in one way or another.

'Right then, what shall it be?' Ada asked, hands on hips and tossing out casual hellos left and right. It seemed she knew nearly all in the place by name.

'Champagne would be a delight,' Pitch declared.

Silas stared about the room, taking it all in with a look of great satisfaction. It was certainly the daemon's type of place. There was a sensual undercurrent about it that even Silas could not deny. Near to the modest stage, which would struggle with more than four actors at a time, a piano was being played by a hunchbacked chap with a shock of curly black hair. His body jerked with his enthusiasm for the notes. A small crowd was gathered around him, singing along, and Silas was quick to see that among them two men were entwined, darting quick kisses at one another, teasing the other with offering their cigarette, only to whisk it away at the last and offer their tongue instead. They were beside themselves with mirth, in the way of the inebriated, and no one paid them any mind save to glance over and grin at the drunken silliness of it all. The gentlemen's attire held all the extravagance of the stage, with flounces and bright colours and sparkling jewellery. They were corseted, with one wearing a skirt with no front panel, revealing trousered legs.

They were not the only ones dressed in such curious fashion. Others were dotted about the crowd, women in breeches and tailcoats, a willowy man in a lace shift. Others wore far less clothing than was really suitable for a December night.

Lucky thing it was so darned warm inside. Silas tugged at his collar.

'Stifling, isn't it? Perhaps we should get you out of those clothes.' Pitch's eyes danced with mischief, and it seemed no accident that his hand brushed against Silas's trousers.

Ada stole Silas's chance to reply, returning with a bottle of champagne and two stunning Bristol blue glasses.

'Now, if you don't mind, I'd like to give you the best seats in the house for the show.' She chuckled. 'Don't get too excited though. It's no Theatre Royale here, but the private box is just that. Private. I thought that might be to your liking.'

'Oh, there's really no need –' Silas began.

'That sounds sublime,' Pitch overrode him. 'We'll take it happily. Would I be right in assuming this a burlesque show of sorts?'

Ada winked at him. 'You know your theatre. Though we like to think our shows press a little harder at the boundaries of respectability than most. Our travesty roles are quite the drawcard. You've spotted some of our performers no doubt. You'd not bring your mother to a show here, not unless she was liberal in her tastes, or quite blind and deaf.'

No wonder Pitch seemed so pleased. He was gleeful as a child with a half-penny in a candy store. Silas took his hand and could not resist pressing a kiss to the smooth white satin which covered it, causing the daemon's grin to widen.

Ada motioned for them to follow, and they made their way across the floor. The drinks were flowing, and had been for some time Silas suspected. He had to pay special attention as they moved and more than once needed to sidestep a patron who was attempting some awkward dance in between the tables. Silas took care to ensure Pitch was out of the way. It had not escaped his notice how annoyed the daemon had gotten with the number of boots landing on his skirts at the station.

Ada led them to the far side of the room, where a spiral staircase was nearly hidden by drapes of fabric and an astonishingly large Boston fern set on a high, audacious marble pedestal.

'Up you go, then,' Ada said. She handed Pitch the bottle and Silas the glasses. 'Mind your head at the top there. Like I said, it's not much. Normally Nancy and I sit there, but I'd like to speak to her about her trip to the city, so we'll be going somewhere quieter. How about we have a late supper after the show? I'll come find you when it's done, an hour or so. Anything you need, tell Phyliss at the bar that it's on my tab.'

'Very kind.' Pitch grinned. 'Oh, actually I wonder if there might be a telephone here I could use? It's probably best I let my aunt know we won't be back this evening. She's a grumpy old thing, a spinster, you see, so she has nothing else to do but bully me about.'

Silas smirked but was pleased he didn't have to talk the prince into calling Lady Satine to tell her not to expect them back at the Village this evening. It was one thing to take matters into their own hands. It was another entirely to disappear off the face of the Earth.

'There's a telephone up in the private box actually,' Ada replied. 'A little luxury of ours. We unhook it during the shows of course. You are very welcome to use it.'

Silas stepped closer to Ada as she prepared to leave. 'Forgive me, it's likely none of my business, but I do hope that all is well with Tilly?'

A shadow crossed Ada's face, but she banished it quickly. 'Sweet of you to ask, Arthur. Tilly has had a few little issues. A rash on her skin we can't seem to budge, and a tendency to prefer waking over sleeping.' She gave him a rueful grin. 'Both of which make her very uncomfortable at times.'

'Sunlight,' Pitch said, one foot upon the first step. 'More sunlight is what it needs, I'll wager. A trip to the south of France should fix things.'

Ada was kind enough not to show it if she was annoyed with Pitch's flippant diagnosis. 'Fixes most things, I'd say. I guess I'll hear soon enough from Nancy what the doctors suggest.'

Pitch shrugged as though he'd given them the answer they needed but was not going to waste any more time convincing them of it.

Ada turned to Silas as the piano man had a slew of song suggestions shouted at him. 'Don't worry now, Arthur, and thank you for your concern. Go and enjoy the night with your fellow. And don't be shy about it.' She leaned in closer as the bashing of the piano keys began again. 'Thaddeus is very lovely, and most people in here can't keep their eyes off him, but he's only got eyes for you, lucky chap. You can relax here, the two of you, I promise. Enjoy each other.' With another wink, of which she seemed overly fond, Ada headed off.

'Come on then, Artie.' Pitch nudged the head of the bottle against Silas's arse cheek. 'Up you go. You're not scared of heights too, are you?'

'Of course bloody not.' Actually he wasn't sure. They'd not yet had to climb out on any ledges or stand on any craggy mountaintops, but the staircase was barely a floor high anyway. It was the width of the spiral that bothered him. 'This staircase is very narrow.'

'Then wiggle your hips a bit.'

'How will that help anything?'

'It won't most likely, but it will make the view very entertaining.'

And as Silas would rather choke on his champagne than allow his laughter to escape, he began to climb.

CHAPTER 13

The journey up was a short one. Silas may have stumbled once or twice, with Pitch at the ready with the bottle, jabbing it into his backside with far too much glee and telling him to 'giddyup' like he were a packhorse moving too slowly. But Silas intentionally kept the pace slow. The steep steps would be a problem for the prince with his uncooperative joints, whether he'd admit to it or not.

At the top, beneath a low ceiling, there was a short platform which took them to a charming white door painted with embellishments of gold. The door handle was a clear-cut glass, cool to the touch as Silas opened the door. He'd expected there to be only a balcony with their seats but was pleasantly surprised to see that they were entering an ante-room. He presumed the balcony lay beyond a lovely bamboo screen and assembly of potted palms, which hid the room's occupants from prying eyes in the main auditorium.

'Oh, marvellous,' Pitch declared, pushing past Silas in a blur of smoke-grey and hushing taffeta. 'I must say, I didn't expect this.'

The room was dominated by a splendid blood-red chaise, roomy enough for three sitters at least and adorned with gold cushions.

'Someone is quite enamoured with gold and red,' Silas noted.

'Someone knows how to stock a liquor cabinet.' Pitch set the champagne down next to an array of crystal decanters and bottles, all perched atop a mahogany cabinet with slender turned legs and exquisite shell marquetry on its panels. 'Can you pour our drinks while I make the call?' He sighed with all the drama he adored. 'I know you are trying very hard not to look relieved about me contacting Satty. But don't get too excited, I'm not calling her –'

'Pitch –'

'It's Thaddeus, thank you. Or is it Margaret? I'm utterly confused. Anyway, I'm calling Mr Ahari. I'm enjoying this evening too much to have the Lady screeching in my ear and demanding we come back at once, like we're escaped fucking slaves.'

Silas doubted that was how the conversation would go, but he'd not argue the point.

'Go on, then. Let's be done with all that.' Silas waved Pitch towards the other side of the room where a telephone perched atop a small but elegant oval table. The telephone's base was wood, chestnut he suspected, with a large rounded brass dial, and the earpiece a chunky combination of both those materials.

'Have my glass full by the time I'm done, won't you.' Pitch swept his hand across Silas's back as he moved, a touch so light he thought it may have been accidental were it not for the lingering glance the prince threw over his shoulder. Silas only just stopped himself from reaching out there and then, taking Pitch's arm, and pulling him in close. With the steady thrum of music and the scent of cigars and fine spirits on the air, the atmosphere was conducive to playing about. Telephone call be damned.

'Put me through to The Atlas Public House, please,' Pitch told the operator.

Silas wrestled with a cantankerous cork, one that was not yet ready to relinquish its stopping duties.

'Who's that?' Pitch asked. 'Oh, Kaneko...is Ahari there?' A pause, then, 'What do you mean, who is this? It's Tòbias. Get me Ahari.'

Silas shook his head at the daemon's curt tone. From what he knew of the surly bartender, that tone of voice was not likely to get Pitch far. He walked towards the screen which hid the entrance to the balcony, bottle still in hand, wriggling the cork as he went and trying to persuade the object it was time to let go.

The entire area was little bigger than his bedroom in Holly Village, but just like that room, it was cosy and most definitely private. A perfect place to, as Ada had suggested, enjoy one another. Silas put his elbow into freeing the cork, trying to ignore the quickening of his pulse and put from his mind thoughts of tasting the prince again. How things went this evening was entirely up to Pitch as he continued to see his way clear of Gidleigh Park House.

The cork shot from the bottle and zipped through one of the potted palms to smack against the screen, making it wobble on its stumpy footings. Silas rushed to steady it.

'Well, what time do you expect him back in?' Pitch said, his annoyance bright and clear. 'It's nearly one in the morning, isn't he too old for flouncing about? No need to use that tone with me, Kaneko. I can stay out as long as I bloody want. Fine...give him a message for me.' Pitch had the cord twined tightly around a pointed finger. He was gripping the receiver like he thought it might fly away at any moment. 'Tell him that Silas and I shall not be returning to the Village this evening... If I wanted to tell the Lady, I would have rung her directly, wouldn't I? Isaac was to tell her we would be late. It's hardly the first she knows of it. Fucking blazes, are you taking this message or not? Tell them there is no need to turn London upside down looking for us, we are fine. We have what we came to find, let them know that. And we shall tell them all about it on the morrow. Is that too many words for you to handle? Such language, Kaneko. Truly, I'm blushing.'

'Pitch,' Silas sighed. 'Your champagne is getting warm.'

Actually the bubbles had spewed forth from the bottle rather quickly, and a good portion of the champagne was soaking the carpet.

'No, there is no number to contact us on.' Pitch continued his battle with Kaneko. 'We are free spirits this evening. Going where the London nightlife leads us, and into as many beds as we can manage to play with as many cocks and cunts as we can handle. Just read the gossip columns tomorrow if you want to learn of our exploits. Our reputations shall be utterly ruined.'

Silas winced against his mouthful.

'Fine,' Pitch sighed. '*Silas's* reputation shall be ruined, then. I'll not argue your point about mine.'

Beyond the palms and bamboo screen, beyond the twin seats that sat like plain thrones upon the small balcony, a gentleman in an exotic Russian kaftan stepped onto the stage. His clothing was a deep burgundy with a thin belt slung around his hips, a lighter embroidered panel on his chest giving it a military feel. There was nothing military about his make-up though. His face was painted stark white and each cheek marked with penny-sized portions of black kohl. He welcomed the raucous crowd, and the whoops and hollers made it difficult to catch a word.

'Welcome to the last extravaganza of the evening at the Crimson Bow, ladies and gentlemen. We have our actors ready and raring to entertain you...and I do mean raring.'

The crowd went a bit mad, banging on tables and sounding like a baying pack of hunting hounds.

'Kaneko?' Pitch shouted. 'Are you there?' He slammed down the receiver and turned to Silas with a broad grin on his face. 'Done. Happy now?'

He strode over, and Silas handed Pitch a glass. 'I am, though not because of your eloquent telephone conversation.'

'He was there tonight, did I tell you?'

'Who and where?'

'Kaneko, at the Charters' soirée.'

The show had begun. A lady was belting out a jolly tune from beneath a swathe of feather boas which did a poor job of concealing the fact she wore very little clothing. 'Really? Why was he there? I'm assuming he didn't recognise you?'

'Delivering some catering I believe. And didn't give me a second glance. Which was rude, really. Considering I am a picture.' Pitch took a sip. 'Oh good gods, this is decent stuff.'

'Indeed. Why didn't you say we were here in Cambridge? Do you have concerns about Kaneko?'

Pitch fluttered his hand, lips brushing his glass. 'I don't think so. But it didn't feel right to broadcast it to him.'

'Were you worried Lady Satine would have the sirin fly in another carriage to retrieve us and send us straight to our rooms with no supper?' Silas was only half joking.

Pitch's unfamiliar, but still striking, honey-brown eyes watched him over the top of his royal-blue glass. 'If she sent us to the same room, I suppose it wouldn't be so bad. But I prefer it here, don't you?' Pitch moved closer as he spoke, making a very warm room so much more stifling.

'It's certainly jovial.' Silas swallowed a decent mouthful, the bubbles tickling at his nose.

The crowd joined in with the chorus being sung, something about a certain member of Parliament having an enormous stick to poke about.

'I want you to take off your coat, Silas.'

Sweet mercy. 'Take off...my...'

'Coat, the long thing hanging off your back.' Pitch's smile twisted about. 'The idea you had about putting the watch in a lead box was wonderful, but it's still quite –'

'Oh shit, yes of course.' Silas slammed down his glass, fearing for a moment the force had cracked it.

'And take my cloak too, if you wouldn't mind.' The prince was attempting to undo the clasp whilst still holding on to his glass, which was likely going to mean more spilled champagne.

'Here, let me do that.' Silas draped his coat over his arm and placed his fingers on the simple clip at Pitch's neck. The job was easy enough, but he was suddenly very aware of how close they stood, and that the daemon's eyes were on him, and his hands were not as steady as he would like. Pitch cupped Silas's elbow with his free hand.

'Tricky little contraption,' Silas stuttered.

He was on the verge of tilting into those impossibly bowed lips. But Pitch was preoccupied with taking those lips to his glass and moaning in an unnecessary way as he declared the drink luscious.

The clasp unfastened. The cloak was removed from slender shoulders, and Pitch exhaled as he stepped back. Silas hurried the clothing away, searching for a coatrack and spying one to the right of the door. But it was too close. 'Maybe I should put the coat outside? Or in the cloak room.'

'Oh yes, perfect place for death's scythe and Raph's trinket.'

'Shit, terrible idea. You're right. I'm more tired than I thought, I suppose.' Or all the blood had simply left one end of his body for the other. He placed the coat onto an iron hook shaped like an elephant's trunk. When he turned about, Pitch was dropping a long, slender silver pin onto the table that held Silas's abandoned drink. He removed another pin from his wig and then pulled the entire mass of black ringlets free, followed by the white skullcap underneath. He shoved his fingers into his flattened natural waves, ruffling them back to life.

'Oh fuck,' Pitch said. 'You have no idea how good it feels to be rid of that.'

Perhaps not, but Silas *did* know how good it was to see those light waves again, Pitch's hair tinged ever more golden since the harrowing times in Devon.

The music's tempo shifted. Violins joined the fray to play out a waltzing tune as the bawdy singalong continued. Silas stepped around the screen to take in the show and avoid staring too hard at Pitch as he continued to fuss with his hair.

It turned out more than four people *could* fit on the stage. Six couples were costumed in screamingly bright fabric, some crowned with pretty tiaras, waltzing about the stage as the crowd clapped. What he'd thought was a young man in breeches was in fact a young lass, with no effort being made to hide the swell of her bosom beneath her clinging shirt and vest. Her partner, at a second glance, was found to be a member of Old Bess's club. A sturdy man with a thin moustache wearing a gown of sunrise pink, a single feathery plume jigging atop an enormous wig of white, like a snowbank parked upon his head.

No wonder Nancy and Ada had had no quarrel with Pitch's costume. It was more of a wonder they had not invited him onto the stage.

'This music...' Pitch was suddenly right beside him. Taking his hand. 'Dance with me.'

At once Silas's pulse was a runaway train. 'What? Oh, I'm a terrible dancer I'm afraid.' The marquess's ball was testament to that.

'But will you dance with me anyway?'

Christ, he'd march into Elyssiam as a one-man army if the prince kept looking at him like that. 'You'll regret asking.' Silas was oddly nervous, about the dance more than anything.

'I doubt that.' Pitch held out his hand, fingers like slim lengths of ivory, and Silas's hesitation fled.

The daemon was, of course, adept at leading Silas about. The ankou only stumbled a handful of times before they found a semblance of rhythm. He had one hand braced about Pitch's lower back, the other clasping the prince's warm palm. The daemon's softness threw him every time. It was so unexpected on a creature so harsh in word and deed.

Around and around they twirled, in a space far too small for such things. Once Silas overcame his worry that he'd tread on Pitch's feet and break a toe, the flow of their movement was hypnotic. Never once did Pitch's eyes leave his face as ivory keys were struck and strings of horsehair plucked. The moment was utterly frivolous. This was not where they should be nor what they should be doing.

But he'd be nowhere else.

Silas urged Pitch in closer, so there was no space between them. The prince came readily, pressing in until the hard lines of his body beneath the gown were evident against Silas's hip. His head was tilted back to look up at the man towering over him, and though he was not smiling, there was no mistaking his happiness. Silas took hold of the moment and kissed him, a brush of lips that slid quickly deeper, to where the air was thin and they were both drawing it in with tiny gasps. All the while, much lower down, the rub of their bodies was making Silas's limp and untroubled parts stiff and bothersome, an embarrassingly evident arousal only stoked higher by the sway of Pitch's hips against him. They danced all the while exploring the heat and dampness between one another's lips.

The prince pulled free with a breathless sound that had Silas's mind spiralling into raw and needy places. Pitch lifted his hand from Silas's shoulder and spun away, returning in a whirl of cloudy grey promise. His smile was tight, purposeful, and full of wicked intent. He shoved his freed hand against Silas's chest with a strength that rocked the ankou onto his heels. Silas uttered a cry as he staggered. The back of his knees struck something hard, and he was going down.

'Shit,' was all he managed before he was on his back on the chaise, sending golden cushions scattering where they were not trapped beneath the weight of his shoulders. A flurry of grey engulfed him. Pitch clambered on top of him, settling his weight where Silas was rigid and straining. The prince planted his hands either side of Silas's face and leaned down low.

'So clumsy, my dear Sickle.' His kiss came with a teasing brush of tongue before he was lifting away again. He shuffled himself down onto Silas's thighs, peeling off his gloves as he did so. 'But as you look so comfortable...' The prince tossed the satin gloves and gathered up his skirts, bunching them against his belly so that the front of Silas's trousers was visible, peaked with stiff want. Pitch's fingers fluttered against a cock that ached to be freed, and Silas crushed a soft moan against the back of his teeth. The daemon had the buttons loosened quicker than an eye could blink and grasped the pillar of flesh that sprang free.

'Oh god.' Silas lifted his hips as the daemon rubbed him in slow strokes, applying only a subtle pressure. 'Pitch...Christ...'

'Do you not like it?' The daemon stopped his attentions, batting his lashes in playful astonishment.

Silas's laughter mixed with an agonised groan. 'You know very well I like it.' He propped himself onto his elbows. 'But you have already spoiled me well...' Silas swallowed, certain of what he wished to say, but shy with it. 'If you will allow...I should like to give you a turn.' He reached to run his fingertips along the cut of Pitch's jaw, down along the smooth material that covered his neck. Silas was rewarded with a shudder. 'Tell me what would be acceptable, and I will do it most gladly. Anything at all.' Silas rubbed at one of the buttons on Pitch's bodice. As stunning a woman as the daemon made, Silas missed the man beneath.

Beyond the privacy of the room, a new act was being announced, something about riding crops and naughty nuns. The crowd rumbled with anticipation, stamping their feet upon the floorboards.

'I know what I would like.' Pitch's fingers remastered their hold on Silas's member. 'But it may be too much.'

He flicked his thumb over the slick head of Silas's prick, and the ankou slumped back onto the cushions, turning to mush beneath the daemon's caresses.

'If it is what you want, then it is not too much,' Silas slurred through his pleasure.

Pitch leaned down, bringing his mouth to Silas's ear. 'I want us as close as can be,' he whispered. 'I want to feel you inside me.'

The band struck a raucous note, loud enough to cover up the strangled sound that escaped Silas. His head was spinning, his vision clouded at the edges so that all he could see was the daemon, with his rouged cheeks and glistening Cupid's bow lips.

'Are you certain?' Silas managed after a time.

Pitch chewed at his lip and withdrew his hand. Silas nearly cried out with the loss.

'I am certain, but it seems you are not.' Pitch moved to sit up, and Silas went with him, stilling him with a firm hand against the sway of his back.

'You misread me. I am very certain.' He ran his hand along Pitch's spine, lightening his touch where he knew the scars from the halo to be. Light-headed, heart galloping. 'I've not been more sure of anything since I found myself returned.'

Pitch relaxed against him, like butter melting in a warm pan. He danced a kiss against the tip of Silas's nose. 'I want you to take me away from this place.'

Silas's hand stilled. 'Of course, if you wish to leave, we shall.'

The daemon chuckled, and Silas's skin prickled in all the very best of ways. 'Gods, Sickle, if you can move anywhere, you are a better man than me. Feel the state of me.' He took Silas's hand, leading it beneath the skirts. Pitch wore no drawers, only gartered stockings that clung to his firm thighs. There was nothing between Silas's fingers and the place where the prince was every bit as hard as he. 'I mean that I want you to fuck me so deeply I have no room to think of anything else. Make me forget all that we are, and all others wish us to be. I want to feel nothing but you. Nothing but us.'

Silas forgot how to blink. How to inhale. He had his hand, at last, upon the daemon's cock, something he longed for so often, but he just held it there. Unmoving.

'Good...lord...' The words barely scraped up his throat. 'Will you...will you take off the bodice, I need to see you.'

Pitch laughed softly. 'As you wish. But I'll not take off the skirts nor the corset. They stay.'

There was a hint there, an undercurrent of subtle darkness that Silas would not challenge. Pitch could do as he wished, as he needed.

'I'd have it no other way.'

Silas took a firmer hold of Pitch's warm, rigid flesh and rubbed his hand up and down its length. The prince uttered the most precious sounds of delight as he worked his way along the plentiful number of gleaming buttons on his bodice. One by one they came undone, from bottom to the top. Silas ached, watching the slow and steady undress. Pitch's mouth was parted, his hips shifting lazily, his gaze heavy as he looked down at the ankou who had him in hand. He was forced to look away when he reached the last button on his gown, high on his neck, setting his chin at a tilt to reach it. Pitch shrugged the bodice open, wriggling it over his shoulders. He rocked harder into Silas's handiwork, making soft sounds of approval.

Under the bodice, Pitch wore a simple black satin corset, with no chemise beneath. The padding that had been arranged to give the illusion of breasts now tumbled free, folded ribbons of material that Silas cast aside. There was no need for illusion here; what form the daemon had chosen for himself was all he desired. Pitch's skin, normally pale as snow, was red where the fabric had pressed him. His nipples were bright pink, their nubs flattened by constant pressure. Pitch arched his back, still working himself free of the bodice's sleeves. Silas sat up, needing to be closer to where muscle hinted beneath smooth white skin devoid of any hint of hair. He helped Pitch rid himself of a cloying sleeve, and as the daemon shifted to free himself at last of the bodice, his chest moved so damned close to Silas's mouth, there was only one course of action a man could undertake. He took his lips to one of the bared nipples.

Pitch hissed between clenched teeth, tossing the bodice aside. Silas worked his tongue around a tightening bud of flesh. The prince slid his fingers into Silas's hair, holding him fast, and rocking his hips into the ankou's grip. The taffeta swished around them, the hush like the distant crawl of a wave on the shore.

'Harder.'

Silas took the sensitive skin between his teeth and bit down. The whimper it elicited was enough to send a man mad with want. He quickened his strokes, tightened his grip, felt the ripples and ridges on the daemon's prick and savoured every one.

At a distance, the crowd broke into applause, shouting their delight at whatever fancy was upon the stage. The reminder that an audience was so desperately close caused Silas to shiver, his cock to pulse. It was a fucking delight to throw all caution to the wind. To be so overcome he could not have cared if he were laid bare on that stage, so long as Pitch was still astride him.

The prince's mutterings were growing more urgent.

Dear god, Silas longed to hear him lose himself to ecstasy. Sheer ecstasy this time, though. Not as it had been in the carriage, where the daemon had worked his own release and his cries had been tinged with darkness, with hurt.

Silas loosened his hold and dragged the pads of his fingers over that most sensitive furrow that ran along the underside of Pitch's cock. He knew that place well upon himself. That delicate skin where the nerves lay so close to the surface.

'Do you like that?' he murmured against Pitch's chest.

But he needn't have asked. The sounds coming from the man who rode him were answer enough. Tight, exasperated gasps mingled with whimpers.

'If you dare let go, I'll...' What the daemon would do was lost to the rise of another moan.

Silas, panting against warm damp skin, kissed his way from one nipple to the other, a breathy touch of lips that had the prince trembling and jerking. The abandoned swollen nub of flesh was glistening and red from

Silas's attentions. Pitch throbbed in his hand and writhed against him. He was mumbling, barely coherent, but Silas heard enough.

The prince wanted him. Needed him. Did not want him to let go.

The blood roared through Silas's veins. There was a pressure building down low, a pulse at the base of his shaft that would soon become unstoppable.

'Come closer,' Silas whispered.

He wrapped his arms about Pitch's backside, gathering up lengths and lengths of sublime cloud-grey fabric and urged his hips forward. The daemon obliged. Silas's breath hitched as their cocks met.

He was so stiff it pained him, but it was the right sort of pain. One that intensified as he allowed his thoughts to move to what Pitch had asked of him. He wanted Silas to take him.

Christ almighty, it had him breathless and terrified of where all of this would ultimately lead.

Silas wrapped his hand around them both, his thumb hooked about his blood-taut member, while the rest of his fingers cradled Pitch's cock. Silas resumed the slow up and down, a caress that pleased them both in unison.

'Oh fucking gods, Sickle.' Pitch drew his hands from Silas's hair and grabbed at his shoulders, digging his fingers in. 'You're a fiend in a gentleman's clothing.'

With a grin painting his lips, Silas firmed his grip. He tilted his hips back and forth, rubbing their lengths together. The result was sheer heaven, enough to make eyes roll and nonsense flow from open lips. But as simple as it would be to bring them both to climax there and then, Silas stilled and released his hold. A disgruntled harrumph came from his daemon.

'What an odd day to die again,' Pitch grumbled.

Silas laughed, his nerves making the sound waver. 'I have not forgotten what you want.' He took a breath and sent his hand to trace a path beneath skirts and petticoats, seeking out the jut of a hip bone and finding a way down to the swell of a tight arse cheek. Silas closed his eyes. He was no stranger to the feel of a man. He knew it. When he'd lain with

Charlie, it had not been without its pleasures, but he'd been like one of the actors upon the stage. Playing a part. Not truly himself.

The room shook with another rowdy cheer from the crowd, as though urging him on.

He teased his fingers in between swells of velvet skin.

Pitch sighed. 'That's it.'

He leaned into Silas's shoulder, his arse lifting, inviting the ankou to explore deeper. Silas needed no encouragement, easing his fingers down to find the clenched swirl of muscle. The ankou teased a fingertip at Pitch's entrance. The prince sucked in a breath, and Silas felt him tense.

'Is everything all right?' Silas opened his eyes.

Pitch was clutching at one side of his gown.

'Would you like to remove the skirt after all?' Silas asked.

He would not mind. Pitch was a vision when laid bare, delicate and yet diamond hard.

'No. That's not it.' The daemon's grin was a salacious curve. 'I have something we need. Aha!' Pitch pulled a tiny bottle from the folds. Pale amber glass with a silver stopper and no bigger than a thumb.

Silas stilled his fingers. He frowned.

'Rose oil,' Pitch offered.

'I know what it is, and what it is for. Why on earth do you have it on you?' A dreadful thought gripped him. No one but Silas knew of all that had happened in that room at Gidleigh Park House, a secret he'd take to a thousand graves if the prince wished it. But what might those who did not know expect of a daemon renowned for his ability to get what he wanted through seduction?

'You took it to the soirée? Surely there was no suggestion you should —'

Pitch pressed a finger to Silas's lips. 'Jane came across it while she helped me dress. She offered it to me, thinking perhaps you and I may have need of it. Nothing more or less. I accepted because...well, I hoped she might be right.'

The admission robbed Silas of any ability to put a sentence together.

Pitch took Silas's hand and pressed the bottle into it. 'The show will not last forever. Will you take me now, Sickle? Or would it excite you to hear me beg?'

Silas curled his fingers around the bottle. He kissed the prince's cheek and found some words at last. 'You have no need to beg anything from me. You are the master here.'

CHAPTER 14

Pitch watched Silas flip open the lid of the bottle with his thumb and drip the scented oil onto his fingertips, coating them. His gave his cock a quick once-over, doing it all with a surety that spoke of experience in such matters. Silas discarded the bottle and then dove his slicked hand beneath the folds of taffeta, which gleamed like quicksilver in the candlelit room.

Removing the skirts and corset would have been practical, but Pitch was not practical by nature and was not yet ready to be so exposed. A ludicrous part of him could not disconnect such nakedness, such exposure, from Gidleigh House.

But he wanted this...to be with Silas...so very much, and refused to allow the daemon to steal that from him too. So, if he and the ankou needed to get tangled up a little to make it happen, then so be it.

Pitch rose up on his knees and spread his legs wider. The restrictive width of the chaise prevented him from moving far, but that did not seem to bother the ankou. Silas's fingers found their way, cool and slippery, to Pitch's entrance. And this time, when he pressed against the tight knot of muscle, there was give. He pushed one finger inside slowly, ever so slowly, easing Pitch open. Silas was no small man. Nor were his beefy fingers.

'Fuck.' Pitch groaned, and of course the oaf was bothered.

'Is it too much?'

'If you dare remove it, I'll slap you. Very hard.'

Silas's chuckle rumbled through Pitch's body, and gods it was wonderful. 'And you say *I* am terrible with threats.' He ran his tongue over Pitch's nipple, which still tingled from earlier attentions.

'A slap would stir you, then?' the prince said. Silas edged in deeper, and Pitch tensed around his finger. 'Oh sweet gods...'

'Perhaps you can help me find out in time all the things that stir us both.'

Pitch exhaled hard. 'You are not making it easy for me to relax.'

'I think you're doing very well.' Silas kissed his chest, a fiendish distraction, as he pushed a second finger into Pitch's entrance. Gently, of course, there seemed no other way for the ankou to be, but even so, the stretch was considerable. Pitch clenched his jaw, riding out the discomfort, determined not to let it show.

'Breathe for me,' Silas whispered.

Pitch could not help a jerky laugh. 'The last time you said that, the circumstances were quite different.'

'And there too you handled things admirably.'

When Lucifer's dark talk had stirred Pitch's beast, Silas had subdued the inferno with words alone. *Breathe, come back to me.*

Pitch raised his head and sought out the ankou's lips. He dove on Silas's mouth as though he'd not tasted it in months and could not be parted from the iron-tinged earthiness he craved a moment longer. It was true enough. His body thrummed with the rising heat of arousal. The sting between his cheeks faded, as he relaxed into the ankou's intrusion.

Silas sank his fingers deeper, and Pitch's thighs trembled so hard he had to lean against the ankou.

Their tongues teased and explored, and the sounds escaping their lips grew more indiscernible as each man began to drown in his urgency. Pitch wrapped his arms around the wide, steady shoulders of the ankou, clutching at his back.

'Closer. I want you closer.' He nipped at Silas's lip. 'I'm ready.'

The ankou's strangled cry sent fiery pulses to Pitch's groin.

Beyond the screen, the show hit a crescendo. The thud of drums and the clash of cymbals rang out as what seemed like an entire orchestra hit their notes. The audience sang along, bawdy and ravenous for the irreverent pantomime being played out. Silas embraced Pitch's waist with his free arm. He pinned the daemon close as he turned them both about and planted his feet on the floor, his back against the chaise's curved cushioning.

Silas made the adjustment without interrupting the kiss or taking his fingers from Pitch's arse, using only his brute natural strength to carry off the move, as though the daemon were an extension of himself and they could not be parted. It was titillating beyond words.

'Fucking gods,' Pitch muttered against Silas's mouth. At this rate, he would last all of a few seconds once he had the ankou inside him. 'Silas –' he hissed.

'I know.' He withdrew his fingers. His knuckles glanced against Pitch's balls as he took hold of his own cock. 'I want you to guide me. Is that all right?'

Sweet taints of the Archangels. This man's tenderness was going to kill him.

Pitched swayed like he'd swilled the bottle of champagne alone, and his heart pounded in time with the music played for the stage. He nodded and searched for the prize beneath the taffeta, finding Silas's hand wrapped about a heated, weighty pillar. He trembled as he lifted himself, tilted his hips, and drew the ankou's straining cock to where widened muscle lay.

Silas's whimper was a beautiful thing.

And Pitch could wait no longer.

He drove himself down onto Silas's oiled length. Taking all of him at once. Crying out at the fullness, the burn that tore its way through his insides.

Silas threw back his head, the veins in his neck bulging. 'Jesus.'

'Fuck.' Pitch hunched forward, impaled and aching.

Silas's fingers had been nothing in comparison to his shaft. Pitch held still, waiting for the shock of sudden expansion to pass. Silas was shaking, Pitch could feel it through his cock, a delightful tremor that told a story of a man teetering on the brink. He raised his head. Silas was watching him now, his breath stuttered, his upper lip damp with sweat, his eyes blown wide with his arousal. And oh, how the man was aroused. The swell of him within seemed to take the daemon over.

Pitch found himself in this position rarely. Usually at the behest of a demanding angel who, it seems, had also enjoyed setting fire to Pitch's soul as he fucked him.

The ankou smiled, just a quirk of his lips and Pitch twisted into sweet knots. *There* was the reason he wished Silas to fill him. *Needed* Silas to try and fill the hollows and cracks Pitch felt so thinned by. This was no battleground, here with the ankou. No harm would come from opening for this man.

Silas's fingers brushed his cheek. The scent of him was near to overwhelming. Mingling with the rose oil the ankou's desire was as sweet as any Pitch had known. He'd not fed from Silas since the encounter in Lady Howard's carriage, not taken a sip as they shared kisses since.

He'd frightened himself with how thirsty he'd been in that carriage. How readily he could have abandoned himself to lust and drunk too deeply from Silas's want. He'd blindfolded the man and held him at a distance. Pitch had not trusted himself to know when to stop. He'd been mad with the need to rid himself of the taste of the Alp, to take control once more. The ankou's desire had freed him with breathtaking ease. Silas was delicious, in all senses of the word. His taste could so easily become an addiction, and that sort of hunger was dangerous. Pitch had seen the witless husks left behind when an incubus became an addict.

He would curb his craving, keep the impuissant need in check. Fucking could be enjoyed without gorging.

But by the gods, the oaf was not making it easy.

'Do you think us close enough now?' Silas was glassy-eyed and wearing that look he reserved so often for his broken prince. One of adoration and marvel.

'Yes,' Pitch whispered. 'Are you all right?'

'Very much so.' Silas was gravelly, choked by his desire.

He laid another kiss on Pitch's lips. One that filtered right through the daemon, and shattered the stillness between them. Pitch rolled his hips, grinding up against Silas's belly, pressing his own shaft into firm flesh.

Once the movement began all sense and sensibility fled.

'Oh Christ.' Silas exhaled. 'Don't stop.'

Pitch could not have stopped if Samyaza himself strode in right then and there. He cast his hips back and forth, eyes clenched shut, head lowered so he was almost cheek to cheek with Silas. He could feel the ankou's breath against his ear, sending shivers down the side of his neck. Pitch shoved his hands under Silas's shirt, needing to feel the firmness of that body, the surety of it. He splayed his hands, running them over the tight clench of Silas's stomach and up into the dark licks of hair covering his chest. Pitch anchored himself there, where he could feel every breath Silas took and feel the faint thud of the ankou's heart beneath his palms.

Pitch kept his movements even, controlled. He did not yet dare rise up and down. For once that began, he'd be shouting into his release, the moment would be over, and he was not willing to part with it yet. Pitch sank onto his haunches. He gasped as Silas's length pushed deeper, teasing at the place within where mad abandon lay.

The ankou's lids were heavy, and he groaned in time with each gyration. He let Pitch use him, keeping his own hips anchored. His hands stroked along Pitch's back, running up over the stiff cage of the corset to brush at bare skin between sharp shoulder blades.

Silas was hungry with desire, there was no doubt of it. His stomach was taut beneath Pitch's fingers, and his face was flushed with yearning. But he was not forceful. He did not rush.

Instead, he relinquished control. Handed it to the daemon, who needed it most.

Pitch's cock jerked hard, his balls tightening. He was going to lose the control he'd been given very, very soon. The base of his spine was afire; all manner of fervid sounds were pouring from him. He rose up, dragging himself along the length of Silas's cock before plunging down. The ankou shouted at the roof, his fingers digging into the corset. Pitch rose up again, and drove Silas deep inside, shuddering as he found the rhythm which banished everything but this painful ecstasy between them.

Just as he'd desired.

He rode Silas faster, his entire body bristling, burning with the galloping approach of climax.

But he needed more.

He wanted to ache for days. So when those days darkened he'd remember this. Remember it was possible to feel so godsdamned euphoric.

'Your turn,' he whispered. 'I need you to fuck me hard as you can.'

The ankou didn't hesitate, gathering his lover to him, rising to his feet easily. As though Pitch were light as a lost soul. The daemon gasped and wrapped his legs tight about broad hips, panting like a hunt-weary hound.

The ankou did not put him on his back, as Pitch thought perhaps he may.

Silas knew better.

He kicked away his fallen trousers, and carried Pitch over near to the bamboo screen. The late-night crowd were singing themselves hoarse. He leaned Pitch's shoulders against the wall, pressing one hand alongside the daemon's head, the other supporting the small of his back.

'Tell me if it is too much.'

It could never be too much. Pitch wanted every inch.

Silas thrust into him. Hard, precise jerks that sent the tip of his cock slamming into that riotously sensitive place, high inside the daemon's passage. Pitch squealed, clutching at Silas's shirt, legs squeezing like a vice around his waist.

'Is this what you want?' the ankou panted.

'Yes!' Pitch shouted. 'Yes.'

The pounding was relentless, its tempo unfaltering. Pitch's vision was a blur, his head filled with a roar that did not come from the jubilant showgoers.

Gods, he was going to erupt, shatter into a thousand pieces.

Dribbled words escaped him. He had no clue what he was muttering, and it didn't fucking matter. So long as Silas did...not...stop.

Another brutal, sweet thrust and Pitch was lost.

He screamed, or Silas did. Someone was losing their mind. Likely they both were. Silas definitely swore, his body rigid. He slammed himself deep. And Pitch came.

Fierce and jarring and utterly without elegance. It was glorious. Eyes closed, body jerking like a fish on a hook, he fell into the abandon of release. Letting all guards down. Giving in to the ridiculous motions.

Turning to jelly, sobbing a little. Because it was safe to do so. Because it was Silas who held him.

Pitch bucked and hissed like a wildcat as he spent himself. The waves tore through him. Crashing and rolling in unrelenting flows. He gritted his teeth and relished it, eyes still tightly closed. Gods, he was drenched. Dripping. The skirt was sticking to him, and Silas's spend was hot and thick between his cheeks.

He opened his eyes to find they were on the floor. Or at least Silas was, on his knees, with Pitch still straddling his lap. His head rested against Pitch's shoulder, and he gulped in heavy breaths, his body still twitching.

The music had stopped, the murmur of the crowd far too quiet. If the patrons hadn't heard at least a little of a daemon and ankou's mating cry, they'd be lucky. Pitch laughed, and his amusement made him jerk. Rubbing the petticoats against a painfully sensitive cock. He whimpered.

'Are you all right?' Silas raised his head. He was red as a beet; a bead of sweat dangled from his chin. 'My bloody legs gave way.'

'I am far more than all right.'

'That was...truly...' Silas pressed his forehead to Pitch's damp chest, his own chest heaving. 'Good god, Pitch.'

He grinned into the ankou's damp, mussed hair. They cradled one another in near silence, their attempts to catch their respective breaths loud and rasping, now the music was quieted. The show had come to an end at some point along the way.

Silas raised his head and was sheepish as he spoke. 'I got a bit carried away. I hope your shoulders aren't bruised from the wall.'

'Oh I have bruises all right, but not from the wall, and not on my shoulders.'

The teasing did not sit well with Silas. 'Shit, I was too rough, I knew it. I don't know what possessed me –'

Pitch stopped him with a kiss, wondering if he could ever tire of this man's lips. 'You are still inside me, we have just fucked each other to our knees, and do you see me complaining? If you were too rough, I would have let you know.' He paused. 'You have some experience lying with men, evidently.'

'Evidently.' Silas was still caressing him, featherweight touches along his back.

'Your skills are quite satisfactory, I'd say.'

Silas's eyes widened. 'Satisfactory?' He was incredulous, and it was adorable. But he recognised he was being teased quickly, and went all loose-limbed with relief. He laughed. Heartily enough that it dislodged his cock from where it was very comfortably slackening inside Pitch. 'Oh, damn. I didn't mean to do that.'

'Well, you had to get out of me eventually, I suppose.'

Silas glanced up from beneath lowered lashes, a coy pose he rarely adopted. 'A shame that. Wouldn't you say?'

Pitch grinned like a cat with the cream. Far too much cream really. It was slick between his arse cheeks and thighs, and cooling fast. 'My goodness, Mr Mercer, you'll make me blush.'

Silas snorted. 'I've already succeeded there. You are quite pink in the face.'

They were both so damned full of queerly shy smiles and furtive glances. Still clinging to each other despite how fucking uncomfortable it was now, damp and sore, the corset pinching at him and his hip starting to murmur its discontent.

It was ridiculous to be so bashful with one another. This was hardly the first fuck for either of them. Silas, it turned out, was no virgin dead man. But they were both jittery, far too giggly and silly, and Pitch was suddenly terror-struck that they may not get to fuck like this again.

If he could have locked them in this room until no one remembered they existed and Samyaza's halo became someone else's problem, he'd have done so.

Sobered by his thoughts, Pitch let his hands fall from where they clasped Silas's neck. 'Right then. You may just need a quick wipe down, but I am a dripping, reeking mess. Jane will kill me for what I've done to her dress. I need to change. Do you think –'

A hard knock came at the door, and they both jolted.

'Oh shit.' Silas was on his feet, bundling Pitch with him like a babe in arms.

'Set me down,' the daemon protested. 'I have legs I can use.'

140

Soft laughter came from behind the door. 'It's only me...Ada. Now, I'd be mildly insulted that you didn't watch a minute of the show if that scream hadn't told me you had found far better ways to entertain yourselves.' Muffled chortles followed. Two people stood outside the door. 'Just thought we'd check everything was truly all right.'

'Bloody hell, were we that loud?' Silas whispered. He released Pitch, keeping a steadying hand against his back as the daemon's supposedly reliable legs betrayed him with a wobble.

'We were *that* loud.' Pitch cupped his mouth, calling out, 'We are fine, thank you. I had a dreadful fright, that's all. I was convinced that I saw a snake, but it was just my husband.'

Peals of laughter came from beyond the door, and from behind the bamboo screen. He'd spoken loudly enough that those last to leave the now relatively subdued little theatre had caught his words too.

'Christ, you are terrible,' Silas moaned, bending to fetch his trousers, his rosy-pink cock limp and glistening between his thighs.

'And you like it.'

'Where is your evidence of that?'

'Running down my legs.' Pitch enjoyed every inch of the mortified blush covering Silas's cheeks.

'It is such a pity you must leave us tomorrow,' Ada called. She had definitely enjoyed a few gins. 'For I think, Thaddeus, your acerbic wit would be a perfect fit for our stage.'

Silas mouthed a horrified *Did they hear that too*? Pitch's answering smirk had him pressing his trousers over his face, sending a fresh moan into the fabric.

Pitch settled his skirts and strode over to the door, wincing as tender places made themselves known. Riding a horse on the morrow was going to be a challenge.

'Don't you dare open that door,' Silas hissed, dancing from foot to foot as he rushed to pull his trousers on.

Pitch opened the door; it was too amusing not to. But he did not open it so wide that the ankou was in any danger of being seen. Only, Silas didn't know that and was making a dolt of himself trying to hide behind the low chaise and drag his clothes on.

'Hello, Ada...Nancy.' Pitch watched the women's eyes flick to his hair, taking in the lack of black curls. The club owner and her paramour moved almost as one, their gaze shifting down to his corseted torso, where his nipples were still a rubbed-raw shade of red. Likely the same shade as his lips, which had enjoyed as good a ravishing as his arsehole. 'Nothing you'll enjoy here, I'm afraid.'

'But someone did.' Nancy was a giggler and had enjoyed her absinthe well. 'Will you join us for one final drink for the evening?'

Surely it was nearer morning than evening?

'Or are you quite exhausted now and would prefer we just show you to your room? We've only made up the one room. That seemed the obvious decision.' Ada was probably grinning, but drunk as she was, she just appeared a bit mad.

Which had the Fulbourn tearing its way into Pitch's evening, its looming spectre a cruel slap to the face of a pleasant night.

And all at once he *was* exhausted, weary to the marrow. A lingering consequence of the Gu perhaps...or just the past few years of his existence slamming up against him, bitter that they'd been forgotten while the ankou fucked him senseless.

'I can't speak for Arthur,' Pitch said. 'But I think I am done for the night. Could I trouble you for a change of clothes perhaps?'

'Another dress?' Nancy gestured to his crumpled, stained skirt. 'That is truly gorgeous.'

'Wash it thoroughly and keep it, or burn it if the stains won't shift. It's yours, though the corset stays with me. A suit would be wonderful, if you can manage one?'

'We'll manage.' Ada nodded. 'For Arthur as well?'

Pitch glanced over his shoulder. Silas held their respective coat and cloak over his arm and was shaking out Pitch's bodice.

'I'm all right, thank you,' he replied.

'A cloth and basin of warm water will do for him,' Pitch said, enjoying the fresh glow on Silas's cheeks.

The women chattered about suitable attire for Pitch as they made their way back down the winding staircase. Ada planted her hands on Nancy's shoulders, their banter easy, their affection clear.

He turned back to Silas. 'We should try to get at least an hour or two's sleep before we head off. I can't imagine it's much before dawn now.'

'Agreed. I'm quite knackered, I have to admit.'

'You've been a busy boy.'

With a roll of his eyes, Silas held up the bodice so Pitch could slip into it. 'Are the arrangements all right with you?' He adjusted the lacework on the high collar as Pitch began to do up the tiny sparkling buttons.

'Arrangements?'

'The sleeping arrangements, the one bed?' Silas said. 'I will not be insulted if you need some space and would rather –'

'I would not rather.' Pitch only bothered with half the buttons, too tired to deal with the fiddling. 'Would you?'

The ankou was terrible at hiding his relief. 'No. I doubt I shall ever rather again, if I'm honest.'

Pitch held out his hand. 'Then let us go to bed, Silas.'

CHAPTER 15

V assago stood upon the clifftop, the Lethe River churning so far below he could only just feel its heat. He watched the Nephilim fall: a grotesque, enormous twist of stony limbs, an unholy scream coming from the dying creature. If the fall into molten, churning fury did not kill it, the vicious wounds he'd landed with the vestige definitely would. Vassago had hunted down the Nephilim until it was exhausted, giant legs buckling beneath it. The monster had stared at him with blind eyes green as manticore piss, lidless and always glaring. The gurgled sounds coming from its rolling black tongue might have been pleas for clemency. The Nephilim had strayed too far beyond the borderline marked by the Lethe River. It had been alone on enemy territory.

And there would be no return to Elyssiam.

Vassago had struck at the towering creature, a blow that had severed a limb as hard and rocky as a mountainside and carved off much of the Nephilim's chest with it. He had kicked the keening creature over the edge, sending it down into the river.

Now Vassago stood, his vestige held aloft, the curved blade lighting up the surrounds so brilliantly it was as though the solstice star had fallen.

He had destroyed another of Samyaza's vile children.

Giants formed from the egregious, treacherous union of purebred and angel.

Lusus naturae of both worlds.

They had no right to exist.

No right to threaten Arcadia as they did.

If any of the Nephilim had taken after their sire more fully, the Severance War would have been over before it began.

Elyssiam victorious.

But the battle was not over. Thank the gods.

Vassago punched his vestige at the air, screaming his rage, his delight, his never-ending hunger for the chaos of war.

This one small victory made him ravenous. Stoked the wildness within to lofty heights.

He was so very close to the Elyssiam border. Just beyond the Lethe lay the quagmire of emptiness unclaimed by either Elyssiam or Arcadia, a land of neutrality where every sorry bastard who found himself there fought alone, for his masters would not step foot in that place.

But beyond that...beyond that lay the Exarch's throne. Where Azazel watched for Arcadia's armies.

Vassago's flame pulsed.

The angel did not search for a lone Dominion who had abandoned his legion and ignored his commanders and their carefully laid campaigns to stalk Arcadia's furthermost boundaries.

Azazel's eyes were turned to distant skirmishes and focused on greater assaults.

Vassago listened to the last of the Nephilim's death screams on the wind. His flame was alive and roaring within, goading him on.

Cross the river.

Seize the throne.

He ignited.

Vassago leapt from the cliff. Incandescent savagery held him aloft, soaring him towards the enemy line.

And the angel was right there. Rising up from below, appearing in his path.

Trying to stop him.

Vassago swung.

Seraphiel screamed, words that burned up before they could reach a Dominion who refused to bow to his master. The inferno built between them, entwining, one and the same. Vassago drank in the angel's rage, and its taste was strikingly familiar to his own. The firestorm between them fed upon itself.

The beast within was crazed, blazing with discontent. But its frenzy perplexed him, even in the midst of madness. For he thought, for a moment, that the wildness did not seek to devour the angel but rather kneel before him.

The Berserker Prince would not kneel.

He whipped the flame into a firestorm. His vestige an aureate curve, seething with a lust for destruction.

Seraphiel was still shouting, raging so his words might be heard. And this time, *this* time they were.

Heed your master. Stand down. Destroy the prince, destroy the life I gave you.

What followed was called out in the language of the Seraphim, bringing forth a surge of powerful magick.

Seraphiel loosed his halo's wrath upon the errant, rebelling daemon. Vassago swung around, throwing himself from the line of fire. He did so too slowly to escape fully intact. A grievous agony blazed at his back, one that should have ended him at such close quarters.

But the angel must have been careless, for the prince lived to retaliate.

Vassago drew on all that he despised, all he abhorred about his existence in this place. A world where his masters sought to break him. To stifle him. He took his rage and fed it to the beast at his heart. It always ate greedily. Straining for release. And again there came the vague sense of confusion within the wildness. The power uncertain of its desires. Of whether to kill or subvert. But *he* was master here. And Vassago knew what he wanted. To decimate. To consume.

He opened the cage, unleashed his power, and threw the might of his flame through the vestige. Sending it straight at the angel who dared get in his way.

Beyond that, the only screams Vassago heard were his own.

CHAPTER 16

Pitch's muffled scream shattered the peace of the bedroom, pulling Silas from a dreamless sleep with shocking veracity. His arm was draped over the daemon's backside. They had drifted off to sleep with Pitch lying on his front, Silas beside him, rubbing at his back until at last the daemon slept.

But now the prince's nightmares had found him.

He kicked his legs, trying to untangle himself from the sheets, which had wrapped about them. Something Silas knew would send him into an even greater frenzy of panic if he awoke fully to find himself trapped.

'Pitch...' Silas shook him, seeking to pull him from his nightmare. 'Pitch, it's me, it's Silas. Wake up now.'

The prince was drenched in sweat, his naked body slippery beneath Silas's hands. He'd been dreaming for some time. Pitch rolled onto his side, facing away from Silas, and kicked back with his legs.

'Shit,' Silas grunted at a blow to his knee. 'Pitch, come on now.'

But whatever the daemon was running from, he had no intention of stopping. He clawed his way to the edge of the bed, and Silas tried to restrain him in a way that would not see him grow more desperately violent in seeking to escape. The bedroom door opened, and Tilly pattered into the room clad in a linen-and-lace sleeping shift, a nightcap upon her head.

'Tilly, stay there, little one.'

With his attention shifted, Silas lost his hold on the struggling daemon. Pitch slipped off the bed, dragging all the sheets with him, and falling with a solid thump onto the floor.

'Bump,' the little girl said, pointing at the fallen daemon. 'Big fire go bump.'

Or at least that is what Silas thought he heard. He was more concerned with keeping her away from the prince, who was liable to lash out if he woke to a stranger's face over him. But Christ, if she *was* talking about fire, did that mean she'd seen Pitch's eyes?

'Tilly, stay there, sweetheart.' Silas jumped off the bed, grateful he'd fallen asleep in his drawers, and knelt beside Pitch. He was breathing heavily, but at least his manic attempts to escape seemed ended. He was curled up in ball of damp sheets and waft of exertion.

'Pitch?' Cautiously Silas hooked his finger into the wavy locks that covered the prince's face, drawing them back. His eyes were closed but he stirred.

'Silas...'

'I'm right here.' He touched his hand to Pitch's shoulder and barely stifled a gasp. The daemon was burning up. 'You are safe, no harm will come to you.'

'No,' he whispered. 'The harm's already been done.'

A cold prickle brushed the back of Silas's neck, a chill that contrasted the worrying heat of the daemon. 'What did you say?'

'I dreamed of the cliff again...and I saw it all plainly this time...I heard him.'

'Seraphiel.' No need to make a question of it. No one plagued Pitch's nightmare's like the angel he had felled, and Silas despised the angel more with each passing day. 'Tell me what you saw. Do not carry this alone.'

He searched for the child. Tilly was sitting at the dresser on the far side of the room. She'd removed her nightcap and was rummaging through a jewellery box, talking softly to herself in the mirror. Paying them no mind.

'It was different to how I recalled.' Pitch pushed onto an elbow but kept his head lowered, the tips of his hair glancing at the floor. 'I could hear him...so clearly...' He looked up, and Silas did his best not to flinch.

The daemon's eyes flared with all the hues of a furnace. 'I knew he cast magick that day...that much I recall. I remember wondering how the blazes he'd not obliterated me at such close quarters. I remember thinking him an old decrepit fool who would rue his failure to destroy me.' Pitch stared hard into his memories. 'Raph was shouting...screaming at me to stand down...there was so much *noise* that day, so much rage....it was deafening. But in the dream there was not so much chaos...I heard his voice...his words.' He turned away, staring down at the rug, his finger tracing the pattern. '"Heed your master", he said. "Destroy the prince, you destroy the life I gave you."'

Silas frowned. 'Whose life? Who was he speaking to? Was there someone else with you?'

'No. We were very much alone. Neither of us were where we should be.'

'What strange words. Heeding your master, I can understand, but—'

Pitch's gaze, still fiery, sliced at him. 'Seraphiel was never my master. Lucifer yes, Enoch certainly. But not him. The Seraphim do not interfere with the Dominion. We belong to the Daemon Kings'...that is how it *should* be at least.'

Silas winced at the idea of one such as Pitch being owned by anyone at all. He kept as close as he dared without touching the prince. The daemon still shook with the rigours of his dream. His nightmare.

'What then do you make of his words?' He kept his voice low, aware of their petite audience. Tilly was sorting necklaces and laying earrings in their pairs. The set Pitch had been wearing, glittering diamonds and sapphires, took pride of place at the centre of the assembly.

'Gods, I don't know. So much of it is different to the memory I've held so long. Some is the same...Seraphiel appeared suddenly, right in harm's way, catching me unawares.' Silas knew this well enough. Pitch had been paralysed with fear at the graveyard where they met with the skriker, when he thought he'd struck Silas with his flame and made the same fatal mistake again. 'And I've always believed I was so intent on destroying the Nephilim, so possessed by the need for a kill that I ignored all else, that I heard nothing but my own rage. But I heard it all. And the monster was long dead in this dream.'

Silas itched to touch Pitch, provide a little comfort, but he curled his fingers into his palms, aware of the great weight carried by the prince.

'Dreams are masters at contorting the truth,' he said, gently.

'And at revealing it.'

'You think...the events of your dream are real?'

'Perhaps.' Pitch ground the heels of his hands into his eyes. When he looked up his eyes had returned to some semblance of calm, honey-brown, the vibrant natural green still hidden. 'The greensward stirred some of your memories. Well, for me I think the watch is doing the same. There is something I haven't told you about the soirée.' Silas tensed, but nodded and waited. 'When that moron cracked my head on the desk it loosened more than my back teeth. I recalled some of my time at the angel's Sanctuary...all of it rather unpleasant.' He hesitated, and god it was a struggle not to reach for him. 'Seraphiel cast his magick upon me there. But not some piss-weak incantation to make a more manageable warrior of the Berserker Prince, as he had Enoch believe. This was cultivation, raw...savage...magick that he sent to where my flame is most deeply embedded. I remembered how fucking painful it was when he touched me, how his magick plundered me, how foreign it felt as it worked its way through to the flame. I thought I knew what it was to burn, but I was quite wrong. Do you recall what my dear sire said, that day in your cottage? That Seraphiel made a monster of me?'

It was hard to forget. 'I do.' Silas placed his hand on Pitch's shoulder. The prince was trembling. 'But he was very wrong, Pitch.'

The daemon glanced away. 'You've not seen the things I've done, Silas. I was the Berserker Prince long before Seraphiel showed interest in me. My flame has always tested me, pushed at the limits of my control and escaped it often.' Pitch shook his head. 'Seraphiel knew this when he came to me, talking of tasting forbidden fruit, of wanting to fuck me simply because Enoch forbade the union of high angel and daemon. I was hardly going to deny him. His desire was intoxicating, or I was intoxicated...I'm not sure which now. But he didn't just want me to bend for him when he called...he wanted far more. I see it now, he had designs, just as Satty said. He wanted my flame. He coveted the wildness within me for his own means. And though I do not know *what* Seraphiel has done to me, I know for certain that it has been done.' Pitch touched at his belly, looking every inch as sickened as he'd done with the Gu. 'Never, in four hundred years, has it been so overwhelmingly difficult to control my flame. Without the amuletum I doubt...' The prince raise his head, his anguish evident. 'It fights me, constantly. Seraphiel *has* made me his monster, Silas. But it is not in the way Lucifer believes. I think I am a vessel...a part of a monstrous whole.'

'Oh god, Pitch...' Silas tried to pull the prince close but he met firm resistance. He took his hand from Pitch's shoulder, searching desperately for anything that might dull the knife-edge of this line of reasoning. The angel's violation was appalling, beyond comprehension, and it came on top of all else Pitch had endured.

'I am glad he's dead.' The words flew from Silas. 'It is nothing less than he deserved for the way he's treated you.'

'But what am I left with, Silas? He's gone but his curse is still with me. His wish is still my command, for here we are...running after whispers.'

To see Pitch so desolate cut at Silas like nothing else. The lump in his throat made it difficult to swallow, his eyes stung with the press of unshed tears. Christ almighty, what awful things he wanted to do to that bastard of an angel.

Then Silas saw a light in the miserable darkness. He touched his fingers to Pitch's chin, making sure he had the daemon's full attention. 'Do you know what is *not* your burden to carry? His death. Seraphiel's own manipulations are to blame for that. What happened that day cannot lie on your shoulders alone, for you were not yourself. The angel saw to that. We *know* that now.'

Pitch sucked in his breath, parting the full pink lips Silas had explored so well last night. He wrapped his fingers around Silas's wrist. Holding on as though the world were suddenly spinning.

'You may be right.'

'I know I am right.' Silas leaned down and brushed a kiss over the prince's lips, resting his forehead against Pitch's brow, letting the words he'd spoken sink in. Hoping the daemon might believe them as fervently as Silas did.

Tilly chatted with her reflection, oblivious to the enormity of the hushed conversation. Silas tucked a strand of Pitch's tangled hair behind his ear.

'What do you wish to do?' he said quietly. 'Are you ready for the Fulbourn or would you rather some more time?'

Pitch shook his head. 'What point in a delay? Nothing has truly changed. I have another memory, a tiny piece of an angelic puzzle, but I am no less a pawn in this game because of it. At least now there is some explanation for this intolerable chaos inside me.'

The child cooed at herself, admiring the earring she held to her ear. The least sparkly of the entire choice on offer, a teardrop of amber which clipped to the ear by way of a single gold leaf.

'Pretty,' she declared.

Silas helped Pitch to his feet, securing the sheet about him and steadying him as he sat on the edge of the bed. The daemon was deep in his thoughts, and didn't utter a word. Silas gathered up the blanket and draped it around Pitch's shoulders, noticing the way the daemon still trembled.

A small vision in white ran at the prince. Pitch pulled his arm from the blanket and balled his fist.

'No!' Silas cried. 'It's Tilly.'

The daemon froze, his knuckles mere inches from her face, his eyes ablaze. But the child did not flinch.

'Why is it in front of me?' Pitch hissed.

The amber earrings dangled from her tiny earlobes, their weight dragging them long. Her cheeks were ruby red, a thin line marking where she'd slept upon a seam on her pillow. Pitch shooed her away, but the little girl smiled at him and pulled herself up onto the bed.

'What is it doing?' Pitch leaned against Silas as she wriggled in alongside him. The child reached for the daemon.

'Tilly, little one, come now.' Silas moved to intercept, but the changeling shook her head, her face wrinkling.

'No touch.'

Silas pulled back at once. The last thing they needed was a screamed tantrum. And he did not mind so much how Pitch pressed up against him, seeking protection from the dastardly infant.

'Go away, damn you.' Pitch flicked his fingers but Tilly was determined.

'Hug.'

Without further ado, Tilly clambered into his lap.

Pitch inhaled sharply, hands raised as though it was dirty laundry in his lap, not a grinning child. 'Silas, for fuck's sake.'

'Language, please.'

'Fire man scared.' Tilly was on her knees. Pitch's lap was buried beneath the bunching of blanket and sheet, his nakedness thankfully, for Tilly at least, covered. The child pointed her fingertip against his chin, and he tried to shake her off by tilting his head right back. 'No be scared now.'

'I'm not bloody scared, thank you very much,' he told the ceiling. 'And I'm not a fucking fire—'

'Pitch, for god's sake, don't swear in front of her. She's referring to your eyes. She must have seen them. You were upset—'

'I'm still upset. She is digging her knee into my co—'

'Don't you dare say it.' Silas lifted Tilly from Pitch's lap, away from his glare. But the child was not happy about it.

'No, no. Fire man.' She tugged one of the earrings free, one plump hand extended towards Pitch. Clearly she wished him to take her little gift. A tiny flower was encased in the amber, a daisy perhaps. Silas was too busy keeping his eye on the unhappy daemon to discern. Tilly's bottom lip began to quiver when Pitch made no move to accept her offering.

'Oh goodness, Pitch just take it.'

'It's ugly. I don't want it.'

'Well, that is patently untrue. It's quite unique,' Silas said. 'Do you wish to make her cry?'

'Fuck no.'

'Then take it.'

Pitch scowled and snatched the earring from Tilly's fingers. The child nestled against Silas with a contented sound.

'Pretty fire man. No scared.'

A faint voice reached them.

'Tilly? Are you there my darling?' Nancy called from somewhere distant. 'No more hiding now, my love. It's getting late. Time for your breakfast.'

'No breakfast,' Tilly said, swinging her feet either side of Silas's knees.

'We need to go, Silas.' Pitch smoothed his thumb over the drop of amber, staring down at the entombed flower entombed. 'Now.'

He seemed quite calm when he said it. Silas suspected he was anything but.

'Of course. I'll take Tilly to her mother. Ada offered us a pair of horses last night. The asylum is a twenty minute ride out of the city.'

'No. No riding.'

'Why-ever not?'

Pitch's face brightened with his grin. 'Because I rode you far too well last night and if we broke into a trot, I think I would split in half.'

'Oh god, stop.' Silas clamped his hands over Tilly's ears, nearly dislodging the other earring in the process. He coughed down his laughter, his cheeks growing rosy under the daemon's bemused gaze. Tilly shook him off, brushing at her pale hair and checking to make sure he'd not thieved the earring from her lobe. 'A hansom cab it is, then.'

He set Tilly down so he could pull on a robe. When the young fae wandered back to her pile of gathered jewellery he decided it safe enough to ask a very personal question of the prince. 'You're not terribly sore, are you? I mean I didn't—'

'I am, which is exactly what I wanted.' He stood up, rising to his tip-toes, and planted a firm kiss against Silas's cheek. 'Let's go and get this over with so you can set about making me sorer still. Perhaps nail me to another wall or three.'

Tilly clapped her hands. 'Nail.'

Silas nearly tripped over himself in his haste to bundle her up.

'High time we get you back to your mothers,' he declared, though very much enjoying the tingle of the daemon's kiss against his skin.

'Tell them she needs more sunshine,' Pitch said, offhand, opening the wardrobe where Ada said there were clothes they were welcome to. 'She'll not thrive otherwise.'

Tilly tried to wriggle out of Silas's arms, intent on the daemon once more.

'Hug.'

Silas sighed. 'I'm afraid that is not going to happen, little one.'

By the time he found Nancy downstairs, Tilly was red in the face from crying, clinging to her amber earring like it were a favoured toy.

'I'm so sorry,' he said as Nancy peeled Tilly's hands off his lapel. 'She wanted Pi...Thaddeus, to hug her but he's not one for children or hugs, I'm afraid. And Tilly was adamant.'

Nancy smiled. 'She's a stubborn one, that's for sure. She knows her own mind.'

'She and Thaddeus have that much in common, then.'

Silas passed on Pitch's advice about the sunshine, leaving the sniffling child with her mother. As he headed back up the stairs Nancy asked Tilly if she would like to take a trip to the seaside when it was sunny once more. The little fae agreed, but on one condition. The fire man must come too.

'He is very sad, Mumma.'

It rent at Silas to hear it. For he knew the changeling was right. And though he'd fight the gods if it would change things, Silas feared the path of Prince Vassago was set, and had very little room for happiness.

CHAPTER 17

Silas asked Pitch to read the sign at the Fulbourn's front gate.

'The County Pauper Lunatic Asylum for Cambridgeshire,' the prince said, lacing his words with acid.

Silas shuddered. 'How awful.'

Though admittedly the grounds were not so. There was no sign of the actual asylum, named the Fulbourn for the village nearby, with only an expanse of greenery and a low stone fence in sight.

The coachman set them down at the front gate just after ten in the morning. They'd sent him on his way with a considerable tip for his troubles. He'd driven his roan hard at their request, after they had departed Ada and Nancy's residence later than intended, even having declined breakfast. Pitch was partly to blame, with his fussing over his clothes. He'd not wished to wear tweed, and was tending towards the most lavish of costumes that Ada laid out for them until Silas pointed out that they were trying to be furtive in this visit. Pitch stood out at the best of times, let alone without wearing a stunning teal coat with fur trimmed cuffs.

With time on his hands, Silas had decided on a change of clothes after all. He opted for a plain brown frock coat with black velvet lapels and cuffs, essentially the only size he found that would fit him, and deep pockets that held the bandalore and the watch in its lead box.

Pitch kept on the black corset of course, and laid it over with a cotton shirt and plaid tailcoat of navy and subtle lime green, and matched those with pale cotton twill trousers. Ada had provided a man's short black wig when requested and was too discreet to enquire as to why Thaddeus chose to hide his brown-and-gold-tinged waves beneath it.

Silas had been a curious combination of tension and happiness on the carriage ride. He was nervous about whether they were still concealed by the elixir, among other things, but very happy to sit so close to the prince on their way. Pitch did not seem to mind too much either, not protesting when Silas's hand rested against his thigh.

As it turned out, contrary to Silas's fears, the elixir was in fact still serving them well. They came to a stop at an intersection, where another hansom pulled up alongside. Its passengers were two women dressed in sombre church-going shades. The one in a severe black bonnet was a dokkaebi, according to the notes that trilled in Silas's mind, a mischievous member of the goblin family originating in the Orient. She offered only the barest of nods when Silas bade them a good morning. Pitch assured him the creature would have done far more than that should it have recognised them. Mostly in her own drawers. Daemons tended to frighten many of the naturals, evidently.

They walked down the asylum's long drive. The road meandered past an established apple orchard and a kitchen garden that backed onto a small, open field, where winter wheat showed off fledgling stalks. Dotted around the grounds were several brick houses, presumably for the employees of the Fulbourn, nurses and doctors perhaps, or groundskeepers for what seemed to be an extensive estate. A gardener was hard at work trimming back a camellia bush, but the man didn't even glance their way as they passed by.

Silas kept his eye on Pitch as they walked, the prince not protesting when the ankou brushed his hand on occasion and or touched the small of his back to ensure he did not trip on the uneven surface. In truth the prince's limp was not too bad this morning. But his distraction was very evident. He withdrew something from his pocket, twiddling it between thumb and forefinger with his gaze fixed on the road ahead. It was the earring Tilly had given him.

'I thought you had left that on the dresser?' Silas nodded at the teardrop and gold leaf setting.

'I did. Clearly the child will make a wonderful pickpocket, because she slipped it back in my pocket without me knowing. Have you checked to make sure you have still have our pieces?'

Only several hundred times. 'Yes. Still there.'

'Hmph.' He returned to spinning the smoothed amber between his fingers, the flower contained within was like a tiny carriage wheel going round and round.

'Well, this does not seem such a horrid place outside at least,' Silas said.

'Hmph.'

They walked for nearly ten minutes before the eves of the main buildings peeked over the oak trees lining a right-hand curve in the road up ahead. They were led further down to where a circular drive wound around a statue of a maiden pouring a flute of water from her shoulder. The entrance to the Fulbourn loomed over her. A bright green door marked the entrance.

The facade of the asylum was impressive: a three-storey central building flanked by double-storey wings, with elaborate stone latticework trimming the eves. The sandstone was shot through with red brick, and squared turrets marked each corner of the main building's roof. It was impressive. But something of the place had Silas on edge.

A nurse and a frail woman stepped out of a doorway on the left wing, the patient's sobs audible from where they stood some distance away.

Silas wanted to take the prince's hand, perhaps give him a reassuring kiss, but it was ill-advised considering how many windows looked down on them, and how many shapes moved back and forth behind those panes. More noises pushed from the Fulbourn to join the trickling fountain and the crying, unhappy woman. Strange sounds mingled with the murmur of voices. Some akin to the bark of a distant dog, the others higher, more frantic, closer to the squeal of a piglet.

'Are you ready?' Silas knew his own answer to that.

'No.' Pitch shook his head and marched as well as his limp allowed up the short flight of worn steps to the front door. He pushed at the painted green wood. Silas right behind him.

They stepped into a tidy, dark-lacquered hallway. A navy-blue runner covered the length of the hallway, where portraits of stiff-looking gentlemen lined the walls in precise rows. Between each of the paintings were closed doors with gleaming gold plaques nailed to their middles.

'Are these the doctors' rooms?' Silas stepped on a floorboard that protested his weight with a screech.

'Seems so.' Pitch moved on, peering at each of the plaques as he went.

Silas spied a vacated desk at the far end of the corridor: a secretary, or receptionist perhaps. A steaming cup of tea sat near a sturdy telephone of black wood and silver trim and not for the first time did Silas wonder if another phone call to Holly Lodge might be in order. He leaned in to make the suggestion to Pitch.

'Can I help you, gentlemen?'

They both swung round at the same time, bumping into one another. A prim lady had stepped out of a side room, carrying a plate stacked with shortbreads. She wore a smart dress suit of grey with white collar and cuffs, a gold-link chain about her neck, hanging to her waist. She had the type of face that immediately put one at ease, the type that seemed to rarely be without a smile. She peered over her spectacles to look at them.

'Do you have an appointment?' she prompted, with both Silas and Pitch failing to have answered her first question.

But now Pitch found his tongue. 'No, no, I'm afraid we do not.' He poured on his congenial charm. 'We've come quite a ways. I hope it won't be too much of a bother to see one of your patients?'

'Let's see what we can do, shall we?' She smiled at him, her eyes never leaving his face. 'Do you have a doctor's name?'

'Dr Severs? I think that's right.'

Eyelashes batted.

And Silas hid his smile.

'We do have a doctor by that name. He's only been with us a few months, and he is already a favourite of many of the patients. I can see if he is available to speak with you. What patient are you hoping to see?'

Pitch's inhale was evident before he spoke. 'Edward Charters. Mrs Charters told us he was here, and we simply had to come and see him.'

The woman showed no sign of recognising the name; likely the lieutenant was just one of hundreds of troubled admissions in a place this large. Which drew Silas to another consideration. The bandalore was quiet. His senses unfazed. For such a place, he would have thought for sure there might be a lost soul or two about. *His* kind of lost soul, not the poor troubled wretches installed here.

'Very well.' She nodded. 'Could I have your names please?'

'Thaddeus Yates and Arthur Knight.' A good thing Pitch seemed to have kept track of their names.

'Would you wait for me here a moment please?'

'Of course.' Pitch stood aside, tilting as she passed. She tossed him a coy smile, patting at her perfectly coiffed caramel-brown locks.

The woman strode up to the third door on the right and knocked before leaning through to speak to the occupant. She was there for some time.

Silas glanced at Pitch. He was chewing on his bottom lip, watching her. His lack of sleep was showing, with dark rings beneath eyes still tinted honey brown. Silas missed his emerald gaze desperately. Had missed it last night even as the prince rode him so beautifully, so deeply. Silas pinched the back of his hand, settling his thoughts. Hardly the time.

The woman stepped back into the corridor and waved them forward. 'This way please, gentlemen. Dr Severs is on his rounds, but his assistant, Mr Weatherby, can see you now.'

Silas saw the shadow cross Pitch's face, and spoke up quickly. 'Wonderful, we appreciate that very much.'

She stood aside, waiting until they had entered the room before closing the door with a quiet click behind them.

Silas's eye was drawn to the office's floor-to-ceiling bookshelves covering all walls save for the one where wide windows opened out onto the driveway they had just traversed. There was a sprawling desk set in front of the view, covered in loose papers and opened books, with a smaller writing desk off to one side. Dr Severs's assistant was at his employer's desk, just setting the telephone's receiver into its cradle. His melody struck out at Silas.

Kitsune. Yako.

He struggled to compose himself, darting a quick glance at Pitch, whose smooth expression belied nothing.

Mr Weatherby was of the same natural kind as Mr Ahari.

'Gentlemen, please take a seat.' The kitsune had a surprisingly high voice and unexpectedly long nails. A striking chap for his aquiline nose, bowl-cut black hair, and sharply cut suit of chestnut brown. 'Miss Grindel says you are asking after Edward Charters?'

For no reason in particular, it bothered Silas to hear the lieutenant's name on this man's lips.

'That's right,' Pitch said, showing no sign that there was anything untoward about finding a kitsune here in employ at the asylum. For all Silas knew, it was quite common to find naturals pursuing a career. 'We'd like to see how the poor chap is settling in. If only for a minute or two.'

Pitch seated himself in one of the leather armchairs set in front of Dr Severs's desk, making it clear he was prepared to wait. Silas followed suit and eased himself into the spare chair, which creaked with his weight.

'Absolutely, of course. Perhaps it will do him good to see some familiar faces. He's rather morose.' There was something unsettling about the way Mr Weatherby's eyes darted between them. Every movement he made was rapid, like the way of a lizard. 'I've put a call in to the nurse's quarters to see where Dr Severs is on his rounds. He's finishing up in the women's wing and will come by to collect you on his way through.' He made his way over to a rounded table that held a floral teapot and assortment of cups. 'The water is still hot. Tea, gentlemen?' He was pouring before they could reply. 'Sugar anyone? Slice of lemon, dash of milk?'

'A dash of milk for me, thank you.' Silas was not in the least bit thirsty, but he accepted the cup and took a few sips. The brew was hot, with a hint of cardamom. He stared out the window as Mr Weatherby poured a cup for Pitch, adding the five heaped teaspoons of sugar that had been requested. A few nurses and patients strolled the gardens, taking the air in the weak sunshine on offer. Silas studied each of them, looking for sign of Edward, of course, but for Charlie also. Wondering if the lad might have secreted himself into the asylum somehow.

If he was here at all.

Silas took a big gulp, letting the scalding heat melt his sudden panic. He'd been holding on to the hope that Charlie was here, somewhere, and now he was about to find out if he'd been a fool.

'And how do you know Mr Charters?' Mr Weatherby was asking.

'Just family friends,' Pitch replied.

'I thought the family had decided to keep his admission very confidential. You must be close to Mrs Charters.'

A prickle of unease lifted the hairs on Silas's neck. He decided it best to say nothing and let Pitch handle the conversation.

'To be honest, I rather think that too much whisky and gin was to blame for the mention of it. I had a conversation very late in the evening with Mr Fothergill at a party and rather hammered him until he told me where Edward had gone. He's not to be blamed. I can be quite insistent when I wish.' He was not batting any lashes here. Throwing his enchantments at another natural was hardly wise, considering they still had the elixir's disguise. 'And Edward and I have been firm friends for a long while. We've been through much together. I'd like him to know he has my support. I'm also prepared to contribute funds to his care, if need be.'

Mr Weatherby seemed happy with that. 'Truly? How very kind, but I do believe Mr Fothergill has it all in hand.'

'I'm sure he does.' Pitch sent a pointed glance towards the mantel clock. 'Do you think it will be long?'

'No, no.'

But it wasn't a short time either. They sat in quiet, awkward silence for another ten minutes, with Mr Weatherby's beady eyes flicking up from his cup to watch them both, and Pitch's tapping foot becoming more than a little irritating. Silas finished his second cup of tea, the daemon refusing another. By the time the telephone rang, he was close to dozing off and nearly leapt out of his seat at the calamitous disturbance.

Mr Weatherby answered. 'Yes, Doctor. I see, yes. Yes. No, no, they are quite content.' Pitch scowled at that. 'I'll bring them along now, of course. Yes, we're just finishing off a cup of tea.' His glance slid to where Pitch was stealing another spoonful of sugar, adding it to the dregs of his tea. Silas should be used to the way that Pitch was stared at by those around him. He was beguiling, no matter the wig on his head or the coat on his back, but seeing the way Mr Weatherby regarded him had Silas rising to his feet and moving to the window so as to promote distraction. 'Very good, sir. We will hurry along.'

The kitsune hung up the telephone, and the sojourn in the office was over.

'This way, if you please. And I must warn you, some of what you will see is disturbing. Some of our residents are very unwell.'

They followed after him. Silas stood back to allow Pitch ahead of him. He touched at the daemon's back in that place he favoured.

'Should we be worried?' he murmured, sending a pointed glance towards the kitsune.

'Of that runt?' Pitch shook his head. 'Not in the mood I'm in.'

'Are you all right?'

'I will be when this is over.' He touched Silas's arm. 'And we are back to ruining each other. Perhaps it's your turn for the saddle this time?'

He strolled ahead, leaving a flustered ankou in his wake.

'Good god, let this be a short visit indeed,' Silas muttered.

He gathered himself and followed after the prince.

CHAPTER 18

Weatherby led them down the hall, and Pitch followed along, trying his best not to betray how utterly uncomfortable he was with the incessant scratch and pull at his back. Since they had walked through the door of the Fulbourn, it had stepped up a notch. Like salt water hitting open skin.

Edward was here, somewhere, and each step Pitch took towards him felt leaden. Unwanted.

They walked past Miss Grindel, who was busy on the telephone and trying hard to appear that she was not interested in the passing trio at all, on to a doorway which Mr Weatherby set about unlocking with a set of jangling silver keys.

'Now once we are through to the ward, keep close to me and don't wander off. It's not safe.'

The kitsune smiled his disingenuous smile.

'Very well,' Pitch said. 'Though I'm sure we will be quite fine.'

He thought he caught the edge of a smirk on Weatherby's face as he fumbled with his keys.

The kitsune were a branch of the djinn family that Pitch had never had much time for. They tended to have little interest in the pursuit of carnal pleasures, which meant they were very dull company for an incubus. The yako were a type of kitsune known for their deceitfulness. Most took pride in being tricksters. Mr Weatherby had likely snaked his way into his position with tall tales and false credentials, seeking to see just how well he could fool the purebreds into believing he had the slightest experience in matters of the human mind. The yako enjoyed the sport of such falsities. It was not a huge surprise to find one playing his games here. But that was not to say it did not worry Pitch some.

If the elixir had waned, there was a slim chance the creature had fooled them into thinking he'd not noticed a daemon and an ankou in his office. But it was slim indeed; more likely they were still shielded by Satty's brew. For now.

In the light of day, with his veins clear of champagne and cocaine and lust, Pitch was much keener to be cautious. The sooner they were in and out of this place, the better.

Weatherby finally had the lock turned, and he pushed the door open. The weight of it seemed substantial, with the slight fellow having to put his shoulder into the job. Another charade, for the kitsune were not without decent strength.

'Come through quickly, if you wouldn't mind.'

It did not take much guesswork to understand why Weatherby had them hurrying. The reek of the Fulbourn struck hard and fast: the cloying scent of unpleasant circumstance, the faint waft of shit and piss beneath the bite of sweat. And it was not difficult to see the cause.

The ward was horrendously overcrowded with all manner of unfortunates. It was nearly as crowded as the platform for the train to Cambridge, though here most of the people milling about were not so adequately clothed. The white cloth gowns that many of patients wore were in varying states of disrepair. There was a chap with terrible pockmarking on his face, whose gown only stayed on because it was hooked about his elbows. He stared up at them as they passed by, crouched like a farmhand trying to shit in the fields, scratching so hard at his bared chest that some of the welts he inflicted were bleeding.

Pitch eyed him with some empathy. The peculiar prickling at his own back grew more intense with every step. Even though the pendant watch was tucked away beneath lead, he might as well have been wearing it for all the good Silas's box was doing here. Pitch longed to tear at his skin as this wretch did. What he wouldn't do to just tear off his clothes and have someone scrub at him with the hardest bristles they could find. Maybe then the infernal combination of itch and crawling skin would cease.

A nurse hurried to the crouching man's side, her face a mask of restrained fury.

'Enough of that I said.' She swatted at the chap with what looked to be a rolled-up newspaper. 'Leave yourself be now, or we'll have to get the cuffs out again.'

Pitch glanced back at Silas, knowing the dismay he'd find there. The ankou's brow was furrowed beneath strands of his unnatural grey, his eyes narrowed. Only a daemon's hand stayed him from marching over and demanding the exhausted-looking nurse leave the vacant-eyed man be.

'Let it go, Mr Knight,' Pitch murmured.

Silas, ever to the rescue. There had been no coincidence in the name Pitch had chosen for him.

He managed to get Silas moving on, but Pitch held back. The nurse had moved on to her next reprimand, and the crouching fellow was alone and back to tearing at his skin. Pitch slipped the earring from his pocket. The curve and weight of the stone was oddly soothing to hold and run a thumb over. And it wouldn't get beneath the nails as flesh did.

'Here. Distract yourself with this.' He dropped Tilly's ugly offering into the folds of the man's drooping gown and hurried on, before the glistening he spied in the fellow's eyes turned into a flood of godsforsaken tears.

Weatherby was clearing a path through the swaying and at times bellowing crowd. Animalistic noises came from many a patient. A young man stood facing a wall, knocking his head hard against it and baying like a hound with each strike. Another stood in the centre of the corridor, swaying but going nowhere, rubbing at his arms like he felt every inch of the chill. At intervals he squawked like a frenzied monkey.

The corridor was terribly long, its end hidden behind the meandering bodies that filled it. Plain white doors, all with narrow viewing panels, stood like pale sentinels along the way. The rooms that Pitch could see into held a mix of camp beds and wrought-iron dormitory beds, crammed into every available space. One particular room emitted the most pungent odour of piss, and Pitch considering pulling up his lapels and hiding his nose.

He glimpsed a skinny fellow laid out in another room, naked and with a chain about his wrist, its other end about the bedhead. Pitch looked away quickly, not liking how it reminded him of his incarceration at Harvington Hall.

'This is horrendous,' Silas said at a whisper. 'We cannot leave him here, surely?'

Pitch stayed quiet. He had no idea if they were on a rescue mission or simple reconnaissance, and he'd make no false promises to Silas. But he agreed, the place was dire. Pitch did not know whom he was most furious at: himself or the lieutenant's family for reducing the man so low.

Silas touched his hand to Pitch's arm, encouraging him to slow.

'What is it?' Pitch asked.

That Silas looked worried was hardly unexpected in this place. 'It is strange.' He was leaning close, speaking at a whisper, and Pitch savoured the warmth of his breath against his ear. 'The bandalore is acting very strange.'

Pitch looked up at him. 'As opposed to what?'

'I could swear I felt it move about in my pocket a moment ago.'

'A teratism is near?' Gods, that would be all they needed right now.

'No. Nothing like that.' Silas shook his head but had no opportunity to say any more as a shockingly overweight man, with feet bright pink and shedding cracked and dry skin, shoved his way between them. He was crying, calling out for his mother.

Weatherby stopped at the only door that did not have a viewing panel. 'Mr Edwards was taken to one of the padded cells for his own safety. We will need to go down to the lower levels.'

'Is Mr Charters attempting to harm himself?' Silas's horror rang clear. 'Why is he in need of a padded room?'

Weatherby nodded, his most fitting expression of moroseness in place. 'The new patients often have some difficulty settling in. He's had a bit more issues than most.'

Pitch pulled his gaze away from a young man barely old enough to have the fuzz growing upon his face, who was picking at his thumbnail so hard it was dripping blood onto the floor. 'Because he does not wish to be here?' Pitch was caustic. 'You can hardly call the man mad for that.'

'But we can for a variety of other reasons. Paranoia and dreadful melancholy, not to mention believing he has fornicated with a being of transcendent beauty and light, one he believes might be a god.'

Pitch focused very hard on not reacting in the slightest.

'How many levels does this place have?' Silas asked, a hint of worry there. After so much time spent in his grave, the idea of heading underground must be unpleasant.

'Just the one subterranean level.' Weatherby was casual, almost flippant. Something in the way he spoke had Pitch giving him a second glance. 'Some patients cannot tolerate daylight well, nor the noise. The lower level caters better to their needs.'

The fellow was unctuous, no two ways about it, but Pitch could not decide if that was what bothered him, or something more.

Weatherby's gaze flicked between him and Silas, never landing too long upon one or the other. It would be most inconvenient if their true auras were starting to show, but Pitch had doubts that was the case. The chap was edgy about *something*, no doubt, but he was not nearly so fearful as a lowly yako would be were he to come face to face with a daemon and an ankou, let alone those from the Order. The yako were generally fearful of the shadows they did not have. Pitch shrugged his shoulders, trying to stretch the skin pressed tight his corset. Anything to alleviate the blasted intolerable itching at his back.

Pitch cleared his throat. 'Do you think we could hurry along?'

'Of course, of course,' Mr Weatherby sniffed, rattling his keys.

Pitch glanced at Silas. He was uncomfortable. The ankou's signs were becoming more apparent to Pitch with each passing day. He chewed at the inside of his cheek, which usually meant unhappiness at something. Pitch was considering having him wait behind, to save Silas the trauma of heading underground when the ankou himself ruined the plan.

The moment Weatherby had the door open, Silas stepped through and headed at once down the dimly lit set of stairs. Pitch confused himself with which bloody name to call out, and by the time he'd settled on Mr Knight, Silas had disappeared.

'Fuck.'

He hurried past Mr Weatherby, who stood holding the door whilst warding off an elderly man with a gruesomely twisted spine who was coming to investigate the new exit.

'Back you go, Zachary. You've had more than your fair share of time down there. Go on with you.'

Pitch glanced up the stairs to see Weatherby give the old man a bodily shove which would have thrown him off his feet were it not for the fact there were too many people milling about for there to be space to fall. The door clanged shut, the sound echoing down the stairwell.

Pitch decided he did not like Fulbourn at all.

'Mr Knight, what is your hurry?' he called to Silas, who had already found the level corridor and had not stopped to wait for him.

'I'm not certain...I just...I'm just rather curious...'

If Pitch were closer, he would have given the ankou a very hard nudge in the ribs. What the blazes had Silas so bloody preoccupied?

The stairs, and indeed the hallway ahead, were lit with a mixture of candles in brass sconces and oil lamps. But despite the ample number of them along the way, the hall was not chased free of all its shadows. There was a weight to the silence down here that Pitch did not like. And he could not hold back the nagging inclination that they'd made a mistake in coming here.

He opened his mouth to call Silas back when a man stepped out of the shadows, not far from where the ankou walked.

'Best you stay together now.' He appeared out of what might be an alcove or another passageway. Nothing was quite clear, despite the shudder of so many flames. 'Quite the maze down here if you don't know your way about.'

He was a solid-built man, stout and evidently human. His shadow waved like a flag as all the flames were disturbed by so many visitors. His heavy, dark muttonchops curved towards a square chin and framed dull brown eyes placed too close together on a face sagging with jowls. His coat was a size too big for him, a deep brown with oversized black buttons gleaming. He extended his hand to Silas.

'I'm Dr Severs. Mr Charters's psychiatrist.'

Silas took his hand. 'Mr...Arthur Knight.' The stumble over his own name was horribly evident, and a look passed between Weatherby and the doctor.

'Thaddeus Yates.' Pitch made his way to Silas's side. The ankou was clearly distracted. 'We thank you for allowing us to visit with Edward.' He poured on the charm but did not risk using any enchantment with the kitsune there.

'No trouble at all,' Dr Severs said. 'Mr Weatherby said you are friends of the lieutenant?'

Gods, had they not had this conversation a dozen times? 'We are, and quite anxious to see him, if you don't mind?'

Dr Severs rocked onto his heels. 'I'm sure you are, sure you are.' He peered up at Silas. 'Quite a large man, aren't you, sir?'

He was not so small himself.

'Hmm?' Silas was busy peering down the corridor. 'Oh yes, I am.'

'How did you say you knew Mr Charters? You see, I must be thorough about whom I bring to see him. I wouldn't want to upset him any further.'

Silas paid attention to that, perhaps sensing at last the strange air down here. 'We would not want that either.' He glanced at Pitch. 'Mr Yates knows him far better than I, I'll admit. I am here to support him, as these types of visits can be quite distressing.'

'Oh, very distressing indeed.' Dr Severs nodded, but he did so just a tad too slowly.

Pitch felt the walls pull in tighter around them. 'Do you know, I do not feel at all well...I think it's the paraffin.' He grabbed at Silas's sleeve. 'Would you mind terribly if we went back out into the fresh air? It's very stuffy down here.'

'That would be a shame, you are so close.' Mr Weatherby tsked.

'Only a few doors down.' Dr Severs gestured to the corridor where the doors had much larger viewing panels, more like windows so the occupants could be clearly observed. 'If you can bear it a moment longer down here, Mr Yates, I'd be forever grateful if you could come and say hello. Perhaps seeing you shall cheer him?'

Pitch nearly laughed out loud. He doubted very much his arrival would cheer Edward.

'He is just along the way. He was crying himself hoarse. I came to give him some more sedatives, to help him relax, but I'd be quite interested in seeing how he reacts to someone he is...close with, as you claim yourself to be.'

'Why would I claim such a thing if it were not true?' Pitch watched Dr Severs very carefully.

'Of course we will see him,' Silas said but Dr Severs blocked the way. 'Take us to him now, if you would, please.'

Dr Severs's face was rather blank and difficult to read. More tiny shrills of alarm went off inside Pitch's head. But he had to exercise restraint. If he struck out now, there would be a mess to clean up and far too much attention drawn for the Morrigan to notice.

If they had not already.

The doctor stepped to one side, gesturing for them to go ahead, glancing over Pitch's shoulder as he did so. Turning about, Pitch swore under his breath. Mr Weatherby was nowhere in sight.

Gods, they had made a terrible mistake.

'No,' Pitch said. 'That's quite enough... Come along, Mr Knight, we are through here.'

But Silas was already on his way with the doctor.

'There you are, the last one on the left,' Dr Severs said. 'There're no other patients down here at the moment. You can't miss him.'

Silas reached the room indicated and peered through the viewing pane. He went perfectly still.

'This isn't the lieutenant,' he whispered.

'No?' the doctor replied. 'Then who is it, Mr...Knight? Do you know them?'

'He should not be here,' Silas shouted, rattling at the door. 'Release this man at once.'

Pitch raced to his side, shouldering past the doctor.

Through smeared glass, he saw a figure seated at the centre of the cell, wrapped in a straitjacket, his ankles bound to the legs of the chair. There was a strip of leather across his brow, pinning his head back against the high-backed chair, another across his mouth, stifling anything he might have tried to say had he been conscious. His eyes were closed, but there was no need to see those cornflower blues to recognise who sat there.

Charlie was a very unwilling guest of the Fulbourn.

CHAPTER 19

Silas pounded on the viewing pane, only stopping to thrust his hand into his pocket. Going for the bandalore no doubt.

'No.' Pitch grabbed at him. 'Stay calm...keep your head.'

'Stay calm? Do you see who they have in there?' Silas was frantic. 'Where is the key, damn you?'

'Do you know this boy, Mr Knight?' Dr Severs was a winter frost. And evidently a stupid one at that if he did not already know the answer.

'Of course I bloody know him.' Silas glowered. 'And you had best not have harmed Charlie in any way, or so help me –'

Pitch dug his fingernails into Silas's arm, hoping the sting might reach the ankou where he was drowning in anger and fear. It was too late to pretend they didn't know Charlie, but until they had a finer understanding of the doctor's agenda, the less else they gave away, the better.

'What is the meaning of this?' Silas squared his shoulders and took a threatening step towards the doctor. 'Release him, right now. You have no right to hold him here.'

Rightly so, Dr Severs was backing away, but Pitch thought the man should have been far more fearful than he was. He looked more like a man who had struck gold.

'You know him. So it is you for certain.' Tilting laughter came from the doctor. 'Silas Mercer comes to the Fulbourn.'

Silas was far too riled up to have the sense *not* to react when his name was called. The ankou's face was a calamity of confusion. The doctor took a few more steps backwards. He pressed his hand to one of the crude bricks, and a harsh scraping announced the slide of a barred door across the passageway.

'What the fuck are you doing?' Pitch lunged for the shifting metal, but he was too far away and the moving parts too quick. The surge of his temper threatened to bring the flame to hand. He shut down the glow at once. He did not intend to give away that advantage yet, not until they knew Edward's whereabouts.

The metal latch clunked into its lock.

The bars shutting him in were mere inches from his face. Pitch stared at the tiny rounded etchings carved into the dark iron.

Fuck. This was maleficium. He'd recognise the markings anywhere. The gods knew he'd stared up at similar etchings long enough at Gidleigh House. These sigils were faint, barely a shade lighter than the metal, and covered every inch of it from base to roof.

By Enoch's shrunken cock, the Fulbourn had the Morrigan's claws upon it, and they had just sauntered across the fucking threshold.

Pitch's pulse quickened, his throat barely capable of allowing his words to escape. 'Believe me, Severs,' he said. 'You have chosen the wrong side if you stand with the Morrigan.'

He heard Silas's sharp intake of breath. 'What?'

'Silas, our dear doctor has chosen poorly. There are sigils carved into the bars. I think he's hoping to extend our visit somewhat.'

'Shit,'

Pitch's gut was a maelstrom. Gods, fucking gods. Was it Charlie's search for Edward that had brought the pair to the Morrigan's attention? Severs knew the lad's connection with Silas evidently.

Pitch was going to kill Tyvain anew for this.

The doctor cleared his throat. 'You'd both do well not to make any moves I might find disturbing, or quite dreadful things will happen in that cell to your friend.'

'Harm him and I'll kill you.' The venom dripped from Silas's words. 'Why does he not wake? What have you done?'

'It's not so much what we've done,' the doctor declared. 'As what we will do, should you not cooperate. My god, we thought we may have some guests from the Order come to look for this pair...but I'm not sure the mistress herself thought we'd be so lucky as to snare one of the Horsemen. For that's what you are, are you not, Mr Mercer? You have some type of disguise upon you to make it harder to see, but I've seen you close enough to be certain such a big, strapping lad can be no other.' His gaze slid to Pitch. 'And we know how very beautiful the daemon is...how very stuck to the ankou's side he is these days. I dare say, beneath the illusion, you are he.'

Fucking gods, Pitch had never despised himself more. His arrogance was astonishing. Why the fuck had he not told Kaneko where they were?

He gathered himself and spoke with no hint of his agitation. 'I'm not sure who you think yourself to be, dear chap, but a human could get themselves very hurt indeed, becoming involved in what you have.'

The doctor was human, was he not? Or had the Morrigan found a way to hide a natural's aura just as Lady Satine had done?

'A human likely could be hurt, you are quite right.' The doctor smiled. 'Now I'd like you both to hop in that cell behind you there, Mr Mercer. There will be a short wait.'

'You can rot,' Silas snarled.

'No, I rather think that's what you shall do.'

'Listen here, you piece of foetid shit,' Pitch said as the wildness stirred, a lazy shift of awakening. 'I don't like to be pissed off, and right now, you are truly pissing me off. You have exactly five seconds to unlock this gate.'

Dr Severs had the audacity to appear amused. 'Or what, Mr Yates, is it? What will you do? I'd truly love to see it again. It is quite spectacular when a daemon loses his temper.' Who the fuck was this bastard? 'Perhaps you should have stayed in London as you told the bartender you were doing. Bed hopping to your heart's content, was that not what you said, Mr Astaroth?'

It was indeed. Nearly word for word what he had told Kaneko in the phone call from the Crimson Bow. The tsukumogami truly was a turncoat? Kaneko was a miserable bastard, but he'd been at Mr Ahari's side for hundreds of years. He was trusted implicitly by the old man.

Pitch had held back their location out of sheer selfishness, a need to keep Silas and their night to himself. Not a real conviction Kaneko was the traitor. To hear it said was a punch to the guts Pitch did not need.

'Now, how about you wander into the cell as I asked? It really would be in your friend Charlie's best interest to do so.'

'And it would be in yours not to threaten the lad again.' Silas still stood at Charlie's cell door, but the weight of his anger filled the entire corridor.

'Come now, Mr Mercer. You went to such efforts to protect him once. We both know you'll do nothing to jeopardise him here.' Dr Severs tugged at a chain around his neck that had been concealed beneath the layers of his clothing. He withdrew a talon, at a wild guess Pitch would say a raven's claw, which dangled from the fine silver chain. 'Perhaps I just need to make this more convincing.'

Dr Severs moved out of view, down the same narrow passageway he'd stepped from when they first arrived. Pitch leaned close to the sigil-impressed bars, trying to see where the doctor had gone. He dared not touch them, for he did not fancy being knocked senseless or whatever else the sorcerers intended.

'Over here...' Silas hissed.

Pitch hurried the few steps it took to bring him to the ankou's side.

'The wall, behind Charlie,' Silas said, his words tight. 'There's something off with it.'

If by 'off' the ankou meant it was rippling like the surface of a pond disturbed by a stone, then yes, there was definitely something off with it.

Silas shouldered the door. 'We have to get him out of there.' The dull thud that came despite an ankou's angry weight told of a door not easily moved.

The rings of motion spread out, distorting the hewn stone of the wall so it appeared like sand viewed through a clear wave.

Dr Severs stepped through the epicentre, emerging from the wall like he might a parted curtain.

'I shall ask you again, gentlemen, to step into the cell.'

Silas's breathing stuttered. He looked to Pitch, his pupils wide with barely suppressed panic. 'Can you do something?'

Pitch had considered drawing on the flame many times already, testing the barrier that stood between them and freedom, but Charlie was a vulnerable hostage. If Pitch made the wrong move and the lad was hurt...or killed...Silas would never forgive him.

And Edward was here too. Somewhere in this dingy, ruinous place.

'I don't think it's wise.' Pitch shook his head. 'We don't know what magicks they have installed here.'

Dr Severs stood right behind Charlie, who was so utterly still it was hard to say if he breathed or not. Pitch was struck by the grisly notion that perhaps they were worrying over a corpse. He touched his hand to Silas's hip to brace the ankou for what he would say next.

'You may well have stuck a dead body there. The lad is stiller than a statue,' Pitch said, trying to ignore the distressing sound that came from the ankou. 'You'd best give us a reason to act like mindless slaves to your whims, or you'll find us very disagreeable.'

'The lad is not dead,' Dr Severs scoffed. 'Your pet is the strings, you are the puppets, as it were. It's hardly the time for cutting any ties just yet.' He muttered a few throaty words and touched his finger to the side of Charlie's neck.

The lad's eyes flew open, so wide the whites showed in a clear circle around his irises. His blue gaze landed on Silas. He blinked, and his face creased with confusion.

'Charlie!' Silas banged at the door anew. 'It's me, it's Silas.' The bewilderment slid from Charlie's face, and desperation and relief replaced it. Stifled sounds followed as he sought to be heard through his muzzle.

'Charlie, it's all right.' Silas was anything but all right himself. He sought to shake the place apart.

'Steady there, Mr Mercer.' Dr Severs scowled. 'If you don't behave, the delinquent will suffer.'

Charlie shouted against his gag. He wriggled madly beneath the jacket, the veins in his throat standing out as he cried himself hoarse behind the leather. The lad's anguish spilled in a steady flow of glistening tears.

'It's all right, Charlie. We're here.' Silas ceased his assault on the cell door and worked instead on a forced calm. 'Stay still, Charlie. We will have you out of there in no time. Do you understand?'

Charlie nodded, wetness running from his nostrils. His eyes darted to Pitch, and once again he seemed unsure, reminding Pitch of how different they must appear.

'Satisfied?' Dr Severs said. 'Alive, as you can see. And no doubt ruing the day he hid among my patients, thinking the chaos here would conceal him from notice.' The doctor's carefully cultivated veneer of calm slipped. His scowl held an undercurrent of something far more dangerous. 'Now, I grow tired of your disobedience. Get in the wretched cell.' He took the talon and pressed the tip to Charlie's neck. Even through his gag, the lad's terrified cry was evident. A thin line of blood ran the short length of his exposed neck.

'No! No. Stop.' Silas's distress buckled his cry.

'We will step into your precious cell.' Pitch held up his hands and took a step towards the cell opposite. The door was open, the interior as plain as the one Charlie was being held in. Plainer, for there was no chair in sight. 'But tell your master they best hurry this along. We don't have all day.'

'No.' Severs's grin was lascivious. 'You certainly don't.'

Pitch grabbed Silas's arm and pulled him away from his continued efforts to take the door off its hinges. 'Come, Silas. Let's humour this dear chap.'

'But Charlie –'

Pitch drew up close to the ankou, hissing in his ear. 'Is at their mercy, as is Edward, most likely. Which means, for now, we are too.'

Silas took some dragging, all the while assuring Charlie he was not being abandoned. Making promises about the lad's safety that Pitch was afraid they could not keep.

The doctor watched them go. His calm was not admirable; it was unnatural. If this man was purebred, then the sorcerers must have spliced the fear out of him, because he had not so much as flinched while Silas turned himself into a battering ram against the door. Nor when he'd stared Pitch down and suggested he knew exactly who the daemon was.

Dr Severs took his bloodied talon and pressed it against his own fingertip, drawing new blood. He brought the talon near to his mouth and began to speak.

The words were strange, as though they sought to be familiar but failed. It reminded Pitch of when Silas went on and on about the botanical names of his beloved plants, the unfamiliar names not quite foreign enough to be unrecognisable, but nor did he understand what they referred to. What was far more troubling than the words themselves was the tongue they were spoken in. Dr Severs was speaking Arcadian with impressive mimicry. The man's precision with the accent was disturbing. How were the sorcerers learning Azazel's magick? Pitch stared at the doctor, who in turn did not look away as he continued to whisper to his talon. The man's mastery of the Arcadian tongue seemed too adept to have come simply from reading a grimoire.

The door slammed shut, the bolt turning.

'My god, what have we done?' Silas whispered.

Pitch had a direct line of sight to where the doctor stood beside Charlie, the lad manic in his attempts to find a way out of his restraints, throwing his hips and shoulders about in a way that would only see him hurt himself. It was a terrible waste of his energies. The Morrigan had no intention of setting him free. But for now, at least, they had use for him alive.

'Gods, I'm so sorry, Silas.'

For Pitch had fucked things up supremely, and if ever an apology was to grace his lips, it should be now.

But he did not learn if the ankou heard him.

The door to their cell crumbled away, pieces falling soundlessly and vanishing before they struck the ground. There should have been a gaping empty doorway left behind, but now there was only stone, great bricks of rock identical to the rest that made up the walls of the cell. One small gap remained at the centre, just wide enough to see the doctor across the way.

Dr Severs smiled, a self-satisfied smirk that Pitch would one day burn from his face. 'Until we meet again, gentlemen. Behave now, won't you? She doesn't like belligerence.' He uttered one last word. Hammered one last nail of maleficium home to seal them in.

'No!' Silas ran at the wall, one arm thrown forward as though he thought to punch his way through the gap, the other pulling the bandalore from his pocket, the blade unfurling like a flashing silver flag.

'Silas, don't be a fool!' Pitch shouted.

The final stone appeared, slotting into place by magick's unseen hands.

Sealing them in.

Silas lashed out with his curved blade. The clang of metal against stone was raucous.

Pitch planted his hands over his ears. 'Stop, you idiot,' he shouted.

'Why aren't you doing something, damn it?' Silas turned, his coat-tails whipping about, his face reddened with his fury. 'Don't just stand there. *Do* something.'

Pitch rushed at him, grabbing at his collar, wrenching him in close and sparing little thought for the sharpness of the blade in Silas's hand. 'Do what?' he hissed. 'Tear this place down around our ears? Have it crush to death those we seek? Not to mention the hordes they have crammed into the corridors above us. Do you want that, Silas? All those humans in the rubble? We have no idea where they've taken Charlie, certainly not Edward.' He shook the ankou, needing to clear the haze of panic from Silas's eyes. 'When I *do* something, it causes havoc, destruction, in case you have not noticed. So we wait, we let them show their hand. We see our enemy's face.'

Silas's struggle weakened. Silver flashed as the blade settled back into its bandalore form. 'They are so fragile, Pitch.' He shook his head. 'They are vulnerable. Charlie and Ed–'

'They are the strings, we are the puppets. Did you not hear the doctor's pathetic analogy? They are safe so long as we play this game. And when the game is over, when the Morrigan have shown their hand, then I will *do* something, Silas. Trust me on that at least.'

The ankou still held doubts, for they were writ large upon his face, but he nodded. Even managing a weak smile. He wrapped his thick fingers about Pitch's wrists and leaned in to bring their brows to touch. 'I trust you on everything.'

'Because you are an idiotic oaf.'

'Who was almost no good to you at all.' Silas exhaled, and Pitch's lashes fluttered against the warmth. 'I am more frightened than the day I woke in my grave.'

'I'm not exactly the picture of serenity I appear either, but we must keep our wits. Do you hear me?'

The ankou nodded. More resolute this time. Pitch slid his cheek across Silas's own, his lips close to the ankou's ear. 'I'm going to take the watch back now.'

Silas tensed. 'But does it not –'

'Kiss me.'

Pitch gave him little option in the matter and hoped to the gods the ankou understood soon enough. Silas jerked back at first, trying to mutter into the sudden embrace. Pitch pressed a hand to the back of his neck, keeping him close, while the other dropped, searching for the ankou's coat pocket. Silas's protest was short-lived, and he yielded, tilting into the kiss now with decent fervour. He cupped the back of Pitch's head with a broad palm.

'Left pocket,' he mumbled.

The ankou threw himself into the performance, keeping his hands up high and busy, drawing the eye should anyone watch them through the cracks. He touched at Pitch's neck, his chest, going so far as to peel off one shoulder of his coat as though he were about to ravish the daemon there and then.

Gods, if only.

Pitch worked quickly, slipping his fingers into the ankou's coat and fiddling with the iron box there. Pulling it open, clasping the watch within. The mark on his back shocked with painful pinpoints.

Pitch whimpered and Silas soothed away the discomfort with gentle touches of his tongue. And it was so very tempting to stay here, dissolving beneath the ankou's hands. But Pitch had what he needed.

The show need not go on.

As though it were a curtain call, dust swept in through those very same cracks in the wall Pitch had imagined. It rushed at them from every angle, a sudden storm of sandy grit.

'Shit,' Silas grunted.

Pitch had but a second to realise what had been sent at them before his eyelids were as heavy as the stone surrounding him.

The need to sleep was overwhelming.

The ankou staggered, his weight pressing on Pitch's shoulders. 'What is...happening...'

'Pixie dust,' Pitch spat. The tiny particles coated the inside of his nose, his mouth, filtered into his ears. 'Gods damn...'

Silas tilted like a tree awaiting the last swing of a farmer's axe. Pitch grabbed for him but only managed to topple with him. They collapsed, Pitch barely managing to avoid being crushed by the ankou's weight. He was half-buried beneath Silas, who had already begun to snore softly. The potent dust doing its work.

Sleep was rushing in. An irresistible fatigue.

But Pitch was determined to see one last task done. Concealed beneath Silas's body, he pushed up a sleeve and pressed his longest nail into the fine skin beneath his wrist. He ground his teeth and bore down, slicing his fingernail through flesh, opening a wound deep enough to hide his treasure.

Beneath the slumbering weight of the ankou, Pitch moved blindly, unable to keep his eyes open any longer. He pressed the pendant watch into the deep incision, hissing his displeasure as the points on the crown snagged on vulnerable flesh. He shoved it deep, to where it nudged at the bone. Pitch brought a pinpoint of flame to his fingertip, just enough to cauterise the wound. His prowess for rapid healing would do the rest.

He entombed Seraphiel's trinket in his body as surely as he and Silas were sealed in this gods-forsaken room.

Sleep hit in a swamping wave as he tugged down his sleeve, dragging Pitch down far below the surface, where he could not fight anymore.

CHAPTER 20

S ilas sought escape from slumber the same way he sought to escape
drowning at the hands of his brother in each of his deaths.

In a frenzy of mindless panic.

Reaching for the surface with a desperation that was all consuming.

His eyes flew open, his mouth wide, gasping for breath. And the name
flew from him before he took stock of where he was.

'Pitch. Pitch, where are you?'

Silas blinked, his voice echoing around him. The light was too bright
for him to see clearly.

'Here...I'm here,' came a slurred response.

Silas tried to turn and move towards where the daemon was, somewhere off to his right, and found the bite of iron digging into his wrists.
He grunted. Christ, he was groggy, his head filled with cotton. Or bricks.
His skull was so bloody heavy. He wondered if he'd ever be able to lift it
again.

Silas blinked once more, willing himself back to sensibility. He concentrated on breathing in air that no longer held the coarse and nefarious
dust.

He was not lying on the ground. Pitch was not beneath him, as he'd
been when sleep overcame them both. And this room, wherever it was,
was far brighter than their stone cell.

He could not make out much of his surrounds but knew now he was on his knees. His coat was missing. Which meant his bandalore was too. His pulse thumped harder, and he had to work at keeping down the nameless panic once more. Silas breathed, as he so often told the prince to do. The Morrigan had already tried to take the bandalore from him. It was not so easy as it seemed. The scythe would find its way back to him. He must believe that, more fervently than ever before.

His arms were pulled out at an angle to his sides and held fast. He swayed, trying to keep steady enough to put up a decent struggle against the weight dragging at his wrists. The rattle of chains came with his movement.

Silas blinked more furiously. The sting of brightness faded, his vision clearing a little – though, he might have preferred it had not.

The prince was a few feet from him, also on his knees. His wig had been removed, his light waves a knotted mess. His coat was gone too, and his wrists bound in iron cuffs linked to chains that were anchored to the floor. A wooden floor, polished and gleaming.

'Are you all right?' Silas called. 'Can you hear me?'

Pitch shrugged his shoulders, his chains clinking. 'Fine. Fine. But I'd be better if left to my dreams.' He turned his head and emerald glinted, the Lady's alterations no longer evident. 'You were doing marvellous things with your –'

'Your eyes,' Silas hissed. 'They are green once more.'

'You sound upset about that,' Pitch said, swaying side to side against his chains. 'You were not so in my dream, Sickle. Gods, you were –'

'Stop.' Silas did not mean to shout it. He glanced about, but the glare was still too much to see far. 'Please, say no more. You need to rouse yourself –'

'I was doing fine with that thanks to your –'

'Dear god, stop talking. You're half-asleep still. Wake up.' Silas halted, thinking he'd heard something in the far recesses of the room.

A large room he surmised, from the way it had made his voice echo when he first called for the daemon.

'Fuck my head hurts.' Pitch shook himself, and the jangling of chains was like a badly orchestrated violin concerto. 'Gods damn it, we're in chains.'

'Yes. I know.' Silas exhaled. 'And we've been moved. Do you have any idea where this might be?' He squinted, which was helpful. He could just make out the spread of honey-coloured floorboards and white walls with fanciful gilded embellishments. Not sigils, thank Christ, rather the ordinary type of gilding one would find in a London ballroom. At the far end of the room was a raised platform, empty save for a smattering of potted palms. The sight tickled at Silas's memories. His squint turned to a frown, and he tilted his head.

Three chandeliers ran the centre line of the ceiling, fine pluming displays of cut crystal. Despite the glare filling the room, they appeared unlit, and with only a few paltry sconces along the walls, their flames tiny and frail, the reason for the brightness in the room was puzzling.

'Why are we in a ballroom?' Pitch grunted. 'Are they going to try to dance us to death? Make our brains bleed through our ears after countless hours of Brahms?'

'I doubt that is their first choice in punishment. Does this place seem familiar to you?'

'In the way of half the ballrooms in London.'

Silas looked to him. 'Are we back in London, then?'

'Not unless they have used their pissy magic to make pixie dust far more enduring than it is. It lasts an hour or two at most on any natural I've known. A handy come-down when one has indulged too hard in snowier things.'

'So we are unlikely to have been shipped back to London,' Silas said.

'Very unlikely.' Pitch ducked his head, wincing. 'Gods, my head. It is positively splitting. I think they struck me.'

'While you were sleeping?' Utter bastards.

'More likely because I was not. I've used the dust so many times...maybe I didn't sleep as deeply as they'd have liked.'

'It seems so bright in here. Yet there are only a few candles lit.'

'That's the dust. The sensitivity to light will fade quickly. Which is good, because right now, you look a fool with all the squinting.'

He stared hard at the daemon. 'Really? That's all you can say at a time like this?'

'Apologies, should I mention again that we are chained? Like goats set out to tempt the wolves?'

'No.' Frustration and panic raised Silas's tone. 'Bloody hell. You should be talking of ways to extricate us from this predicament, damn you. Saying something useful instead or resorting to pointless dribble about goats.'

Despite his best attempts to steady his breath, to try to stay the terror that bubbled inside him, Silas's lungs were tight to the point of suffocating.

'Pointless dribble?' Pitch sniffed. 'Says the man who can wax lyrical about a weed all bloody day. Oh, or a gooseberry bush. My gods, that day you tried to convince me of their merit was excruciating.'

Silas glared. 'Damn you, it was not a gooseberry bush. I knew you weren't listening to a word I said.'

'I didn't care to hear about your weeds.'

'It was not a weed. It was a blackberry bush.'

'Either way, it had prickles which you did not warn me about.'

'I told you several times the blackberry had them.' Christ. Even at a time so dire the prince was infuriating. 'But you insisted on snatching at one without so much as your gloves. I distinctly told you to be careful.'

'I think I have the thorn still in my thumb. It pains me to this day.'

'*You* pain me, honestly.' Silas shook his head, edging about on his knees so he could better turn towards the daemon. He forgot for a moment what dug into his wrists. 'And that thorn is long gone. At least the blackberry thorn is. Who knows what else you've been up to. I removed it and recall it distinctly because you actually thanked me for it. An event so rare as to be memorable.'

'Clearly the toxin from the shrub had gone to my head.'

In spite of it all, a laugh spilled from Silas. 'They don't bloody have toxins. The berries are really quite...' He fell silent. The tightness in his chest had eased, he had a crooked smile on his face. He nodded at the prince, who was smiling too. 'Thank you.'

The ludicrous conversation had him breathing again. He blinked and the glare deadened. The room was actually in the grip of twilight, as though only one or two shutters were opened to allow the day in. But there were no shutters nor day, just the smattering of candles in their sconces to cast shadows across Pitch's face as he watched Silas.

'It shall be all right, you'll see,' the daemon said. 'But keep yourself clear-headed for me, my knight. Put your fears down deep as you can and lock them away, for there is no place for them here. You'll not be able to help Charlie if you cannot rescue yourself.' He paused. 'Stay with me. Keep to my side, and I promise you, we shall meet this challenge as we have all others. Do you understand me?'

Silas stared at him. *Now* he could imagine Vassago at the head of his legion. A glorious vision, his words dripping like honeyed wine, stirring his soldiers on.

'I understand,' Silas whispered. 'I will always stay with you.'

They knelt there in their chains, gazes fixed upon one another. A heaviness hung in the air between them. Silas's pulse danced all manner of acrobatics.

'You want to kiss me, don't you?' Pitch said.

He could think of nothing to say but the truth. 'Among other things. Yes.'

'Then best we are done with this place sooner rather than later.'

The daemon's smile made the room tilt, and Silas had to look away.

A pair of mirrored doors halfway down the right side of the ballroom flew open, and the kitsune waltzed in with a grand flourish. 'Gentlemen, I'm so sorry I was not here to greet you when you woke. Terribly remiss of me, but the preparations for your incarceration have us all run off our feet.' He strode across the dance floor with all the surety of a consummate host, spreading his arms to take in the room. 'Wonderful, isn't it? Marvellous job she's done, I must say.'

'Has anyone ever told you your voice is terribly jarring?' Pitch declared.

'Goodness me.' Weatherby's grin was stitched in place. 'I should have hit you much harder, shouldn't I?'

'Oh, you have no idea.'

'Perhaps when Madam is done with you, there might be something left for me to play with.' The kitsune paused to scuff his shoe at a mark on the floor, staring down in some wonderment. 'Right down to the heel marks, quite remarkable, the details.' He straightened and clapped his hands. 'Comfortable?'

Neither Silas nor Pitch answered him.

'I'll take that as a yes.' He glanced over his shoulder and frowned. 'Come along, then,' he called, to someone or something beyond the open doors. 'Are you there? I did ask you to follow, very nicely I might add, but I suppose you may have trouble hearing me. '

'Where have you taken us?' Silas demanded.

'Oh, here and there, but not very far.' Clucking his tongue, Weatherby heavy-footed it to the door. 'Hello? Are you there? You're not the one meant to be lost here. Do keep up.'

The dense clatter of what sounded very much like hooves upon a road echoed into the room.

'Oh shit. A step too far, Weatherby.' The kitsune spun on his heels, mouth agape, arms paddling at the air, as though that might give him greater speed to escape what was approaching. He raced through the gap between Pitch and Silas, just as the very last creature one might expect to see in a ballroom burst through the doors.

A powerful roan steed, its coat tinged blue, cantered across the floorboards, hooves leaving no trace upon the wood. The animal's mane hung almost to the ground, and the feathers at its hocks were astonishingly long, like bunched serpents about its hooves. But the horse was not so remarkable as its rider.

For the man in the saddle had lost his head.

The rider guided his mount with hands upon the reins and no eyes upon the way. His cloak whipped out behind him, snapping dully at the air, the high collar ringing nothing but empty space where a neck should be. A whip was coiled at his hip, one made of thick segments white as chalk. They were wide up high near his hand, but their girth shrank the nearer to the arrowhead-like tip they were.

The tune of the headless rider played to Silas: a haunting singular note that shattered into a plethora of fleeing, desperate sounds.

Fae. Unseelie. Erlking's servant.

'Dullahan,' Silas said, reading the clearest of the scrambled notes, the one that squealed the highest. This creature's melody was terribly confused...not quite so badly as Lady Satine's had been, but enough that Silas was not certain of all that stood before him. The tune said nothing of death. Nor of a teratism.

'That thing is fucking fae,' Pitch growled.

'In part,' Silas said. 'I'm not sure it remains entirely so.'

'Uh-ah, gentlemen,' Weatherby tutted. 'This is really not the place to be bad-mouthing the Unseelie Court, I assure you.'

Silas frowned into his thoughts. He had only the faintest sense of knowing the Unseelie Court. The Erlking. A king of the fae. An elf? It was all dim, far too distant. But what sense of it remained was far from pleasant, like biting into a rotten apple.

The Dullahan sat easily upon his restless steed, and the roan tossed its head, mane cascading like water thrown from a bucket, eyes black as coal. Though the Dullahan had no face, no eyes to see with, Silas had the disconcerting sense that his attention was set on Pitch. As was Weatherby's. He'd not missed how often the kitsune's gaze darted to the daemon.

Pitch seemed unperturbed by the scrutiny. 'Are we meant to feel intimidated by that horse and his headless rider? Or are we being offered free pony rides?'

The chandeliers overhead burst to life, the candles flaring without the touch of any evident match. The crystals cut the light into dazzling pieces, illuminating the entire space like it were the middle of a summer's day.

'Right then, gentlemen, she is ready.' Weatherby adjusted his jacket, his face a serious model of concentration. 'Shoulders back if you will. Try to look smart.'

Pitch made it clear what the kitsune could do with his instructions. And Silas was about to add his two pennies' worth when his head was turned by movement beyond the flick of the roan's tail. The horse danced on its hooves, suddenly ever more restless, prancing off to one side and affording Silas a clear view now down the length of the ballroom.

The platform with the plant life was no longer empty. A figure cloaked and masked sat upon a scroll-footed chair, their pale hands draped over the edge of cushioned arms. The chair's crest rail arched above their head, the elaborate carving giving the whole arrangement the air of a throne.

Weatherby cleared his throat. 'Gentlemen, I present to you, Macha of the Morrigan.'

CHAPTER 21

A cold chill settled on Silas. The sorceress did not stir any revealing tune within him. The absence of a melody for Pitch was a puzzle, but Silas was less confused when it came to the necromancer. Her magick was a learned skill, bestowed on her bloodline by Azazel's teachings. But this sorceress, like her siblings, was born a purebred.

Macha.

Sister to the sorceress Nemain, who had been so delighted in outdoing her sibling when she trapped Silas in her greensward. She had been scathing of Macha's failure to bring the ankou down with her ash men.

Clad in identical costume to her siblings, with a heavy cloak and a feathered mask that shielded the eyes, Macha had painted her lips a complimentary black hue, all the more prominent against her bone-white skin.

'Mr Mercer, so lovely to see you in the flesh.' The sorceress had an annoyingly pleasant voice, one that would fit nicely in a Mayfair parlour. 'You looked ever so well when I saw you last through one of my children's eyes, but I must say, you present far better in actuality. I do like the shaven face. It is very fetching. Not certain about the grey-speckled hair though.'

Pitch rattled his chains. 'This is how you are going to do it, then? We are to be destroyed by a church bell's inane chatter.'

Black lips flirted with a smile, and Macha spent far too long studying the prince before she spoke. 'We weren't sure who was coming to the

Fulbourn. Mr Fothergill told us a fine specimen of a woman had been asking after Edward...a beguiling lady whose rather burly brother arrived in quite a huff, making all kinds of untoward accusations about the treatment of his...sister. Amusing, certainly, but hardly concerning. A pretty lady seeking a reunion with her once-lover, only to find herself being pawed at by a drunken man of business. Hardly enough to pique my interest.' Macha crossed her legs, and her cloak slipped from her knee, revealing black trousers and thick-soled boots. 'And I had to sit through Mr Fothergill's endless, dribbling apology, for divulging Edward's location. We'd made it very clear he was to fob off any queries, and pass on the names of those who were asking to Dr Severs, or he'd lose the reward we were paying him to ensure Mr Charters came into our care. The silly chap went on and one, I was hardly listening...said he didn't know what had come over him. Felt like a man possessed. That was when he had my interest. I thought to myself, what on Earth would cause a man's tongue to run away from him like that?' Macha tilted her head, her gauze-hidden eyes very clearly set on Pitch.

'I can't imagine,' Pitch said, as caustic as he'd ever been.

'No I don't suppose you could, if you were truly the frail human you've tried to appear. Mr...what was it now?'

'Thaddeus Yates, madam,' Weatherby added, most unhelpfully.

'Thaddeus...goodness.' Macha uncrossed her legs, parting them to lean her elbows against her knees and lean forward. 'You cannot lose the grandeur, even in disguise.' She flicked her fingers. 'Whatever little trick you conjured to conceal yourselves has failed you now. But I was quite sure we'd snagged a true prize when you asked for five sugars in your tea, and then heaped in more when you thought no one was looking. Very incubus of you.'

Silas decided there were moments where nothing needed to be said. He took in the surrounds, noting that Weatherby now stood near the door he'd entered through, looking, to Silas's mind, a little anxious. The Dullahan was not much more than a statue upon his restless mount that shifted about on Pitch's far side, too close for Silas's liking. But more worrisome was how, behind the dais, the shadows were fluid, changeable things. Shapes of all sizes, but with no clarity he could determine.

'Are you seeking a round of applause?' Pitch was haughty. 'A small token of reward for your guesswork perhaps?'

'I have my reward already.' Macha seemed to find the whole occasion quite amusing. 'I have you both. And truly, I could not ask for more. I am still rather gobsmacked that you both just waltzed into my humble abode the way you did. So soon too...that caught me off-guard, I'm not too proud to say, and with no fanfare, no djinn horses, not even a note home to tell your masters when to expect you back. What naughty boys you are.' Her laughter cracked against the walls and he thought it echoing through the vast room until he recognised the trill of childish laughter joining in with that of the sorceress. Silas grew ever colder with dread. She had harpies with her, hidden in the shadows.

'Oh you have no idea,' Pitch replied. 'I can be shockingly bad when the occasion calls for it.'

Macha rolled back in her chair, still chuckling away at how reckless the Lady's Horsemen had been. Silas found it far less amusing, but no less true. The plan to sneak off to Fulbourn whilst still masquerading as human had made some vague semblance of sense at the time. But he'd been too absorbed with needing to find Charlie to keep his wits about him, and the liaison with Pitch at the Crimson Bow had certainly done nothing to appease the situation. The prince could have talked him into standing on his head after they were done with ravishing one another. He'd been too cock-teased to consider how deeply the Morrigan had dug themselves in. Too absent-minded to suppose Fulbourn might be every inch the trap Gidleigh House had been.

They were not naughty boys, that was far too kind. They were imbeciles.

'Oh your badness is quite legendary. The poor lass at the Moon Inn will not be the same, I'm sure,' Macha continued. 'That will teach her for peeping, I suppose. And goodness, wasn't she upset that you had passed her over in order to pound the lieutenant into a mattress instead. A woman scorned, and all that...was quite handy when it came to loosening her tongue. But her story wasn't all that interesting to us at the time. Just because you are rumoured to fuck anything with a pulse, dear daemon, doesn't mean you don't say no to a lass every now and then. But to say no and then ask the poor, heartbroken thing to watch over your lover after you paid for his room and board...now there is something worthy of note. Tobias Astaroth giving a fuck about who he fucks? Well, that made Mr Charters a touch more interesting. It was rather a boon when he needed committing, as I just happened to already have a perfectly wonderful little asylum to put him in.' The giggles rose again out of the shadows, and a thin girl and a boy with his arm in a sling clambered up on the stage, coming to sit beside Macha's poor attempt at a throne. They were dressed in ragged, dirty clothes, which seemed to be the harpies' preference when in their human form. The boy's shirt might have been white in another lifetime. Now it was marbled with unpleasant smears and run through with tears. The sling was flecked with what appeared to be blood, or raspberry jam. Whichever it was, no attempt had been made to clean it away. The sorceress reached for the nearest, the girl, and twined dirty, oily strands between her fingers. Both the harpies gazed up at her with toothy grins. 'He did bad things to your brothers and sisters, didn't he, the nasty daemon?'

Two heads jogged in vehement agreement. The girl picked at a nail on her dirt-stained foot.

'If they are feeling left out, I'm very happy to see to it that they join their brethren.' Pitch's eyes danced with hard shards that caught at the glitter of the chandeliers.

Macha laid a kiss upon the top of the girl's head. 'Did you hear that? He's being ever so mean, isn't he? Would you like to see me hurt him?'

The cackle that spread through the entire blasted ballroom had every inch of Silas's skin crawling. For it was not only the sound of harpies, dancing about in delight at the suggestion. Another throaty shudder of laughter joined them from the shadows behind the dias.

Macha played at a put-upon sigh. 'Oh goodness, all right. I suppose we shall know then for certain that we truly have Onoskolis's pretty daemon in our midst.'

Silas's breath froze beneath his ribs, but his body had no such care for stillness. He lunged forward, caring little for the savage wrench to his shoulders. 'Leave him be, you wench.'

'Steady now, Mr Mercer.' Pitch's laughter held a hollow ring. 'I don't need you defending my honour. There was none to protect to begin with.'

It was a curse and a delight to know the daemon so well now. For Silas could hear more clearly when he was pained. Silas pulled forward, the drag of metal at his wrists taking skin. Bloody hell, whatever these chains were forged from it was formidable metal.

'Be done with this posturing, sorceress,' Silas said. 'You are boring us all with your ceaseless chatter. Do what you intend.'

There was a pointed silence. Macha returned to her elbows-to-knees stance and steepled her gloved fingers. 'My, my look at you, Mr Mercer. All hot and bothered. Anyone would think you cared. Did the daemon get what he wanted, then? I've been told our friend stood right to attention at the thought of fucking you.' She glanced over her shoulder to where the shadows swayed. It was evident she looked to someone there, her rising smirk turning Silas's stomach. 'Which, I'm also reliably informed, was ever so useful when it came to riding him –'

'Enough.' Silas wasn't even sure the voice that left him was his, it bulged with acrimony and wrath. His blind rage gave him the false belief he could get to his feet. He lurched up, his view crimson, his strength testing the binds. The crack at his shoulder came with a blinding flash of pain, the wrench of a joint pulled from its socket. The end to his show of temper was rather humiliating, a topple onto his backside that jolted a grunt from his lungs, his shoulder throbbing.

'Gods, stay still, you moron,' Pitch hissed. 'If her words alone can send you this mad, then you are lost.'

Silas was far from lost. Certainly not mad. He was very, very clear about what he wished to do to Macha and her words. The pain stemming from his dislocated shoulder was eye-watering, yet his head had never felt clearer.

'Don't ruin the fun,' Macha said. 'I'm enjoying this show very much.' She made a theatre of her shuddering. 'I do pity you a little though, Mr Astaroth. For the incubus in you. How tiresome it must be to be ruled by carnal pleasures. All that exchange of bodily fluid and rubbing of bits really does nothing for me. The grunting alone makes me gag. It is tiring and messy and left me feeling quite disgusted when I tried it.'

'Perhaps you should have chosen somewhere other than a pigpen for it, then.' Pitch was smooth and icy as a winter pond. 'Leave the swine be, and see if you can fool a man or woman into having you.'

Macha did not hesitate to roar with laughter. 'It is a pity you are on the wrong side of this. You are ever so amusing.' She poked a finger beneath the feathering of her mask, evidently wiping at a tear. 'No pigs or people for me. Fucking makes me feel quite wretched. But shall we get back to you?'

'I don't see any reason why not,' Pitch returned. 'I can regale you with all my fornicating forays if you'd like, though we will be here awhile. Do you have time?'

The Dullahan's horse pawed at the floorboards, violent grabs at the wood that should have made a scratch at the very least, but not a single mark appeared.

'Well, I do. But regretfully, you do not. Palatyne is dealing with final touches to the Sanctuary, and your accommodations will be completed very shortly.'

Pitch sagged against his restraints. And a trickle of despair ran through Silas. He knew what a Sanctuary was capable of. And learned it in places built by allies. Who knew what horrors lay within a Sanctuary constructed by an enemy?

'Palatyne has a very particular skill of which you will become acquainted with very shortly. Do you not appreciate the work done here already?' Macha's delight was like mould sullying a piece of fruit. She spread her arms, indicating the entirety of the ballroom. 'I fear you do not. This is where we first laid eyes upon you, Mr Mercer. Watched you danced so very poorly, upon so many feet. We'd heard the Order were to be guests of honour at the marquess's ball, and we do like to keep or eyes on the Lady's bunch. Didn't expect the air elemental to show up with a new acquisition upon her arm.'

Silas gazed with fresh horror upon the surrounds, seeing now how the chandeliers might resemble the ones at the Marquess of Ailsa's ball, but far more sickened at the notion that he'd been watched from the very beginning.

Macha propped one foot upon her chair, watching him over the top of her knee. 'I doubt you would have noticed the exquisite satsuma plate displayed upon the wall.' She waved her hand towards the ballroom's left-hand wall. 'Somewhere about there I think. Always handy to have a tsukumogami in place to keep an eye on the Order's comings and goings, but you seemed rather dull for too much attention. More fool us, hey?' She did an odd little shudder and whipped her gaze to Pitch. 'I don't suppose you will just tell me what it is about the purebred that has you trotting up here all on your lonesome?'

Pitch copied the tilt of her head. 'He was a very good fuck. Flexibility like you wouldn't believe. I had hoped to find him sane enough to take back into my bed.'

She exhaled with a hum, dropping her foot back to the ground. 'The ankou disappoints you, then? After all you've done for him?'

'He has no predilection for cock.'

'Very sad for you, indeed.'

The grins they traded were inches from becoming snarls.

'Intensely.'

'Do I waste my breath asking again what it is you want with Edward Charters?'

'You do.'

Macha played with one of the feathers that splayed out from her mask. 'Very well. You may feel differently later on. And I can always wake Eddie to ask him directly.'

'If you wish to hear the ramblings of a lunatic, go ahead.'

The sorceress tugged the feather, pulling it loose. 'Oh I very much do.'

Silas had the sense of being amongst two powerful serpents, who were each coiling around one another, searching for a weakness at which to strike. To give her her due, Macha was impressively calm in the company of the daemon, considering what she knew of his skills.

'So, let's return to you then, Mr Mercer.' She cocked her head, reminding Silas of the raven that had perched upon her sister's shoulder at the greensward. 'We had thought Mr Charters rather a long shot, I'll be honest, despite the connections. He's such a bruised chap, full of gaping holes, and really is quite mad. His need to be here is legitimate. I wasn't sure he was worth the bed. We could watch him well enough in London. But then we noticed a new face among our patients. He might have stayed hidden if he did not insist on sneaking down to visit Mr Charters at every available moment. You know who I mean of course. The lad in the straitjacket...Charlie? Is that not the creature's name?'

Silas curled his fists, very aware that Pitch was sending daggers his way, daring him to be stupid enough to allow Macha's taunts to anger him again. It was so very tempting.

'The lad has no part in all this...' Silas formed the words as calmly as the maelstrom within would allow. 'Let him go.'

Macha tittered like she'd heard a pleasant joke at a garden party. 'Oh my dear, the lad clearly has a very large place in *all this*. Was he not with you when you first met my merry bunch of revenants...and destroyed all of them? Which I'm most unhappy about, in case you hadn't gathered. And did he not traipse off with you to Harvington Hall –?'

'By chance.' Silas shuddered to wonder how much of their lives were known to this sorceress. 'He was at my side through chance alone. I took him to the hall to ensure his safety. Charlie should not be punished simply because his path crossed mine.'

Macha dug beneath her cloak and pulled forth a slender stick. Or rather a reed, thought Silas, noting the knuckled joins along its length. She danced it about in the air like a conductor with an invisible orchestra, whispering as she went. The moves were distinctly circular, but Silas could see no other notable feature to the seemingly random movements. She darted the reed forward, pointing the tip towards the open floor that lay between the dais and where he and Pitch were chained.

And where there had been nothing before now lay two glass structures, wedge shapes he could think of as nothing else but coffins.

'No...Charlie...' His words died upon his lips.

The lad lay in repose, hands folded on his chest over the thin cotton of a patient's shirt and pants, but the straitjacket was gone at least. He looked peaceful, if Silas were to choose a word, the auburn flecks in his hair standing out as much as the freckles on his cheeks.

Silas needed to take a breath, to inhale before the white spots in his vision grew worse, but his shock kept his lungs still.

His gaze moved to the second glass coffin, with its edgings of silver, very like the prism that had held the spirit of the forest. The lieutenant was similarly laid out, his face drawn and rings the colour of bruises beneath his closed eyes. He wore the same simple garb as Charlie, the material faintly chequered and the dreary colour of duck eggs.

Bile struck the back of Silas's throat. His bones felt turned to jelly, save for his damaged shoulder, which burned well as any bloody campfire.

'They were innocent.' He gagged upon the past tense. 'What have you done?'

'Ensured her own demise, if ever it had been in any doubt.' Pitch spoke so coldly Silas shivered where he knelt.

'Oh gracious, don't fret so. They are not dead. Not yet.' Macha sounded frighteningly disappointed about that. 'They are merely sleeping...the sleep of the dead, as it were.' She giggled at her own black humour. 'I've a talent for slumber hexes, as you know. If you recall, your steeds were dreaming of sunshine and hay whilst we dealt with you at Gidleigh.'

Silas pictured wiping that grin off her face in the most dastardly of ways.

'But never mind all that. Now come, come, ankou. If your little pure-bred friend was there *only by chance*, are you suggesting his presence here...at my asylum, offering words of encouragement to the daemon's whore is utter coincidence too? You best think carefully before you insult my intelligence.'

Silas couldn't think at all. He stared at Charlie, searching for a sign the sorceress spoke truly, looking for a rise of the chest that would denote the lad still resided in the land of the living.

Christ, he lay so still.

'Pitch, what do we do?'

The daemon didn't answer. He was watching the sorceress on her dais. His face as lifeless as Edward's and Charlie's.

The male harpy toddled to the sorceress's side, and she leaned so he could whisper in her ear. 'Very well, then. I did promise you that you'd see the nasty daemon punished for what he did to your kin on the greensward. And I'm ever so keen to see that Mr Mercer knows he cannot go around ruining my revenants. So best I get to it.' She stood up. She was not tall, no greater in height than Charlie, but her presence was much, much larger. She touched the tip of her reed wand to her lips, whispering a word that did not reach them, and pointed it once more at the glass coffins.

A cry wrenched from Silas as the lad and the lieutenant vanished as though never there at all.

'Where have you sent them?' he demanded, venting some of his frustration towards Pitch, who was frustratingly quiet. Usually the bastard couldn't hold his tongue to save himself. 'We must do something, damn it.'

'Oh, they are around.' Macha leaned down to reach for something beneath her chair. Her cloak flowed out around her on the dais like a spreading stain. 'Here we are.'

She held aloft a macabre trophy. A severed head, one that had long since been separated from its body. The skin was the colour of an abandoned campfire, all various shades of black and grey, and clung so tight to the bone it looked set to tear across razor-edged cheekbones. The sorceress held the head by long lengths of pale auburn hair tied up with a clashing vibrant pink ribbon. Not, Silas decided, an original feature.

A black tongue, like a deformed truffle, poked from between slashes of flesh that once were lips.

The Dullahan's mount let out a piercing whinny.

Macha puckered her lips, and with the head dangled high, she pressed a vile kiss to a sunken, shrivelled cheek. Hard enough to leave behind a mark of the black rouge from her lips.

'Dullahan,' she cried. 'Your master, the Erlking, has made you beholden to the Morrigan, so heed me now. I wish to see the ankou and the daemon punished for the atrocities they have inflicted upon us.'

'Oh fuck.' Pitch tilted his head 'Truly you do go on.'

Macha pointed a black-gloved finger at the daemon, only to let it slide a path through the air to land upon Silas. 'I have not begun to go on yet. Ready yourself, Dullahan. Let us see if the daemon has such a sharp tongue when his ankou screams.'

The Dullahan's mount reared up, pivoting as his rider gave the reins a vicious tug. With flashing hooves so near, Silas shrank back, only to cry out as his damaged shoulder roared with pain.

'Careful, witch. Your next move may be your last.' Pitch loaded each word with rich contempt.

Macha laughed, the harpies grasping at her legs. 'Oh I doubt that very much. But it may be yours. How mad can we drive you before you are lost? For you do tend to lose your mettle when poked hard enough, don't you? And you don't recover quickly. Disappeared for days into Harvington Hall after you went berserk and caused such a fuss at that farmhouse. And when your man here bundled you into the carriage at the greensward, you did not look well at all.'

Silas ground his teeth, holding very still. Macha reminded him of the raven more and more. Beady-eyed and ever watchful.

'I'd like to get to know you, whoever you are, Mr Astaroth. You have great power obviously... You had them all running like the hounds of hell were on their tails when you slipped your leash at Gidleigh, and you have showed a resistance to the Gu that is astounding. You had what? A stomach ache for a few days after, and that was that?'

Silas worked on staying still, but his mind churned. Only those in the Village knew anything of Pitch's illness after they'd returned from the greensward.

'Never mind how you destroyed my sister's precious magick circle and annihilated her panlong, which I will never hear the end of, mind. She had an unhealthy liking for that serpent and was quite beside herself when you turned it into sashimi.' She brandished the head. Eyes red as cherries...or blood. 'You are mercurial and fearsome, and I heard you once nearly strangled a boggart to death because he dared suggest you were a deserter from the Berserker Prince's legion and every bit as mad as that prince.' She paused, licking her lips. 'That seemed to me an instance of the lady doth protest too much, don't you think? Shall we see if the boggart was right?'

One of the shadows behind the dais stepped forward, emerging as though from behind a curtain. Their blurry image sharpened, and a woman with sun-darkened skin and long jet-black hair teased high upon the crown emerged.

Her tune was the harsh random rub of horsehair against strings. An off-key affair that had Silas wincing.

Daemon. Alp.

'As pleasing a sight as it would be,' she said, her voice deep and rolling, 'perhaps it is worth taking a moment to think it through, my dear.'

Pitch inhaled, and dread pounded through Silas's veins. The prince had his gaze fixed on the new arrival, pinned there the way a lion might stare when sighting prey. He was so very rigid, the veins in his neck evident. And his face, that was the worst of it. For he'd shut himself away entirely. There was nothing to read there at all. The sheen of emerald was dulled as though the light within were suffocating.

Oh god, Silas knew for certain now who this was.

He ignored the deafening pain of his shoulder to lean towards the prince. He ached to be closer, to place himself between Pitch and the villain upon the dais. For if anything would see the daemon lose his tenuous control, it was Onoskolis surely.

'Pitch, look to me. Not there,' Silas whispered urgently. If he could just get the prince to shift his arrowed gaze, to see that he was not so alone as he had been in Gidleigh House. 'I am here. Please, look at me.'

But it was as if he was held in a trance, his hatred and fury binding him up and giving him a feral air. As though he were one heartbeat away from going wild and losing himself to the monster he believed he was.

The woman sauntered her way across the dais, her movement liquid. She was clad in a simple satin gown of ocean blue with a criss-cross of black ribbons at the bodice that dangled untied, as though she'd not quite finished dressing. She sidled up to Macha and ran a fingertip along her arm, easing in very close. She tilted her head as though she were considering laying a kiss upon Macha's neck, and her hair shifted, revealing the nubs of horns hidden among the strands.

'My mistress, best we stay with the plan Nemain laid out, don't you think? Palatyne is moments from being ready to accommodate our guests.'

'Oh don't patronise me, Oni. You know it pisses me off. Are you worried I'll break him too much for you to play with again?'

The daemon slid a glance to where Pitch looked set to launch himself at her. 'Oh I'm not interested in tasting him again. He's far too bitter for my liking.' Eyes of slate grey found Silas, resting on him with a weight that crossed the divide. 'Perhaps, though, the ankou might be sweeter?'

A guttural, primal sound rose from Pitch, and he wrenched so hard against his chains a lesser man would have broken the bones in his wrists.

'I suppose he might,' Macha replied. 'But he is not for you to toy with. Mr Mercer is mine, and he owes me.'

Silas kept his focus entirely on the prince, tight as an arrow set in the bow, who had to fight so valiantly not to lose himself on the best of days. And this was far from one of those. 'Please look at me, Pitch, I beg you. I need you to see me...not that creature up there. She ran from you screaming that day, remember? A coward in all ways. One who hurt you but did not best you. Pitch, look at me.' Silas was so certain he was not getting through that he startled when Pitch looked to him.

'Silas...I can't...' The prince was breathy, struggling.

'You can. And I am right here, Pitch. You are not alone.'

Macha and Onoskolis carried on, not paying any attention to the whispered exchange.

'Owes you?' The horned daemon frowned.

'For all the children he took from me.' She waved off Onoskolis's caresses. 'Do you have any idea how many revenants he destroyed? What resources we lost when those bodies were ruined? That is days and days of my precious time.' She shooed the harpies out from beneath her cloak where they huddled. 'The ankou needs to suffer.'

A terrible darkness crossed Pitch's face, a cracking open of something excruciating. He threw his all against the chains, light emanating from his hands as though he clutched candles in his balled fists.

'Now if you will, Dullahan.' Macha raised her hands, a conductor of the strangest orchestra known. 'Punish the ankou and make them both suffer.'

The blow came at once. A pain like that of a dozen arrowheads struck Silas in the back. He roared, arching against the onslaught.

Christ almighty, it was grievous.

He jerked as whatever pained him was yanked free, the withdrawal as harrowing as the arrival. Shit, it felt as though some ribs had been removed with it. The shock filled his vision with white speckles. He needed to turn around. To face this enemy. But his mangled shoulder would not heed the order.

The next strike followed closely after the first and was no less intense. But with one advantage this time. The punch to his body was so violent it snapped his dislocated shoulder back into its socket.

His scream soared. Silas was thrown forward, his head down, catching a glimpse of feathered hooves studded with rusted nails. And glancing along the ground with them, like a ghost-white snake slithering, was the end of the Dullahan's whip.

He had a moment to realise what made the weapon. Bone. Spiked pieces of bone. Great rounded chunks like those from a spine, from one or many creatures.

The headless horseman struck again.

The breath Silas had not yet gathered was taken from him. Awful gurgling, heaving sounds came as he fought to take in some air. The pain was stealing it all. Stealing his vision, his hearing too. All was muffled as though he were back beneath the dreaded waters of the greensward's pond.

But he knew Pitch's voice. Heard the prince's enraged cry. Felt a heat beyond that of his own pain coming from where he knew the daemon to be chained.

How mad can we drive you before you are lost? The sorceress's words.

She sought to launch him into a frenzy from which she knew he may not return. The sorceress was as mad as any of the tormented souls above them, but she was also right.

'Pitch...' Silas spat blood. 'No flame. Stay calm. Do not give –'

The Dullahan raised his whip once more. He heard it claw its way across the floorboards and creak and groan as the fae king's monstrous servant prepared to strike again.

Silas's bellow filled the chamber. His eyes watered through the pain, blurring everything around him. The agony was so intense as to be paralysing. He could not breathe, his cry jamming his throat full.

But he heard the sorceress far too clearly.

'Strike him again.'

He felt the sear of Pitch's heat.

Silas flung out the words as the whip laid into him. 'Pitch, I beg you. Hold back the flame.'

CHAPTER 22

Pitch clenched his fists so hard his nails broke skin, blood warm and oozing upon his palms. But it was insignificant compared to what Silas was enduring.

Hold the flame. Was Silas mad? Did he expect Pitch to do *nothing*?

The ankou's back was sliced open, deep ugly gashes that flowed with blood, deepening the hue of his trousers to an unsettling mahogany. Pitch was not sure if the glimpses of white within the ruined flesh were strips of the ankou's shirt buried deep or hints of ribs.

The cruel tips of the bone weapon made light work of firm muscle and sinew. Silas could not hold back his cries, and each one had the wildness at Pitch's core crashing itself against the confines of its cage. Gods, he burned to release it. To tear apart this whole miserable fucking place and take the sorceress apart, one vile piece at a time. The Alp would go next. He'd rip out her black heart with his own hands and shove it down her fucking throat.

It would be easy...so, so easy, to let the madness take him, here and now. To release whatever maniacal strength Seraphiel had imbued him with. To give up trying not to lose himself to the maelstrom of it. Pitch's hands were aglow, flame licking beneath the surface.

But the oaf was telling him to hold back. *Begging* him.

And damn him, Silas was right.

The ankou, Charlie, and the lieutenant were all far too close to the Berserker Prince to survive if Pitch let go.

The sorceress chewed at her lip, watching wide-eyed with delight the punishment of the one responsible for killing her grotesque children. The Dullahan's head dangled from her clenched fist, swinging as she was absorbed by the torment she had ordered. She glanced at Pitch, watching for sign that she'd tipped him over the edge. Onoskolis hovered at her side. The only light in this darkness was the look upon the Alp's face. She was harried. This was not a part of the plan. Her mistress was playing out of turn.

Pitch fought to tune out Silas's screams, working up a brittle smile. 'Dreadful racket he's making, isn't it?' he said. Oh gods, the things he would do to these sorcerers...to the Alp...when the path was clear.

'It does have a nice ring to it though, don't you think?' Macha was a lunatic. It was there in the twist of her mouth, the mania that clung to her voice.

Onoskolis went to whisper something, but Macha elbowed her away. The Dullahan's head snagged on the Alp's gown, which, Pitch was most pleased to see, aggrieved the bitch very much.

'Macha,' she snapped. 'Enough. Send them on, now. The others will be here before long and will expect them ready to be sealed away.'

The sorceress raised her hand, lifting the Dullahan's red-eyed head. 'Cease.'

The rider heeded her at once and reined his horse in, the roan sinking back on its haunches as it danced backwards.

Silas slumped, arse to heels, toppling forward, his forehead hanging just shy of the floorboards as the chains held him from total collapse. His breathing was a ragged, choppy hacksaw. His groans made as much of a mess of Pitch's insides as the wildness which bayed for blood.

He will heal. He will heal, Pitch told himself. *He cannot die from this.*

But he could not stop the unbidden voice whispering in return, *But he can suffer. Silas can certainly suffer.*

Pitch dug his fingertips into the cuts he'd already made. He needed...wanted...to be hurting too.

'There, it is done,' the Alp said. Onoskolis stroked the sorceress's arm, long soothing strokes, as though Macha were as volatile as any prince.

He took careful note. For the maleficent woman may be powerful, but he saw in the Alp's treatment of her what he'd seen himself many times in White Mountain. The cautious way those around him moved, as though he were liable to come undone before their eyes if they so much as blinked the wrong way.

Beneath Silas's groans hung the drip of liquid. His blood marked a steady beat as it dropped to the wood.

'Silas?' Pitch fought to keep his face clear of any distress. His insides, though, did not fare so well. 'Can you hear me?'

A muffled grunt came from the ankou. A twitch of his head that might have been a nod.

'Did we break your favourite toy, my sweet one?' Onoskolis called out.

Pitch despised himself for flinching at the name she gave him. The flame grabbed at his ribs, took hold of his innards, and demanded its freedom. He swallowed his reply for fear the words would turn to fire and obliterate them all.

'He hides it well,' the Alp told her mistress. 'But I've seen beneath his pretty, vapid mask. I've felt the hard truth he thought he could conceal. That glorified corpse is under his skin. I assure you, my dear, you are punishing the daemon well with this.'

Macha cocked her head as though she'd spent far too much time with the raven. The taut hold of her body slackened, her manic fervour subsiding. 'Yes, but I was hoping to see better sign of it, Oni.' She pouted. 'He doesn't seem fit to be called a Berserker Prince's soldier at all. It's quite disappointing.'

'Well, maybe Palatyne's Sanctuary will change that. Best we put them where the others expect them to be, wouldn't you say?' She played with a feather on Macha's mask. 'I don't know about you, but I'm relishing the look on Nemain's face when she sees what you've achieved here.' She leaned closer and whispered. Pitch barely caught it. Something along the lines of *closer to our king*.

Macha brightened like a child catching sight of a pile of presents. 'Oh gracious, yes.' She brandished the head. 'And she'll adore this idea, don't you think? Giving the Dullahan his name.'

Onoskolis crooked her finger and rubbed at Macha's cheek. The connection between the two eluded Pitch: at times sensual, though Macha professed to hold no such desires; at others akin to mother and child, or older sister to younger. Whichever it was, it was as twisted as the two creatures themselves.

'Absolutely,' Onoskolis said. 'Now, shall we see that done? And then we can send these two away.'

Silas groaned, trying to sit up.

'Stay still, you fool.' Pitch's concern made him sharp.

'Are you...all right?' Silas coughed and his lips were bloodied.

Fucking stupid, ludicrous man. Did he ever think solely of himself?

'Of course.' Pitch eyed the Dullahan atop his mount. Still too close, his bone whip smeared with crimson evidence of the blows it had dealt. 'Save your strength.'

And heal, curse him. Silas *had* to heal.

'I'm...fine...'

'Fucking liar,' Pitch hissed.

The wildness moved like spears against his gut, trying to prick its way free. His fury was making him desperately unstable, but how could he be anything else but furious here?

'Oh, isn't that just so sweet?' Onoskolis had a small smile upon her vile lips. He had never despised another so greatly as he did the Alp. 'Half the skin torn from his back and he's hoping you will believe everything is fine. You two are truly adorable.'

Pitch glowered, hoping she could see all the vicious things he wished to do to her in his eyes. The wildness rolled in his hatred, eating at it greedily. 'Lady Satine will not think much of your treatment of her Horseman.'

The ankou twitched and moaned behind clenched teeth. He was trying his best, but for Pitch, each sound he made rang as loudly as a church bell on a Sunday morn.

'A pity both her Horsemen forgot their horses,' Macha returned. 'The Order must have turned half of London upside down searching for you by now. I almost wish I could be there to see it. But I like the view better here, I think. Lady Satine will know soon enough that her time of keeping us from the Watcher King is over.' Macha stretched her arms overhead, rolling her shoulders. The cloak slid back to reveal a tunic, dark as tar like all the rest, over her trousers. The basic attire of the country folk. 'Samyaza's call grows stronger each day. Neither Satine nor the angels she serves can keep us from him much longer. Not now I have all I –'

'Macha, my dear.' Onoskolis reached again for the sorceress, entwining their fingers. 'Careful now.'

Macha raised their joined hands and kissed at the daemon's knuckles. 'I merely wish them to know a few paltry Horsemen will not be enough to keep us at bay.' She dropped Onoskolis's hand like it burned her. 'But don't interrupt me again, Oni. I really don't like it.' Pitch relished the sudden rebuke for the way it clearly irritated the Alp. Macha returned to him. 'No matter who you are or what pretty fires you can start, you and your ankou are not enough, Mr Astaroth.'

'You seem so very sure of that.'

Macha peered down her nose at him, tapping her foot. 'Feel free to convince me otherwise, for I'm quite underwhelmed so far.' She glanced over at where Silas struggled to keep his head much above a few inches from the ground. 'Oni insists you give a shit about this sod and that it pains you no end to see him hurt so.' She huffed. 'But your man has his ribs on show crying like a babe, and you're just kneeling there with a piss-weak little flicker of flame and doing fuck all about it. I wanted to see you glow, little daemon.' She actually stamped her foot. 'He's no fun at all, Oni.'

'The naming, Macha.' The Alp was gentle with her reminder. 'Do you remember that is what you wished to do next?'

'Yes, yes. Of course I bloody remember.' Her lips twisted as she studied Pitch awhile longer. 'You had best glow for me before the others arrive to seal you away. I want to see your pretty colours. It's not fair that the others have seen them and I have not.'

The Alp darted a look at Pitch, who gave her his widest, brightest smile. He was seeing what she clearly hoped he had missed; her mistress was volatile and quite unhinged.

'They will be here before long,' she muttered. 'Come now. Don't you want to see them run like rats in the maze?'

Macha let out a delighted squeal. 'Did Palatyne have time to do the oubliettes, do you know?'

His already-tormented skin prickled ever more. Oubliettes were this world's paler version of an abaddon. Deep prisons where inmates were sent to be forgotten. The flame darted against his ribs, testing soft places for escape.

'I'm not entirely sure,' Onoskolis said. Pitch stopped breathing as her gaze brushed him. He'd not be seen to tremble. 'But then the Sanctuary itself shall be close enough to one when the seals are in place.'

Macha nodded, pleased. 'Weatherby, gather what I need now please,' she called.

The kitsune had been so quiet and still that he'd blended into the walls it seemed. Pitch had no idea he'd remained in the room until he suddenly stepped forward, adjusted his coat, and promptly shifted his form.

His clothes peeled away, like skin from an orange. There was a pop, a dull spring of light like a torch passing behind frosted glass, and the creature was on all fours, scampering across the room, his trio of tails sweeping about like a thick peacock's tail. His pointed ears were too big for his head, and the single streak of white upon one of his bushy tails reminded Pitch of a skunk rather than a fox.

Weatherby made his headlong way, straight at Pitch.

Barely was there a chance to tell the pathetic creature to fuck off and Weatherby was lunging, jaws agape, yellowed teeth glistening wet. His damp nose brushed Pitch's neck first, then the kitsune laid his teeth in, biting down and tearing free a sizeable chunk of flesh.

'You fucking piece of basilisk shit!' Pitch roared. He let the flames erupt from his hands and realised quickly how utterly useless that was, for it only scorched the floorboards, threatening to set them alight. He curled his bloodied hands while fresh, warm blood ran down the side of his neck. What the blazing fuck was that all about?

211

'Good boy. Bring it to me now,' Macha directed.

Rather than run at the dais, Weatherby shot past his pile of clothes and rushed straight out of the ballroom doors that swung wide to accommodate his departure.

'I am not the only one anxious to acquire your company, Mr Astaroth.' Macha set the Dullahan's head on her chair, shifting some lengths of hair that had fallen across the blood-red eyes. 'The Unseelie Court and the bluecaps are close cousins. The Erlking was very, very unhappy about what you did in those mines. I mean he was rather miffed you killed them all, but worst of all, you reneged on your deal with their queen, an unforgivable insult to all the races of fae. They do not like a cheat.' She tutted. 'The oath you broke with the bluecaps now belongs to the Erlking. You are rightfully his property to claim now, Mr Astaroth. Aren't you honoured? Being so sought after by so many?'

Fucking gods, the Forest of Dean would never cease to plague him. 'The best of luck to him in claiming me.'

She shrugged. 'He's aware it is unlikely, but very happy to add to your misery during your stay with us. And as the Unseelie Court has been so good to us, who am I to deny His Majesty?'

'Who indeed?'

This stupid bitch could talk the spines off a hedgehog. Pitch glanced at Silas.

The ankou was more upright, slumped back on his heels, but his head hung far too low, and his body swayed too much. The Alp whore was right about one thing. It *did* pain him to see Silas so, like a butcher's hook sinking deep into his chest. The ankou turned his head as though sensing Pitch's gaze. With his hair cut short, there was no hiding behind its strands. The agony was writ large across Silas's face, glazing his eyes, pinching at the corners of his mouth.

The wildness hit Pitch deep down, a blow that caused him to shudder. And he struggled to remember why he should not just let the inferno loose.

'No...Pitch,' Silas wheezed.

Now the ankou was a fucking mind reader apparently. But likely it was all in the eyes. Pitch could feel the heat behind his lids.

'Ah there you are. Excellent, thank you, Weatherby,' Macha said.

The black fox padded up onto the dais, its teeth bared as it clutched its piece of daemonic flesh between them. Pitch frowned at the roundabout delivery. Weatherby could have crossed the dance floor and been done with it.

'Good boy.' Macha patted his head, laying out her other hand to take the bloodied prize. Though Pitch's neck blazed with pain, the portion that was stolen was small, a penny size at most. She knelt beside the chair and placed her lips close to the ear of the Dullahan. She raised the crimson flesh to his mouth and whispered. The dark scratches that passed for lips opened. Onoskolis watched on with a smirk as Macha pressed Pitch's flesh into the widened mouth.

'Christ, that's vile.' Silas coughed, sending a fresh speckling of blood onto the floor.

'Rather.' Pitch was silently pleased the ankou could find the strength to comment at all. 'How are you faring?'

'I've had better days,' he grunted.

'There we are, then.' Macha clapped her bloodstained hands. 'When you are ready, Palatyne. Dullahan, perhaps one more strike for the journey, seeing as our ankou seems fit enough to speak again.'

She wiggled her fingers, not any great move of maleficent magick, but a condescending wave.

The Dullahan raised his whip, curling it in the air in a lazy circle. Silas muttered something beneath his breath, his body shaking, curling in against the oncoming blow.

The bony protrusions struck the ankou's back. Pitch was sure he heard the chandeliers shudder with the weight of the blow.

Silas did not bellow or scream or cry. He sobbed.

Pitch's vision went white with fury. He lurched against his binds, determined to break his fucking hands if need be to free himself. But he didn't get the chance.

The manacles fell away. He barely managed to plant his hands down before he copped a mouthful of floorboard. Pitch leapt to his feet. His flame roared up through his middle, searing his ribs, the prickling at his arm and back vanishing beneath the onslaught.

The beast stepped one foot out of its cage. The twisted distortion Seraphiel had made of his flame sought freedom. Pitch inhaled the calamity. This may be the very worst of ideas if the wildness slipped him, but for now it was the only idea that would stop the ankou's torture.

Pitch turned on his heels, hands ablaze. The Dullahan readied another strike.

'Enough!' He thrust his hands forward. Twin torrents of crackling rage burned towards the Dullahan. They struck the fae king's minion, and the creature burst alight. Headless or no, the creature managed to sound off screams that were unholy. The whip was a snaking ribbon of fire that twisted and corkscrewed through the air in a desperate but vain attempt to rid itself of the flames consuming it. The Dullahan's mount reared, legs thrashing, its mane and tail burning with a white-hot fire, its squeals joining that of its rider.

Silas lay beneath them, trying desperately to move himself, but the wounded ankou was too close.

Furious, Pitch struck out again. He cared so much less how violent the flames became or how much of his skin they consumed. He sent the torrents of heat and destruction outward and used them like a lasso. The moment they struck the Dullahan, wrapping like ribbon around an unwanted gift, sparks of white set off amongst the blaze of autumn colours. The fae's magick sought to repel the force of a Dominion and angel's monster both.

Pitch sneered and raised horse and rider off the ground. Fuck. The arsehole and his mount were near as heavy as Goodrich Castle. Jaw clenched, veins bulging with the duress of flame and burden both, Pitch caught sight of the dais.

Macha and Onoskolis had not moved an inch. The sorceress's expression was hard to read, but he did not see any fear there, and he despised her for it. The Alp...that bitch of a creature was smiling. By Enoch's taint, he wanted to gouge her eyes from her skull, burn her lips clear off her face. His fury sent fresh licks of heat racing through him. The beast was reaching through the bars, lunging at the collapsing resolve of the daemon prince who kept it chained.

He was dangerously furious, more so than when he'd feared Silas dead at the greensward. Because here the ankou suffered because of *him*.

The dark shadows at the edge of Pitch's vision were creeping in, narrowing his view down to pinholes.

A tiny part of him still spouted caution, still tried to call on him to hold back. This was madness, his sensibility whispered.

He would *become* madness, if he did not calm down.

But he was tired of this place. Of the need to be here to begin with.

Seraphiel's quest be damned. Let the Blight make monsters of all humankind.

So long as the ankou still existed to deal with them.

A dull throb came from Pitch's back, along the length of the spine. The amuletum pushed to its limits. But fuck the damned enchanted ink. He manipulated the flames to raise the Dullahan, horse and all, up into the air. The blue roan's legs scrambled madly, but the rider made no move to leave the saddle.

Pitch released a cry that ripped at the flesh of his throat, and he hurled the Dullahan across the room. Straight towards his tormentors.

The creature flew like a blazing comet, illuminating everything in its path.

Which was...nothing...

The Dullahan careened across the width of the room.

The *empty* width of the room.

No dais. No sorceress or odious daemon. Not even a pestiferous harpy in sight.

'Bastards.'

Through his sputtering, cooling fury, Pitch understood why the kitsune had left the room to deliver the flesh to his mistress.

Macha had never been here with them.

Nor had the Alp.

They were as much an illusion as the glass coffins and Charlie pinned in his straitjacket.

The Dullahan took an inordinate amount of time to collide with the far wall, as though the entire room had stretched while Pitch was busy losing his temper. The shape of the creature became less distinct, as did the flames that were seeking to consume it. The sparks of white coming from the fae grew more pronounced as the long path of the Dullahan stretched longer. The wall was right there, Pitch could see the blasted thing, but the Dullahan was yet to strike it.

'Pitch.' Silas's voice was the groan of a rusted gate.

Pitch spun about. The ankou's chains were gone. He was on his feet, but barely so. The back of his shirt had been destroyed entirely, the rags draping at his sides like limp, broken wings. Blood ran from his mouth in a drizzly line to the floor, and he wobbled about like a child who'd not yet learned how to work his legs.

'Careful, you fool.' Pitch struggled against the flame, which bucked and scrambled still to escape him. He was merciless with pressing it down, punching in into submission, so he might reach for Silas.

He so very nearly had a hold of him, was so very tantalisingly close, when the first of the cracks formed. There in the floor where Silas stood. As though it were not wood he stood upon but ice.

'Silas, don't move.'

The cracks snapped and popped, their veins spreading further. One raced out from beneath the ankou to serpentine across to Pitch's boots.

'Pitch?' Silas raised his head, his eyes reddened, his pain holding a vice grip on his face. 'I don't think I can...'

He toppled forward.

And there was no fucking way Pitch was going to watch him fall. He ran for the ankou.

The ground shattered, like a struck mirror, and nothingness opened beneath them.

CHAPTER 23

They fell. Pitch shouted his fright and irritation and bare horror into the darkness. Silas, somewhere nearby in the pall, did the same.

And they kept falling.

The descent dragged on. And on.

Pitch ceased his cries, and their echoes were swallowed by an inky gloom so thick it seemed to caress his skin. His fury had been whipped away with the shock of the sudden fall. But he was still aglow, a falling star of light, the blackness a thick curtain that doused even his truculent flame, for only the immediate area around him was brightened.

'Silas?' he called.

'Here.' Though where exactly *here* was, Pitch could not tell. The darkness took their voices and bounced the sounds about like balls on a court. 'Do you think...they were dead?'

Pitch blinked against the weight of the blackness. 'Who?'

'Charlie...and Edward...'

'Fuck...we are falling into an abyss, you are in pieces, and that's what you are thinking?'

'Were they sleeping as she said...or were they dead, Pitch?' Silas shed his usual endless patience. 'The question is simple. Alive or dead.'

'Alive.' He'd not explain why he believed that. He did not wish to say aloud how the prickling at his back and at his arm where he'd buried the pendant watch beneath his skin was more akin now to someone rubbing him down with an exotic cactus that had been soaked in acid. Not pleasant at all. But sign, he was sure, that Edward at least was still alive and well. 'Edward is alive.'

'And Charlie?' Silas sounded so small in the darkness.

And gods damn it, Pitch hesitated too long.

A sob danced against the blackness.

'I'm sure he's...fine...' Pitch rushed out the unconvincing consolation, but the truth was he had no clue. The truth was if he were in Macha's place, he would kill the purebred now. Charlie had served his purpose. Drawn in the targets. 'He was likely sleeping.' Gods. He'd always thought himself a masterful liar, but he was failing abysmally here. But, in fairness, he *was* rather distracted about the never-ending fucking fall.

Utter silence came from the night around him.

'Silas?'

'Can you not throw out your light further, damn you?' the ankou snapped. 'I can't see my hand before my face.'

There was no trace of his usual impeccable tolerance of a daemon prince who could be, they both knew, a monumental pain in the arse. Silas was hurting. This was the precise moment Pitch should find soothing words, offer some gentleness, as the ankou had done so often in reverse.

Pitch wanted to, he truly did, but he was talentless in such things, and his bloody tongue had a life of its own. It had defied a curse, after all. 'I am not a living torch, you prick,' he spat.

'You have fire in your veins,' Silas shot back. 'It is exactly what you bloody are, but you are very poor at it right now.' His voice boomed around whatever strange place this was.

In the past, perhaps Pitch would have beaten a man to a pulp for such insolence. But not now. Never with this man.

He smiled, pleased to hear the vigour in Silas's tone. 'I suppose you are right.' The ankou was pissed off, very much so, but that meant he was not fading away, torn into pieces by imagined loss and the Dullahan's whip.

'And why the fuck are we still falling?' Silas hollered.

His rare ribald language pushed strained laughter up Pitch's throat. Gods, Silas never ceased to surprise him, delight him. And if the Morrigan tried to touch him again, he'd not bother trying to hold back the Berserker Prince at all. Never mind the consequences.

'I have no idea,' Pitch replied. 'I'm beginning to think they are sending us to the centre of the Earth. I shall need to take a piss soon... That will be interesting. I hope you're not above me.'

A mangled version of laughter came from the surrounds. Then a hiss of discomfort.

'Shit.'

'Are you all right?' Foreign words for Pitch. More foreign still, the need for an answer.

'No.' Silas paused. 'That whip made a mess of me, I fear... I'll be quite useless till these marks heal. If we ever bloody stop falling, it might be best if you –'

The blackness gave way to low yellow light, and the nothingness gave way to the solid press of ground at last. Pitch's feet hit the slight cushioning of a rug a second after he caught sight of it. The landing was not so terrible as it might have been, as though he had actually dangled only a few inches above the floor all along, the sense of falling one of pure illusion.

Gods damn it. Illusion, indeed.

Between the sorceress's skills with deceiving the eye, and the talents of the Children of Melusine who built the Sanctuaries, Pitch was wary that anything at all here was entirely real.

Sanctuaries were built with a unique vein of magick wrought from an ancient purebred and fae union, and were inherently unpredictable. Unstable if firm foundations were not set. The more reliable Children of Melusine could be counted on to bridle the magick adequately and ensure Sanctuary residents didn't wake to find themselves bricked into a wall or lying beneath the foundations. Old Bess built into his mansions and castles an innate desire within the bricks and wood and mortar to protect the inhabitants.

But the reverse could also be designed.

Silas's halt was not as elegant as Pitch's. The ankou's thump upon the ground was weighty. He staggered. A wall rose up behind him, and he landed against it, squarely against his ruined back. His scream filtered between hard-clenched teeth, and he was toppling forward in his haste to be away.

Pitch was at his side in two strides, searching for somewhere to lay his hands that would keep Silas upright but go nowhere near the ghastly wounds. The ankou's blood made a garish design upon the white wall.

'I have you. Steady now.'

'I'm all right.' Silas gasped. 'Just need...catch...breath.'

He slung an arm over Pitch's shoulder. Pitch could not wrap his arm about the ankou, so he held on to Silas's forearm, tilting himself forward as though the man were a weighty sack of potatoes he had draped over his shoulder.

'I'm sure Charlie was sleeping,' Pitch whispered.

But damn the ankou. He was not paying a single snippet of attention to Pitch's attempt to redeem himself. Silas braced one hand against the wall, busy peering up and down the corridor. His frown appeared partly borne of confusion rather than just his pain.

They had landed in a corridor. Doorless and windowless, with evenly placed gas lamps throwing subtle patches of yellowed light upon a dull brown hall runner. Wood panelling along the wall reached to hip height, Pitch's hip at least, with white plaster above. Stark, save for the crimson inkblot showing where Silas had landed. It could be a hallway in any number of homes they might have visited.

'Did she not speak of a maze? This looks nothing of the sort,' Silas declared. Pitch's words had not reached his ears, and it brought a selfish pang of relief.

'So long as it remains roomier than the oubliette she threatened, I'll take whatever they throw at us.' Even just saying the word made his pulse stutter.

'You do not like them much.'

'Oubliettes? What utter moron would *like* them?'

'I saw your face when the sorceress spoke of them.' Gentle as the proverbial fucking lamb, of course Silas was, even as blood dripped from his shirt hem. 'I've heard talk of the abaddon in Arcadia...where you were imprisoned... I wonder if –'

Considering Silas would have felt Pitch tense beneath his arm, what point in denying it? 'If I was left to rot in an inescapable tomb much like an oubliette? Wonder no more. Now shall we get on with this so we can find what we came for and leave this place?'

Silas sucked in his breath. 'Of course. I'm sorry.'

Pitch was too irritated to admonish him for apologising. He glanced back behind them. The carpeting was just as bland there, a cheerless brown runner with a hint of black patterning through it.

'Do you feel drawn either way?' Silas asked. 'Any sign of what direction to take?'

Pitch touched at his arm absently. The irritation of the pendant watch was steady and not too bothersome, all told. With the benefit of hindsight, he realised it had not grown any stronger when Edward appeared in his coffin, which should have told him there and then that the spectacle was nothing but an illusion. 'No, but I think you have the right idea.' Seraphiel's trinket desired to be with Edward. Perhaps it could prove more compass than pain in the back. 'Shall we pick a path and see what happens?'

'Absolutely.'

Their progress was slow, to say the least. With the injury-laden ankou keeping such a miserable pace, Pitch could walk without hint of a limp. They made their way along a corridor that stretched on as far as Pitch could peer, with no deviation from the blandness. The ankou insisted on trying to keep some of his weight off Pitch's back, despite being told numerous times it was all right to do so. Silas walked with one hand braced against the wall, pausing occasionally to cough into his sleeve, blotching it with strawberry-coloured stains.

He did so for the third time, wiping at his mouth and smearing blood over his chin in the process.

'Don't do that. Can you brace yourself a moment?' When Silas nodded, Pitch manoeuvred himself around so he stood facing the ankou and tugged at his own shirt sleeve so the cuff gathered in his hand. The material was frayed and rubbed grey where it had been caught beneath the manacles. The *nekhri* manacles. So the Morrigan had arrowheads *and* cuffs and chains. Not exactly a calming thought. Arrowheads might be found in private collections. There were enough of them shot during the Severance War's beginning, but he very much doubted the chains that had been the perfect lengths to hold a slight daemon and an oversized ankou just happened to fall into their possession. Which meant someone in the sorcerer's merry bunch of arseholes not only *had* the metal but knew how to forge it.

Silas swayed on his feet, and Pitch hurried to tend to him. He pressed the material-covered heel of his hand to the ankou's chin, where the blood was thickest and dampest. He dabbed at it in what he hoped was a helpful way, very much aware of how the ankou watched him.

'Does the flame trouble you?' Silas said softly. 'What of your back?'

'Aching but no more than usual.' Luckily Pitch was a proficient liar. 'My little monster is back in its cage. Fear not.'

'I don't fear you, Pitch.' Silas grimaced as Pitch moved to his neck, near to a gash that trickled like a stream.

'Sorry.'

'It's all right, Pitch.' But that was hardly true. Silas leaned heavily against the wall, and gods there was just so much blood coming from the man. 'You did so very well for so long when the Dullahan was –'

'Tearing you to shreds?'

A soft chuckle squeezed another grimace from the ankou. 'I know it could not have been easy. You were fighting enemies within and without, but you handled yourself remarkably well. I was so bloody proud of you, finding the strength to fight against Macha's madness and the flame. You kept your calm for so long.'

Pitch's cheeks flushed. The ankou had found time to be proud, even whilst being flayed open by the Dullahan? Honestly, this man was beyond comprehension.

'Well, keep your pride, for in the end you suffered needlessly for too long. The calm was never going to last. I should have acted far sooner –'

'No. You shouldn't have. Now both the Morrigan *and* the flame know it is not so easy to taunt you.'

He spoke of Pitch's fire in the way Pitch thought of it himself. As though it were a separate entity, a challenge to be handled, an adversary to be managed. For the first time since he'd first felt the shift in his power, he was not alone in trying to hold himself together.

'Even when you did relent,' Silas went on, 'you were precise, not mindless. Besides, you could not have done anything sooner, for you were in chains. Astonishingly strong chains. They can't have been human-made?'

'They were nekhri, the same as those blasted arrowheads... But I could have ruined them.' His cuff was soaked through with blood, making his attempts at cleaning detrimental now. 'I could have broken free, if I –'

'Let go entirely? Let the wildness take over?' Silas shook his head. 'You were right to restrain yourself.'

Pitch gave up with the cuff and used the pad of his thumb to vanish a tiny speck of blood that hid in the faint bristle of Silas's already-returning beard.

'Edward or not, if they touch you again like that, I shall reduce this place to ash.'

Silas tried awfully hard to make his smile reach his eyes, but the attempt was a failure. He looked dreadful. His skin held a tinge of greenish grey, and the ring of black around his irises seemed thicker, pressing in on light brown as though the darkness they'd fallen through had seeped into him.

The ankou touched his hand to the wound on Pitch's neck where the kitsune had taken his bite. 'I wasn't sure this had truly happened,' Silas said.

'On account of being thrashed to senseless by that piece of shit upon his horse?'

'Was the rest of it true? The Erlking claiming our deal with the –'

'Can we focus instead upon the task at hand here, instead of fae nonsense?'

Silas did not seem keen to do so, his eyes still fixed on the wound, which was really not much more than a graze now.

'Silas?' Pitch nudged him.

'Yes, yes, of course. Edward and Charlie.'

'That's the pair. Do you have any idea where they might be?' He fluttered his hands. 'Does your bond with the vagabond tell you anything? Perhaps you set some of your ghostly friends to work to find him?'

'I am not connected to Charlie in that way, though I wish it were so.' Silas wrinkled his nose. 'And as for the ghosts...that's the odd thing. I've yet to sense any lost souls here at all.'

'Why is that odd?'

'So many must have died here...so many unhappy souls. And not one lingers in a place like this? Neither in the corridors upstairs, if we are still under the asylum as you believe, nor down here. That strikes me as surprising. But then, most everything about the Fulbourn is an unwelcome surprise.'

And by the Archangel's cockheads, Pitch should have known it would be so. He should have taken Silas back to the Village. Bend for him there until he was so punch-drunk from fucking he could do nothing but sleep like the dead he loved so much. Then Pitch could have crept away to make this foolish journey on his own. Dealt with the repercussions of his arrogance and petulance alone. But he had not. And here they were. In the veritable lion's den. So they must take from that what they could and survive to tell the tale.

'Can you walk on, do you think?'

'Yes.' Silas nodded, tending more of his weight towards Pitch. 'The healing is not so fast as I'd like, but the bleeding has stopped I think.'

'Shall I check?'

'No, it will be ghastly to look at.'

'I manage well enough with your face each day.'

Silas laughed, and it really was a cruel thing to make him do, but by the gods it was wonderful to hear.

'Oh shit,' he gasped. 'I think I'd rather the pain stop than the bleeding.'

Pitch gave him a moment to gather himself, and at his nod, they set off on their snail's pace again.

The corridor stretched ahead into a narrow point of darkness, places where the gaslight could not seem to penetrate. It was the same behind them too, Pitch noted. As though the lights had been snuffed out as they moved along. There was not a painting upon the walls nor a plant in a pot upon the floor. And not a single door. Nothing to indicate they had moved at all. Each step they took just delivered them to an identical place. As though they were walking on the spot.

'This feels rather pointless,' Silas said after a few quiet minutes. He leaned his weight towards the wall. 'Are you feeling any kind of pull towards one direction?'

'No. No, there's nothing.'

Silas sighed. 'You'd make your way a damned bit faster if I were not holding you back. Perhaps you should –'

Pitch jerked to a halt. 'Go, and leave you here like a fucking bear caught in a trap, ready for the hunter to come along? I'm not averse to hitting an injured man, Silas. Keep that up and I shall consider you warned.'

Silas's snort was cut short by the evident pain it caused. His eyelids were heavy, and a grimace contorted his lips. 'I've tried calling for the bandalore, but it won't...or can't, hear me. And in this state, I am –'

'Dare say useless or a hindrance and may the gods help you, Mercer.' Pitch hissed. 'Never tell me to abandon you.' He was perhaps tugging too hard at the ankou, who was feeling increasingly like a sack of bricks. 'You will heal.'

Spoken as a command, and filled with gritty determination.

Silas nodded, though his head seemed too heavy for him to move with ease. 'I will. But the injury is deep. I need time that we do not have. The lieutenant needs you.'

'Fuck the lieutenant.'

Silas's inhale was wet and ragged. 'Well, I'd say the horse has bolted on that one.'

The unexpected sordid humour put a hole in Pitch's expanding temper. But he refused to be distracted. 'I'm not leaving you. You will heal.' He said it again. Maybe the gods would hear this fucking time.

'Well, that settles that, then.' Suddenly, and very much unexpectedly, Silas pressed a kiss to Pitch's temple.

The daemon ducked his head, doing his best to look mightily annoyed, which he was not in the slightest. 'Hardly time for that, Mercer. And gods, man, you can lean on me more. I'm sturdier than I look, and you know it full well.'

Silas obliged, leaning into Pitch, his hip brushing very close to where the halo's mark stirred and prickled and caused strife. But Pitch was not about to tell him, for he'd want to change position immediately, and with the state Silas looked to be in, he'd likely pass out.

'I don't think I like Sanctuaries much,' Silas said, his wheezing returned. 'All the ones I've known have worked me far too hard.'

'Can't say I'm overly fond of them myself. I much prefer theatre boxes, I think.'

This time Silas's sigh-mingled-with-groan came from a lighter place. 'Bloody hell, that feels like another lifetime away, does it not?'

Pitch's lips twitched. 'Not according to my arse, no.'

Silas squeezed his arm against Pitch's neck. 'Don't. I really don't want to laugh.'

'I wasn't joking.'

Something odd, like a whimper and a sneeze conjoined, jumped from the ankou. 'Should I assume, then, we shall not engage again in –'

'Make such an assumption at your peril, Mr Mercer.'

Pitch soaked up the satisfied little harrumph the ankou made, and for a while they continued in silence, each to their own thoughts.

'Do you know,' Silas said after a while, 'I believe I've seen this hallway before.'

Pitch sighed.

'No, no, I'm serious,' Silas said. 'I thought it when we first arrived but was more concerned with not passing out. I'm certain that The Atlas threw me into just such a hallway when I first tried to visit Mr Ahari.' Pitch felt the ankou's tension at his back. 'Would this Palatyne, if they are the architect here, have been in The Atlas?'

'Highly likely. It's open to all naturals.'

'Even those who would work with our enemies?'

'The Children of Melusine are loyal only to gems and coins. Why do you think Old Bess is always dripping in overstated jewellery? The Order keeps him in the fashion to which he's accustomed. If the Morrigan have the right coin, Palatyne would likely build them whatever they want.'

The same as the Child who had built Seraphiel's Sanctuary...or prison. Pitch had never been able to decide which. Whoever they were could likely retire from building for eternity having had the angel as a client.

Silas brought them to a stop, planting his hand to the wall, noticeably breathless. 'Old Bess doesn't seem so –'

'Mercenary? Well, he's always been an odd fish, and he has a soft spot for the Lady, the gods know why. I don't recall this hall in The Atlas.'

'Did it lead you up a hundred flights of stairs and send you all about?'

'It wouldn't dare.'

'Then you haven't seen the half of it.' Silas rolled his shoulder, gingerly, as though testing just how badly it would hurt to do so. Evidently not too badly, for he moved the other soon after. 'But then I suppose it need not have been the Child who was in The Atlas to begin with. It certainly wasn't them in the Village to know that you had been laid up by the Gu. Did you hear that said by the sorceress? She knew you had been unwell.'

Pitch nodded and could not help but think of Kaneko at the soirée. The tsukumogami had been in Mr Ahari's employ an untold number of centuries. As little as Pitch liked the surly prick, even *he* was not certain the wretch would turn betrayer. But maybe he was sick of tending the bar. Ahari might well have tasked him with securing the akaname from the black market, told him of their purpose in healing a sick daemon. Kaneko could have described The Atlas to the Child so as to include its halls in this wicked place.

And it was Kaneko who had taken Pitch's call at The Atlas. Even if he had told the tsukumogami where they were going, chances were the message would never have been relayed.

They'd still be as they were now. A tad bit fucked.

'There are many eyes upon us, Sickle,' Pitch said quietly. 'And less of them can be trusted than we knew, it seems.'

They continued their aimless stroll in a thoughtful silence, on a path that never changed, the same section of panelling repeated over and over. Until Silas gasped.

'There, do you see it?'

At long, long last a change in scenery. Up ahead lay a clear shift in the passageway. A right-hand turn.

'About bloody time.'

Silas's arm jerked against him, the ankou stiffening. 'Shit,' he whispered, struggling to look back the way they had come.

'What is it?' Pitch helped him turn about. He scanned the corridor, but all he could see was more drab-brown floor runner, more wood panelling, and tarnished sconces with spitting gaslight.

'Christ, Pitch. There are teratisms down here.'

CHAPTER 24

S ilas had tried hard, for a long while, not to crush Pitch as they
walked, but between the god-awful pangs at his ruined back and
the sudden clanging in his ears, he barely had the energy to breathe. He
stumbled, but the prince had no trouble righting him.

'A teratism?' Pitch twisted about, scanning the corridors, which hinted at no end in sight. 'Fuck, are you absolutely sure?'

Silas nodded, swallowing as the back of his throat burned with threatened bile. The notes had begun a few moments ago. Faint, like they were
merely the echo of a song and not the tune itself. The bandalore had so
far ignored, or could not heed, his summons, but he knew now, with so
many of his death memories loosened by the Morrigan's dire pond, that
the trinket was only one part of the scythe. He was as much a part of
death's weapon as the blade itself. There was no need to hold on to it to
know the cry of the Blight's afflicted.

'Where are they coming from?' They had halted beneath one of the gas
lamps, its tiny flame jigging about like a will-o'-the-wisp seeking escape.
Silas did a double take, just to make sure that wasn't the case. It seemed
the sort of place where such things might happen. But it was a simple
flame there, and no such creature.

'I can't tell yet.' He frowned, touching his fingers to his temple as
though he could coax the details from his mind.

'How many? Is there just the one?'

'I'm not sure...' Silas's finger trick was a failure. 'It is loud but so contorted...I just don't know.'

'What *do* you bloody know?'

He ignored Pitch's waspish question. The daemon was bothered, and rightly so, but Silas needed a moment to focus on the melody. It was the scratchy, offbeat song of the teratism for sure. But it was like half an orchestra tuning their instruments before a performance, all kinds of twangs and trills mismatched. It may be one tune, or it could be several played at once.

Whichever it was, the sound of the unsettled orchestra played at his right. It was coming from beyond the turn in the hallway.

'We need to go that way.' He stabbed his finger.

Back the way they had come.

But Pitch made no protest, turning them about. The ease with which he was able to manoeuvre a person nearly double his size still managed to astonish Silas. So many of the prince's strengths did.

'You are taking us *away* from it, aren't you?' Pitch said.

He moved them down the corridor at a quickened pace, but not so fast as Silas would have liked. The notes were clearer now but no less garbled and repulsive to the ear. They were being followed, there was no doubt, but by how many of the blasted things?

'Yes, I'm sorry. I can't face it now. I need more time.' He was near to fainting away with just hurrying. He ran one hand along the wall, using the lip where wood met plaster as a brace.

'Sorry you aren't going to try and wrestle a teratism with your bare hands, in your current state?' Pitch's laugh was brittle. 'Gods, Sickle, your need to apologise for all and sundry never ceases to amaze me.'

'Pitch, we need to move faster.'

'I'm sure we do, but you cannot see your face.' The daemon glanced up at him, at just the perfect moment for the gaslight to flirt with the colour of his eyes. The brilliant green had returned in full, disguised no more by Lady Satine's camouflage. A superlative sight that made Silas forget that he was in more pain than he'd thought a body capable. 'You do not look well, Sickle.'

The daemon's face grew shadowed. He looked away, taking his brilliance with him. And Silas was as he had been, nearly doubled over with his agonies of body...and of the mind. His fears for Charlie were like nails hammering deep, and they would cripple him if he considered them too much.

'I just need time, that's all,' Silas huffed, his lungs tight. 'The wounds will heal, but I need time. Damn it, does this corridor go on forever? There are no doors?'

Pitch adjusted himself beneath Silas's arm. 'No. No doors nor windows. No clear route to escape. It might as well be a fucking oubliette...or the abaddon.'

Silas moved his hand, which dangled over Pitch's shoulder, to rest against the daemon's chest. That small contact was all he could manage by way of comforting gestures. He would have preferred to gather him up in his arms in a hug that Pitch would have viewed as a gesture of pity and despised. But His Royal Highness would need to get over his irrational aversion to affection, for Silas had given up trying to ignore the impulse to touch him, comfort him.

'I am so sorry you had to endure the abaddon...along with everything else.'

It was a wonderful surprise when Pitch covered his hand with slight, warm fingers. 'Your coffin can't have been a wondrous thing either.'

Silas grunted and immediately regretted it for the way it jerked his ribs and sent flashes of hot pain scouring through him. 'I don't think of it fondly.'

A wave of dizziness struck, and Silas found himself flailing. The prince hissed his surprise at finding all the ankou's weight upon him suddenly. They staggered a few steps like a pair of drunkards lost on their way home from the pub.

The calamitous melody roared up the corridor behind them. Tenfold louder than it had been.

'Shit, Pitch...' Silas gasped, exhausted by the effort it took to stagger. 'It is much closer.' He tried to peer back down the corridor, but his wounds did not like the movement at all. He took a sharp breath, swearing as well as any sailor. 'We must move faster.'

'Faster may be an issue. What the...well, fuck...that's inconvenient.'

Silas lifted his head, and his knees buckled at the sight.

A steep staircase stood just a few paces up ahead, where a moment ago there had been flat, endless corridor.

'Oh god,' he whispered.

'It's all right, we'll get you up there.' Pitch was steely. 'Come on now.'

Silas faltered, nearly at a stop, and the daemon tugged at him, urging him closer. But just laying eyes upon the narrow steps and sharp incline had his shoulders sagging. He clutched at Pitch, who pulled him along determinedly, but each new footfall jarred at the broken and torn ruin of his back.

'I don't think I –'

'Don't think. It's dreary. Just move with me.' Pitch had a tight hold on Silas's forearm, but his other arm slipped low across Silas's back, bracing against the curve of his arse. His fingers hooked over Silas's hip. 'Is that low enough? Am I clear of the wounds?'

'Yes.' Silas swallowed thickly. He could not take his eyes from the staircase, which disappeared up into shadowy darkness, no landing in sight. He knew what The Atlas had done to him with its stairs, sending him upwards, upwards until he thought his lungs might burst. That day at Mr Ahari's Sanctuary had left him gasping for breath with its test, and he'd been fit as a fiddle.

The pressure of Pitch's arm across his buttocks increased as the daemon braced him. It seemed he intended to push Silas up the stairs.

But there was not even a banister to brace upon. The staircase was slotted between walls covered in a ghastly, elaborate wallpaper. Blue waves curled along the base, while above them flouncy pink birds with necks like snakes stood among brilliant green foliage. Silas raised his foot to the first step, knowing exactly where he'd seen such a print. It had been the cause of Baron Faversham's ill-health, arsenic, if he recalled, being used to create the vivid verdant pattern. A lost soul had shown Silas the way, a young girl who'd begged for the scythe when her life-saving task was done. Silas's first seance, in this reanimation as ankou at least.

It was where he'd first laid eyes upon Tobias Astaroth.

'Bloody hell.' Silas was sufficiently distracted to manage to climb the first few steps. 'Do you see this? The wallpaper?'

Pitch was strained as he replied, 'How could I damned well not? It's an assault on the eyes, terribly garish and vile.'

Silas agreed mostly, but the verdant hue was not so far removed from that of Pitch's eyes, and he thought them astonishingly beautiful. The jarring melody of the approaching teratism brought him back from his wayward musings. The raucous notes were no closer though; the creature had not gained on them. With their pace so near to a standstill, that hardly seemed possible, unless their hunter was so certain of a kill that it was taking its time to stalk them.

Shit...could he be killed in this state? Silas stifled a cough. 'I hoped you could see it too. I thought maybe they were toying with my mind somehow. I'm sure it is the same design I saw in Baron Faversham's residence...where I dealt with my first lost soul.'

'Oh, they are playing with our minds all right. I suppose Macha thinks herself very clever, adding little pieces of our past to this pissy attempt at a Sanctuary.' Pitch's arm tightened against Silas's backside as the ankou wavered, light-headed suddenly. 'Take it easy, Sickle.'

Silas shifted his weight closer to the wall, fingers nearly clawing at the wallpaper, as though the smooth surface might give him some purchase. The daemon was doing a damned good job of keeping him going, but he did not wish to burden him any more than necessary.

'We are being hunted.'

'Yes,' Pitch agreed easily. 'There is likely no way out of here, save for the one I could burn for us.' He raised his tone, placing a question there subtly.

'No.' Silas's toe clipped the next step, but he barely staggered as Pitch quickly steadied him. 'There's no telling how much of you that would demand.'

God damn it, how he wished his skin and bones would knit quicker. He was useless to the daemon in this state, and it was infuriating. He shrugged his shoulders, as much to shake off the needling melody that followed behind them as to shift against the strange twinges and pinches that came at his back. He *was* mending, he knew it, but it was far too bloody slow.

They climbed. And climbed some more, and even Pitch was muttering about his thighs and the infernal things he would do to the Child of Melusine who had made this place when a thought struck Silas, defying even the calamitous noise filling his head.

'Harvington Hall,' he said in a rush.

'Stay with me, Silas. Keep your wits,' Pitch replied. 'We are not at the hall.'

'That's not what I mean.' Silas planted his feet and edged about gingerly to face the wall, forcing Pitch to move onto the step above and bend awkwardly so he might still keep his arm about Silas. 'The walls...the spectre showed me how to move through them.'

'You have just thought of this now?' Pitch said, exasperated. 'We've been walking for hours.'

'A slight exaggeration, and I was preoccupied with trying to keep my ribs from skewering my lungs.'

Silas was snide, but he'd not deny it felt as though they had trekked across the damned Sahara by now. His face was damp with sweat, glistening with the effort of ceaseless climbing. He darted a glance down the staircase, where the steps sank down into a pit of shadows. Any trace of the corridor was gone. He squinted, peering into the gloom that clung like a fog over a field, hiding all beneath. There might have been a swirl of movement there in the bleak depths.

'Wait...do you see down –'

'Shit, Silas!'

He had leaned forward, teetering dangerously. The prince grabbed at him, trying to find purchase as Silas tottered.

And Pitch's fingers sank deep into flayed flesh.

Silas's punished lungs released a sound that trembled between a roar and a scream. So loud it succeeded for an instant in drowning out the drumming notes of the teratisms below.

'Fuck, fuck. Gods, Silas I'm sorry.' Pitch had already withdrawn the offending hand and darted to stand one step below Silas, both hands pressed to his chest to prop him upright. The fingers on his left hand held a gory glove of red.

'I'm fine.' Sweet lord, he was nothing of the kind. Tears blurred his vision.

'And a fucking terrible liar.'

Panting, his body shaking, Silas shook his head. The white blur at the edges of his vision faded as the pain subsided. 'They are close, Pitch... We have to find a way out of here.' He wiped at the tears. 'We can't follow the path being set us here...but perhaps...I can...'

Silas pulled himself upright, trying to grapple his thoughts into something more coherent than panic. At the hall, he'd been desperate to find Pitch, and no wall could have stopped him.

He was desperate here. Perhaps it was enough. Silas pressed both hands to the wallpaper, which stilled the trembling in them at least. He splayed his fingers, gritted his teeth, and focused on the black-tipped beak of one of the birds in the wallpaper.

'Silas? I don't think you can glare a hole in the bloody thing.'

He shrugged off Pitch's attempt to move them both on and leaned his weight into his hands. 'You will not keep us,' he whispered.

'Oh gods, Mercer. A thoughtful idea, but you are not so large you can shoulder your way through a wall, especially not in a place like this.'

'I found you at the hall.' Silas blinked. He'd found Pitch through sheer desperation. *Do not stop when it seems you must,* the spectre's words as he urged Silas to overcome the barriers put before him and find the daemon. *If you wish to reach him, you must keep going.*

His overwhelming desire to reach Pitch had driven Silas then. He needed such a passion now. Silas closed his eyes, drew a stuttered breath, and allowed himself to think of Charlie. Of the lad lying in the glass coffin, so still and quiet.

He imagined it was death there, and not slumber.

He imagined Charlie gone.

A quiet fury bubbled along with a stinging grief, and the sweat on his face all at once felt dreadfully cold. He pictured the corpse of the lad in his mind, letting the spears of grief drive into him. The pain of mourning trumped anything the Dullahan's whip could deliver.

Silas's fingertips sank into the wall, through the arsenic-embellished wallpaper.

The teratisms' refrain grew louder, a clatter and bang of nonsensical notes like the orchestra had lost all semblance of sanity. He felt Pitch shift beside him and heard the daemon curse beneath his breath.

'My dear,' he said. 'We have to go. I think your monsters are here.'

A heated tear slid down Silas's face, and his hands sank from sight. He was buried to his wrists in the wall. The staircase shuddered beneath his feet, a great weight setting upon them.

The bone-jarring cries of the teratisms rang again, and he felt Pitch startle. The daemon heard the Blight's creatures now too.

'Silas, if we are going, we go now.'

'Hold on to me.' The wallpaper curled in torn licks around his arms, as though seeking to tear itself away from his invasion.

'Hold on to you?'

'Quickly, Pitch.' He pulled one arm free of the wall and grabbed at the daemon, catching the lip of his corset, gripping it tightly. Pitch let out a startled cry, noticing for the first time Silas's arm sunk into the wall, nearly up to the elbow now.

'Fuck, Silas, what –'

'It's all right, Pitch.' The stairs shook with the thump of heavy foot-falls, the groan of timber mixing with the calamitous songs. 'Don't let go of me. Stay close.'

'Of course.'

Pitch trusted him easily, readily, and Christ, it made the ankou tremble. The prince found his place beneath Silas's arm, and his warmth chased away the chill.

Silas shut his eyes and fell once more into his well of sorrow, floating in the embrace of death, feeding on her exquisite agonies as he thought on his friend, taken too soon. Silas allowed his grief to coax from him the spectre that he was. The Nephilim spectre he had been for thousands of years. He'd forgotten it all. But he remembered so much more now.

He was death's messenger.

He was Samyaza's monstrous creation. A forging of skin and bone and angelic ambition.

An anomaly of life and death.

Silas swept an arm about the daemon and gathered up his slight but weighty body, fairly certain he'd lifted Pitch off his feet, but he needed him close. He wanted to feel him living and breathing against him. He knew exactly who he was around the daemon prince. A protector. Guardian.

The teratisms shrieked, and the walls shuddered. Silas did not waver from his introspection, eyes shut fast. He could count their number now.

Three calamitous, contorted ghouls came for him. He glimpsed them in the darkness behind his eyelids. Sallow and pitted faces, haggard with the bereavements that had transformed them into inhuman tragedies.

'Hold tight, my dear,' he whispered to the prince, who nestled in tighter against him.

Silas edged himself so that he would meet the wall first, and with teeth bared, he drove them both into it.

CHAPTER 25

P itch pushed up against the ankou as the teratisms lurched out of the darkness. Claws that would have made Black Annis wild with envy swiped at his ankle, nicking thin skin. He swore, but the curse didn't have time to leave his lips before they were slamming into the wall.

Or, as the case may be, *not* slamming into the wall. Silas clutched him close and drove them into the tasteless wallpaper. There was no neck-jarring, skull-cracking thump of their bodies against it. The wall seemed to give way, the air pressure altering as though a door had been opened somewhere and a powerful draught let loose.

It turned out that moving through the walls of a Sanctuary was as unappealing as it sounded.

Pitch retched, stomach rolling. He was dizzier than when Jane had swept him up in a whirlwind after discovering he'd stolen a pair of her favourite heels.

What would the air elemental think of her favourite ankou now? Likely far too much. For Silas was astonishing. He was dragging them both through a fucking wall...in a Sanctuary no less...like they were mere beams of light through glass.

A pity it was not more pleasant.

The world was a blur and came with the unpleasant sensation of tiny insects upon the skin, crawling all over him, up his nostrils, skittering across his eyeballs. The toe-curling sensation was momentary, thank the gods. Their surrounds rushed back in, frigid and gloomy. Their momentum sent them staggering across a narrow, compact room, towards a looming wall of grey stone.

Instinct had Pitch shrinking in on himself, raising his arms to protect his face from striking the rough surface. But Silas stole any need for that when he angled himself at the last minute and took the brunt, his shoulder and hip taking the impact that loosened stones and dust from the wall. They rebounded, and Silas's knees went from under him. Pitch grabbed his arm – he'd not risk touching anywhere else again – and tried to ensure the ankou's fall was steady and measured.

'Are you all right?' Silas didn't even give the daemon a chance to fuss before he himself was at it.

'Yes, yes.' Pitch could still feel the odd sensation of movement beneath his skin. Even the beast at his core seemed to dislike it, hunkering down deep in its pit, seeking distance. A boon. One less discomfort for a body that was filled with them. 'I'm fine. And you? Let me look at you.'

The only illumination came through cracks in a wooden door behind them, the peachy hue of distant candlelight. He took Silas's chin, tilting his head up until he could catch the light. The ankou's face wrinkled with a grimace.

'I just need a moment to gather myself, that's all.' He gave Pitch a weak smile. 'Are you sure you have no ill effects?'

'I'm quite sure.' He'd not mention the crawling skin nor that the watch pin was doing all manner of unpleasant things, and the halo wound was mumbling through the weakening of the amuletum.

Silas studied him a long moment before he turned his attention to the room, apparently satisfied the daemon was not cracked nor chipped any worse than before. He seemed to be searching for something. Pitch could see the exact moment when Silas realised it was not here to be found, for he shrank a little, deflated by what he was missing.

'What is it?' Pitch asked.

The silence in the compact space hung like a shroud. Every breath they took was evident.

Silas shrugged, planting one of his wide hands upon the stonework, readying to stand. 'I just...I thought maybe...Charlie might be here.'

'Why would you think that?' The question was said too curtly. There was something between Silas and Charlie that left Pitch feeling...well, damn it...not so front and centre as the ankou normally made him feel. Pitch had developed a taste for Silas's silly fond looks, and he did not like sharing them with others.

'I thought I needed something to focus on...like I did at Harvington Hall when I searched for you.' Silas used Pitch's shoulder to brace himself, and together they got him to his feet. 'So, I thought of Charlie. And I had hoped...maybe I might –'

'Find him.'

'Yes.'

Pitch breathed through a wave of guilt. Silas was bereft, and here he was lamenting not being at the centre of the ankou's world for a brief moment. Gods. 'Well, did you find me straightaway? At the hall?'

He almost applauded himself when he saw a little brightness return to Silas's face. 'No. No, I didn't. It took quite a few attempts to reach you.'

'Then we just do it again... Well, *you* do it again, whatever the blazes it was that you did. How is it you can walk us through walls?'

Silas cleared his throat. 'I don't understand the how entirely, but I know why.' He paused and did not seem happy, despite his marvellous talent. 'When I am as I am now, in between lives, I am neither here nor there. I am neither corporeal nor ethereal. I rest somewhere in between. I have no idea how I brought you along with me. I wasn't sure it would work. All I knew was that I had to have you there, that I wasn't leaving you behind.'

A new warmth slid beneath Pitch's skin to hear it. 'Well, shall we do it again?'

Silas picked at a hangnail. 'I don't think I can. It takes energy...like being out in the sun too long on a summer's day. I feel weak now...well, weaker than before. I don't want to risk us ending stuck in a wall because I've run out of puff.'

'Not high on my agenda either, I assure you. I'm more than happy to walk.'

Silas turned, dragging his hand over the wall's uneven stone. The room was barely bigger than Pitch's water closet at Holly Lodge. And even though Lady Satine's builder had been uncommonly generous with dimensions there, it was not a place one would choose to linger.

'Walk to where?' Silas exhaled. 'Tunnelling through a wall is one thing. Finding where they have Edward held is entirely another.'

'And Charlie,' Pitch said forcefully. 'Charlie can be saved yet, Silas.'

A muscle fluttered in the ankou's jaw. 'We must hope so.'

Pitch stood just enough behind him to see the utter disrepair of his back. There was slight improvement, if one squinted. Not so much hint of deeper muscle, perhaps bone, on display. But the strips of skin were still far too loose, the wetness of the blood too evident. And some deeper gouges trembled like tiny jellies when he moved. The shreds of Silas's shirt hung at his sides like a woman's used rags.

Pitch was struck by an uncommon desire to find his way to Silas's side, to tend to him. But he held still. What he was looking at was the result of becoming too close to begin with. Silas might have escaped the lashing if the Alp had not informed her masters the ankou was the way to piercing a daemon's heart.

And what riled him most? The three-penny-upright whore had known it first.

'Do you think you have the means to find him?' Silas made his way, alone, about the small space, using the wall as his crutch. He was presumably headed towards a crude door set opposite to where they stood. He didn't seem to trust himself to walk unaided the three or four strides needed to reach it. 'We don't know for sure they are even still in the asylum. The illusion could have them anywhere.'

'He is here.' Pitch was firm. The tug of the watch was far too bloody irritating for it to be otherwise.

Silas turned. 'You are sure?'

Pitch nodded. 'Very much so.' He moved to where Silas had paused against the wall, and tried not to think too much on how those few steps seemed to exhaust the ankou. Time, he'd said. Silas just needed some time. 'But before you get your hopes up, it's not exactly ringing out a Morse code with directions.'

'But could it, do you think?' Silas asked. 'Where is it hidden?'

Pitch took Silas's hand and placed it over where the watch lay beneath his skin. Silas winced with understanding. 'Very well. Do you think...if you listened closely enough...you might learn more from it?'

'I doesn't work like that,' Pitch returned, oddly irritated by the line of questioning. It was a decent enough suggestion.

Silas took his other hand from the wall and laid it gently against Pitch's cheek. 'Do not take this the wrong way.' Pitch tensed, for nothing good ever came from such a sentence. 'But is there a chance you are choosing not to listen?'

'What bloody –'

'Please, Pitch, hear me out.' Silas was close, and the rusty hint of blood came with him. 'I know how much this whole quest of ours disturbs you. And I do not in any way blame you for that. I'd be as furious as you to be in such a position. I wish I had had the balls to refuse to allow Lucifer to set foot in our cottage.'

Our cottage. All manner of pleasant tingles joined Pitch's general discomfort. 'Don't be a fool.'

Silas brushed his thumb over Pitch's cheekbone. 'That proves difficult for me.' Another of his watery smiles. The smears of darkness beneath his eyes were like makeup gone awry. 'You are frightened of finding him. You are angry at the angel. I understand. And you are powerful, my dear. So very beautifully so. Might it be possible that the watch could lead you, if you chose to allow it?'

How easy it would be to snarl and throw the tantrums he was renowned for were he standing before anyone else. Pitch stabbed back the flicker of anger, ushering it back to its corner. He had no need for it here, because the ankou was not so terribly off the mark. From the moment Lucifer handed him Seraphiel's gift, Pitch had been filled with the impulse to run. As far away as he could. To vanish into the human world, find an opium den, and smoke himself out of contention for any mad attempts to set right a wrong done so long ago.

He was frightened. Very much so. He was angry on a level that even he could barely fathom and struggled to banish thoughts of what lay inside him. What Seraphiel might have placed there, violating him every bit as terribly as the Alp had done.

Pitch's fear and anger could very well make him his own worst enemy here.

'Perhaps you are right.' He was as quiet as the tombs Silas relished.

The ankou squeezed his arm. 'I find no happiness in that, I assure you. But if there is a way, I know you will find it. And I shall not give up the search for Charlie. We will find them. I'll not think otherwise.'

A coughing fit had him pulling his hand from where it warmed Pitch's cheek. Silas hacked and spluttered, but the attack was brief. He exhaled. 'That didn't hurt so terribly this time. A good sign, I'd say.'

Pitch tipped his head in a noncommittal way. The ankou could not see what he saw, the pulpy mess upon his back that was far from healed.

Silas gestured towards the door. 'This place feels very' – he searched for the word – 'unfinished, don't you think?'

'There is certainly no refinement here,' Pitch agreed.

The door was crudely built, like something a hermit living in the deepest forest might fashion. The wood bulged as though water-damaged in places and did not fit well into its arch. Soft light seeped through large splits at its centre.

'Do you recognise this room? It is no place I know.' Silas looked to Pitch. 'Or is this perhaps the true state of this Sanctuary, without the illusions?'

'It could well be.' But something of the place was vaguely familiar. It was not an Arcadian structure certainly, and really it could be any of a number of ruins or old castles in the British Isles. 'You may have upset Palatyne with your wall trick. The Child did not have much time to make our cage for us, Macha said as much.'

Silas made the odd decision to try to open the door. Odd because he was barely managing to stay upright and looked pale to the point of translucent. Pitch had to bite his tongue to stop from telling him to be careful. He'd be damned if he was going to be the fusspot here, but truly Silas's back was a wretched sight.

The ankou caught him looking. 'Is it that ghastly still?'

'I'm afraid so. And bleeding quite badly.'

Silas made a face, nodding his head. 'It does not seem to be healing as quickly as I'd like. Perhaps it's the fae magick in the Dullahan's whip.'

'You're an expert on these things now?'

'Knowledgeable, not expert. My experiences at the greensward seem to have rattled things loose in me.' He paused as though to catch his breath. 'I wonder...could the wounds be cauterised?'

'With what? Do you have a hot poker in your pocket I don't know about?'

'I thought...maybe...you could use your flame.'

'You want me to set fire to your open wounds?'

'Cauterise...not set fire, thank you. The procedure is simple. Humankind has used it for centuries.'

Pitch shook his head in astonishment. 'Not using the creation fire from beneath the Ophanim throne, they haven't.' He glowered. 'And certainly not using a flame that's been manipulated by a lunatic angel. I'm not burning you, Silas. Don't be an idiot. You don't want me for your nursemaid, I assure you. You said yourself you just need time.'

Pitch edged around the ankou, pushing at the door, which swung open easily for him. He stepped out into a tunnel with the same rough stone walls, only here there were lit torches set along the way. And it struck him again, the sense of familiarity with this setting.

Silas followed after him, dragging his stupid idea with him. Actually, it was not a terrible idea at all, only the suggested execution was awful.

'Here.' Pitch flourished a hand towards the wall. 'I can grab a torch and set it to your back, if you like?'

'You know that's not how it works. We'd need a cautery. Could you not use your hand, your fingers perhaps?' His slight shrug said he was not any surer of this than Pitch.

'How much blood have you lost, Mercer? You are talking nonsense.' Though not entirely. The idea was not without some merit.

'A great deal, I think. I'm starting to hear voices. Will you not consider it?' Then Silas cut right to the chase. 'You just need to tell me if it is too much for you. I know that encounter with the Dullahan must have taxed you.'

'It's not too much. I'm not a helpless fop.'

'Then you do not trust yourself to do it?' He was gentle with the accusation.

Pitch whirled to face him, stepping up close now so he could hiss his reply. 'No. I do not. Not here. They are seeking to unhinge us, Silas. Unhinge *me*. There is too much uncertainty.' He stared up at Silas. He was so close to the ankou that Silas's breath caressed Pitch's forehead. There had been a subtle change in Silas since the greensward, a hardening of his resolve. He was not so afraid as he'd been, not of their enemies at least. But sometimes Pitch thought he caught a glimpse of a different sort of fear lurking in Silas's eyes. The pained glances he sent Pitch every now and then. Silas had learned more of himself than he was saying, and he was not happy about all the memories.

'Pitch, please help me. I can't...' He paused, his eyes taking in every inch of Pitch's face. Silas ran his tongue over his bottom lip before continuing. 'What will unhinge me is anything happening to you while I am stumbling about like an invalid. Christ, Pitch. Failing Charlie is bad enough. Failing you...I'd break, and Izanami herself could not put me back together again.'

Pitch stared at him, mouth agape and his reply a knotted lump at the back of his throat. What the blazes did Silas expect him to say to that? This was not the time for sappiness and sweet nothings. The ankou was certifiable.

'Turn around.' Pitch was hoarse. 'If this hurts, do not blame me.'

'I won't blame you, I promise.' Silas's gentle smile was infuriating. He turned around and planted his hands upon the wall, digging his fingers into the stone, keeping his feet further out so he was tilted at an angle that saw his arse nearer to the centre of the passageway. 'I'm ready.'

Pitch blinked. If he ignored the blood and flayed skin and dire circumstances, the ankou presented quite a picture. One worth returning to if they survived this.

'Pitch?'

'Yes, yes. Gods, are you in that much of a hurry for pain? I didn't peg you for a masochist.'

'Get on with it.' Silas rubbed at his ear. 'Are you hearing anything?'

'Apart from your heavy breathing? No. It's altogether too quiet. Are you?'

'I think so. Whispers. Since we passed through the wall.'

'The teratisms maybe?'

'No. Different to that. There's no melody...' He shook his head. 'Never mind that now. Maybe it's another of Macha's games. I'm ready when you are. Just do what you can, no more.'

Pitch summoned up the flame, bringing it to the tips of his fingers until they glowed as surely as any cautery. He glared at his own power. This rickety, unreliable power that the Morrigan knew was his greatest strength and most formidable weakness. So help him, if they chose now to test him, he would turn the fucking fire on himself and be done with this whole damned mess.

'I'll count to three.'

Silas shifted on his feet but said nothing.

On two Pitch pressed his fingers into the ankou's ravaged flesh. Silas bucked, hissing and whimpering behind pressed lips as Pitch melted his body in the name of repair. The stench was awful, but Pitch kept his breathing measured, his hand steady, for if the ankou must bear the pain, he could at least bear the odour. He touched his fingers to the worst of the bleeds, where the pulse of blood from the vein was visible to the eye, like a tiny water pump at work.

'Oh god.' Silas sagged, his knees threatening to give.

'Steady, almost done.'

Pitch wrapped his free arm around Silas's waist, taking his weight while his fingers danced over the worst of the ankou's wounds, attempting a patchwork repair. Silas endured, allowing himself only the barest of moans, clutching at the wall as though he dangled from a cliff. By the time it was done, they had both sunk to the floor, Silas now clutching at Pitch's arm about his waist, leaving marks sure to bruise.

'It's done, it's done.' Pitch kissed Silas's shoulder, resting his head there as the ankou breathed heavily beneath him. 'Well done.'

'Thank you,' Silas whispered.

'See how terrible the scarring is before you get all thankful.'

Silas pulled his nails from Pitch's arm, reaching back to find the daemon. His hand landed on Pitch's arse, and he gave it a squeeze. Pitch kissed his bloodied shoulder again. The waft of burnt flesh did not manage to stifle Silas's earthy scent entirely.

'We should keep moving,' the ankou said.

'Can you stand?'

'I can.'

Pitch helped him to his feet and tugged one of the torches from its bracket, just in case their hosts decided on plunging them into darkness again. They headed in the only direction afforded to them.

Silas seemed better able to keep up with the pace Pitch set and was not leaning so heavily upon the wall as he went. They walked on. The entire place was silent, and Pitch longed to hear something, anything, that would distract him from what he knew to be true.

That he had led Silas beyond reach of the Order and into intolerable danger.

'Did that cause you any pain?' Silas's voice, coming from close behind, made him jump. 'Using the flame on my back?'

'No.'

'There was no strain on the amuletum?' he whispered.

'No.'

The ankou grunted, clearly not believing a word, but fell back into quietness.

Of course there had been a damned strain on the amuletum. But he was certain Silas wasn't lugging about a vial of the stuff as he'd been on their misadventure to Devon, so why worry him with something that could not be changed?

Pitch needed to choose his use of the flame wisely. The Morrigan, blast them, knew what state he was left in when the beast within slipped its chains. He was less sure they knew of Silas's calming influence in such matters. But if they did, was being left together now just another cruel play? Would they whip the ankou away at the very moment Pitch would need him most? Strike Silas down and then sit back and watch as a Dominion lost his infernal mind?

A touch to his shoulder had Pitch stifling a scream.

'It is just me, it's all right,' Silas said. 'I thought you had stopped because you see it too.'

Pitch had no idea he'd come to a standstill. 'See what?'

'Where they have put us.' Silas pointed slightly upward.

Pitch's gaze first went to the lengths of ivy that coated the walls. The tunnel had given way to an open area with high walls made of imposing stone stretched high above them and no roof in sight. Further along the way lay a great pile of fallen stones, the remnants of a wall that had collapsed, the opening now a gaping hole in the structure. An all-too-familiar place.

'Goodrich.'

'Mm-hm. This is where we climbed in.' As though Pitch might not recognise where he'd carried a trembling ankou on his back.

'We need to keep moving.'

Silas nodded, though he seemed intent on where his fingers dug into the gaps between the pillow-sized bricks. He was thoughtful as he pulled his hand away.

Pitch quickened their pace along the cluttered corridors of Goodrich Castle...or at least, the illusion of the castle. The ivy was memorable enough, clogging up the pathways more and more as they moved, catching at his toes and causing him to trip and curse more than once.

He was not going to dare use the flame to clear a path, tempting as it was.

'Just one moment,' Silas said.

Pitch halted, realising he'd set far too rapid a pace. Silas was a ways back, half a dozen steps or so, but he was upright and seemingly in control of his faculties. He stood with both hands braced against the wall. Or, at least, Pitch supposed it was the wall, for the ankou's hands were hidden beneath the swathe of greenery.

'Do you need to rest?' Pitch glanced up ahead, where there appeared to be a widening of the passageway at last.

'No. I'm fine.' His cauterised wounds were ugly swells of red, but there was no sign of fresh blood flow.

'Then what are you doing?' Pitch's frustration seeped into his words.

The ankou shook his head. 'I can hear something behind these walls. The whispers are real, I'm sure now. The despair...it's...familiar.'

'Despair?'

Silas nodded, standing straighter than he'd done yet since the Dulla-han's attack. 'All of the lost souls have a trace of it, and with the teratisms it's overwhelming.'

'So there are teratisms behind that wall?'

'No. But I believe there are lost souls...a large amount of them.' He cocked his head. 'I'm beginning to wonder if it might explain why it's so bloody quiet upstairs. I think maybe the lost souls are all trapped down here.'

'The dead from the asylum are down here in the Sanctuary?'

Silas had said he thought it strange such a place as Fulbourn had no ghosts, something Pitch had to agree with. If death and despair did not exist there, then it should exist nowhere else.

'Yes...well, perhaps.' Silas adjusted the front of his shirt, which was mostly in one piece, though sweat and pink smears made it cling to his chest. 'Shit, I really don't know for sure. Normally I hear a melody. Maybe this is illusion too.'

'Deception seems to be favoured by the sorceress.' Pitch discarded the torch, the flame all but extinguished, but the ivy held a faint glow, a sickly green that did Silas's unhealthy hue no favours. 'She's likely passing the time sending us on wild-goose chases while she waits for her charming family to arrive and do with us what they will.'

A screech tore through the castle, like that of a pig stepping on a trap.

'Is that one of yours?' Pitch shook his head, trying to dislodge the ringing in his ears.

'I'm afraid so. They've come out of nowhere. I had no chance to tell you before they were on us. They're close.'

Another cry, harsh as sheets of tin dragging against one another, rico-cheted off the stonework.

'You don't say?' Pitch yelled. 'How many?'

Silas clutched at his temples. 'It's distorted... At least two I would guess.'

And likely two too many for a half-recovered ankou.

'Come on, move, Silas.'

Pitch hurried him away from the sound, towards where a ragged arch-way marked the entrance to a grander space that was all too familiar. The cobbled courtyard with its central well held one notable difference from the last time they'd stepped foot in it. There was no prism of glass holding the spirit of the forest hostage. But otherwise, even the lighting was the same, the tint of silver upon everything as though the moon were actually overhead...as it had been that night.

The rasping cries of the teratisms crashed against one another, making the noise infinitely more terrible.

Silas ran panting into the courtyard just behind Pitch. Two other corridors offered escape. The one to the right had, in the true castle, led to where the giant drawbridge had been fastened tight to shield the main entrance. The left was where the archer had stood in the shadows to hurl arrows their way.

'Head to the drawbridge!' Pitch shouted.

'Why?' Silas shouted back, barely heard over the din. 'They are hardly going to let us just walk out the front gate. I can face them.'

Pitch whirled on him. 'You are barely stitched together after the Dullahan, and without the bandalore.'

'What choice do I have?'

A bellow rattled debris loose from the walls. A towering man entered from the passageway that would have led them to the drawbridge. The new arrival was a Silas and a half in height but slender to the point of skeletal. Perhaps a man once, but now he was more akin to something that had been dragged from the bottom of a swamp and then dunked in acid. He had eyes like giant dirty pearls and was caked in a grey-green slime which dripped from hands gnarled and crooked, arthritic as a hundred-year-old man. All his features seemed partly melted. The bottoms of his eyelids dragged down to his cheekbones, earlobes dangling beneath his chin, which in turn was far too long and large to exist on a true man. His hair was no more than duckweed, in desperate need of a trim, brushing at the backs of his knees. He was hideously naked, with a swinging set between his legs, ball sack elongated as though filled with lead. The cock's tip was dark as a gangrenous toe.

'Get behind me, Pitch.' Silas elbowed him out of the way.

'Don't be bloody ridiculous. You need my help.'

250

A shriek that hammered at the eardrums came from the left passage-way. Another similar creature stood there, though this one was plainly female, with breasts like vile pendulums and a tangle of duckweed be-tween the legs that looked like it could snag a man whole.

'You saw how it was with the Verderer. You cannot deal the death blow. Don't waste your energies here.' Silas's command lit the air between them, firm and undeniable. And damn if it wasn't rousing to see the gleam in the ankou's eyes.

'Fine!' Pitch yelled over the racket of the approaching teratisms. 'Still nothing from the bandalore?'

'Nothing. I'll have to do this without it.'

Silas spun about and ran, with no hint of distress, at the dripping menace that approached. The creature moved with far more grace than it seemed capable of, using its long, twisted arms upon the ground to speed its pace, rolling into a gait not unlike that of an ape.

Pitch edged back into an alcove that might have held an ornate sculp-ture at one point. He was infuriated at being set on the sideline but equally as mesmerised by Silas's foolhardy yet stirring assault on the teratism. He was far too busy staring at the ankou to notice the ivy slip about his ankles and wind about his legs. It was halfway up his calves by the time he looked down in alarm and swore.

'What the –' Another strand of the greenery came from higher, slip-ping about his throat. 'Fuck,' he coughed.

Caught unawares, and with the wicked shrubbery moving with aston-ishing speed, he was forced back into the alcove.

Pitch's hands tingled with the pressure of the flame, but the arrow was faster.

It slammed into his chest, the arrowhead piercing a hole right along-side his calamitous heart.

CHAPTER 26

T he daemon's rage-laced cry reached Silas through the cacophony of the teratisms.

'Pitch?' he shouted.

A grunt and then, 'Fine...fine.'

If it were a lie or the truth, Silas could not discern, for he dared not turn his attention away from the disgusting work of the Blight that was upon him. A teratism most foul, one that smelled of ditchwater and rotting fish, a viscous liquid spraying off it as it moved. The creature's tune was higgledy-piggledy, a jumbled mess and just plain wrong. Or at least it reeked of *wrongness*. The clarity was distorted. The melody of the teratisms he'd met before were ripe and clear with consuming grief, full of cracks where the Blight had seeped in and poisoned the soul. This though...this tune was distorted, as though the musician were playing by ear a tune they had once heard but could barely recall.

Not unlike that he'd heard with the Verderer, a teratism unnaturally conceived.

Silas wiped at his face, his hand coming away slime-coated and reeking of maritime decay. Jesus Christ, the Morrigan had grown more adept in manipulating the Blight and had chosen their souls with nefarious intent. He would bet a fortune that this once-mortal soul had met his demise in the water. Death by drowning. The sorcerers were keen to unravel not only the daemon but his ankou too.

And the bandalore was nowhere to be seen to put a swift end to the misery they had created.

Silas balled up his fist and levelled a punch straight into the strange, hanging flesh of the creature's gut. An horrific caterwaul left the teratism. Silas's knuckles sank into the spongy flesh, and the rest of his hand followed. He found himself buried to the wrist in the creature's belly, his fingers encased in a substance that clung to them like hardening mortar.

'Shit.' Silas grunted, trying to wrestle himself free and at the same time fight off the teratism's own wretched hands that clawed and nipped and sliced at him. Though they looked like the hands of a terribly old man, they were strong, and their shortened nails deceptively sharp. Silas danced about, trying to angle himself in such a way that the creature would not find the still-healing wounds upon his back. The other teratism stood not far away, swaying on its feet but showing no sign of attacking. Fear raised the goosebumps on Silas's flesh another inch.

'Pitch? Pitch, where are you?' Silas sought to crane his head to get a glimpse of the courtyard, but the creature had turned him about and stood blocking his view.

'Right here.' A grunt, then a vile curse. Silas had never heard such a sweet sound. The daemon was in control of his faculties enough to reply.

Pitch might have shouted something else, but the teratisms managed to synchronise their horrendous cries this time. It was as though the entire world rocked on its axis, tilted by the unsettling sounds.

Silas pressed his lips tight and dragged his hand free of the teratism's gut. His skin was coated in a thin film of residue, the colour of mould on cheese.

He kicked out at the creature's legs, the violence of the blow sending the gangly limbs out from beneath it. It landed with a thump upon its back. Silas straddled the teratism and hammered his fists at the creature's face, careful not to press too hard lest he found himself up to the elbows in god-awful sludge inside the skull. The blows were swift and punishing, as though his hands now held the strength of the bandalore. When the teratism's eyes rolled back in its head, revealing a hideous veining of red, Silas lunged and wrapped his hands about the narrow neck.

The other teratism bellowed again, though in protest or attack, Silas couldn't tell. He liked to imagine he heard Pitch's hollering there too, but he couldn't be certain.

Silas squeezed the teratism's throat. Something cracked under his fingers, and the teratism writhed beneath him. Silas squeezed harder, and the creature's tune changed to a higher, more desperate key, overpowering the bellows of the second creature.

Damn it, he could not hear the daemon. Pitch should have been shouting all kinds of foul things as he stoushed with the other teratism. Silas dared turn his head, as much to avoid the spittle that flew from the violently shaking creature as to search for the prince.

He ran cold with the horror of what he saw.

Pitch was backed into an alcove, a space barely large enough to contain even his slight figure. He was tangled in the ivy. It wrapped about his neck and legs but teasingly left his arms free.

Free to clutch at the arrows embedded in his chest. Two of them, nearly side by side.

His shirt was soaked through with blood, a deep scarlet that veered towards black in the light of stuttering torches. His face was a mask of confusion, his eyes wild.

'Christ. Pitch.'

The teratism bucked weakly beneath him, in its last throes, while the other stood by, watching the daemon prince pressed into his corner, a cruel smile upon its lips. Silas scanned about wildly for the archer, but the shadows made for drapes in all the corners he could see.

A terrible gurgle came from the teratism he straddled, and Silas tightened his grip. His fingers sank into the melted wet wax of the creature's flesh.

God damn the bandalore for not heeding him. And bloody hell, why would this forsaken creature beneath him not die?

The courtyard lit up with amber-yellow light, the prince's flame burning bright.

'Hang on, Pitch.'

'Fuck, cunts, this ivy...' Pitch cried. 'Tore this castle down once before...do it...again.' He was gasping, spitting with a fury that could so readily consume him.

'Keep calm, Pitch. I'm coming.'

But the light only brightened, harsh enough to have Silas blinking where he clung madly to the teratism's neck.

A ribbon of flame shot out and wrapped around the teratism that stalked the prince, causing it to screech like a cat tangled in carriage wheels. He lifted the creature off its gangly legs, the duckweed swaying and dripping.

The daemon's scream came a moment later.

Another arrow had struck, this time in his thigh. Pitch's eyes blazed like a blacksmith's furnace. He was beyond any semblance of calm. Macha's archer had pushed him towards the edge.

A knot clenched in Silas's chest, dragging at something weighty within and hauling it to the surface.

With a roar, he bore down with all the might the goddess had invested in him. His fingers hit bone, a spinal cord perhaps on this vile manifestation. It crumbled at his touch. He wrenched his arms upwards, and the teratism's head came away, the lengths of duckweed flapping about and catching Silas in the face with the wild swing of his arms.

He thought for a moment he heard a voice at his ear, a whisper so hushed he could make no sense of it. A chill struck him, one that sank into his marrow.

The teratism's crooked melody, faulty and strange, ceased.

But there was no silence.

Fire hissed and popped and crackled, and the teratism screamed its agonies. Pitch held the creature before him like a shield against the archer's arrows, the remnants of the ivy that had bound him now hanging like scarves of charcoal. He had made the contorted soul as much of a fireball as the Dullahan had been. But just as it was with the fae, a daemon's flames offered only temporary eradication of the pest. And with the teratism ablaze, Silas had no hope of getting close enough to cease its existence.

'Set it down!' he shouted, trying to make himself heard over the woeful squeals of the burning soul. 'Stop the fire.'

'Archer!' Pitch shouted back. He tried to take a step, but his arrow-punctured thigh put paid to that, and he went down onto one knee.

Silas dashed towards the daemon, flinching at the pure unrelenting heat that came from the burning teratism. The creature's sky-rending cries had fallen silent. It burned at the centre of Pitch's shield like a grotesque coat of arms.

'Pitch, steady now.'

Every inch of visible skin on the daemon glowed. The emerald in his eyes was entirely submerged beneath the glare of gold.

'Then they best stop shooting fucking arrows at me.' The prince spat a glob of claret that landed near Silas's feet. 'Did you see the archer?' Still holding the burning teratism aloft, he wrenched the remaining arrow from his thigh with his free hand. In his chest, the twin punctures were gelatinous, bloody holes, more disturbing to Silas than his own act of severing a teratism's head with his bare hands.

'I haven't spotted them.' Silas shook his head. 'But they can only be in one of those two passageways.' He gestured, though it was difficult to see much at all through the hovering inferno. 'I was near the third. There was no one there.'

Silas wiped at the cascade of sweat running down his temples. The heat from the flaming corpse was overwhelming, but he kept himself edged as near to Pitch as he could bear, adding another shield to protect the daemon from whoever lurked out there with their nefarious bow and arrows. Arrows that taunted.

And aimed to push a fatigued and fearful daemon to his limit.

'We should head for that passageway,' Silas said. 'Can you run, do you think?'

'And go fucking where?' Pitch's flamed snapped with his irritation. 'If they wish to see how pissed off I can get, then so be it. Stand aside, ankou.'

Silas shuddered at the impersonal naming. The daemon was losing himself.

'Hold on to your temper, Pitch, I beg you.'

'I'm tired of holding back, Mercer.' The flame poured from the prince's fingertips, his upraised arm shaking. 'I don't give a fuck what becomes of this Sanctuary...the asylum...or anyone in it.'

His eyes were entirely consumed now, heated furnaces that could melt any who dared to look into them too long. The prince's rage, and rage it was, rolled off him in searing waves of heat.

Silas could *feel* the prince drifting from him.

'Of course you bloody care.' Silas was steely. 'That is your fury talking, and it does not own you, Pitch. Do not *let* it rule you.'

Pitch glared at Silas, and it was so bloody hard to stare into that sun. A rippling beneath the prince's skin contorted his features, as though the beast he spoke of, the wildness he feared was not entirely his but something placed there, lurked just beneath the surface, seeking escape.

'Don't you dare lose yourself, Tobias. You must not be overcome...by any of them.' Suddenly Silas was furious – at the Morrigan, at the daemon for not fighting harder, at himself for the very same fault. Silas grabbed Pitch's collar and shook him. 'God damn it, Pitch. You are stronger than any blasted angel or sorcerer. I've seen it. I know it. Do not leave me. I'll not lose you. I cannot.'

The prince's expression changed at once from murderous to disoriented. Traces of jade pierced through the furnaces. He blinked like he'd been staring too hard at his own flame. And the torrent of fire coming from his extended hand stuttered, the burning shell of the teratism dipping almost to the ground.

'Why are you shaking me?' His temper still crawled beneath his words, but Silas was not a pile of cinders, so there was that.

Silas exhaled a lengthy breath. 'I thought you'd kill me for sure if I slapped you.'

'Too right.' Pitch's eyes widened. 'Look out!'

He slammed himself against Silas, throwing the much larger man off his feet. What seemed like an army of arrows whisked overhead, one catching at the hairs atop Silas's head as he was hurled sideways. Pitch discarded his teratism shield and let loose with bursts of flame from each hand, merciless fireballs that lit up the courtyard. In the brilliant glare, Silas caught a glimpse of a figure standing in the archway that was the target of Pitch's assault. Clad in black of course, masked as well, the only difference here was their shield. The colour of bone and just as dull, but the black lines carved into it gleamed like polished onyx, the sigils all too clear.

Despite the hurtling, oncoming flames, they did not move.

As the glare brightened, the stonework around the archer shimmered, duplicating itself, knitting fragmented pieces together in a blur of movement.

Pitch's flames hit a solid wall of brick and were immediately repelled.

'Oh shit.' Pitch dove in front of Silas, placing himself in the way of the roaring returned daemonic flame. He raised his arms out to his sides, both limbs entirely on fire, forming a barrier behind which Silas stared, gobsmacked and dripping with sweat. The heat was phenomenal. He should have covered his head, perhaps cowered a little. But Silas could not drag his eyes away. And the daemon would never let him burn.

Pitch's returning flame struck him. The prince staggered. There was a hissing sound, like water poured on hot coals, as the returned fire was absorbed back into the prince and sank back down to wherever it lay within him. Pitch grunted, found his feet, and extinguished the barrier. Now there was nothing but the soft crackle of the burning teratism, the creature twitching where it lay.

Silas got to his feet slowly, wanting to touch the daemon but filled with the sense that it was best to keep his distance for now. He peered around Pitch's still-outstretched arms. Smoke billowed from an enormous scorch mark upon the wall. But it was a wall no longer reminiscent of Goodrich Castle. Now it was entirely nondescript, simple red brickwork with mortar bulging like grey worms in places.

Pitch pressed his hands to his knees, gasping, and Silas forgot the change at once.

'Can I touch you?' he asked quietly.

A nod was the reply.

Gratefully, Silas laid an arm across the daemon's shoulders, holding him steady. Good god, the heat coming from the prince's skin was enough to warm a room on a middle-winter's day. His slender neck was riddled now with scratches from the ivy, along with the kitsune's fading bite. His shirt held two awful polka dots of red where the arrows had embedded so close to his heart, the blood flow making strange tie-dye patterns on the once-white material which clung to the corset beneath.

'Tell me there was no Gu on those arrows.' Silas's stomach turned at the idea.

Pitch grunted and shook his head. Ash flew from his hair. 'No. I suppose I should be grateful for that.'

Silas tucked his finger beneath Pitch's chin, needing to look in his eyes. Verdant irises greeted him, barely a trace of ember in their depths. A tilted, unsure smile rose on Pitch's face.

'I'm still with you, Sickle.'

Likely it was too rough for the stained and gasping daemon, but Silas wrapped him in his arms and kissed him hard, tasting grit and ash and divine bittersweetness. He pulled back, just an inch, and whispered into the warm space between them.

'My heart.'

Silas froze. Christ, had he said that out loud?

Pitch raised his head, Cupid's bow lips still perfect, despite the ruin of the rest of him, and damp with Silas's kiss. 'What did you just call –'

'I said...my heart cannot take much more of this place.' Silas tugged at the rags of his shirt, the strips plastered to his damp body. 'Let's move on.'

And pretend he'd not just let his tongue run away with him.

The daemon gave him an odd look and brushed off Silas's attempts to assist him. 'Do you not see they are running us like rats in their maze? Just like Macha wished. The necromancer and her Child are deciding our every turn.'

Silas glanced at the brickwork, a strange scar against the rougher grey stone of the castle, as though it had been patched up badly and without any regard for the original materials. And blast if he did not hear those whispers again, coming from behind it.

'Macha is not deciding everything.' He stalked across the courtyard, up to the red bricks to where the daemon's flame had left a sooty mark of night black. Silas pressed his hands to the wall. His fingers were sticky with what was left of the teratism.

He listened, eyes closed, dipping himself into the bleakness behind his lids, seeking out the hint of desolation and despair that seemed closer to him now. Clearer.

He ran his hands over the space where the entrance to the passageway had gaped not so long ago.

There. Faint but sure, as though the sound were the very last resonance of an echo. Silas dug his fingers into the blackened wall.

'What is it?' Pitch asked, coming to stand behind him.

'I can hear lost souls again... I think perhaps they know I am here.' He glanced at the ashen remains of one teratism, the pulled-apart ruins of the other. 'There was something very wrong with the songs of those. I wonder...' Silas swallowed. For century after century the cursed halo had found those most vulnerable among the souls, those with all-consuming rage and resentment, and slowly poisoned them. Turning them into monsters. The Morrigan were meddling with that process. They'd been testing it with the Verderer. But had they perfected it here?

'You wonder what, Silas?' Pitch was busy with wrapping a torn strip of his shirt about the wound on his leg.

Silas balled his fists, too preoccupied to answer.

These were *his* lost souls. Silas was their guide, their light in the darkness, the goddess's messenger. He could give them resolution and peace, but Macha was stealing that from them.

From him.

'Silas?'

Silas felt Pitch's warmth before the daemon reached his side. 'She is not just stealing corpses,' Silas said quietly. 'She has been gathering souls too. There are so many of them here...too many to be natural. And those teratisms that attacked us...they were...wrong. They were not as the others I've met.' He paused. 'She is making them. The Verderer was not an anomaly. She is striving to create teratisms. If ever there was a hell, then we have found it.'

A heated hand was placed over his. 'And I dare say they'd like to keep us in it. But could not a horde of lost souls be of use to you? You seem quite popular with them.' He flung his hand towards the decapitated teratism.

'When they've not reached the stage where you need to rip their heads off.' He raised his eyebrows. 'That was quite the display, my dearest.'

But Silas was distracted by his horde of lost souls.

'Suppose they can tell us something of this Sanctuary? Perhaps even the part of it where Charlie and Edward lie?'

'You are the ghost whisperer, that's for you to learn. Do you want to drag us through this wall?'

'I think it is the way we should go, yes.'

Pitch sighed. 'Wall walking is not pleasant, I have to say.'

'There's something I must do first though.'

Silas left him to move quickly to where the teratism still smouldered. All sign of flames were gone, but a smoke the colour of dishpan water lifted from the body, dirtying the air. The teratism's dreadlocks of duckweed had burned clear, and the head was nothing but the stark white of an exposed skull. Actually that could be said of most of the creature's body, a skeletal ruin. But the hands still twitched, the body jerking and shuddering. True death had not yet come.

He knelt at the side of the teratism. It was odd how the burned flesh did not smell truly wretched. The creatures had smelled far worse when dripping with the horrors of the Blight's contortions. Silas placed his hands just below the exposed jaw. He flicked his wrists and pulled away at the same time, his formidable strength severing the head from the spine in one quick motion. He set down the head gently, cleaned off his hands, and moved back to Pitch.

'Is that what shall happen to me if I step out of line again?' he quipped.

'Macha has tormented that soul long enough. I'll not see her monsters being made to suffer any longer than they must.'

The prince's full lips pressed into a thin line. Silas flinched. Replace Macha with Seraphiel, and he could have been talking about Pitch.

The sharp clip of hooves upon cobblestones rang out, and the high whinny of a horse bounced along the only remaining passageway on the far side of the courtyard. Gooseflesh rose along Silas's arms.

'The Dullahan...again already?'

'Fuck.' Pitch wrapped his hands about his middle. 'Silas, I can't face him right now, nor can you. And if he catches me too weakened, there's a chance...'

Silas stared at him. 'Surely that was puerile nonsense spoken about the Dullahan claiming you for the Erlking?' He waved his hand near the faint wound on Pitch's neck. The kitsune's attack and Macha's talk of Pitch's oath to the bluecap queen being owned now by the Erlking had come as he'd barely clung to consciousness after the Dullahan's whipping. It was all terribly vague. 'I don't recall precise details about the Unseelie Court –'

'Well, I assure you, all fae are ridiculously precious about oaths made to them, and the Unseelie particularly so.'

'You are too strong for them surely –'

'Not always.' Pitch set his teeth into the words. 'You of all people know that. And if the Erlking has played a part in keeping the sorcerers hidden from the Order for untold years, I am not keen to test the limits of what else his court is capable of right now. Are you moving us through the wall or not?'

Silas braced against the wall, which felt less like coarse brick and more like a dry sponge beneath his palms. This time he did not hesitate. There was no need. There was no time.

He honed in on the wail of the lost souls and allowed their despair to fill his senses. With shoulders set and the daemon tucked at his side, Silas pushed into the red brick.

The Sanctuary worked against him, a thick, syrupy sensation that pushed and fought back, refusing to be manipulated by him.

But it was not enough.

There had been a shift within, strengthening him. Silas had felt it with the snap of the first teratism's neck. Like a rusted lock finally giving way to the insistent jostling of a key.

They fell through the wall, barely keeping their feet as it gave way and tumbled them into a small room, wood beneath their feet, the cobbles vanished. Silas kept his arm about the prince, aware he may need to rush them on again.

A simple bedroom lay before them, where a single window was covered by a thin length of cloth, making the room dim. There was a low chest of drawers with a tarnished mirror opposite a wood-framed bed set over a rug of startling white fur. Upon the mattress, a figure lay flat upon his back, naked as the day he was born, with arms splayed as though he'd fallen, exhausted, and not bothered to settle in properly. His fists were tight bunches, one grasping at the corner of a pillow that lay askew. The sheet beneath him was rumpled and had tugged free of one of the corners, while a top sheet tangled itself around his lower legs. He lay with his head turned away from them, the hair about his temples flecked with grey and damp against his skin. His member, only half slackened, was such a pronounced shade of pink that Silas could not help but notice it nor the dampness upon the skin that glistened under the glow of a sagging cluster of candles perched on a mantel over a small fire.

Silas averted his eyes, mortified by what felt like a blatant intrusion upon a very intimate moment. In looking away, his eyes fell upon Pitch. He frowned at the uncertain horror writ upon his face.

'Pitch?'

'Shit.' The prince tried to free himself from Silas's hold. 'Let me go, damn it.'

'What is it?'

'Not what...who.' Pitch pulled from Silas's slackened grasp and took a couple of limping steps towards the bed.

'Pitch, be careful.' The room held a stifled but scentless air he did not like. The fire in the hearth did not dance as it should either. The flames were too bolt upright, like stiffened orange soldiers. 'We cannot trust this place.'

'I'm aware.' His voice was tight. He took another step but did not place his boots on the pristine white fur rug. 'Edward?'

Silas took a startled step forward, moving so he might see more of the man's face, trying to stifle the silly flicker of something akin to jealousy that came with Pitch recognising the lieutenant so intimately.

The man shifted, and Pitch stepped back. The supine man rolled onto his side, and Silas sucked in a harsh breath. There was no doubt it was Edward, though the man looked more hollowed out than when Silas had last seen him. The shadows beneath his grey eyes were darker, certainly, and he'd lost enough weight about his face to make his cheeks sink in above the rough scraggle of three-day growth.

'Tobias.' The lieutenant pressed a hand into the mattress and made his wobbly way onto his knees. The rattle of a chain marked his lethargic movement, and the sheet slipped, baring his legs and revealing a shackle around one ankle. 'You're here at last. I've been waiting for you. I knew you'd come.'

He lifted his arms, reaching towards Pitch, who had moved no further. The daemon barely seemed to be breathing. In turn, Edward's eyes were unfocused, and he swayed as he knelt there, causing his stiffened cock to rub against his belly. Silas blinked, unsure if the man had been quite so aroused a moment ago. There were scratches too that Silas must have missed in his haste to offer some modesty by looking away. They scoured the man's belly, his chest, and worst of all, his collarbones. They were crescent-shaped wounds, the unmistakable pinch of fingernails. Silas bit his lip, feeling heat seep into his blood. He'd seen such marks before. He glanced at the daemon. The Alp had sullied Pitch's body with the same cruel cuts.

Silas's chest tightened. It was hard to breathe. Nearly impossible to hold on to a modicum of calm. No wonder the prince held himself so rigid.

'Do you see where we are, Silas?' Pitch said, holding on to each word as though they were horses threatening to bolt.

Silas glanced about the room again and grimaced, spotting the hole in the wall to his left. One that would afford anyone in the neighbouring room a fine view of the goings-on in here. He'd not looked hard enough when they first arrived, but he saw where it was the Sanctuary wished them to believe they were.

The Moon Inn.

'I see it now.'

If the peephole were not enough, the unusual carving of the bedhead, all rough whirls and knots, certainly was. It had been carved as though the maker sought to make the room seem more refined than it could ever be. His room had held one similar. They knew already that the sorcerers had visited the place, asking questions of Mabel that the lass had not hesitated to answer. But this was a well-timed reminder that the Sanctuary was a place of illusion, enjoying every moment of its game with them.

He regarded Edward anew. The last they had seen of him, he'd been sleeping in a glass coffin. There was a chance he'd been revived and brought here to taunt them, but why would they give up their prize so easily? Far more likely this version of the lieutenant, the one bearing Pitch's wounds, was a very cruel illusion.

'Pitch, what sense do you have of him?' Silas kept his words low, for the daemon alone. Hoping perhaps the watch hidden upon him might shed them some light.

The prince opened his mouth to answer.

'Tobias!' Edward cried. 'Why are you just standing there? Don't leave me here another moment, I beg you.' The lieutenant's voice shivered dangerously, his eyes glassy. He clutched at the sheet, pulling it to him but managing not to cover himself any better than before, leaving his wounds and arousal on equal display. 'She uses me...I am her slave, and I cannot bear it. You know whom I speak of. And she is not so kind to me as she was to you at Gidleigh House.'

Silas took an enraged step forward, and Pitch stopped him with a firm hand. The lieutenant shuffled towards the edge of the mattress.

'Do you not see how she hurts me?' He let the sheet fall away, revealing inner thighs running with thin rivulets of scarlet.

Silas gaped, repulsed by the abuse it suggested, caught up in the sheer horror of it before his sense kicked back in. Illusion. His gaze flitted to the sheets. Rumpled but unstained. The deception had not been thorough enough.

'She says you are to blame, Tobias, for refusing to submit. Now I must endure what was meant for you. It does not stop. She allows me no peace, and I cannot take much more. You know though, don't you, Tobias? What it is like? To be held down...to be forced against your will. You should have stayed on your back for her, Tobias. You are stronger than I. And now I suffer in your stead.'

Pitch swayed as though he'd been struck. He made a strange, garbled sound, and glints of amber yellow quickened on his palms.

Macha and her Alp daemon were beyond abhorrent with this. Their cruelty was breathtaking. And precisely placed if they wished to see a prince come undone.

Silas thrust himself between Pitch and the lying atrocity upon the bed. 'Shut your fucking mouth!' He grabbed the creature, clamping down on thin, bare shoulders. 'Say another word, you piece of piss, and I'll break your jaw. It would have served you well to know the true Edward Charters, then perhaps you'd not have failed so miserably to mimic the man.'

Edward would never have brought himself to say such brutal things. Silas had seen the way Edward Charters looked at Tobias Astaroth. It was nothing like this strange, vapid yet fevered stare, which began to subtly alter as Silas's crushing grip deepened on his shoulders. The smoky grey of the lieutenant's eyes had once caused Silas to recall a lost memory of smoke curling from an autumn bonfire, laughter and music from company long vanished. But now it leaked away, seeping from the gaze of the impostor and leaving a thin remainder of colour that could not conceal the depths beyond, dark and fathomless. Black as onyx.

What kneeled upon the bed was a reanimated corpse. A revenant.

An ash man.

A guttural growl crawled from the creature, its lips drawing back against gritted teeth, and it was hard to imagine how they had ever mistaken this creature for the lieutenant.

Pitch uttered a soft curse, his hands still aglow with a subtle but unmissable illumination. Christ, what effort it must be costing him not to explode in the face of such heinous taunts. The Morrigan had stooped to a fiendish low. Silas needed to remove the prince from this room, this goddamned asylum, at once.

Silas dragged the revenant off his knees, lifting him up so they were nearly eye to eye. The ash man did not fight him. Rather he dangled there, limp as the puppet that he was, with his eyelids heavy, as though he were nearly falling asleep. Silas gave the creature a violent shake. Its head snapped back and forth with an audible crunch.

Leaning in so he would fill the creature's black vision, Silas addressed the sorceress watching them. 'You and your whore daemon should relish the hours left to you, Macha. For I assure you, they are numbered.' His voice reached a deep timbre, not far removed from a snarl. Silas tightened his grip and felt bone snap.

With the breaking of its collarbones, Macha's creature came to life. Wriggling about, it was all loose-limbed and frantic, but its smile was still in place. Good god, that lip-splitting grin would haunt Silas's dreams. The illusion cracked and fell away in places, ruining the pleasantness of Edward's face to make it a patchwork of deathly horror. The gums were toothless, speckled in places with an odd mossy green, while the grey it mixed with would have matched the tombstone the ash man should be lying beneath.

A gurgle came from Macha's creature. 'Come into the fold.' A cackle rent the air, twisted as a crow's caw. 'Samyaza will reward all his children when he returns.'

The words jolted Silas, held him locked for a moment. Oh god. Did the Morrigan know his truth? Silas's unsteadiness was all the ash man needed.

Needling hands found Silas's neck and snapped around them like an iron collar. The corpse dug its nails in, and strange, nonsensical words flowed from the creature's bleeding lips. A chant that made Silas's flesh crawl.

'Silas,' Pitch cried.

'Stay back,' Silas coughed. He wrapped his hands around the ash man's wrists and crushed bone, but the revenant's hold on his neck was unmoved. 'I have this.'

No sooner were the words spoken when the ash man's mouth opened wider than unbroken jaws would allow. A rush of foul, acrid air struck Silas in the face. The onslaught was instant, pure, intense, and devastating.

Good god, the anguish. He was fury, he was resentment and unimaginable loss. And each tangled up against one another so tightly they were a beast unto themselves.

Cries of torment scratched at him, utter anguish mixed with a seething rage and a blazing, righteous indignation.

Fucking hell. They had struck him with the Blight.

Silas buckled in on himself, trying to make himself smaller so this despair could not find so great a target.

There was no hope here. No light. Barely air enough to breathe.

There was only ruination. Utter and total. Defeat.

Little wonder this drove the lost souls mad. The legacy of a ruined angel. A legacy of loss. Of failure. Of Samyaza's sheer and undeniable hopelessness. And not just his, but of all those who had followed the Watcher King and died for him.

Silas staggered, knees giving way beneath the onslaught of such unbridled grief. The ground seemed to shudder with the force of his fall.

Somewhere in the distance, way, way off in the black cloud that had filled the room, Silas heard a voice.

'Hold on,' it commanded. 'Do not let go.'

Silas blinked through the haze, one formed by his own tears. The ash man was gone. He did not grip broken bones now, but hard wood, the edge of a gaping hole in the ground. The floorboards had vanished beneath him. There was ash everywhere, black specks floating like rotten snow about him. He dangled in a pit, crying, with just one hand fastened to torn and splintered wood. He struggled to work out why he should not just let go. The weight of the Blight's despair urged him to let go. What point in holding on?

'Fuck, Silas. Give me your other hand.'

A beautiful green-eyed man appeared overhead, his hair a lovely tangle about his sublime face. A stirring of happiness came with looking at the man. So odd and misplaced amongst the doldrums.

'Give me your other hand.' His pretty mouth uttered a fierce directive. 'Don't you dare let go.'

Silas felt a pain at his chest, a sharp thud of his heart, and he sobbed. He should reach for this man.

A force tugged at him from the abyss below. *Here is where you belong.* The harsh, grating sound was barely a voice at all.

The wood at his fingertips crumbled away.

Come home.

The words cut at him, sure as the tip of a blade, and set his very blood to quivering.

And the darkness grabbed his ankles and wrenched him down.

CHAPTER 27

S ilas fell. His tears streamed, falling with him.

The beautiful man cried out with a desperation that the Blight thrived upon. He shone like a summer morn, brilliant and wild-eyed. But a great shadow appeared at his shoulder, looming over him thick and heavy as a storm cloud. A headless figure upon a horse, arm raised, a whip streaming overhead like a strand cut loose from a maypole.

Silas saw only a glimpse. He opened his mouth. To say what?

Utter a warning?

Yes.

He wanted to warn the beautiful man. He wanted to protect that precious soul like he did no other.

Silas sobbed. The desolation of insurmountable grief dragging at him. Pulling him down. He had dared to let go; he'd defied that glorious face.

Now he was tumbling down, sinking. To somewhere he hoped this grief, this agony of loss, might not follow.

Return to whence you came.

Silas winced at the added blow of misery the voice brought. And his fall quickened.

It took him beyond the touch of the one who had reached for him, moving him to where he may find respite, but too far from the man who had cried out for him.

Fight it, ankou. A new whisper struck, sure as an arrow, through the gloom of his tired soul. This one a gentle caress, where the other voice had been a striking blow. *You must not fall. Find us. Save him.*

Silas coughed, and out of him came a mouthful of gritty water. The water forced itself out of him, pouring from his nose, pushing itself through his teeth, though he fought to clench his jaw. Christ Almighty. He could not stand it. Drowning again.

Return from whence you came. The brutish voice returned. *Child of mine.*

And Silas tried to cry out his despair as understanding swamped him, but his throat burned with the all-too-familiar sear of cold, slamming waters.

He knew to the depths of his aching heart he would find no freedom in that voice.

The voice of the Blight.

The voice of the Watcher King.

The voice of his sire. Or, at the very least, a remnant of what Samyaza had once been.

Silas would find no home nor freedom if he listened too carefully. Silas had *seen* what the Blight's call did to a soul. And now he *felt* it too.

He shook himself, tried to breathe despite his lungs telling him it was impossible. He was drowning. There was no air here, could be no air here.

But he was not sure. Not sure...bloody hell...what was he not sure of? It was so dark, so cold, so heavy down here, it was as though the thoughts were being squeezed from his mind by the pressure. He shook himself, trying to peel off the layers that grief and mourning had folded over him, weighing him down. He rubbed rough hands against his face. His face was soaking wet. With tears...no, with the waters of the loch...as he sailed ever downwards.

Bloody hell. Was he crying or drowning? He was impossibly sad. Desperately so. Did he cry because he was drowning? Or drowning because he didn't wish to cry anymore?

This wasn't right. Silas shook himself again.

The grief felt like a shrugged-on coat. One not made for him. One that did not fit quite right upon his shoulders. And he was not truly sad. In fact, if he pushed back against the pressure in his skull, he found something quite the opposite. He'd been happy. So much so.

With the man who'd begged him not to let go.

Awareness snuck in, burrowed its way via the cracks formed by the crushing weight of sorrow.

The Blight might be leaden, but Silas was strong.

He was a Horseman.

Child of mine, the Blight had whispered.

No.

Samyaza may have given him life, but he was not there when it was taken away. It was the goddess who had kept Silas. Izanami had given him *another* life. Given him power. Made him *less* of a monster.

'I am death's messenger, Watcher King.' Silas reached into the darkness, defying the water that sought to choke him and throwing off the mournfulness that clung to his pores. He sought something solid to cling to. 'You lost this child long ago. I am not yours to take.'

Well fought, brave one. The gentle whisper returned, brushed his cheek, and wiped away his tears. Lost souls. *Find us. Fight, Sickle.*

Sickle.

The name punched at him, drove through the darkness and clutched at his stricken heart. That is what the beautiful man called him. The precious soul he'd left behind with a monster closing in.

Silas arched his back and roared, 'Enough!'

A rumble moved the air around him. And his hands struck solid, *real* stone. The darkness peeled away as he spat out the last of the waters and shook off the illusion of being sunk deep. He found his feet. The strike of them upon hard ground was brutal, sudden, and utterly sublime. He choked back a sudden desire to laugh wildly. The remains of the melancholy drifted like skin peeling after a day in the sun.

They had tried to use his past against him again, but they'd failed this time. The Blight was formidable, the Watcher King's legacy bruising, and the Morrigan was clearly an enemy not to be underestimated, but none of them had bested him here.

These fiends were not insurmountable. And would be even less so with the daemon prince at his side.

'Can you show me where Pitch is?' Silas whispered, hoping the lost souls who had called to him would listen.

He stood in another endless stone corridor. No ivy, which was a welcome change, nor any sign of teratisms accosted him. No melody announced their approach.

But there *was* a welcome sound. A reply.

Find us, ankou. Set us free.

An answer, but not to the question he'd asked. 'And I will, but I need to find my companion.' How vapid that word was, how hollow. One's heart did not stutter to think on a mere companion. 'I need to find Pitch.'

Another rumble ran through the Sanctuary. Silas brushed his hands over the uneven surface of the walls, where sections of packed dirt replaced some stonework, giving an air of incompletion to this area of the Sanctuary, just as there had been in the room with the crude door.

Beneath his fingers came a very definite vibration. As though giants walked above.

Silas shivered. That didn't bear thinking of. Did the Morrigan have a damned Nephilim hidden in their Sanctuary? *Another* Nephilim? he wondered. Would it be a creature like him? Large, but not monstrously so. Or a true giant? For he knew the Nephilim to be feared for their immensity and angelic fortitude, but his infuriatingly selective memory failed him thereon. The shape of Samyaza's spawn escaped him. He recalled none other but the one he glimpsed bleary-eyed in a morning mirror.

Another deep shudder moved through the Sanctuary, and Silas was struck by a fresh, terrible thought that had him wishing for giants alone to be the cause of the disruption.

Macha wanted to see the daemon glow. She wished to push him to his limits and cause him to lose all control.

What if the ugly scene with Edward's image and then Silas's disappearance had done so? Silas could still hear the desolate cry Pitch had made as he'd slipped from his grasp.

'Shit. Shit.'

He set off at a run. Choosing right over left, he ran, and ran, until even his near-immortal lungs could bear it no longer.

'Fuck!' he shouted at the stillness in the plain, dreary passageway that was cool as an autumn morning. Silas punched the wall, and his fist sank all the way in. He shoved himself between the Sanctuary's folds, passing through one passageway, then another, cursing all heavens and all hells while the Sanctuary shook itself around him. Sprinkles of dust were loosened with the vigour of the tremors that held the Morrigan's labyrinth in its grip.

Stop running in bloody circles. That won't help no one.

He tumbled into a foyer and rocked to a stop. A grand marble staircase dominated the entry space, which held altogether too much white along with searingly bright floral rugs. This was Knighton House, he thought absently. The house in Leicester where he'd met the ghost who urged him to face up to Black Annis. Somewhere at the top of that stairway, in the real residence, was the painting of Edinburgh Castle he'd admired and wondered at the recollections it stirred.

'Who's there?' In any other place, he'd be sure he knew the answer already – a lost soul calling to him. But nothing was as it seemed in this Sanctuary.

Promise you won't get mad and pull out my fingernails?

Silas frowned. 'Good god, why would I do such a thing?'

Your face is angry.

'It's not...' Silas shook off the denial. 'What do you want?'

Because it certainly wasn't to intimidate. Perhaps this was another distraction, a fake offer of assistance? He eyed the hallway warily, but what all his instincts crowed, what his gut assured him, was that he was encountering a lost soul. One of no danger to him.

Hungry ones are gunna find me and eat me, if you don't hurry yourself.

The wall rumbled, and Silas pulled his arm clear. He peered about. 'Where are you?'

Right here, Mister.

Despite the fact he was death's messenger, Silas jumped. The apparition stood right behind him, so close and so small he'd likely just peered straight over the top of them as he looked about. The top of their head barely reached Silas's belly. The child, for that is without doubt what they were, was covered nearly head to toe in soot, clothes black and somewhat tattered, their sleeves too short, with twine where buttons should be upon their shirt. The area around their mouth was all that was clean about them, the skin as white as chalk. They clutched their cap in hand, craning their neck to look him in the eye. They peeled back their lips as they squinted up at him, revealing missing teeth on the top front row.

You need to come with me, instead of running about like a chicken with its head cut off.

'Come with you where?' Silas tried not to snap; the child ghost looked fearful enough as it was. He couldn't tell if it was boy or girl beneath all the grime, and it hardly mattered. Death did not care for such detail.

To free the ghosts that's left, like they've been askin' ya. One Limb Jack said you'd come with me because you're the ankou on the Pale Horse. Silas had no wish to discover why One Limb Jack deserved such a name. *Saving souls is what you do. You should be freein' them, not scampering about trying to find your daemon.*

'My daemon?' Silas's pulse resumed its hurried tempo. 'I must find him. Do you know where he is?'

One Limb Jack sent Tommy to look for him. The child ghost shuddered. *Poor little shit doesn't stand a chance, between that daemon and the hungry ones. Tommy'll be chewed up and shat out for sure, or we'll find him turning over a spit, with the devil's flames beneath him.*

'Bloody hell...Pitch will not roast your friend.'

One Limb Jack said he might, said he's half-mad, that daemon.

'He's not mad.' Silas prickled. 'And this One Limb Jack would do best to stop talking such rubbish. He is brave and doing the very best he can. You have no bloody idea what he's endured, so watch your tongue.' Silas blinked, startled by his own vehemence.

Well, well then. One Limb Jack wasn't just making up tall tales. He also said you was giving each other gooey eyes earlier on, and that you'd be cock deep in each other soon as this was all over.

'Christ.' Silas gaped. 'You're a child for god's sake –'

Listen, Mr Horseman Mercer, I haven't been a child since I got stuck up one of the Fulbourn's chimneys and choked to death on soot. Must be more than ten years ago, if I was bothered with counting such things. I'm as unhappy about it now as I was then. The ghost child glanced over their shoulder, wiping at their nose once more. *Me name's George, I'll be thankin' you. George Brewster.*

Silas nodded. 'Pleased to meet you, George.'

You don't seem so pleased.

'I've had better days, I'll admit.' He forced his temper to cool. 'My companion and I are under some strain at the moment.'

Righto, well let's move on, shall we, and get this done? Sooner it's so, sooner you can be getting back to playing with your companion's tackle. Half ya luck. I died before I knew what it was like to hold a girl's hand, let along stick my pillar in her basket. Silas widened his eyes, but stayed silent. *You need to set the others free.*

'I will.' He nodded. 'Do you know what they are doing with all these souls here?'

They'd been collectin' all sorts of body parts too. Not sure what that's about, but the souls they took from them, the witches are turnin' them into monsters.

Silas knew Macha to be making teratisms, but what of the creatures this soul feared?

'But the hungry ones...they did not make them.' A butterfly-like thought found a place to land in his mind, settling with a tickle at the back of his skull. A *knowing* that the hungry ones were a particularly horrid type of soul that did not need the Blight to make it so. The souls of murderers and sadistic men and women whose cruelty held them fast to this world. With the sudden return of the knowledge, Silas wondered how it had ever eluded him. Understanding the ethereal world was innate, intrinsic to the thud of his pulse. 'But you should have no reason to fear a hungry one –'

Let's call them what they are, shall we? Cannibals.

Silas frowned. 'They consume souls, yes. But only those vulnerable, those so weak they are barely a smear in this world. The hungry ones could not touch a strong soul like yourself. And they are so very rare.'

The tickling at his skull continued, nuggets of knowledge pushing to the surface. He knew the hungry ones rare because *he* made it so. When Izanami woke him, it was not always to hunt teratisms, certainly not always to ride for the Lady Satine. They had, just as the Lady said, met so very rarely. But the goddess had not kept him idle in his graves.

The rush of conviction rocked Silas on his feet.

He'd used his scythe upon hungry ones.

When those venomous ghosts had grown too gluttonous and eluded the other ankou too long, Izanami had raised him. As though to give Silas a chance to stretch his legs and swing his arm while the world slept quietly without the Blight's stain upon it.

Well, they ain't rare here. Nor weak. That necromancer is making a mess of the order of things, for sure. So you can see, Mr Horseman Mercer, that it's a damned shitty place to be, and only gettin' worse, especially since they done it all up to cater for you and your...companion.

'Done it up? So this Sanctuary was not formed to imprison us, then?'

The ghost spat laughter. *Bleedin' hell no, been here awhile. But it's gotten all kinds of fucked up since you arrived. Now come on, will ya? Between your daemon setting fire to the headless horseman again and the witches trying to cut down that tree, this place ain't likely to stay long on its foundations.*

'He set fire to the Dullahan?' Silas's heart bullied its way to the back of his throat. 'He has bested that creature again?'

If you're meaning the headless horseman, yes. Your fellow put paid to him.

'And...the daemon...he is not still burning...'

The Sanctuary ain't on fire, if that's what you are askin'.

Exhaling a breath of relief, Silas asked, 'What of the tree you spoke of?'

Only heard about it secondhand... Apparently, it just started growing out of –

An unholy bellow smothered the ghostly explanation. A roar like a tin shack being torn to pieces. Not a teratism, Silas knew it unequivocally. But what the hell was it?

Never should have said I'd come find you. The child squealed. *Should have stayed in my bloody chimney like Tommy said. We've been dodging the hungry ones and the witches for months. A few of us have managed to stay free, and that crazy necromancer bitch didn't seem too bothered about huntin' us down... Don't think we was what she was lookin' for anyways. So I survived all that, only to become gristle in a hungry one's tooth because we wanted to stop you running around in bloody circles.*

'*That's* a hungry one?' It was all terribly wrong.

The ravenous creatures grunted, snuffled, then moaned a little as if they were truly starving, but he'd never heard a hungry one sound like a dragon disturbed from hibernation.

Another bellow, this time undoubtedly coming from somewhere beyond the top of the marble stairs. And certainly much closer.

Shouldn't you be breaking out that blade of yours about now, ankou?

George wobbled like jelly and clutched at Silas's trouser leg. He felt the tug of the material, a touch on the corporeal world that was almost as rare as the existence of hungry ones. George Brewster was a poltergeist, one of those noisy, restless spirits who was capable, through some strange quirk, of being able to interact with the world they had left behind. Usually through small, relatively irritating ways: a smashed dinner plate here, a slammed door there, with the rare few making themselves heard in ghostly whispers.

Silas turned over the thoughts in his head like they were precious gems. He could have cried with the relief it was to no longer be so in the dark, so blank of mind.

Where's your fucking blade? I don't wanna be gobbled up and shat out like a cowpat.

Sweet Jesus. What unpleasant detail.

'Just take me to the lost souls. I'll deal with the hungry ones if the need arises.'

Judging by the proximity of the sound, the need would be arising very bloody soon if they did not move. Now. The bandalore was not answering him, not even a hint to say it had heard a word of his pleas to return. But he was not about to admit that to the nervy ghost.

'Go!' Silas shouted.

The ghost child ran at the wall to their left, vanishing into the woodgrain. Silas sent one last glance up the staircase, but there was no hint of the hungry one. He stepped through the wall. Right at the moment another shudder ran through the Sanctuary.

'What is causing that?' he shouted. The child dashed on ahead, slipping across a hallway and into the next wall that lay in his path. 'It sounds like the place is about to come down on us.'

The witch is trying to bring down the tree. That's what One Limb Jack said, anyways. And it's pissing her off no end. That's why the others thought now was the time to sneak out and find you. While Macha and her minions are distracted.

'I need to know more of this tree.'

Jack said there's a tree growin' where it ought not be.

That hardly took genius. They were buried beneath an asylum.

'What sort of tree?'

One with leaves and branches, I suspect. It would account for how he knew it was a tree to begin with.

Silas ground his teeth. 'Now is really not the time for –'

Idle chatter? I agree entirely. You're a grumpier bastard than I imagined. If I were a bettin' fellow, I'd say you haven't got yourself between that daemon's legs yet and you're all pent up.

Jesus, this chimney sweep had a one-track mind.

'How dare you,' Silas spluttered and then made a damn fool of himself. 'I'll have you know you would have lost your bloody money.'

Good for you, Mr Horseman Mercer, good for you. A fine arse on that one. I'd go there in a heartbeat, if I had one. A heartbeat, I mean. Though I'd need an arse too I suppose –

'Good god.' Silas was choking. 'Get on, will you?'

His cheeks were roasting. From the hurried pace, he liked to think. And not because of the appalling conversation with a ghost who had the face of a twelve-year-old and the mouth of a dockworker.

They moved through another wall, then ran down a stony corridor, this one made from the plain coarse stone that Silas was beginning to believe was the Sanctuary's bones, the sections that had not yet been cast with any illusions. Each time they pushed through to yet another passageway, he held on to the frail hope that he might run straight into Pitch.

He bit at his cheek, trying not to imagine he may well be moving further and further *away* from the daemon. Leaving the prince to fend off the Dullahan and whatever else the Morrigan had in store for him on his own. A wretched notion that made Silas feel ill.

He needed to be returned to Pitch's side. But it certainly felt as though they were headed to the centre of the earth.

'Do you truly know where you are going?' Silas was waspish, unsettled by all his worries.

You can hear 'em, can't ya? 'Course, I'm going the right bloody way, you tosser.

Silas *could* hear the whispers, but only if he strained to do so. They were far less coherent than before, a jumble of murmurs like a hive of bees somewhere up ahead. Perhaps they'd spent all their energies on reaching him the first time, urging him to their rescue. A tug of guilt took him. This One Limb Jack fellow was not wrong. Saving souls was what an ankou ought to be doing, and Silas had perhaps not tried hard enough to reach them. Scampering about, as he'd been reprimanded, trying to find the daemon. But they'd be damned grateful for his scampering if it got him to Pitch before the daemon loosened his rage on the Sanctuary.

A violent quake gripped the passageway, strong enough to shudder great chunks of stone from the wall above.

'Shit.' He dove forward as rock toppled, the cut of stone glancing at his heels. With a thump, he landed on his belly on the packed earth, the breath shocked out of him.

He was barely on his feet again, still catching his breath, when the melodies came.

Three teratisms at least, with perhaps another tune mingling there, lighter than the rest. But it was clear enough. He was being hunted again.

'Oh, Christ almighty. This place is a nightmare.'

The songs of the teratisms were harsh and shambolic, curt notes, sharp as blades. Just like those of the Blight-born creatures he'd already dispatched.

Keep going, not far now. Come, come. Hurry up.

'I'm hurrying, damn it.' Silas felt like he'd not stopped hurrying in days.

The roar from earlier found them anew.

And fresh peals of terror came from his ghostly guide. *I'm going to die, I'm going to die. I'm going to die and be shat out of a hungry one's stinking arsehole.*

'Let me deal with what arrives.'

I intend to, believe me.

Silas decided against pointing out the very obvious. That death had already visited the ghost child when he was stuck in the chimney, choking on soot. He had been offered a chance then to bow to the scythe and escape all this, but the sweep had defied death. There were always consequences. One way or another.

Stonework fell around them. The Sanctuary groaned and creaked and showed itself to be no less happy than the ankou. The ground was damp here, as though water had washed through and the packed floor had not yet dried.

The hungry one came out of nowhere.

Well, not precisely. It lurched out of the wall, right alongside the ghost child, who only had time for one note of a scream before he was stifled.

Silas broke into a run, covering the short distance between them quickly.

The hungry one's name belied its appearance, for it was stout rather than gaunt. Its rotund belly ploughed into George first, and they fell in a terribly messy collision of limbs which saw the child crushed beneath the weight of the hungry one. Silas could just see one small foot poking from beneath the more mammoth body of his assailant, a fellow bloated by his hunger, like the carcass of an animal inflated by sun. The beast was filled to popping with murderous intent, rage gone absolutely mad. Hungry ones were touched by evil, one that warped them in life and pushed them to terrible acts. This creature's head was swollen to a grotesque size, making his neck seem reedy and far too delicate to hold the weight, with thighs and calves like bulging pillows, his feet nearly captured in the folds of flesh. There was nothing beneath the garish, mottled grey skin, Silas knew. The hungry ones were hollow, and always seeking to fill the void at the heart of their evil natures.

Ankou! George screamed. *Help me, you sod!*

Silas halted a step back from the writhing bundle of ghostly bodies. The hungry one either did not know, or, more likely, did not care that an ankou stood so close, with its ravenous hunger superseding all sense. All the hungry ghost knew was the desire to devour a soul so that his own might be filled. A foolish endeavour for certain. To feed upon a lost soul only meant filling themselves with angst and regret, anger and despair. Hollow food indeed.

Silas straddled the pair. The ghost child stared up at him, face awash with naked terror. The hungry one pushed its sausage-fat fingers into the child's mouth, using its other hand to pin the wriggling, desperate soul to the ground. Instinct drew Silas along with a rush of powerful certainty. He planted his hand to the back of the hungry one's head and dug his fingers in. His nails sank in through the stretched flesh, puncturing holes.

The hungry one fought a bit, but it was as though it knew itself done in. The struggle was a token gesture, an instinctual thing that was snuffed out quickly.

Silas's touch, the *goddess's* touch, drained the soul from the puffed and malformed shape it had taken, reducing it to a limp and boneless wreck. He felt the movement beneath his skin, the drag of death through his veins.

Wrinkled fingers slid from the child's mouth, and George retched.

Get it off me, get it off me.

'Let me finish.' Silas felt the chill at his fingertips, the rush of frigid air that escaped the body, the cocoon the hungry one had made for itself. Silas inhaled deeply, dragging in the precious scent of mortality, even its faintest, vilest strains as they vanished for good.

He *was* the bandalore. The scythe. The final nail driving into the coffin the creature should have been laid in well before now.

'Are you all right?' Silas pushed the carcass aside. The weight slopped heavily, with a wet sound, the flesh dissolving even as he reached to help George to his feet.

Not in the slightest. I thought you were going to let it eat me.

The petulant reply caused a pinch in Silas's chest. The snide words would have been at home upon Pitch's lips. God, he'd been away from the daemon far too long.

'Let's move on.' The ground shuddered. 'There are teratisms approaching too.'

Coming here?

'I thought that self-explanatory, but yes. Where do we go?'

George spared a moment for a nervous glance up and down the corridor as another disturbing grinding of stonework came from further up the passageway, where the masonry was shaking apart.

Well, we're right on top of where we need to be. It's here. Follow me.

Of all places to go, the ghost child went down. Sank right into the floor, a waving hand the last of him to disappear. Silas sighed and took one last lingering look about, searching for a glimpse of a gold-threaded head of hair, a flash of emerald, and a careless wave. The teratisms sent their song ahead of them. Their caustic melody filled the passageways as they worked their way through the labyrinth that was this Sanctuary, finding their way slowly but very surely towards the ankou.

With a grim set of his mouth, Silas concentrated on the floor beneath him. He sank into the ground, shifting himself so easily and readily he might have thought it marvellous if he were not so twisted with worry for the prince who faced this Sanctuary's cruelties alone.

CHAPTER 28

Pitch was dragged facedown along rough cobblestones. The Dullahan's whip impaled him where it coiled like an enormous viper around his chest and thighs, pinning his arms to his sides. So long as he kept his head bent back at an excruciatingly uncomfortable angle, he was not in danger of having his face scrubbed off by the asperous surface. And with his hips lifted, his prick wasn't in any similar danger of being whittled away. So far, the majority of his trousers had escaped utter ruin.

But those good fortunes aside, there was not much else to be said for the situation.

He kept playing over in his mind the image of Silas being wrenched away. The sudden savagery of it widening the ankou's eyes to saucers, his mouth like the teacup to pair with them. But the stupid, stupid oaf had been so bloody absorbed by something Pitch could not discern, he'd not even been holding on properly, dangling like an enormous apple ready to drop.

The Dullahan dragged Pitch across a pothole as wide as his hips, and the resulting thump of his body had him crying out with the vilest admonishment he had the energy to summon. The segments of bone that made up the whip were considerable. Evidently, it was a spinal cord, though of what monstrous creature, he could only imagine. Nephilim crossed his mind, but he did not like that idea and threw it away. It was bad enough to know the Unseelie Court played their cards with the Morrigan. Spiteful, vain, duplicitous creatures the Unseelie were.

The piece nearest the Dullahan's hand was double the size of his fist, and even those smaller sections nearest the tip were thick as Silas's wrist. All were spiked like cudgels, as though the creature had been inflicted with a deforming disease upon its bones.

Pitch was trussed up like a bird being prepared for a roast. His arms were pressed tight to his sides, his corset and shirt ruined, his trousers heavy with blood. He was growing rather tired of the sickening dig of the spikes, gouging soft flesh at every bump. Of which there were a tremendous amount.

Making it all tenfold worse was the halo wound. The absolute prick of a thing pressed like an iron, fresh out of the oven, against his skin. The amuletum's normally soothing influence stretched taut and thin. Pitch quashed a scream at the back of his throat as a particularly harsh jolt had the still-knitting wounds from the nekhri arrowheads tearing open anew.

Oh fuck, it would be terribly easy to just throw open the cage and set the wildness running rampant. The gods knew it strained to do so.

Pitch could destroy the Dullahan again, that was not in dispute. But in doing so, he would push himself ever closer to his rapidly approaching limits of control. The remains of the amuletum were a flimsy barrier, fluttering like a torn veil between a prince in vague control and utter mayhem.

The Dullahan raced him along like he were a plough meant to till the cobblestones. Fine. Let the fucking Dullahan run itself ragged with a good gallop. They both knew he wasn't about to die from being dragged. And if the servant of the Erlking thought this might make him suitably weak enough to enable it to haul a broken daemon back to the Unseelie Court, the headless cunt was to be very sorely disappointed. The Dullahan may have his name, the Unseelie Court may have taken over Pitch's broken oath to the bluecap queen, but a Dominion prince would need to be good and pummelled before they had any chance of claiming him.

Which was exactly Macha's intent, wasn't it?

Goad on the crazed daemon until he was lost to himself...to whatever Seraphiel's interference had made him...and place him in danger of succumbing to a rage that yearned to devour him.

The sorceress wished to see beneath his skin and ruin him in the process.

'If you are trying to upset me,' he shouted, 'I must say you are terrible at it.' He might have sounded impressive had they not hit another depression in the cobblestones. The jolt made his teeth crash, and he uttered an embarrassing squeal.

The Dullahan said nothing in reply of course. The fiend had no head nor tongue to speak with. It made for a dull journey. But perhaps it was for the best. It was far easier to keep some modicum of calm when your opponent was not egging you on. If the Dullahan had laughed and told him that Silas had been harmed, sent to the bottom of the black pit he'd fallen into, Pitch might have grown angrier. If the Dullahan said there was no way out for the ankou, that Silas was trapped, as Pitch had been in the abaddon, he may have found himself pissed off beyond measure.

Pitch swallowed, his mouth rich with copper and bitter things.

He truly must not think on all the torments the sorceress and her daemon strumpet might be casting on Silas. He should be thinking on the watch, should be listening carefully, trying to decipher a pattern in the pains it sent to him. But still...

What if that darkness they'd sent Silas into was unending? Oh, gods.

What if they plunged him into a vast lake at the bottom of that pit...a place to drown a man endlessly...

Pitch coughed against pungent dread. The flames sparked to life around the beast's cage. 'Shit,' he hissed through clenched teeth. *Stay calm, stay fucking calm, idiot.*

Keeping calm involved chasing his thoughts from the ankou. He twisted his hips, knowing it would drive the barbs of bone deeper.

That would give him something else to think about. Being impaled often did.

Macha wanted to see him glow, and by Enoch's sphincter he wished to show her just how well she could burn, but that was not the game to play here. The sorceress was likely madder than any up in Fulbourn, but she was not a fool.

Onoskolis had torn his weakness from him in violent thrusts, finding Silas there in the cracks Pitch tried to hide, and run screaming. Nemain had feared a daemon taking back what was his.

Macha would keep Silas alive. Keep him here so Pitch would not dare burn her little Sanctuary to cinders before the rest of her vile tribe could arrive – and make this Sanctuary a coffin for Silas and Pitch both.

Another hiss came from him. Not because he was being ricocheted off the walls as the Dullahan's roan cantered down corridors, but because he knew his edges were fraying.

The Morrigan would barely have to work to see him lose control. He'd been dangerous long before Seraphiel's meddling. He'd always been monstrous, the angel had just given him sharper claws, stronger teeth, and manipulated his natural wildness into something malformed and even more horrifying.

Something that could not endure being so helpless for much longer.

Pitch forced the image of Silas into his mind's eye. Gods, let that be enough to hold on to.

The corridor took a sudden, sharp turn right. The Dullahan's horse was not ready for it, and its hind legs skittered out from under it as it negotiated what should have been an impossibly sharp turn for such an animal.

But the steed was about as ordinary as Lalassu and Sanu.

The roan found its hooves before Pitch had time to brace for a nasty collision with stonework. He squeezed his eyes shut, hunching into himself as best he was able. Which was not really much at all.

He hit the wall back first and screamed his unhappiness as the impact crushed the bones deeper into his body, and he was dragged down the length of a new passageway, this one plain dirt. Dusty as a desert. He trailed skin and shirt behind.

'Fuck...fuck.' He spat blood and decided that the next death he delivered to the Dullahan was going to be monumentally miserable. So would the one after that, and the next after that.

The section of dirt ended, thankfully, quickly. Pitch blinked, tears sweeping away the grit in his eyes. Dirt gave way to smooth floorboards, the passageway widening in this godsforsaken Sanctuary. Maybe this is what had happened to the Child Jacquetta, supposedly the greatest of the Melusine builders. Old Bess said she'd been missing for years. Pitch suspected Palatyne had locked Bess's sister in a fucking labyrinth.

'Gods, damn it.' Pitch coughed out the remnants of the dusty corridor. His patience for this carnival ride came to an end.

He brought the flame to hand, very carefully. But therein lay a problem.

He was faced the wrong way for throwing it at the Dullahan.

Pitch strained against the whip's pressured coils, trying to gain some wriggle room, tilting his wrist to attempt to angle it so he could direct a river of white-hot pissed-off-edness at the Dullahan.

The canter turned to a trot, the slam of hooves a calamity upon the floorboards. Pitch, distracted, didn't realise he'd kept sliding over the smoothness of the polished wood, the chalk-white bone leaving gouges in the floor as it went.

He was almost beneath the roan's hooves before he realised it. And to top off his most ridiculously horrid day, he could not move himself to avoid a hoof strike to the side of his head.

The crack was sickening. He definitely saw stars.

And then flames. So many flames.

'You fucking great bastard!' someone roared. Him, most likely, though his own voice seemed to come from the bottom of a well.

He was on his feet – at least, he thought he was. Hard to say with all the pulsing, burning madness around him.

A horse screamed. And the bone whip fell away, puddling at his feet, a glare of white amongst autumn's bonfire. He stood right at the heart of an inferno.

'Fucking cunt.' He chewed up the words and spat them out with all the copper flooding his mouth.

What a waste of time it had been to attempt to stay calm. He'd rather this. Not even remotely placid.

The remains of the amuletum were melting from him, leaving him wide open, vulnerable. He breathed in and kicked at the whip. It crumbled, releasing a puff of white like a pie cut straight from the oven. Gods damn it, he'd lost a boot and sock somewhere along the line. But his corset still pressed him close, held a few shreds of him together. A good thing. If the boning had been ruined too, it would have been the veritable last straw. The gods themselves could not have saved this Sanctuary. He would have razed it. Along with everyone in it.

'Steady, steady,' he whispered to himself, while the beast punched at him, and the pendant watch rubbed at his bone, trying to scratch its pin through to the marrow. The flames snapped about like a ship's ropes cut in a storm, slashing against the helm, making it fucking hard to keep on course.

'Keep it together, you imbecile.'

Breathe. That was important, wasn't it? To keep breathing. The ankou seemed to think so. He'd said it more than once when Pitch lost his hold. *Breathe for me.*

Pitch dragged in a long breath. Filled his furnace lungs. Held the air. Let it bubble and boil.

The torrent of flames escaping his fingertips slowed to a dribble, then a drip, then nothing at all. He was glowing; he was restless and on the brink, but he was not incinerating anything. That was good.

'Very good,' he said to the ash and scorched hallway.

He raised his head, and his satisfied smile wilted away. He'd expected, for a split second, to find the ankou there. Grinning with that trace of smugness Silas sometimes allowed himself, rather than saying outright *I told you so.* Silas, ever ready with a word of praise and a gleam of delight in his eyes.

Shit. Pitch *was* mad.

He was also very sore. In every crack and pore, but mostly at that place upon his back the halo had claimed. The amuletum was all but fired away. Another release of the flame like that, and the pain would be overwhelming, the beast devouring the agony like a fresh carcass.

The strangeness in his arm shifted Pitch from his grim musings. A throb like a tiny, sharp pulse. Seraphiel's trinket was beating. He glanced up, ensuring he'd rid himself of the Dullahan. The considerable smoking hole in the woodwork at the end of the hallway suggested he'd done so reasonably well. It would be nice to imagine that the prick received the message loud and clear this time and would stay the fuck away. But it was a fanciful thought. The Dullahan was obliged to hunt him. The only way to be rid of him entirely was to submit or rescind the deal made with the bluecaps. Pitch's life in exchange for Silas's safe escape. Pitch would never renege on the deal.

The Unseelie Court would never, ever make the oaf their captive instead.

Pitch scowled down at the sharp thumping in his forearm. If he squinted, he was quite sure he could see his skin tugging with each beat. Very precise beats.

Marking time.

The bloody watch was ticking.

He heaved a put-out sigh.

It was entirely possible there was not a single inch of him that did not hurt. His head ached with a passion from the horse's hoof; the punctures of arrowheads and whip both were uncomfortable as they all healed. He was quite sure there was a nasty splinter in his bare foot. The Sanctuary was doing him over well.

Pitch rubbed at his arm, felt the bump like a lost knuckle there beneath the smoothness of his skin.

'I hear you,' he muttered. 'I am listening.'

Pity he could not understand the language of a ticking angel clock.

He turned and decided that of the two choices of direction he had, he would head back the way they had come, keeping clear of the bristled wood torn up by the bones. Pitch took a step, and the mild tick turned into a much harsher tock. A spasm gripped his arm, jerking it back behind him, every muscle stiff as a pendulum in a grandfather clock.

'Gods!' He spun on his booted heel. At once the shallower ticking resumed. The tension eased. 'You have absolutely got to be joking,' he whispered, cognisant he may be observed.

Time was leading him on. Gods, it was just like the Seraph to be so fucking fanciful.

Pitch stomped his way up the corridor. His infernal limp made all the more pronounced by his lack of footwear upon his right foot. If nothing else, he intended to find his bloody boot.

His hoof-struck mind threw an image at him.

Edward.

The very same nondescript picture of the lieutenant he'd seen when he first touched the watch. The man had a faint smile on his lips and was looking at something that pleased him, but there was no hint of background to make what it was clear.

'Well, that's a waste of a vision,' he grumbled.

Find the prophet.

Pitch's carefully tempered breath escaped him in a sharp exhale. He spun around, staring into dust-speckled air, as though there were any chance the speaker might be standing there.

Find the prophet. A faint pull came at the watch, twitching his arm, an urge to hurry forward.

'Who is that?' His own pulse had grown more harried, for that voice was frighteningly familiar.

Find...the...prophet.

It was said slowly, with a dangerous hint of condescension mixed within. Far too reminiscent of a domineering tone he recognised and had only rarely listened to. Pitch shoved his free hand into his hair, finding a true travesty of tangled strands, full of hard pellets of the gods-knew-what.

'You *are* mad,' he admonished himself. 'They've done it. Tipped you over the edge.'

Find the prophet.

'Stop!' He pressed his hands to his ears. Not much of a defence, considering the voice was *inside* his head.

But no. No. This was all wrong. The Morrigan could not know this voice to mimic it so well.

Find the prophet.

There was steel in the command, as though all the previous utterances were a warm up.

With his hands still over his ears, Pitch leaned into the wall.

'Is it truly you?' He was hushed, as near to silent as one could be and still say something.

Find the prophet.

The watch jerked hard enough to pull his hand from his ear. Go. Onward. A lump sat at the back of Pitch's throat, intent on keeping him as light-headed as he'd been when the Dullahan's horse kicked him in the head.

Find the prophet.

Pitch curled his fingers as licks of anger curled about his mood. He glared down at the tiny smear of pink skin that was the only telltale of where he'd buried the watch. Seraphiel's trinket.

Seraphiel's voice.

And what if I refuse? He snarled his thought.

Gods. To hear the angel's voice after so long...after so much fucking devastation.

It felt to Pitch as though the corset he wore were shrinking, the whale bone trying to come together until he was so narrow of waist he could not even think of breathing. He closed his eyes.

Wanting to hear more, terrified he would do so.

There was deep, copious silence.

His arm twitched once more, gathering up to cramp again. He took a step forward, hoping to any gods that were still holy that it was the right direction.

And promptly tripped.

'Fuck, bloody...what the blazes?'

A tree root, of all things. Bulging out of a crack in the floorboards, thick as a hound's tail, and the hue of cedarwood.

Find the prophet.

Seraphiel's voice came at precisely the moment the watch's violent downward motion forced Pitch to drop into a crouch. His hand was drawn towards the root where it peeked like an inquisitive worm. The arrow wound in his thigh screamed indignation at his position, he was tired beyond all reason, and it was incredibly tempting not to just fall on his arse right there and sleep. A movement further up the passageway drew his gaze.

A bulge of dirt pushed through fine seams in the floorboards, bubbling up like a strange fountain. With it, the emergence of another root. Or the very same one perhaps, snaking beneath the surface. Another appeared further along, like a sprout in spring, reaching towards the light. The flicker of movement continued for as far as he could see along the ever-darkening corridor.

Pitch ran his fingers over the wood, which was temperate, pleasantly dry. He rose to his feet.

'Very well, then. Show me to this poor bastard prophet of yours.'

CHAPTER 29

S ilas winced as he slipped between the layers of the Sanctuary with his newfound ease, a wave of whispers coveting his eardrums. The lost souls sensed him and grew ever more hysterical because of it. They were *so* bloody loud, and with the distant hum of the teratisms, his mind was a jumbled mishmash of sounds.

There was little doubt he was growing closer to where the lost souls gathered.

His feet touched the ground in a brand-new chamber just as another calamitous tremor took hold of the Sanctuary. Startled, Silas stepped back, only to find nothing solid beneath his feet. He took a tumble, albeit a short one, which landed him hard on his backside. He stared up at a domed ceiling, where a trio of softly glowing stalactites bore down on him like enormous spears, casting their hue of winter-morn sky blue. He hurried to his feet, dusting off his hands and trying very hard to ignore the cacophony in his head.

For a moment, Silas thought the Sanctuary was taunting him with the illusion that he'd fallen into the chamber of the bluecaps, deep in the mines. If the Child was attempting to mimic the mines here, then they had gotten most of it very wrong.

He had stepped back off a raised platform of smoothed stone that formed the base of a monopteros. The circular colonnade was made of polished limestone and shot through with veins of cobalt. At the centre of the circular gathering of pillars was a carved statue, an angel with wings spread and lifting towards the roof, stone feathers arching over the slender, muscular body of a man with all his assets on display. And considerable assets they were. The figure's face was perhaps not so admirable, an unsettling combination of superb beauty and severe angles. He was carved in fierce lines, mouth opened as though roaring his displeasure, eyes of ruby. Quite literally. The gems fastened into the stonework gleamed a searing red. His hair hung nearly to his waist in coils that serpentined all over his naked body. He clutched a weapon, a spear.

Silas licked his lips, his tongue catching on dry skin. He had an idea who this might be.

The Morrigan were, after all, beholden to Samyaza.

But surely that was not the cursed halo he held? The weapon that had caused all this angst to begin with could not possibly be so...well, so dull in appearance.

Their king, apparently, George whispered, confirming Silas's suspicion without a question asked. *How can a chap manage to be so ugly and yet so beautiful at once?*

Silas harrumphed and nodded. The carving was indeed a juxtaposition, for despite the angered scowl and glaring eyes, there was no mistaking the beauty imbued in this sculpture. The creator obviously held a reverence for the angel, a wariness of his dangerous beauty.

'The Watcher King,' Silas said, for no real reason but to connect the name to the statue out loud. And in part to try to see if he could hear himself over the riotous babble in his head. The lost souls were ever so close. He would not have been surprised at all to find them all huddled in the corners of this chamber. But so far, he saw no such sight.

George shrugged dirty shoulders. *We've heard them call 'im that. Do you 'spose this is what he actually looks like though? If the painters and sculptors who do our queen are anything to go by, then this lot are hardly going to sculpt something that's downright ugly, even if it might be the truth.* The ghost coughed, clearing a throat that had needed no such thing for a long time. *Is it true, then? There's angels about...*

'There are.' Silas nodded, pressing the heel of his hand to his temple. The cacophony in his head was beyond intolerable. The teratisms' notes mixed with a clamour of voices, all speaking over the top of one another and, as a result, saying little at all.

He caught coherent words only rarely. *Here.* And a more desperate, *Help.*

Does that mean there's daemons too, then?

George's sudden question made all the knots in Silas tighten.

'There are.' One of whom had barely left his thoughts since...oh hell, since the day they had first met. 'But I dare say you have less to fear from the daemons than you do the angels.'

George gave a dramatic shiver. *Can't say that's helpful in making me feel any better. So what can you do for them, then? The souls I mean...not the daemons.*

Silas's breath hitched, knowing which of the two concerned him the most. The last he'd seen of Pitch, the Dullahan had loomed, ready to strike the distracted daemon.

You all right, Mr Horseman Mercer? Now's not really the time to go all woozy, if you don't mind me sayin'.

'I'm not woozy.' Though he *was* sick with worry.

Another of the disconcerting rumbles moved through the chamber. A steady thumping sound came from beyond the monopteros, as though someone sought entry there. Either the Sanctuary was seeking to unsettle him with false sounds of carnage, or he should be truly afraid of the place caving in on him.

This place don't seem to like you two very much. So what do we do now?

A good question indeed.

Through narrowed eyes, Silas surveyed the rest of the chamber. The walls were set with carved stone arches, one after another, side by side, like windows in an elaborate cathedral. But instead of a view of the outside world, each held a painted scene. Some were faint, others as though half-completed, but the nearest to where he stood was clear enough. Part painting, part engraving, it was set at the heart of the archway. A monstrous creature dominated the scene, with the etchwork of a forest chipped into the stone. The beast stood upright on legs that were like boulders stacked upon one another. One clawed foot pressed down on a fallen oak, the wood clearly shattered beneath the weight. The creature had massive shoulders and a bulging chest, hairless and craggy as a mountainside. The face was deep crevices of thick grey skin like folds of mud that had hardened, with eyes of onyx the size of golf balls. The creature would be tall enough to stand over a carriage and crush it underfoot.

A giant.

Silas tugged at his collar, seeking air against his skin. There was nothing to say this was a Nephilim, no plaque announcing that the grim beast was a reflection of what Silas might have become, but he did not feel well at all to look upon it. He felt as though the very sight stirred unpleasant things in a locked-away part of him.

Let it stay tightly locked.

He turned his attention back to the lost souls. *Here,* they were saying. The rare evident word he could decipher from the buzz of voices.

He looked to the monopteros anew. On impulse Silas tilted his head side to side, watching the shift of the light against the columns.

He cursed under his breath.

Sigils covered every inch of the stonework, great swathes of design etched into the columns only evident if they caught the chill-blue light of cobalt strains just so.

It was a cage of maleficium.

There, right before him, was the prison of the lost souls.

As though sensing he now understood, the souls roared, and their desperation flooded him. Silas nearly buckled with it.

Took a lot to make themselves heard, George shouted, clearly hearing the wretchedness too. *Can you save them?*

Their despair leaked from between the pillars, their manic clamour for escape now deafening. They were bordering on deranged in their calls now, barely clinging to the sense that had enabled them to reach him. It had taken them, he suspected, their sanity, to find him. There was no hint of the clear, directive voice that had drowned out the siren's call of the Blight as it tried to lure a prodigal son home.

The lost souls had not only guided him, they had saved him too.

Silas riled with indignation.

These were *his* dead.

The necromancer should never have touched them. She would regret it. He stepped up onto the platform and moved close to a column.

The dim light from the cobalt veins struck at the shallow engravings of the sigils, catching in the curls and lines. They covered the stone entirely, seeming woven into one another. Intricate knots and patterns, as delicate as any lacework.

'A seal,' Silas whispered, as the lost souls cried for him. 'Shit...'

Pitch had said it himself. Azazel was a master of seals. The Morrigan had already shown themselves quick learners of the art, with the greensward and its stone circle. Silas had only escaped because of the daemon's intervention. It was *Pitch* who had been formidable enough to destroy the barrier that stood between him and Silas.

And Pitch was not here.

Will you use your scythe now? To break the soul trap?

Silas snapped a look over his shoulder. 'Soul trap?'

There are souls, and they are trapped, what better name for it?

True, but he'd heard such a term used before. Silas struggled to recall, and the memory wriggled from a dark recess to find him. Phillipa, the Lady Howard's ghostly lover, had spoken of there being a soul trap in the Lady's carriage. A means of storing souls as they were abducted from the Devon countryside, before they were carted off to wherever the Morrigan intended.

Before they were carted off *here*.

Silas stared at the raging angel.

This Sanctuary was Macha's foul laboratory.

A new tremor struck, a stupendous affair, a rolling wave that had Silas staggering. He covered his head against a rain of debris, cowering against the pillars. A prickling sensation ran down his body where it was closest to the stone. And the sense of wrongness he'd felt at the greensward returned in a punishing wave. The maleficium hummed with dread and sullen things. The barrier unseen by the eye but felt all too well by all the other senses.

You need to hurry. George huddled at the base of the platform. *It's gettin' worse. Feels like the Sanctuary is dying.*

Silas blinked through dust as the tremor eased, and his thoughts were in a race, towards a place that gave him hope.

The prince had destroyed the bluecaps' mine.

What if Pitch could do the same to this Sanctuary?

Oh sweet Christ. What if he were doing so unintentionally, goaded beyond his limits by Macha and her daemon?

Silas bowed his head, brought down by the despair radiating from the trapped souls. He pressed his hands to his head. 'You should go, George. Find your friends and leave this place.'

You're abandoning them? George cried.

'No. Of course not. But you need to leave... Can you do that?'

George shook his head, sooty face miserable. *Only as far as the asylum, and that doesn't seem far enough.*

No. It did not. But it was better than remaining down here.

'You should go there now, and do what you can to have them evacuate the place.' The poltergeist could manipulate objects in the corporeal world. If the asylum's residents did not already notice its foundations shaking, then perhaps the ghost could frighten them out. 'Quickly, gather the rest of your friends and go. Thank you...for all you have done. I will not forget it.'

There was no way of seeing George's blush beneath the soot, but Silas saw sign of it in the shy bob of the child's head.

Just do your best then, Mr Mercer.

He offered a grim smile. 'I shall. Now go, quickly.'

Silas did not wait to see if the sweep would follow instructions. He turned back to the monopteros. He flexed his hands, running over the options, which, without the bandalore, seemed seriously numbered.

He was not going to abandon these souls, but how the bloody hell did he free them?

The scythe might have been capable of making a dent in this magickal cage, but he wasn't sure his new talent for beheading teratisms was as useful here.

Silas bit at his bottom lip, raised his hands, and took a bet. A bet that Macha, or whichever of the sorcerers had constructed the soul trap, was intent on keeping those things inside trapped there, not assuming they would need to stop someone from trying to get *in* the horrid prison. The monopteros was deep, deep within the Sanctuary. He'd defied its catacomb-like passages to find it and had the help of a rogue ghost to do so. He hoped he could rely on the Morrigan being as unprepared for his ability to defy the Sanctuary as he was.

'Right then, let's see.'

Silas slammed his hands against the thin air between the columns. He closed his eyes tight, his head turned slightly into one shoulder, bracing for whatever might come next.

Which was...nothing of note. Save for the feeling of pressing up against a solid wall and a tingling in his fingers that bordered on ticklish, the end result was surprisingly mild. And extremely disappointing.

The souls' cries rose. And a few words fought through.

Careful, said one.

'Sound advice,' he muttered.

Ankou, from another.

But the last discernible word made no sense.

Sluagh.

Silas braced for another try, using more vigour this time, leaning into the task like a man on the docks trying to shoulder an enormous load. He grunted, and grimaced, and spat all kinds of unpleasant words before he relented. He could not, it seemed, move a mountain with his bare hands. Not a magickal one at least.

'Shit.' Furious, he punched at the unseen barrier, and by god he was sure this time there was a yield beneath his knuckles.

Silas tried again.

And a third time. Feeling for a softness, a tender place, like he knew existed in the walls of the Sanctuary. Unstructured points that allowed him to pass through.

Silas sidestepped around the pillars, testing the spaces in between, one by one. The souls clamoured for him, and there were snippets of coherence within the babble.

Hurry.

Hurry.

Don't.

Leave.

Us.

'I won't leave you.' Silas ground his teeth as another violent shudder took hold of the Sanctuary. 'Pitch, damn you. You had best be causing this strife on purpose.'

Imagining this calamity was intentional was far better than imagining the daemon was being consumed by his wildness.

As he continued his search for the barrier's weakness and his own strength, Silas pictured the prince at his sublime best. In a rage, but in control. Giving this Sanctuary utter hell.

He imagined Pitch tearing that ballroom apart. He pictured the terror on the sorceress's face, the pale horror overcoming Onoskolis as the daemon showed them his true worth.

Silas drove into the ecstasy of his thoughts, as he drove his fists into the soul trap.

There. There it was. A give in the barrier.

He laughed. A startled, rather manic sound. The sound one made when one was so filled with panic they were going to burst from it.

'Easy now,' Silas urged himself.

He returned to thoughts of the prince, to Pitch finding Edward and freeing him. Moving on to what came next.

Surpassing that bastard angel's expectations. Surpassing Lucifer's.

Destroying that damned, fucking halo.

Good lord, it would be magnificent. His daemon would be astonishing.

Silas's fervent punching of the barrier faltered.

He had intended to be at the daemon's side to the very end of all this. Now though...

But he could not leave these souls.

He kicked out at the barrier, the impact vibrating up his leg.

Idiot. He was fooling himself. He was making no headway on breaching this fortress. The tiny give in the magick he'd felt seemed no more than a tease.

The Sanctuary seemed to laugh at him, a deep chuckle that made the stones grind against one another. The platform beneath him juddered, and Silas braced against a pillar. It felt as though a monster were stirring beneath the ground, readying to rise up and strike at him.

Silas glared at the heart of the monopteros, a fire in his belly, fists balled. The statue of the Watcher King had its ruby eyes fixed on him, the twin-pronged tip of the spear aimed at him.

Silas planted both hands against the barrier and spread his fingers. 'Whatever remains of you in this world,' he hissed at the stony Watcher King, 'will not withstand the prince, I promise you. He will rid this world – all the worlds – of you, once and for all. And he does not need me there to see it done.'

'Is that so, Mr Mercer?'

Silas spun about, pulse thudding.

The sorceress stood in front of one of the archways as though she had emerged from the stonework itself.

'Macha,' he breathed.

Christ almighty. He had just handed her Pitch's deepest secret.

CHAPTER 30

Pitch followed the bulge of the tree root and cursed at the stiffness in his hip. His strides were uncertain, tilted and ungainly, made more so by the frequent shivers that ran through the Sanctuary. The forceful shakings had him wobbling on his feet when they struck.

'Fucking place,' he mumbled.

Pitch pinched at the bridge of his nose, seeking to push back concerns that clamoured for attention. Silas could handle himself. He must believe that. Gods, the ankou had taken to ripping teratisms' heads off. If that were not slightly impressive, then nothing was. Pitch's thoughts brought him to a standstill. What if that newfound brutality was not enough?

Gods. Fuck the prophet and fuck the halo.

He'd find Silas instead. Take them both to some distant corner of Arcadia. They could live like hermits and fuck like they had in the theatre. Crash into one another until Pitch did not know where Silas ended and he began. He'd fall asleep with thick fingers caressing him gently and awaken with the reassuring bulk of the ankou surrounding him. He'd ache in all the right places, in all the right ways.

A shiver took him, a brief moment of delight in this intolerable place.

The steady beat of footsteps shook Pitch from his thoughts. 'Silas?' The stranger's approach grew louder, and no reply came. 'Fuck.'

Flame tingled beneath the skin of his palms, and a sharp pang came from the watch, rippling up his arm.

Pitch stared up and down the empty, bland corridor, another of those places that held the air of being incomplete, with patches of the grey stone dotting the plaster like measles on the skin. Hiding was impossible with not even a potted palm to crouch behind nor a doorway in sight.

That was, until a moment later.

The seams of an oak door formed in the wall up ahead, some ways from where he stood. Pitch swore again, flames teasing at his fingertips. His muscles clenched around the hidden watch, a painful contraction that was infuriatingly distracting.

The door handle, a gleaming silver affair, ground like a rusted gate as it turned. Pitch backed up a few cautious steps, stepping over the tree root, only to find it had quite disappeared. It no longer breached the floorboards like the back of a half-concealed serpent.

The door swung open. And Mr Weatherby stepped out. The kitsune was in his purebred form, clad in his chestnut suit, not a fine hair of his severe cut hair out of place. He was busy staring hard at something he held and did not look up as he turned towards where Pitch stood. He marched down the passageway, a hallway that was barely wide enough to have two people pass side by side. Pitch braced, readying for the moment the kitsune would glance up. The little prick would find himself with a face full of daemonic flames.

The beast in Pitch's belly paced restlessly. The wildness had refused to be subdued from the moment he'd first sent the Dullahan soaring across the ballroom. He filled his palms with light, ribbons of dancing flame that were so eager to bloom into an inferno it was almost more than he could bear. At his arm the pinch of the watch was impossible to ignore, like a dozen woodpeckers were trying to open him up and take the trinket for themselves.

Weatherby nodded down at his hand. 'Badh has just arrived, yes,' he said, in that galling high pitch he had. 'He is eager to set the seal in place, having seen the disturbances, but –'

A voice came, seemingly from the palm of the kitsune's hand.

'But Macha is being a petulant menace as per usual.' Masculine, impatient, raspy and deep. And infinitely recognisable, for Pitch had heard it not so long ago as Dr Severs taunted them with the illusion of Charlie.

'There is no time to waste here. We've had word that Ahari has left The Atlas in rather a rush.'

Weatherby paused, barely three strides now from Pitch. The scrying stone he held was more evident now. This one was the colour of moonstone, swirling like a mist was trapped in the rock. 'He is coming here?'

Pitch scowled at both the increasing sting of his arm and the kitsune's apparent blindness, barely taking in the news that perhaps the Order might yet save them. What the blazes was wrong with the kitsune? At the very least he should have sensed the daemon with his fox-sharp sense of smell. Pitch had been told, no end of times, that his natural scent was odoriferous.

'We must assume so,' Dr Severs replied.

'The Fulbourn has deceived the Order for many –'

'Fetch the sorceress, Weatherby.' Dr Severs's voice held an authoritative air that even made Pitch stand to attention, far sterner than anything the good doctor used outside Charlie's cell. 'So help me if I must leave here to drag her to the summoning place myself. She'll not recover quickly from it. She must join her siblings to set the seal at once.'

'She's convinced she must recapture the purebreds. That tree protects them. Edward is clearly import–'

'Not important enough. We have both Horsemen at our mercy. There will not be a better opportunity than this to cut off the Order at the knees. With two of her Horsemen gone, the Lady's lake is vulnerable. Bury the purebreds and that fucking tree with them. It will not matter a damn who or what they are if they are beyond all help. Macha must not jeopardise everything we can do here because she is a spoiled child who does not like to lose unimportant games. And if she dares refuse my messages again...' Dr Severs's anger hung like the weight of a humid summer's day. He paused, seeming to gather himself. 'Bring her to me. Tell her it is a direct command. She denies me at her peril.'

'Of course, yes, sir.' Weatherby hesitated. 'Sir, where is the tree's magick coming from? It is formidable. It feels like this bloody place is going to come down around us.'

'So let it!' Dr Severs shouted. 'We will set the seal and let the Sanctuary crush all of them.' Weatherby flinched, extending his hand so the stone was not quite so near. 'Find Macha, now.'

The kitsune nodded sharply. 'It will be done, Iblis.'

A deep unease ran with the infernal prickling around the watch. Iblis. Silas had spoken of such a man after the greensward. The ankou had told Lady Satine of the Morrigan thanking one named Iblis for protecting them. Satty had said little on it, save for one rather poignant detail.

The only Iblis she knew had been a Watcher angel.

Pitch watched Weatherby slide the scrying stone into his pocket. The fellow muttered under his breath, the harshness of his tone suggesting he had not enjoyed the chitchat with his superior.

A fucking *angel*.

How had Iblis stayed hidden from the Order, and for so long?

The slowly healing marks of the Dullahan's whip twinged, as though to answer that for him. It was possible the Unseelie Court had sheltered Iblis and his fledgling sorcerers. That was exactly the sort of meddling bullshit the Erlking thrived on. Plaguing a world he'd long been banished from was a favoured pastime, with no more purpose than to stir trouble.

Pitch scratched absently at his arm, digging his nail into the fragile scar. Vaguely aware that his arm hurt enormously.

By Enoch's taint, they had been fools. Outplayed at their own game when it came to disguise. Evidently Satty's elixir had a competitor, one potent enough to keep an angel hidden in plain sight.

Dr Severs was not a purebred nor a sorcerer. There was a damned good reason why the doctor had been so proficient with those ancient Arcadian words he spouted to cast his magick. It was his native tongue.

The kitsune adjusted his jacket and glanced up the corridor. Pitch brought the flame to hand, wincing as the burn reached around the trinket.

The kitsune looked away, searching the other end of the corridor. He had no fucking idea Pitch stood just feet away.

A deep, resonate groan moved through the Sanctuary, like a great beast slumbered beneath it and muttered in its sleep.

Weatherby's fright was evident, his nose twitching, the hand that played at his collar tightening around the starched fabric.

'Shit,' he whispered. 'Get on with it, Weatherby, old chap.'

The *old chap* shook himself like a dog banishing water from a pond. His clothes flew from him like they'd been pasted on and the glue had failed. There was the same popping sound as there had been in the ballroom, a dull surge of light, and the kitsune was transformed.

A black fox now stood in the corridor, with its three bushy tails waving about like pussy willows caught in a breeze. The kitsune snapped its jaws, long pink tongue darting to swipe at a gleaming button-black nose. He darted straight at Pitch.

Instinct should have had him readying for attack, but here instead it urged quiet. Stillness. Pitch stayed his hand, teeth set hard against the unnerving sting of the watch.

Without a glance up, Weatherby swerved just before he would have struck Pitch's legs. The kitsune trundled off at fast clip down the corridor without pause and vanished before Pitch had spun about.

'What the blazes...' The incessant pinching at his skin eased, the calamity inside stepping down a notch. Pitch rubbed at his arm, the ache fading. 'If I'd known it could do that,' Pitch grumbled, 'I'd have fucking well used it to get into the Sanctuary to begin with.'

Floorboards creaked behind him.

He spun about. The tree root had returned, pushing through cracks all the way down the middle of the passageway, now with a webbing of finer roots spreading from the main shoot like pulpy spiderwebs. The kitsune had prattled on about a tree during his chitchat with Iblis, a tree with formidable magick. Pitch massaged the muscle around the watch, felt the hardness of it beneath the skin.

'What the fuck are you up to, Raph?' he muttered. 'Am I finding a lieutenant or a bloody tree?'

Find the prophet.

'Oh fucking gods, I'm sick of the sound of that. Answer my –'

A roar this time. *Find the prophet!* Louder than a horny garuda's mating cry. Pitch clamped his hands against the side of his head.

'Shit...bloody...gods, stop! I'll go. I'll go. But you give me something first. Tell me the ankou is unharmed. I'll not move another step until – ahh!'

A violent tug at his ankle jerked him forward. The spray of fine roots had wrapped it tightly. And their message was decidedly clear.

Move on.

A fine, slithering section of roots crept over his bare foot, surprisingly warm against his skin. He kicked out, tearing them loose.

'Enough. I don't need to be dragged.' The roots shrank from him, laying themselves upon the ground and untangling themselves from his booted ankle. 'Is he all right? Tell me. And I'll move.'

He braced, ready to be yelled at again. There was silence but much movement. Ahead, the roots swayed upwards in one great bouquet, tangling up in each other, gathering in on themselves, weaving and ducking.

Knitting themselves into a shape that had Pitch's pulse skipping.

Silas's scythe swayed before him, a topiary of roots that Harvington Hall's gardener would have been proud of. The scythe tilted forward, tapping its point towards the far reaches of the corridor up ahead.

'He's that way?' Pitch was already striding forward. 'Show me the way. Don't dally about it.'

The roots unravelled, like hair brushed free of tangles, and collapsed to the ground.

Pitch set off at a run. The deep groans rose up through the floorboards and seemed to make the entire corridor sway at times. The roots led him up a wide, broad staircase that might have resembled one he'd encountered at Hampton Court a few months back, but Pitch had tired of the games the Sanctuary sought to play.

He wanted to find Edward and get the blasted angel out of his damned head.

He wanted to find Silas. Gods, he wanted that with a longing that was truly abysmal. The ankou's absence at his side was a void that sucked the air from the room and the strength from Pitch's reserves.

And what else he wanted, almost as much as the ankou's return, was a fucking boot to cover his bare heel, which was managing to land upon every trace of grit and stone upon the floors.

'Shit.' He hissed, dancing on his booted foot as he rubbed at the ball of the other. The debris was thickening upon the ground, tiny stones intent on hindering his every move. 'Could you not choose a clear path?' He told off the tree root with a fervour that, along with his patience, was eroding rapidly. He was a paradox of sensation. At his heart he was calamitous, the beast still baying for release; but outside of that cage, he was leaden, sore, and so very sick and tired of corridors and staircases.

Pitch carried on. And on.

The Sanctuary grumbled and moaned and echoed with disconcerting sounds around him. And all he could think on was mention of the seal. Of being shut in this sodding place. Pitch folded his fingers over the watch, trying to rationalise his panicked thoughts. If it was truly Seraphiel's voice in his head, if Edward had suddenly been made a bloody prophet, he had to believe there was more in store for him, for Edward...and for Silas...than being locked up forever in a damned labyrinth.

Pitch turned his attention back to the root. Focused all his thoughts that way, refusing to allow them to derail with the creeping terror that came from imagining forever in these hallways.

At times the root cut a path along the walls, right alongside him, at other times he was forced to crane his neck to search for it upon the ceiling, but it was always there, leading him through hallway after hallway, stone passage after stone passage.

'Fuck this place, with several pustulous wyvern cocks,' he panted, trying to catch his breath as he entered yet another grey-stoned godsdamned passageway. Another thoroughfare with far too many spiky shards of stone upon the floor. If his foot was not bleeding by now, it would be a miracle.

'Wonderful.' He growled. 'I'm more vagabond than Charlie ever was.'

Silas hated hearing him speak of the lad that way. He'd scowl if he were here. Pitch could picture it clearly. The gesture would make his left cheek push up higher than his right. His brown eyes would glint topaz with unhappiness.

Pitch wiped at his face, blinking as sweat trickled into his eye. He tried to ignore the tremble in his fingers and the dull thump of the watch beneath his skin.

'Just find the fucking prophet. Stop pining like a fool.'

He cleared the sweat from his eyes, and the way ahead was clear. Pitch came to a halt.

The corridor no longer stretched like a ribbon of deepening darkness. Several feet ahead, a set of mahogany doors had appeared, cutting off the passageway. Their ornate, thick-runged knockers glinted silver, as though a moon shone against them.

Pitch eyed the new addition warily, as he did most things in this place.

The doors burst open, and a trio of harpies spewed forth, wings slapping about, feathers bunched and ruffled, black beaks wide, screeching as though Silas's blasted skriker were after them.

Pitch came to life, or at least tried very hard to do so. He sought to raise his hands, summoning the flame from where it waited ever so eagerly for his call. A tightness dragged at his wrists, holding him in place. He snapped his gaze downwards. Twin roots were tangled about his arms, rising from the ground like delicate saplings, binding him like a prisoner to the dock. Pitch wrenched his shoulders, struggling to free himself. His right hand was a ball of flame, but at his left there was only the barest glow. And gods, how the thudding beneath his skin there grew. The tick of the watch rattled his bones, sent hot pokers into his skin.

The harpies blustered past him, a wing slicing so close to his ear he was certain some of his hair had been cut. Their screeches were loud enough to make his teeth rattle. But just as it had been with the kitsune, not a one of them showed any sign they'd noticed the daemon standing in the dead centre of the corridor. They swept around, tilting their ragged wings at the very last moment to avoid him. Their stench struck him, shoving its way up his nostrils, coating the back of his mouth, saturating the air even as they left it and continued their manic flight down the passageway.

Pitch spat against the cloying remnants of the harpies' odour and gave the vine-like tendrils an extraordinarily hard pull. His hands came free easily, and he nearly struck himself in the face with his own momentum.

'Christ almighty,' he shouted, echoing the ankou's preferred curse. He'd have said more far less congenial things if he did not at that moment spot what lay beyond the thrown-open doors.

It was the interior of a small barn, light filtering through uneven slates, bales of hay scattered, and a rusty old shell of a plough hulking in a far corner. A scattering of random pieces were laid about, a wheelbarrow here, several empty apple crates there, placed in a vaguely circular shape. He knew at once where the Sanctuary had placed him. This was the barn where he had boxed with half the township of Bishop's Castle, and would have killed its constable in a rage if not for the intervention of the Valkyrie. For one very rare time, he would have done anything to see Sybilla come blazing in here now.

Perhaps the angel could explain the one striking difference between the true barn and this illusion.

The enormous bloody tree that stood at its centre.

A rowan tree with dense green foliage and clusters of red berries that spread out against the slats of the barn's roof. The rowan should not be bearing fruit at this time of year, but then that was hardly the strangest thing about a tree growing underground with no taste of sunlight and soil that looked parched dry of any moisture.

The trunk on this rowan was a great curiosity, up high beneath the branches, it was slender and rather normal in size, but the closer to the ground it went, the broader and less usual the trunk became. The flare of gnarled wood at the base was enormous, like a giant woman's skirts puffed with air, and bubbled in places, the wood bulging high enough that Pitch could likely crawl into the hollow beneath on his hands and knees.

A hushed scraping sound marked the slow recoil of the roots that had led Pitch here, slipping their way back from whence they had come, leaving furrows in the packed dirt.

A searing pain shot up Pitch's arm.

The prophet.

'Fuck.' He jumped, darting a gaze over his shoulder.

It was as though Seraphiel had been standing right beside him, speaking against his ear. Gooseflesh marked his skin, the chill accompanying the angel's voice contrasting the warm trickles of sweat beneath his arms.

'Where is your bloody pr...' He stopped himself.

The Morrigan might intend to entomb him down here, but it would be lunacy to go blurting about prophets in a Sanctuary of this kind.

A tremendous thump, like the heel of a titan's boot coming down upon the Earth, made the entire corridor shudder. The wail of timbers under duress tore the air apart. He could not think too deeply on what those sounds meant, for they held too much of an air of finality.

Pitch dashed across the threshold. The moment he set foot in the barn, the pain at his back and his arm ignited as one.

He released a hollow cry, clamping his hand down upon his arm, squeezing at the watch beneath his skin. By Enoch's fucking arsehole, it was like a stinging ants' nest had cracked open beneath his skin and all the blighters were scattering across his body. He could not find a place to itch at that would settle the sense of something crawling inside him. Pitch gouged at his own flesh, leaving red welts down the length of his arm where he was clawing at the watch. He staggered, trying to keep at least a mildly straight path towards the tree, for whatever this bloody thing was, it was a part of finding Edward.

But fuck, could it have been less painful a place to be? The halo wound was nearly as devastating as it had been the day he'd received it.

Flutters of colour fell about him, seesawing movement that marked the descent of leaves. Sunburned yellows and ember flashes. The rowan had swapped its green spring vibrancy for the crisper hues of autumn in an instant. Leaves fell thick and fast, coming down like soft rainfall and covering the hay-pitched ground like pieces of sunset fallen.

A crack of wood, much closer this time. So close in fact Pitch felt the vibration of it through his bare foot.

He stepped back, lifting his arm to worry at his aggravated back. If the amuletum still worked at all, it would not do so for much longer.

The formidable thump came again, like the throwing of an enormous bolt. The groaning of the wood was almost lost beneath the dire sounds echoing around the rest of the Sanctuary.

Almost.

Pitch frowned, certain he recognised what he'd heard. There had been enough felling of trees with Black Annis as the enraged teratism struck down oaks in her fury.

Sure enough, as he stared up, the shivering branches of the rowan tree loomed towards him, dowsing him with a fresh fall of leaves.

'Gods damn it!'

He dove as the tree moaned and lamented its fall.

Pitch hit the ground at a roll, but not soon enough to avoid the slap of branches against his arse. He yelled his discontent, entirely sick of all the punishment he'd received today, but at least the great weight of the rowan had missed him in favour of smashing to pieces the stored plough.

Pitch cursed every angel he could name as he rolled over the halo's mark, before he thrust himself to his feet, at the ready to face whatever it was that had brought down the tree.

He was entirely unprepared for what he faced.

Pitch's throat clenched.

This must be another of the Sanctuary's cruel illusions.

The tree had not torn its roots from the ground. Rather it was like an enormous axe had made one clean strike through the trunk higher up, cutting it off and leaving the wood smooth. It formed a circular room of sorts, with the entrance being an upside-down V-shape, like the entrance to a tent. And within that enclosure of wood...was one of the glass coffin's Macha had revealed.

Edward lay within, hands lying over his chest. Still as a corpse.

But draped over him this time, clutching at the coffin like a sailor to flotsam after a ship's sinking, was Silas's lad.

Charlie was on his knees, his chest pressed to the flat surface of the coffin's top, his arms reaching as though he sought in vain to cover the lieutenant. His sleeves were in tatters, the left shredded up to the elbow but the right only torn enough to bare Charlie's wrist. He wore a wooden bracelet, a crude twisting of rowan wood and holly.

Pitch knew it on sight.

Silas had worn it in the Forest of Dean. An ugly creation woven by the self-proclaimed forest witch, Ottelie. She had offered it to the ankou to stem his violent sickness as they approached Goodrich Castle and its imprisoned spirit of the forest. Ottelie had insisted Silas take the inelegant thing as a parting gift.

A wave of panic blurred the interminable stirrings of the halo and the trinket and all the wounds he carried.

Fuck. Don't let the vagabond be dead. Silas would be inconsolable.

'Charlie,' Pitch shouted.

Limp and bare foot be damned, he ran.

CHAPTER 31

The sorceress appeared beneath one of the arches, stepping out from the relief as though she were stone come to life.

Silas edged back, uncertain if what he saw was real or another illusion, as Macha walked one purposeful, slow step at a time around the monopteros. She had her hands clasped behind her, lost in the folds of her cloak, her face obscured by the mask of feathers. Only her lips were visible, and they were curled in a small smile. Perhaps – Silas grasped at a rather long straw – he had luck on his side and she'd not heard him speak of royalty.

'You've done very well to make your way here, Mr Mercer.' She waved a hand towards the columns. 'But do you think you are any less trapped than your beloved souls?'

'You have no right to imprison them here.'

'And yet, here they are.' A lopsided grin bared teeth. 'Seems I do not need a right to take what I want. Isn't that wonderful?'

The Sanctuary chose then to rumble through its newest tremor, and Silas relished the slip of the sorceress's smile. The moment was brief though. She regathered her poise in a heartbeat.

'What purpose do you have for all these souls?' Silas demanded. He took another step back as she drew closer. The sway of her coat was real enough to stir dust as she went.

'Oh come now, Mr Mercer. It doesn't suit you to play stupid.' She touched at a column, running black-nailed fingers down its length. The veins of cobalt lit up, and the lost souls raised fear-laden cries. 'The light of Azazel is with me, as it is with my sister and brother both, and you have already seen what it is our lord's magick allows me to do.' She brushed a limp-wristed hand against the next column. The cobalt responded again, highlighting the mass of sigils carved into the stonework. The markings were intricate, all manner of whorls and helixes and loops. All told the designs were elegant and undeniably beautiful, but his gut churned to look on them. 'You know I should be quite upset with you, Silas. tearing the heads off two of my sweet children not so long ago...after I thought I'd taught you a lesson about how unhappy that makes me. But to watch your brutality really was quite rousing.'

He shook off her words. 'You seek to make teratisms of all these innocent souls.'

'Good grief, hardly innocent. Why do you think they are susceptible to the Blight to begin with? These souls are all rotten in some way.' She sighed. 'But as much as I think myself quite useful in crafting teratisms, I can only aspire to the Watcher King's brilliance when it comes to making monsters. For he is the Blight's true master, and I am a fledgling apprentice at best.' She glanced at Silas, a hint of the white of her eyes showing through the mask's netting. 'So, tell me more about how your prince is going to best him, then? It all sounded so very exciting.'

The world seemed to fall away beneath Silas's feet, and his blood turned cold in the vein. His face must have betrayed his horror, for her smile widened.

'So there it is, I did hear you correctly. Goodness, Onoskolis will be delighted to learn she rode a royal cock.' She tilted her head, hand at the ready to stroke at a pillar that was far too close to Silas for his liking. 'But what a pity I shall have to inform Nemain that she was right.' She winced, lips peeling back as though she'd sucked on a lemon. 'My dear sister has had it in her head that Mr Astaroth might well be the famed and feared Berserker Prince ever since Onoskolis came back to us in such a tizzy, claiming it was no regular daemon she had ridden. As Iblis knew of only one higher daemon in Arcadia who could not be accounted for and would have a decent reason to want to hide away...well...'

Silas was silent a moment too long. 'I'd not be in any rush to deliver such news.' He did his best to appear scornful. 'If your Iblis knows anything at all, it is that the prince is imprisoned in an abaddon beneath White Mountain.'

'Well, that is certainly what Arcadia would have everyone believe. But I dare say His Royal Highness is in no such place. Goodness, you don't look well, Mr Mercer.' She tut-tutted, shaking her head. 'You were not chosen by the goddess for your ability to keep a secret, were you? You are absolutely terrible at it.' She laughed, a high and rather too pleasant sound. 'The Order will be horrified with your loose lips, I'm sure. But never mind, you are both idiots, you and the prince. For if you were not, you'd not have travelled here quite so alone.' She reached to touch at the column nearest to Silas, as though daring him to strike out. 'I suppose if you'd not been so idiotic, that boy of yours might not be dead now either.'

Now it was heat roaring through Silas's body, as though Pitch's flames moved in him. 'Charlie.' His voice was scratchy, parched dry. 'If you have harmed him...' Silas threw himself at the sorceress.

Macha raised one hand, palm up, whispered quickly, and blew against it. A puff of yellow dust flew from her palm. The particles swelled, and a buzzing filled the air. Silas braced as the dust took form, and a swarm of yellow-and-black wasps drove at him. Silas waved his arms about like a fool, dancing and shifting around in violent contortions, swatting at the tiny creatures that darted at him. The souls were a bubbling cacophony in the background, unsettled by his assault.

Not.

He caught the word, but it was hardly his greatest concern. The air was awash with insects. They darted at him, driving stinging tails into the backs of his hands and where his neck was bare, no longer hidden beneath lengths of dark hair. For such tiny things, they delivered a whopping pain. It was like being driven at with the sharpest of knife tips. The wasps slashed shallow cuts, making him holler in rage and discomfort.

'Now you will tell me where he is, ankou.' Macha's easy manner evaporated, replaced by an icy steel.

Silas hissed beneath the onslaught of tiny attackers. 'What...do you...mean?' His ankle turned as he was driven off the platform, still slapping about like a deranged scarecrow. Perhaps if he could make his way to the walls, he could escape to another section of the Sanctuary and find Charlie.

The sorceress *must* be lying. Charlie was not dead. He'd know it, would he not? Surely if the lad had passed, Silas would *know* it.

'Shit...damn it...' He swiped at the cloud of buzzing fierceness surrounding him.

A pity he could not see a step ahead to make his escape. He dared not open his eyes too wide for fear of receiving a barb right to the eyeball. His cheeks were on fire from the strikes. The infernal critters were bloody everywhere.

'Tell your pretty prince to come out of hiding, for it will not do you, or your souls, well for him to conceal himself much longer.'

A wasp found his lip, and Silas slapped at his own face to rid himself of it. But his thoughts were not with the attacking insects; rather they were settled on Macha.

Come out of hiding?

Christ. The sorceress didn't know where Pitch was.

It was the very best news he'd heard in a lifetime. The daemon was evading them, here in their very own Sanctuary.

Silas laughed through swollen lips. 'He's outdone you, then?'

The Sanctuary shuddered so hard it seemed to startle even the wasps, which paused for a beat in their attack.

'Hardly, Mr Mercer, for we still have you,' Macha snarled. 'Mr Astaroth will show himself soon enough where you are involved.'

The hubbub coming from the souls grew louder. He strained to make some sense of their cries, but they might as well have been talking underwater. Through the squint of his eyes, Silas noted the brilliance of the room, the cobalt shining like rays of a blue sun. Much brighter than before.

Macha was setting off every column in the monopteros. And he feared he knew the reason why.

Not.

Real.

Stop.

Silas frowned. The souls were making no sense. He clapped at his ear, where a wasp was intent on travelling into the canal. Bloody hell, his body felt as though it had been rolled back and forth on a bed of nails. He fell to one knee, groping about in the vain hope he might be near the wall. His hand swept through empty air.

Not quite empty. There was a thick soup of stingers awaiting him.

Illusion.

Not real.

Stop!

Silas froze with one hand halfway through another manic wave. He was puffing like he'd fought Black Annis twice over and not a cloud of tiny insects.

Illusion.

Silas lowered his hands and pressed to his feet. The wasps clouded the air around him, the ache of their strikes filling him. Their buzzing was so loud it was as though they were inside his head.

He breathed in, calmed his racing pulse. And breathed out.

The wasps were *not* bloody real.

'Not real,' he muttered to himself. 'Not real.'

He refused to rise to the urge to strike out, to defend himself. The attacks lessened, the sound of the insects fading.

Silas opened his eyes.

The chamber was clear, though still a startling shade of blue. He glanced down at his hands, filthy with the dried remains of the teratisms but unblemished by any nicks and cuts. Not a single red welt.

The sense of having been stung at all evaporated, like a hunger sated. The sorceress had played him well. He searched for her.

Macha stood near the relief she had stepped through earlier. 'I will say they do seem to like you more than me, Mr Mercer. Can't imagine why.'

Her grin was lascivious. 'But it hardly matters now.' She threw a careless wave towards the monopteros. 'You are all at our master's mercy now.'

Every column in the monopteros was aglow. The sigils were all high-lighted by the thin rivulets of cobalt that formed them.

'What have you done?' he demanded.

'It is more what I am about to do. Your daemon cannot hide from me forever. And we both know he will not long stay concealed if he thinks harm may come to his ankou.'

The relief behind her shimmered as though it were a reflection atop a pond. A familiar face pressed through the watery image, jet-black lengths of hair framing a sun-touched face, horns parting the silken lengths.

A trace of bitterness coated Silas's tongue. He curled his fingers into fists and imagined them laid into the creature who had brought Pitch such misery.

Onoskolis lifted her skirt to step over the lip of the entranceway, revealing a vile feature; one of her feet was not a foot at all but a dirty white hoof struck through with smears of black as though it had been badly tarred, her thick ankle coated in matte-brown hair.

The Alp glared at him, dropping her skirt quickly. And Silas revelled in letting all his revulsion show.

She glanced away. 'Macha, come. Be done with this. You heard Iblis's order.' The Alp grabbed at Macha's cloak.

'Piss off. He will not order me about.' The sorceress slapped her away. 'I want more time.'

'You cannot have it. Do you not feel what the tree's magick is doing to the Sanctuary?'

'All the more reason to get to the purebreds it covets. We have the ankou. The daemon will show himself if he is endangered and –'

'Iblis grows angry with you. Badh is here and impatient for you to aid him in sealing the Sanctuary. Palatyne too cannot wait on you any longer. We must go. It is over here, Macha.'

'What of Nemain?'

Onoskolis glanced at Silas. 'It has been deemed not wise for you all to assemble in the same place. The Order is searching for their Horsemen.'

Silas's pulse drummed a hopeful beat. Did that mean the Order was close enough to frighten the Morrigan? Perhaps Macha was not the only one who needed more time.

'Nemain needs to be here, damn it.' Macha pouted. 'The three of us could easily overcome that fucking tree –'

'You *need* to survive. The Fulbourn was only ever meant to hold your ghosts and corpses; it was never meant to become a battleground. The daemon eludes us, and the magick that has that fucking tree growing is shaking the foundations.' Right on cue the Sanctuary rumbled like a distant storm, and the lost souls sent urgent whispers to Silas. *Help us.* 'We will have it all come down on our heads if we stay here much longer. Palatyne has done all she can. Your sigils alone are not strong enough –'

'Shut your mouth.' Macha glared at the daemon, her lips an angry, thin line. 'We need to lure the daemon, and this is how we do it.' She stabbed her finger at Silas.

'The time has passed for –'

'He is Dominion.'

Onoskolis looked to Silas, her confusion almost comical.

'Not him, you fool. That daemon you fucked is Dominion.'

Onoskolis's fine-featured face drained pale. Silas had made a terrible mess speaking Pitch's truth out loud, but to see her fear made it almost worth it.

'Dominion...' she breathed, touching a hand to one of her horns.

Ankou, the souls pleaded. Silas peered into the trap. Samyaza's ruby eyes had darkened beneath the cobalt.

'You rode royalty, my dear.' Macha withdrew the white reed from her dark cloak. She held it aloft, as though preparing to conduct an unseen orchestra. 'Mr Mercer very kindly let that particular cat out of the bag. The daemon is a prince of Arcadia.'

Onoskolis's smile had trouble lifting. 'I knew him different...but *the* prince of Arcadia? As Nemain proposed?'

Macha adjusted her hold on the rod, pointing it towards the glowing monopteros. 'Yes, yes. No need to point out that my sister was right. I'll not hear the end of it as it is. The Berserker Prince is not in his abaddon.'

She flicked her wrist, and the lost souls cried in one voice, a voice muffled as though a thick blanket had been thrown upon their prison.

'I see.' Onoskolis swallowed so hard Silas caught the click of her throat, but her agitation was short-lived. She pulled back her shoulders, lifted her chin. And her wide grin flashed sharp teeth. 'Well, if only I'd known. I'd have done so much more to him.' She caught Silas's eye and ran the tip of her tongue slowly between her lips. 'He was a very fine fuck indeed. And I've you to thank for that, Mr Mercer. He was so very hard with his desire for you. I do hope I have not spoiled him for you. You can still get him onto his back, can you not?' She blinked wide, fathomless eyes in a show of innocence that looked ridiculous on her. She breathed in cruelty like an incubus inhaled the sweet things in life.

Silas did not swallow against the bile rising up his throat. He did not move. Not an inch. For the very slightest movement on his part would see his control lost. His rage would escape a volatile stranglehold and serve no purpose but to likely see him screaming and punching at a brick wall as the Alp and her mistress slipped away. He would have his moment with Onoskolis, but it was not here and now.

The Alp looked away, and Silas liked to imagine it was because she saw the darkness of his thoughts.

'Let us go. Now, Macha.'

He savoured the subtle waver in her tone. 'Yes, best you run along now.' He was ice and hatred mixed into a fine cocktail, with a sliver of a smile to match. 'Pitch has told me all the things he would like to do to *you*, daemon, when he finds you. I doubt very much you will thank me for anything at all, once he is done.'

'Oh, Mr Mercer.' Macha laughed. 'You speak as though you have a hope of ever leaving this place.' The rod began to emanate light, a sicklier pale blue than the cobalt. 'Your work for the Lady is done, I'm afraid. And though I shall be sad to say goodbye to the Fulbourn, for I had such fun here, I shall be very happy knowing that the souls I had no use for will serve a purpose after all, for I abhor waste. Goodbye, ankou.'

Macha whispered, so low beneath her breath it sounded more of an exhale than speech, and pointed the tip of the rod towards the monopteros.

Silas's ears popped first. A vibration hummed through the air, subtler than the more violent screeches of the ailing Sanctuary. The cobalt veins brightened. Silas shaded his eyes. The sorceress's wild laughter echoed off the chamber walls as she and Onoskolis slipped back through their portal and vanished.

The moment they vanished, the roar of the lost souls went from faint to raucous.

The unseen barrier that had separated them from Silas fell away, the soul trap gone.

What swept from it was a horror.

Silas was dumped in a seething pool of misery. The angst of dozens of hopeless dead. The roar was deafening to begin with, a disarray of sound that held the lead weight of grief and unspeakable loss. He wished nothing more than for it to end, until the first brittle notes began to appear.

The clattered, uneven melody of Macha's teratisms. Clunky, jarring notes that sought to clamber over the top of one another.

'Christ.' Silas staggered, as much as from the tunes' morose weight as from understanding what the sorceress had done.

She had wielded the Blight like the curse it was...twisting each and every soul that had called to him...had rescued him from her illusion... and forced a transformation upon them.

She had made them teratisms in one astonishing instant.

His throat was thick with the horror of it. The realisation a dagger, its tip sharp and cruel against his heart. These souls had begged for his protection. And he had failed them.

The wave of anguish hit him head on. The mournful arias rose, abrupt, untuned, and wayward, as though the new teratisms were confused by their sudden existence.

Samyaza's statue rocked on its plinth, and Silas braced.

He could run, push through to another place and seek to stay one step ahead of the maddened crowd that was coming for him. But an inner pull held him rooted to the spot, an ingrained compulsion to remain and see that right was done.

He was ankou. He was made to end their torment.

The statue toppled, shattering in huge portions. One chunk skidded towards Silas, and he sidestepped to avoid being struck in the shin by one of Samyaza's wings.

The teratisms spewed forth from their pit, a torrent of umber and sickly greens rising like a burst water main from the monopteros's floor. So many wretches he could not make much sense of any of them until they were upon him. Saturating him with ire, vexation, and enmity, they were as thick as marzipan on a rotten cake.

He reached his hands into the fray and found the neck of a creature whose mouth was fixed open, crawling with writhing worms that spilled over him as Silas crushed its gangly neck. He tore the head free, found himself spattered with something horrid and sticky, and set off using the grotesque battering ram to fend off the multitudes reaching for him. He spun about, seeking to create some space for himself in the vile pile that sought to smother him.

They came for him in a mob. Spindly and graceless, thick and grotesque. All very vaguely human. Enough so for it to send sharp pangs of horror through Silas with each blow. He caught a glimpse of watery eyes, a thin film of white dulling their colour. Fear was so apparent in the gaze that he hesitated and suffered a deep gash to his bruised shoulder when another teratism took its chance. He threw the head with all the might he could summon, sending more than one of Macha's creations tumbling.

A skeletal creature with a misshapen skull ran at him. Silas met it head-on, dispatching it quickly with a moist snap of an elongated neck, the head coming free with a sickening moist sound. Silas grabbed the body before it fell and made it a shield. He charged at the gathering of wailing, tortured souls, seeking to push his way free of this miserable prison.

Bloody hell, there were so many of them. So much death to be wrought. But this was not the pleasant dispatch of a ready soul. Here he must be monstrous, breaking and tearing his way through the group.

And he did not want this. Silas was not a creature of chaos.

He was covered in gore, puce and pea green, drenched in a vileness that did not bear thinking of.

Silas bellowed into the calamity.

He stood at the centre of a hellish circle. Far worse than anything he had faced at the greensward, for he knew that it was not a daemon who could save him here, only carnage itself. A carnage not wrought by a rampaging prince but by an ankou.

Another neck was broken, another decapitation complete, this one setting off sprays of rich crimson that bathed his face with warmth. The tinge of copper clung to his lips, and he may have darted his tongue to taste it.

One of the grief-ridden souls caught at him, latched twisted, rheumatic fingers about his arm, and sought to tug him closer to where sharp teeth and gouged eyes waited.

Silas's cry was unearthly. It tore at his throat as he landed his fist in the middle of the teratism's grey and sagging face. Anger drove Silas's fist deep through sinew and bone still fragile and tender after such a hurried birthing.

He could have freed all of them. Sent each soul to where the goddess waited. Finished their lives as they should have been ended.

But the sorceress had made that impossible.

They had begged Silas for release.

Now he was their destroyer. And the longer this went on, the more his own inner beast roared.

He was torn in two as he broke them apart, savaging their wretched, manipulated bodies with hands that had been made for exactly such things. Silas stumbled. Seeing himself for what he truly was.

He was Nephilim.

A monster destroying monsters.

He was dreadful. He was death. And a tiny part of him relished it.

Another teratism hurled itself at him, the surrounding mass seeming to adopt a twisted herd mentality, awaiting their turn to come at him. All the while their melodies screamed, bastardised by long-held rage and rich with a hopelessness that coated the chamber like soot.

Silas could not discern where one refrain began and another finished. He was a drunkard on his feet, struggling to keep upright as horror after horror came at him. He was saturated with sorrow, fairly drowning in the blood and ruin of the damned. It was staining him, making him heavy and in danger of sinking too deep.

Each strike added another stone to his pockets. Another weight to drag him down.

Silas's sob thrust itself free, making his ribs ache, his eyes water. A saviour, the ghosts of Castle Coombe had called him. Fuck, what would they think of him now?

He shook his head. 'No more,' he whispered, as another came for him.

As another was torn apart by his hand. One after another they came. One after another he took them apart. Their blood and bile running over the shaven contours of his face, his skin a ruin of split flesh, his own blood mingling with those he killed.

'Stop,' he said, weakly. 'Please, stop.'

He cast away another severed head, flesh thick beneath his fingernails. 'No more.' Louder this time.

The stench of the carnage was sickening. The drag of sorrow picking him apart. His feet slipped in cool puddles of entrails, and Christ almighty, it was too much

'No more!' he shouted.

Silas's nails bit into his palms. No one in this cursed chamber should exist, himself included. They would *not* exist, were it not for the manipulation of those with great power.

For the teratisms it was Macha and the Blight.

For Silas it was a traitorous angel. Izanami too perhaps. But at least the goddess had allowed him to keep something of himself when all else was stripped away. He'd lived. Likely loved. Certainly lost.

Another tortured soul took its turn next. A spindly thing, a rag-and-bone collection so fragile to be filled with such suffering. And Silas saw it plainly then. His image caught in the blackness of the teratism's eyes.

They were the same. He and these broken, manipulated unfortunates.

They were, at least in some part, human. Monsters of a very different kind.

Silas separated skull from spine, and he was washed with blood the colour of juniper, thick as warmed honey.

Another tormented creature took its place. There were so few now. Enough.

He pursed his lips, unsure what sound he sought to make until the air was rushing from him.

The whistle was high and as sharp as the bandalore's blade had ever been. Silas played the note across his tongue, and it stretched as long as the horizon. Exquisite and unreachable. A tonality that could be made by no other than him.

Death's chord, for death's envoy.

The creature's head snapped to one side, its face a smoothed, tight sheet of skin with no eyes, no nose, just a tiny hole where a mouth might have been. The teratism did not take another step. And the melodies of the last of the Blight's miserable army faltered.

'No more!' Silas's cry echoed, as though he stood in a grand church, the ceilings high and built for lifting the priest's voice to something nearer to god.

His lips tingled, and he breathed heavily, his nostrils damp. He was hemmed in by twisted limbs and torn pieces. A mountain had grown around him, threatening to bury him more deeply than the Sanctuary ever could.

'That is enough,' he breathed. 'I'll do no more.'

A handful of teratisms remained standing.

They, like all the others here, were weak vessels, made too fast. They'd not been strengthened by decades of the Blight's influence, formed with time into dangerous calamities. Macha's creatures were delicate, coming apart like rain-soaked paper in his hands.

'Stay back.' He drew himself up, hand raised, fingers splayed and palm open. No fists this time. 'No more. Do you understand me?'

The melodies sank low, their tempos hitching, losing their flow.

'Can you hear me? I need you to hear me now.' Silas took shallow breaths, too frightened yet to believe the stillness around him might last. 'Listen to me. Follow my voice, and I will take you out of that darkness. Do not be deceived by the Blight....' He recalled what the ghosts and spectre of Castle Coombe had told him. 'The gloaming, you know it as…but it is all the same. It is a lie. It is deception. Listen to me, hear *me*. For I need your help.'

An off-key note sounded, somewhere in the aria of one of the few who surrounded him. Far too few in a room soaked in catastrophe. But he could not change what he had done, only what he might do next. 'Do you hear me?' Silas's voice cracked.

The stillness was reserved for the teratisms only, for the Sanctuary itself shook like a pot about to boil. He inhaled, his heart at a race in his chest.

The Morrigan were going to seal them in here. He must find Pitch, and Edward and Charlie, before they all learned what a horror it was to be buried alive.

Silas raised his voice. 'There will be an end to the Blight, I know. Because I know the one who will end it. I have been at his side a long while, and I have seen what he is capable of.' His eyes stung with the cold hard prick of loss. 'The prince will not fail us, because he has never once failed me. He is extraordinary. And he is brave. He endures when all have assumed him a lost cause. He is quite remarkable.' Silas had entirely forgotten where he was going with this. 'And it will take far more than divine magick and a headless horseman to stop him. I assure you, there is no other like Tobias Astaroth.'

Prince.

Dominion.

Scoundrel.

Lover.

Silas slumped. Filth and remains clung to every nook and cranny on his body. He was knee-deep in strewn organs and broken bones and only realising *now* what was undeniably true.

Oh bloody, bloody hell.

He loved the mad prince of Arcadia. Loved the fool so very much it hurt more than any pain he'd suffered here yet.

A strange sound hiccoughed from the ankou. 'Shit.' He fought to gather himself and shrug off the ill-timed sensibilities. 'Do you hear me? I need your help to find him. Do you understand?' he demanded, forceful now. 'Listen to me, not the Blight, for it rules you cruelly. Do not succumb to its falsehoods. The Blight is not your saviour.'

Silas's lover was. Every rambunctious infuriating inch of that glorious creature.

The jostle of conflicting emotions played havoc with Silas's steadiness. He was joy and brutal unhappiness combined. And he could not stand another moment absent from the daemon's side. Too much time had been lost here already.

'Help me, please,' he begged. 'Help us stop all this.'

A contorted teratism, with limbs that bent contrary at the joints and a mouth sewn shut with a criss-cross of thick threads, turned so it might lift its crooked arm towards him.

Ankou.

A humpbacked teratism whose chin rested against its chest slithered an awfully long tongue from its slash of a mouth and spoke. *Stop. This. Us.*

'Yes, for good. It must end. Will you help me?'

Silas *heard* the surrender. The collapse of the Blight's hold upon these creatures. It was there in their melodies. The grating, restless tunes finding their tempo at last. Silas took a shuddered breath. Their songs were not lovely, but they were resolute and held a beat that could not be denied.

The Sanctuary shifted with a deep, disconcerting rumble. Silas threw out his hands, certain this was the moment the roof would cave on him. And there was no way on god's green Earth he was going to be ended by damn stalactites.

'We must go.'

Find saviour.

'Oh god, please don't call him that to his face. I'll never hear the end of it.'

A shudder took hold of the chamber. The archway the sorceress and Onoskolis had used cracked in half, releasing chunks of thundering, dust-billowing stone. The pieces skidded as far as they could before the corpse-soaked ground brought them to a standstill.

A gaping wound opened in the wall. An escape. As though the Sanctuary were turning on itself, abandoning its attempts to hinder him.

'Find him!' he shouted, racing at the opening. 'Take me to Tobias.'

CHAPTER 32

Pitch ran at the coffin, jumping over the shattered branches. His boot slipped through piled leaves, the debris catching between his bare toes. His back was plagued with needling points, and his arm...gods, it was like an oversized bird upon a cuckoo clock was trying to hammer its way through his bone. The watch was well aware of who was in this room. But Edward would have to wait.

'Charlie!'

There was a narrow opening in the wood, an upside-down V-shape that demanded he crouch to negotiate it. He grunted his way through, bent knees none too pleased, the arrow punctures on his thigh making themselves known.

'Pissy, fucking, headless fucking horseman.'

He finished his tirade and his squeezing through and stood up just in time to see Charlie attempt to do the same. Only the lad was far less capable of the task. Pitch's naked foot squelched something soft and damp as he covered the two steps needed to reach Charlie. The ground was covered in a thick layer of rowan berries, some of which he'd just pressed like he were making a summer wine.

'Easy, easy.' Pitch grabbed beneath the lad's armpits. He was clad in the institution's garb: starch-stiff linen and a baggy shirt and trousers with unappealing chequered panels of contrasting greys, a size too big for the slight vagabond.

'Don't touch me.' Charlie put up a pathetic fight, despite the fact that Pitch was all that kept him on his feet. The bracelet's holly leaves scratched against Pitch's wrists as he easily overrode the feeble resistance.

'It's me, Charlie,' Pitch said. 'Tobias.'

The silver hue that lit the barn made the lad appear shockingly white, doubling the vibrancy of his cornflower-blue eyes and causing the freckles upon the bridge of his nose to shine like tiny beacons against his paleness.

'Pitch?' Charlie sighed and collapsed against the daemon. 'Thank god. Is Silas with you?'

The question stung. 'No. He's not...'

Charlie inhaled sharply, eyes darting to take in Pitch's state. He was a ruin with his shirt entirely done for, only the corset to cover him in any way, and garish pink wounds and all manner of grime and dirt and blood staining the rest of him. 'You look terrible –'

'It's been a shitty day.'

'Silas...he's all right, isn't he?' Great orbs of blue were set on Pitch.

'Of course he is,' he snapped.

'But he doesn't have this.' Charlie's right hand had been curled in a fist, and he relaxed his fingers now. 'It came to me...I don't understand how...but it saved my life.'

Silas's bandalore sat on his palm. Its mahogany tones were made darker by the wavering silver light, but Pitch would know the damned thing if they were in near darkness.

'How do you have that?' He wanted to snatch it from the lad and only just held himself back. 'He's been trying to...he needed it...' And was still in need of it now.

'I don't truly know... I don't understand how I came to be holding it, but I am so very glad that I did.' Charlie winced as he settled himself.

'Are you hurt?' Pitch had discomfort of his own. The bloody pendant watch was trying to tear a hole in his skin now he was alongside Edward. But the lieutenant showed no sign of rousing. Not even a flicker beneath blue-veined eyelids.

'Just a bruise here and there,' Charlie said, far too wide-eyed, horribly pale. 'But the lieutenant...I don't know what they've done to him. I went to see him in his room. I'd been doing that since they brought him to the asylum.' The lad dashed his tongue against his lips. 'But he was gone, and the next thing I know, I'm waking to see you and Silas peering in through the glass and myself in a straitjacket. Then that tosser threw me in a bloody glass coffin, and next time I woke, I was surrounded by shattered glass with the bandalore in my hand.' He spoke far too fast and feverishly, shaking as he caressed the scythe like it were a damned kitten. 'I don't understand it...but I felt compelled to move. To find Edward...' Charlie pushed up his sleeve, revealing more of Ottelie's braided holly-and-rowan-wood bracelet. There were finer tendrils coming off the larger stems, hints of green at their tips, like new shoots rising after winter, lying across Charlie's skin as fine as spiderweb. 'I found him. The bandalore, it was, god you'll think I'm mad, but it led me to him.' He flicked his gaze to Pitch, who said nothing. 'I found Edward, and when I did...god, Tobias...I could feel the bracelet grow. I felt it take from me, like I was the soil it was lacking...using me to grow...and I didn't mind...I didn't mind...'

The respite from the growling of the Sanctuary's foundations ended, returning with a crisp vengeance. The tremor shook the illusion of the barn with nasty vigour.

Charlie cried out, the bandalore cracking against the glass as he braced himself. Pitch too used the coffin to stay upright, glancing down at Edward. The man was handsome, no nefarious sorcery seemed capable of stealing that, but his hair and beard had gone a shocking grey, as though the colour had fled all this unhappiness.

'Do you think he's...' Charlie rubbed at the bracelet. 'Please tell me he isn't –'

'He's not dead.'

The lad's relief turned his shoulders into jelly. 'Thank god.'

There was very little chance his particular god had anything to do with it. But Pitch was certain: Edward was alive.

A shift in the air above him had Pitch diving for Charlie. 'Look out!'

He threw himself over the lad, plastering him against the flat surface of the coffin. Debris crashed through the barn roof, bringing down slats of wood along with the stones that fell. More than one of the falling stones aimed itself at Pitch's back, striking the soft flesh where the Dullahan's whip had penetrated. Rocks slammed against the glasswork, creating fine spiderweb-like cracks in the surface.

'Edward,' Charlie cried, muffled beneath him. 'We need to protect him.' The lad was trying to wriggle free, but to go bloody where?

'Fuck, stay still.' Pitch grunted. A rock large as a golf ball found the back of his head, and he swore anew.

If the tree was to blame for the Sanctuary's instability, then what the blazes was going on now? And where the fuck was the ankou? Because they needed to leave. And leaving without Silas, even if it meant getting his precious bloody vagabond to safety, was not going to happen.

'Forget me,' Charlie cried. 'You have to protect him, Pitch. You came for him, didn't you? Tyvain said the two of you had to be brought together. I know it's important.'

Pitch was saved from replying by a blow to the small of his back. He loosened a string of bitter curses against the culprit whilst wondering how the fuck the soothsayer, who was generally utterly useless, had nailed this particular foresight.

The onslaught settled. The sprinkle of dust and finer stones around them no longer seemed intent on breaking their bones. Rather, it was just immensely irritating to the nose, and getting his hair remotely clean after this would be a whole new nightmare.

Charlie slipped free, managing to tread on Pitch's bare toes in the process.

'Oh Christ,' he hissed.

'Quickly,' Charlie yelled 'With the two of us, we might get this open. I couldn't do it alone.' The lad crashed onto his knees and put all his paltry effort into pushing at the lid of the coffin, his youthful face wrinkled by his efforts. 'Tobias, help me, will you? Don't just stand there. I think you're probably a lot stronger than me.'

'What the blazes do you mean probably?' Pitch spat. 'Stop that before you burst a lung.' He dug his fingers into the narrow gap between base and lid. 'Move back.'

It was not so easy a task as he'd hoped; the lid was astonishingly heavy. Pitch allowed a modicum of his flame to lurk beneath the surface of his hands, but he'd not be able to keep it there long. Even that slight whisper of fire bullied his control. The unsettled beast awakened the moment it felt him draw on his strength, no amuletum to stifle it.

Gritting his teeth, Pitch hauled up, sparking a quick flare of flame, extinguishing it the moment the lid flipped over on itself and fell with a thud alongside the body of the coffin. His forearm roared with unmitigated pain as though he'd been struck by the very scythe itself.

'Enoch's fucking taint.' Pitch went to his knees, clutching at his arm.

'What is it? The fire? You were on fire...' Charlie hovered in the clumsy way of the useless. 'Tobias...are you wounded?'

Of course he was fucking wounded. He'd barely spent a moment of his existence not suffering from one injury or another.

Blood flowed between the fingers he had pressed to his arm. The cut he'd made to seal in the watch was splitting open. The sense of something with pincers beneath his skin was truly horrific.

The halo's scars joined the fray. They blazed so fiercely he'd have thought he was actually on fire. Pitch doubled over, Charlie's cries ringing in his ears. Gods, it was too much. His lungs were scorched dry of air; he was certain his skin was falling from his bones with the heat.

Give the prophet the relic.

Seraphiel's voice roared with the flames. Brutal and blunt and as commanding as he'd ever been in life. Bending Pitch lower, his forehead near to his knees, his bleeding arm saturating his trousers. Gods, he was so fucking tired of bleeding.

Give the prophet the relic.

Pitch breathed through gritted teeth. The watch's pin slicing him open. Reminding him how little choice he had in all this.

A relic? The purebreds had such things. Bones of their dead saints. But it was a name that could be given to any object that survived from the past.

'Tobias, please.' Charlie's desperation surrounded him. 'I don't know what to do. How do I help you?'

Pitch didn't waste time with a pointless reply. The purebred could do nothing to help him. He lifted a scarlet-gloved hand from the watch's hiding place, and before he thought too much about it, he dug a finger into the sliced-open portion of his skin. Pitch exhaled long and steady and gouged the tear wider, dragging his finger through his own flesh until the hole was wide enough that he could squeeze two fingers into it. Carmine droplets gathered at his elbow, dripping to soak into the crushed rowan berries beneath him.

Charlie whimpered, but to his credit, he did not look away.

Pitch got ahold of the coronet which sat at the top of the watch's design and dragged the pendant from its pulpy hiding place. There was no telling the item was gold, it was so drenched in the deep crimson of Pitch's blood.

The watch slipped from between his fingers, and it was Charlie who got to it first, cupping his hands to rescue the grim token.

'What now?' Charlie might yet collapse in a quivering heap, but for now he was stalwart and resolute as any wartime nurse. He wiped the stained watch upon his clothes as he waited for an answer. Pitch saw then why Silas might admire the lad so.

Pitch sat back on his heels. His body trembled with the forces spoiling beneath the surface, the rising clamour of the wildness and halo's mark had combined into a reckoning he struggled to control. His skin and bones did not seem enough to contain them both.

'Give it to him.' He jerked his chin towards Edward.

Charlie's gaze darted back and forth between them. 'He's asleep... What do you want me to –'

'Pin it on him,' Pitch growled. 'Shove it up his fucking nose...I don't know.'

He just needed it to be done. For this sense of fraying at all his edges to settle. For his body not to ache at every joint and burn in every vein.

Charlie leaned over the lieutenant, speaking to him as he went. 'I told you it would be all right, Edward. They are here to rescue us...just as I said.' The lad swept back a strand of grey hair that had curled across Edward's nose, doing so with a gentleness that spoke of a deep concern for the man. 'We just need you to open your eyes, Edward. Come on now. This will help you...Tobias says.'

Tobias had said no such thing. Tobias...Pitch...Vassago...was an inept wreck at that very moment, barely in control of himself, let alone any rescue. Charlie was careful with his pinning, slipping one hand beneath the lieutenant's shirt to ensure he did not prick the skin, whilst the other manoeuvred the pin into the fabric, the very same fabric the lad wore: unflattering checks of contrasting grey that was the institution's patient uniform.

'Forgive me,' Pitch whispered. For it felt the right moment to say such things. He and Seraphiel had taken so much from the lieutenant. And the stealing seemed set to continue.

'There we go, then,' Charlie muttered, patting at the watch where he'd pinned it to the right-hand side of Edward's chest like one of the medals the lieutenant owned. 'Right...it's on him. What happens...'

Edward's body jerked. He sucked in a harsh breath, and his eyes flew open.

The prophet's irises were a radiant citrine. As unforgettable as the Seraph who had borne them.

He tilted his head, gazing beyond where Charlie had his hands pressed to his mouth. He found Pitch, and a tiny smile curved his lips.

And when Seraphiel's voice came again, it was not from the depths of Pitch's skull but from Edward's own lips.

'Vassago.'

CHAPTER 33

Pitch recoiled from the name...from the angel's voice...as though he'd been struck. All the noise around him vanished, all the heat found a way to leave his skin. Pitch's pulse was manic, the beats blurring to a hum.

'How are you here?' He was hoarse as fear dragged its claws along the bars of the beast's cage.

Edward blinked, and the glare of citrine settled into tiny flecks that floated amongst the lieutenant's own more pleasant grey.

The dazed man struggled to gather his bearings.

'Jesus, my head.' Edward sought to sit up, but Charlie was there first. 'Charlie? Oh thank god you are all right. I thought they had...' He grimaced. 'I thought they had hurt you. I could hear screaming.'

The lad was busy fussing over the lieutenant in a way which would have made Silas proud. Gods, he was going to lose his mind to see the lad upright and in one piece.

'There's been quite a lot of that...' Charlie grew pained. 'But it wasn't all me. I hoped you had slept through it all...'

Edward leaned into Charlie. With the way the lad sat, the lieutenant was hidden from Pitch's view. Which was fine. Pitch was not keen to see those flame-riddled eyes again. 'I drifted in and out... I heard things... I couldn't tell what was dream and what was real.' He ran his hand along the glass rim, his face troubled. 'But I see much of it was not a dream.'

He clutched at Charlie's sleeve. 'He's here now though, isn't he? I didn't dream that.'

'Tobias?' Charlie helped Edward shift onto his knees in a tender way that betrayed his affection.

Pitch watched them, taking note of the gentle air between them. Just one chance meeting in a Berkeley Square pub seemed highly unlikely, with the doe-eyed way the vagabond regarded the lieutenant.

'Yes. Tobias is coming for us, Charlie.' Edward was panting by the time he'd made it to kneeling. He draped an arm about Charlie's shoulder and looked up. The lieutenant's breath caught, and his eyes, still flecked with unsettling gold, narrowed. 'Tobias...oh...you're...'

'I'm what?'

'So...' Edward squinted. 'So very bright. You're almost as bright as he is.'

'He, who?' Pitch spat the question.

'I think you know very well.'

Pitch's temper flared. 'Don't fucking play with me, Charters.'

Charlie's freckled face bunched in a frown, but Edward pressed his hand to his arm. 'It's all right, Charlie.' He turned to Pitch. 'He says not to utter his name here, but he is the one I've spoken of before...from my dreams...the one you said was my imagination struck mad. Everyone said I was mad...' Edward grunted as Charlie helped him sit on the edge of the coffin. He was scowling, but Pitch suspected it was not because of the uncomfortable seat, rather at being condemned a lunatic. 'But I am not. I *never* was. The Holy One says you have always known who it was I saw.'

The fucking Holy One? Seraphiel was an imperious enough bastard to name himself so. Pitch shoved his scarlet-smeared fingers into his hair. 'And this...' He could barely bring himself to say it. 'This *Holy One*...he's speaking to you? He told you I would come?'

'In his way, yes. It's not exactly speaking.' Edward was far surer of himself than he ought to be, what with waking to find himself lying in a coffin, the ghost of an angel inside him.

Waking to find himself a prophet.

What the blazes was happening here?

Was Seraphiel actually using Edward as a vessel again? Pitch clutched at his hair, pulling at the roots. No. That wasn't it. When Seraphiel had possessed Edward before, the man's presence had been pushed aside, tucked away in a corner where it could not bother anyone.

And besides it could not be as before, because the angel was dead. The angel was very, very dead.

'Right, I'm sure you two have lots of catching up to do, but am I the only one thinking this is really not the time or place? And I'm just going to say it, the both of you are really disconcerting to look at right now...Edward...your eyes...' Charlie shrugged off his own confusion. 'Are you feeling all right?'

'My eyes?' He touched at the delicate skin just beneath his eyes. 'They feel fine...' Edward frowned. 'Actually, I feel...quite content. I know that shouldn't make any sense, considering all that's gone on...' He shrugged. 'But you are right. We need to go.'

'Brilliant advice.' Pitch tried to summon the energy he needed to get to his feet. He was not fond of uncertainty nor at having a creature he had murdered fill his life once more, and he was balls deep in both here. 'Did the Holy One happen to shove a map with the exit into your head too?'

Edward shook his head, massaging his temples. 'Not for this Sanctuary, no. He doesn't know this one...only his. And we need to go there.' His head jerked up, and his gaze was unfocused as he spoke. 'You and I...Tobias...I must take you there. That's what I must do... That's what I must do... I know the way... I cannot fail him...'

'Must get me where, Edward?' Pitch said, wanting and yet not wanting at all, to know he'd heard it right.

'His Sanctuary of course. That's what we must do.'

Pitch stared at the man while Edward in turn peered about like he were looking through a fog. His gaze seemed unable to settle or to focus. The flecks of gold were overcome by storm grey, and he must have peered right past Pitch three times before Charlie whispered urgently, 'Can we go, please, Tobias? We really need to get out of here.'

Edward kept working his fingertips against his temple as Charlie helped him to his feet. 'There was someone...she was...oh god...magic...'

Again he was peering into an ether of his own, head moving this way and that as he peered about at sights unseen. 'Magick,' he exclaimed. 'There is magic here, Tobias. Magic intended to hurt you.'

'We could have done with that warning hours ago. The magick *did* hurt us, me and the ankou both.'

'The ankou...Silas...yes...the Horseman.' Edward reached for Pitch but was too far away to have hope of touching, and nearly toppled himself out of the coffin.

'Steady on,' Charlie cried.

'They are going to seal you in, Tobias. I heard them speak of it.' Edward was breathless. 'They have already begun.'

'Again, not news!' Pitch shouted. 'If you want to tell me something useful, tell me where the fucking front door is, Edward. Or better yet, tell me where the ankou is. Can the Holy One find Silas? Tell him I'm not fucking leaving here until we –'

'Tobias, stop shouting.' Charlie spoke with some duress as he took Edward's weight while the lieutenant stepped over the lip of the coffin. Edward's clothes hung off him. The man had clearly lost weight since Pitch had seen him last but was still a decent load for Charlie to carry. He should have offered them some assistance. But he didn't want to touch Edward. He did not want to know what he might see...or feel...if he did so.

Pitch wiped his bloodied hand against his trousers, a pang of melancholy striking as he watched Charlie encourage Edward along, keeping him safe from any risk of a fall. Pitch knew how that felt now, to be handled carefully, to be watched and worried over. There was a gaping void at his side, wide and broad as an oaf, that hurt as keenly as any of his wounds. Pitch blinked, dropping his gaze to the ground – to where Edward and Charlie were barefooted, the soles of their feet scarlet with the stain of rowan berries. And now their knees as they prepared to crawl through the pyramid-shaped hole in the tree trunk. An easier option than attempting to climb over the wooden barrier. Listening to the berries squishing beneath their weight, Pitch was suddenly hopeful.

'What about your bracelet, Charlie?' Pitch said. 'Make it find Silas. Make it grow another tree and send out the roots like it did for –'

'I can't make it do anything, Tobias.' Charlie held his hand over Edward's head, ensuring he stayed low as he crawled through the archway. He made a painfully slow job of manoeuvring himself through the narrow gap. 'That is not how it worked.'

'Have you tried?' he said tightly.

'Forget the bloody tree, Tobias,' Edward snapped. 'And forget your pet, he's collateral. Use your flame to get us out of here. Do it now, that is a command.'

'Edward,' Charlie gasped.

Pitch stared at Edward's arse, the only part of the man he could see. A cold knot gripped Pitch's chest. He could count the number of times Edward had ever raised his voice to him. A grand total of zero. Seraphiel, on the other hand had made a sport of it.

The lieutenant slumped onto his backside, ducking his head to peer back at them through the gap. 'I'm sorry? Is there something wrong?'

Charlie glanced at Pitch, confusion seeing him knit auburn brows together. 'Wrong? You were a bit of a prick just now. I know it's been a bad day, but...we care about Silas. We are not leaving him here.'

Edward's confusion matched the lad's. 'When did I say to leave him here?'

'You didn't. But your dear friend the Holy One seems to have made himself very clear. Give him a message, will you?' Pitch glared at Edward, at whatever he was: the prophet, a vessel for the angel's ghost, the angel himself. None of it fucking mattered. 'Tell him that if he ever commands me to abandon the ankou again, then I will seek out the Morrigan myself and submit to them. I shall be *their* puppet instead of his, and he shall have not one but two monstrous mistakes to be remembered by. Does he understand?'

Pitch rumbled along with the Sanctuary, deep and insidious, and never more clear-headed in his life. They would not take the ankou from him. None of them. Without Silas to steady him, Pitch was only broken pieces, one strike away from shattering entirely. Without the ankou, he forgot why he was even *trying* to hold himself together.

'Does he understand, Edward?'

The lieutenant swallowed. 'Honestly? I don't know...but *I* understand. For now, I hope that can be enough?' He waited until Pitch nodded, then turned and continued to crawl his way free of the tree.

'Ah...Tobias,' Charlie whispered.

'Just leave me be.'

'You need to look up.'

'If you are trying some form of motivational nonsense, I will hurt you.'

'Look *up*, damn it.'

The urgency in the lad's voice had him doing as he was told. 'Shit.'

The barn had vanished, the illusion wiped like a blackboard scrubbed clean. The only source of light now came from the coffin itself, a delicate silver gleam more intense where the silver trim edged the glass. But the faded hue of a full moon only went so far to penetrating the shadows that surrounded them.

Pitch pushed past Charlie, who crouched to negotiate the low-set exit from the trunk's embrace. Pitch scrambled through on hands and knees this time, admonishing the berries as they made the way slippery. He got to his feet and added red berry smears to the bloodstains on his atrocious trousers.

'The barn door was this way, was it not?' He pointed ahead.

'Barn? I saw nothing when I crawled through,' Edward said.

'Not so all-knowing after all, then,' Pitch muttered, for his own benefit and no one else's. He strode forward, heading in the direction he thought the door to have been. He was working on a hunch that though the vision of the entrance was gone, the opening itself might still exist.

'Tobias, be careful,' Charlie called.

'Bloody coddling,' Pitch sniffed. 'He'll be so fucking proud.'

He'd taken precisely three steps, each one punctuated by an unpleasant prick of gods-knew-what against his bare foot and was still within the realm of the silvery light when a branch rose from the ground ahead of him. A considerable limb, one that would rival the width and length of a rowboat's oar. With no rower in sight.

With a sharp exhale, he summoned the flame, trying not to groan with the weight of doing so. Gods, he was so near to done he could fairly taste it.

'Wait.' A shrill cry. The tree limb jabbed at him. It wobbled wildly as though far too heavy for whoever held it, but they were trying to joust nevertheless. 'Stay. Coming.'

The words were snatches of sound, like the sharp bark of a cough or a sneeze.

'Show yourself.' Pitch grabbed at the trembling branch. 'And stop waving that bloody thing in my face.'

Pitch wrapped his smouldering hand about the rough limb, the few clinging leaves crackling against his palm and igniting in flares of abrupt and short-lived flaming life. There was a shriek, and the far end of the branch fell to the ground with a thump.

'Rude.'

He was certain he heard a watery sniff. Pitch dropped the branch, thin lines of smoke coiling from the bark. 'Who are you?'

And *where*? It wasn't so dark he shouldn't be able to see someone right in front of him...and yet...

'George. Friend. Wait.' Three little yaps like it were a tiny dog out there in the shadows.

'Wait for what, gods damn you?'

A chasmal rumble came from the darkness. A potent explosion followed.

A spray of rocks came at him hard and fast.

Pitch threw up his hands, given no option but to spread the flame in an arcing shield. One high and wide enough that there was no chance any of the flying rocks could pass overhead, landing on Charlie and Edward behind him. 'Get down!' he shouted.

The debris smashed against the flames, the force of the blows setting him back on his feet. His insides were a maelstrom, the flame gut-wrenching as it poured from him. This was not a good fucking idea.

The stones hit the firewall, and the impact shattered them, reducing them to coarse ash. It was over as quickly as it had begun.

He snapped off the flame like a nightman capping a gas lamp, and slumped forward, his hands to his thighs, trying to catch his breath and convince himself that his pains would ease.

'My god, Pitch. I'm sorry. Are you hurt?'

The voice stole the air, made breathing impossible. There was only one person who would apologise at a time like this.

'Silas?' Pitch's pulse thundered.

A figure ran from the gloom and dust, and he'd have known that silhouette in any bleak corner of the world. Pitch bit back the cry that tried to work its way free.

He ran over cutting stone and fallen wood, not seeing either, not caring how they both made cruel marks upon his bare foot. His ankle turned, more than once, and he was so driven in getting to where he sought to go he did not see the rock until his toes clipped it.

Pitch grunted, and he was tumbling headlong into the ankou's out-stretched arms.

Silas swept him up in arms strong as girders on a railroad track. An embarrassing whimper left Pitch's lips. He clung there, hanging from Silas's neck, lifting his legs and wrapping them around the ankou's hips. The broadness of the man made his thighs ache, but an ache he would happily endure.

'You're here.' He whispered it into Silas's hair, the shortened strands damp, and not nicely so. It was as though the ankou had finally suc-cumbed to having a bath, but in a pond of slime, slippery and viscous.

'I would be nowhere else.' Silas's chest rumbled, sending a hum through Pitch's body, A lullaby he pressed into, seeking to find a way beneath the ankou's skin.

Finding wetness instead. Silas's clothes were soaked. And there was a ripeness to the man that bordered on very unpleasant. But it would not shift Pitch. Not yet.

'Are you all right?' Silas ran his hands over Pitch's back, a touch so damned welcome the tired and beaten daemon might have moaned. The ankou explored him, searching for his pains. His fingers were far nimbler than their size might suggest, finding their way over bruised and troubled skin. The caress of his fingertips was like tiny kisses, taking in as much of Pitch's body as they could find. Touching at the nape of his neck, caressing the dainty swell of ribs, tracing the boning of the corset. 'Pitch, tell me you are unharmed. The last I saw, that infernal Dullahan was standing over you.'

'He knows better now.' The false bravado suited the moment. Pitch was already too feeble a thing now, coming apart against the ankou. 'I've not seen him in a long while.' He did not want to lift his head, he wanted to stay here, in the curve of Silas's shoulder. 'But what of you?'

'I am much better now, having found you.'

Pitch first grinned against Silas's skin, then kissed it. He grimaced. 'You taste awful.'

'Christ, Pitch, spit it out. Whatever is in your mouth, I assure you it is far from pleasant.'

Pitch pulled away but did not let go. Now he took in the ankou's bloodstained face and glowered. 'What did they do to you?' By the Archangels' taints, Silas looked fucking dreadful and was covered in stains that turned the stomach to look upon.

Silas's gaze dropped. 'I am to blame for this. This mess was made by my own hand... But there's not time for that now.' His fingers caressed Pitch's arse cheek. 'We must try to find our way out of here.'

'How did you find us?' Pitch's flustered thoughts moved on before the ankou could answer. 'Did *you* send George?'

'George?' Silas's caresses faltered. 'Do you mean the ghost? A boy?'

'I suppose. He tried to stab me with a branch and told me I must wait here.'

Silas released a contented sigh. 'I am very glad you heeded him.' His caresses struck up again. 'Is there a chance you found Edward?'

Pitch was still scowling at the splatters upon his ankou, imagining the ways he would pick apart whoever was responsible. And it was just as he was considering how he might pull off their nails one by one that he spied the hulking masses approaching.

'Gods.' He untangled himself from the ankou. 'Look out, Silas!'

CHAPTER 34

T he flame was at Pitch's fingertips too quickly, for it had barely
heeded his demands to sink below the surface to begin with. The
glow cast itself upon the monstrosities lurking behind the ankou.

Four great deformities, every bit as large as Silas but with a decided lack
of his considerable charms.

'No, no. Pitch, stop.'

The idiot, the absolute fool, wrapped his hands about Pitch's wrists,
staying just clear enough of the flames to avoid burns, but far too close
otherwise.

'Silas, damn it.'

'Listen to me. These teratisms helped me find my way to you. Pitch,
they heeded me. They overcame the Blight to *listen* to me. They are not
lost.'

In this den of misfortune, Silas was happy. So very obviously astonished and delighted by his own achievement it was difficult not to grab
at his solid chin and kiss the man soundly. But Pitch had already coveted
the ankou too long.

'I found Edward.' It was blurted from him.

'God, that's wonderful.'

'And Charlie.'

Silas's breath ran uneven. And he seemed to hollow beneath his layers of grime and foul things. 'Alive?' he said, in a voice too tiny to belong to a man so great.

Perhaps Pitch left the air empty a moment too long, but the instant he brought Charlie to life, the ankou would take his soft touch and his warming gaze elsewhere.

Pitch was a selfish prick.

He opened his mouth to unbreak the ankou's heart. And was beaten to it.

'Silas Mercer, you look terrible.'

Gods, the look on the man's face. He knew the lad's voice well.

'Charlie? Oh my god, Charlie.'

He did exactly as Pitch knew he would. The ankou left him. And though he knew, gods, he *knew* he was being irrational and stupid and all the miserable things that came with this intolerable lunacy that was caring too deeply, Pitch could not bear to turn around and watch the reunion between them.

He listened to it. Heard the cries and the sobs and the breathlessness as they embraced. The jumble of words as they spoke over the top of one another. The hurried questions, the rushed answers. The joy of finding one another when all hope had been lost.

And Edward was not exempt. Silas was generous with his happiness, almost as verbose in his delight at seeing Edward again as he'd been with Charlie.

Everyone was so fucking happy. As though they'd forgotten where they were, and how stuck fast in that place they had become.

Pitch stared at the teratisms. Contorted, ugly versions of what they might have been once. And they stared back at him. At least as well as they could. One of them had a smoothed face of skin and no features. For a moment he was jealous of the monster who could see nothing, hear nothing.

'You have the bandalore?' Silas cried.

'I have no idea how.' Charlie laughed, slightly manic in his gaiety. 'I woke to find it with me. I thought perhaps you had gotten it to me somehow...to keep me safe.'

'No...I wish I could say it was...' Silas's confusion played through his words. 'It found you somehow.'

'It saved my life. Well, that and the bracelet...' He held out his arm.

Silas stared at Ottelie's gift, a swathe of emotions chasing themselves across his strong features. Despair, relief, concern, and confusion. He looked so lost.

'Oh Charlie...' Silas said. 'I'm so sorry for all of this.'

The ankou's tedious habit of lending apology to all and sundry shook Pitch from his self-pitying quagmire, and he turned about. 'Now you have the bandalore, maybe you can break through more than a few walls,' he said. 'You need to find us a way out of here.'

And he needed to be nearer to the ankou.

Pitch stepped forward. The grind of his heel came at the same time as a frightening lament rose from the earth.

The Sanctuary keened. There was no other word for it. An awful, rending groan that spoke of the end of all things.

Pitch saw Silas reach for Charlie, then for Edward, and gather them to him. He felt the teratisms sweep past him, their scent a scar upon the air as they moved to their ankou. They assembled around him, arching their deformities over the trio that huddled against what remained of the tree trunk. As though that might be enough to protect them from the Sanctuary as it turned on itself.

Silas called out. 'Pitch, hurry.'

And Pitch was running to him again, dragging daemonic power to the surface once more. The flame tore through his body as the sounds of destruction came from all the darkest corners. Stones pelted down, falling from places unseen, lost to the shadows. White rage gripped him. After all they'd endured, they were to be crushed by something so paltry as a godsdamned rock?

Not so damning for him and Silas as it was for Edward and Charlie. Whatever Edward was, he was not, so far as Pitch knew, immune to heavy, flattening objects.

He slackened his grip on the weakening reins that held the flame in check. His hands were ablaze, snaking lines of fire so long they got in the way as he ran. Pitch got as close as he dared to those of flesh and bone and raised his arms. He sent a plume of melting heat and shielding fire over the huddled group.

'Careful, go carefully.'

It was Edward. Or the angel within. Perhaps recalling how terribly a daemon's control could escape him.

Heat roared through Pitch, the last of the amuletum eviscerated in a heartbeat. A heartbeat Pitch could no longer feel as the wildness tore a hinge off its cage and took one step towards absolute freedom.

The taste of blood filled Pitch's mouth as he bore down, trying to cling to the last of his control. But by the fucking gods, he was losing it.

If the Sanctuary didn't kill them all, he would.

He screamed his fears, his panic, into the crackle and snap of the blaze that fought for its head. Pitch was brittle and thin in places where it was dangerous to be so. He was too weak for this onslaught. He knew it.

The flame knew too and was champing at the bit, eating away at his resolve.

Around them the death cries of the Sanctuary rose. It was as though the place was folding in on itself, precise as origami, taking its corridors and passageways and all the illusions packed into them, and imploding.

He sobbed with the weight of it, feeling his shoulders bend and the protrusions of his spine trying to tear through his skin. Fuck, how Mr Ahari's cane would be welcome now, anything to siphon the flame's torrent, make it barely manageable...instead of this...nearly ripping him apart.

So much for being Seraphiel's vessel. He was useless. Embattled, within and without.

While one beast clawed at his heart, another surrounded him. The fae magick that had made this vile place was transforming it. Reducing it. Turning upon them. Making its endless walkways finite. Pressing them all down on him like he was trapped in a godsdamned concertina.

And the weight was all too much.

Pitch blinked through the glare, a blinding firestorm of his own making. Impossible as it seemed, he saw his way to Silas. The ankou's eyes were fastened on him already, a fierceness in the depths of narrowed brown eyes, a fearsome determination in the set of his mouth. He held his scythe overhead, and death's blade was a wondrous sight. The blade was formidable, the grandest Pitch had seen it. A curving half-moon of razor-sharpness that was deflecting the flame. If it had been stretched straight, it would have easily run the length of Silas's body. The ankou held the crudely carved shaft aloft, a warrior crying out for the charge to be led. The air about the scythe's blade shimmered as the flame was repelled from its surface like the heat off a tin roof on a summer-sodden day.

Silas and his blade were guardians against the scorching heat of Pitch's fire. Charlie and Edward sat as huddles of shaking humanity, sheltering as best they could beneath the scythe's considerable shadow. And around them knelt the four teratisms, staying true to their master.

'What do we do?' Silas shouted, his face glistening. Even the scythe could not protect him entirely from the inferno above. 'I cannot see a way out.'

'Because there is not one.' Pitch grunted, setting his feet. The caps of his knees felt ready to snap, he was bowed beneath the pressure that was closing in, and the flame was scraping him hollow. 'No yet.'

There was chance perhaps that he could blast his way out of this forsaken fucking hole in the earth. In truth he had no bloody idea if such a thing was possible. He was no master of fae magick nor divine, for that matter. But he *was* a master of sheer force.

He'd been made so when he was created Dominion. With Seraphiel's meddling...well, who knew what his limits were? Perhaps Edward knew them. Though right now the man seemed capable only of knowing how to look utterly terrified.

Pitch let out a burdened growl.

Fuck. If he let go...if he bared his throat to the beast tangled about his innards, there would be consequences. Quite possibly terrible fucking ones. He might end up trapping Silas and his motley crew in this labyrinthine nightmare of a place with a Berserker Prince unleashed.

Pitch glared down at the scorched earth, sending fresh heat tearing through his fingertips, his arms aloft. He was on his knees but had no recollection of falling there.

Could he forget himself so thoroughly that he'd harm the ankou?

He'd harmed Lord Enoch's precious Seraphiel.

He'd cared for killing far more than for seeing what was right in front of him. If he let go, he was certainly capable of killing Silas. And the bloody angel too...for a second time.

'Fuck!' Pitch roared, throwing his head back, trying to find a way through his own scattering thoughts.

'Edward!'

Pitch's head flew up at the sound of Silas's cry. The lieutenant was crawling on hands and knees away from the ankou's protection. He was almost beyond the curve of the blade. Charlie lunged for Edward's foot, only to have Silas sweep an arm about his waist and gather him close.

'The heat will kill you!' the ankou bellowed.

'Then help him, Silas!'

'Edward.' Pitch could barely spit the words clear. 'What the fuck are you doing?'

'Hold fast.' Edward's eyes were twin suns. 'They have come.'

Who the blazes were *they*?

Pitch could barely hold his head up, let alone carry this burden any longer. If the Morrigan were returning to finish off what they had begun, Pitch didn't have the strength to fight them.

Tears were scorched dry before they had a chance to fall.

What a terribly fucked-up idea it had been to ever go searching for Edward Charters. Pitch should have thrown the pendant watch back in Lucifer's face.

Edward found a place between two of the teratisms, the creatures staring at him with fathomless onyx eyes. He clasped his hands, fingers entwined, and pressed his thumbs against his mouth. His lips moved, and fine scraps of his words reached Pitch where he bent beneath the folding weight of the Sanctuary.

The words were indecipherable, but the language was not.

The Seraphim and Archangels deemed themselves so far above every other pithy living soul that they had a language for themselves.

The lieutenant spoke the words of mighty angels, rushing them out through mortal lips. Gods, how much power had Seraphiel's relic bestowed upon this man?

Edward unclasped his hands and slammed them against the ground. A glittering, jagged line of deep cerise appeared, like a tiny rivulet carving a narrow path through the ground. The colour altered, capturing all the hues of a winter sunrise as it flowed to a destination beyond the flames.

Pitch stared at the slender path that trailed away from him. Tiny white sparks danced off the surface, like diamonds on the boil, marking the path of the strange stream that stretched into the darkness as far as Pitch's eyes could fathom.

It was a dramatic show. And Pitch had known one high angel who enjoyed cultivating such melodramatic displays of divine magick.

His arms sagged, threatening to lower altogether. He ached down to the marrow.

'Pitch, higher... I can't withstand it!' Silas cried out.

With an effort that left him dizzy, vision blurring, Pitch raised his arms. The punch to his gut rocked him on his heels, winding him. The beast was so very eager, so very near to cracking the final hinge.

He was on the very precipice of losing himself. A choked cry escaped him. 'Fuck.' He hissed, blood spraying and vanishing in the heat.

He did not know Edward was there until the lieutenant was mere inches away.

Blood ran from his nostrils, making a crimson mess of his lips, and his irises were tangles of grey and umber. 'The angel has been called for, she will find us now,' he said damply. He raised a shaking arm.

'Don't touch me,' the prince hissed.

'You cannot succumb, Vassago.'

It would be far from all right if the idiot got any closer to an inferno that must already be far more than his skin could handle. Pitch tried to shift himself, thrust his hip so he might shake the man off, but Edward was persistent. And strong.

'Heed your master,' he whispered, leaning in close. 'Stand down.'

Those same words again. Spoken on a wretched clifftop once, now here, in the bowels of the Fulbourn.

But if Pitch stood down now...if he let go...they would all perish.

'Fuck, Edward...Raph...stop.'

But neither the man nor the angel listened.

The lieutenant swept his arm around Pitch's waist and touched a hand to where the tattered corset covered over the halo's mark.

A white-hot shock bolted through the daemon's body. He went rigid, back bowed.

And the wildness shrank into the depths. Scuttled back into its cage. Heeded its master.

Pitch exhaled hard, buckling forward, the flames stuttering above him. But he had the reins again now, and there was no tug upon them, no fight to be had.

Edward nodded, the specks of vermilion in his gaze washing away and leaving tired smoky hues instead. His eyes rolled back in his head, and he collapsed into a limp pile.

'Pitch, what's happening?' Silas. Looking for answers. For hope.

But Pitch could give the ankou neither. For at that moment the Sanctuary renewed its assault. A death rattle. The last lock on the Morrigan's seal, perhaps, shutting them in here. A place worse than any oubliette or abaddon, for those at least had an entrance to cry out to.

The pressure was tremendous, forcing his knees into the earth. An unpleasant crack came from his right arm as bone snapped. Blots of darkness formed around the edges of his vision.

And the beast was nowhere to be seen. Pitch was in control, but with that control came a lessening of his power. His strength had waned. He was no longer a titan, just a burdened daemon who was likely about to be crushed into the cracks and crevices of the Sanctuary.

Silas's voice reached him. As though it came from the furthest end of the labyrinth's most cursed corridors. 'Pitch, stay with me.'

There was the most brilliant blast of turquoise, all the beauty of the ocean, and another voice. Right at his ear. 'Well done, boy. But best you put that fire away now.'

His thoughts filled, bizarrely, with images of frothing pints and red wine. Pitch sagged, and the blazing torrents he commanded slithered and slipped and shrank until it was only his nails that glowed.

A pressure wrapped around his waist, firm but comfortable.

He had the oddest vision then too. That of the face of an enormous red fox, his snout as long as Pitch's broken arm, eyes the size of dinner plates at their centre and tapering off to fine points. The vast animal leaned in close, its breath cooling against his parched skin.

He felt himself lifted from the ground, pulled from the burrows that had formed around his knees as he sank beneath the weight of trying to save them all. He dangled there, peering down through weighted lids at the fox's broad back.

This fox was friend, not foe. He'd have bet his withered cock on it.

'Take Silas first,' Pitch mumbled.

'There's no first or second,' the fox told him, black lips pulling back over chalk-white canines. 'I'll take you all at once. No time for dallying.'

The kitsune's voice was no different from when he'd heard it last.

Mr Ahari had been in his human form then, of course. And Pitch had been seated by the fire in The Atlas, drinking wine while Silas ate a disgusting-smelling concoction which he claimed was delicious. Pitch had no wish for any more fire today, but by the gods a slice of pie would be wonderful.

'Strawberry,' he slurred.

'Out of season I'm afraid.' The fox's grin was mildly terrifying, but Pitch had never been fearful of Mr Ahari, so would not start now. 'Now, little one, you next.'

Charlie proved he was human by releasing a scream that could have woken all of Silas's dead. One of the kitsune's nine tails, weaving about like a furry panlong, snaked around the frightened lad's waist. Charlie tried to beat it off. And Silas was doing his level best to placate him.

'It is quite all right, Charlie. Look. Quickly now.' He lifted his arms to accommodate the curl of a tail about his own bare waist, which was smeared in all the foul residue of the Sanctuary. He fussed his little undead heart out over his lad but spared anxious glances Pitch's way as he did so.

'I'm all right...stop worrying.' Pitch was slurring. His tongue was too tired to work for him, and he'd not spoken nearly loud enough for Silas to hear, what with all the ominous moans still coming from the Sanctuary.

The ankou was a sight, barely clothed, which was not so bad, but grotty beyond measure, battered and very bruised.

Gloriously alive.

Mr Ahari shouted at them to hold on. That the journey would be rough. That it was not over just yet. Gods, the fool had no idea.

The kitsune broke into a run. Pitch spared the very last of his energy to ensure that Edward was among the dangling trophies Mr Ahari held in his tails. Next to Silas, the lieutenant hung, unresponsive, dangling like a bundle of sopping clothes.

Pitch closed his eyes, listening to Silas assure Charlie all would be well, and let a welcome darkness take him.

CHAPTER 35

Being hauled through the depths of a maniacal Sanctuary by a kit-sune was not an experience Silas would forget in a thousand life-times. The fox's python-like tail was firm around his waist, holding aloft his considerable mass as though he were as feather-light as Charlie. They bounded along in the inky confines, following the narrow trail of altering roseate hues that deepened and lightened as they eddied along.

'Silas, is it going to eat us?' Charlie cried. He had his arms and legs wrapped about the tail, clearly convinced that the loop hold would not be enough to stop him plummeting. But there was barely a distance to plummet. The fox was large, but in the way of a grand draught horse, and they were held but a foot or two from the ground. There was no risk of death in a fall.

'He's not going to eat us, no. Do try to stay still, Charlie.'

Silas was distracted, noting how limp Pitch's body was in the grasp of the fox's outermost tail, a bushy affair that was tipped with white, unlike his own that was coated with black hairs.

Perhaps it was best that Pitch was not conscious, for the prince was bound to be in all manner of pain after that display with the flame. Yet again, the daemon had kept the world from caving in on Silas. Pitch had best be ready for the thanks that were coming his way. Silas would be very thorough. Very robust.

An unnatural moan came from the bowels of the collapsing Sanctuary.

'Now hold on tight,' the fox barked. Quite literally so. The creature bunched up its hindquarters. 'This place is closing in too fast. I'm going to send you ahead. Apologies for the landing. It may hurt, but time and essence and all that.'

Silas looked away from his study of Pitch to find that the sparkling rosiness of the rivulet had altered remarkably.

The thin flow of light abandoned its horizontal path and lifted, spreading out to form a wall of rose and apricot and salmon hues that ran upwards. A waterfall in an upside-down world.

He was so busy marvelling he did not heed Mr Ahari's instructions too well. Silas let out a startled cry as he was suddenly whipped back, only to be violently thrust forward a second later. The fox's tail unwrapped from about him, and Silas was flying, soaring like a fledgling sent too early from the nest.

Charlie released a frantic squeal, and the teratisms who had been secured each in their own length of tail bellowed and bayed like herd animals scenting a wolf. Only Edward and Pitch were silent as the entire group was sent catapulting like inelegant scarecrows.

Silas cowered behind raised arms, ready to be smacked senseless as he approached the shimmering barrier. But the light was purely that. Light. No substance.

The same could not be said for what lay upon the other side.

Silas had a blink's-length of time to make out his surrounds. A room laid out with multiple beds, bedcovers like tangled banks of snow spilling from torn mattresses.

'Oh bloody hell!'

He balled himself up as best he could and became a living bowling ball. Silas crashed into a bed, the metal frame unforgiving against the back of his shoulder. The momentum kept him racing onwards, pushing the bed into the next, and that one in turn into the next, and so it went. He was the caboose on a freight train of springs and thin mattresses and only drew to a halt when the furthest bed flipped up against the wall.

He leaped to his feet, slightly dizzy and needing to hold fast to the nearest upturned bedframe.

They were returned to the Fulbourn, in one of the bleak wards with its drained white paintwork and dreary furnishings. There was, thankfully, no sign of any patients. Nor though any sign of where they had just crashed through the wall. Aside from a few thin seams that might be cracks in the plaster, the walls were all intact.

A thunderstorm was underway, banging and crashing its way about outside like a wild horde seeking to break in. Silas had landed near a shattered window, curtains dancing madly with the wind that brought in icy-cold rain to spatter his skin. He was a walking suit of gooseflesh, the outside world far chillier than the doomed Sanctuary.

'Pitch, Charlie,' he called.

Rich shadows draped the room, lit at intervals by flashes of lightning nearly too bright for the eye to endure. The drum of rain came down with the precision of a military band.

'Mr Mercer, they are over here, my dear.'

The voice was not one he'd heard in a while, and he could have wept as he hurried towards the misshapen shadows further down the ward. 'Bess? Is that you?'

'It is, my dear. Sybilla too, but she's just needing to catch her breath right now. Hurry along, best we get you all out of here.' There was a certain timbre to Old Bess's voice, one Silas had found soothing from the moment the master of Harvington Hall had welcomed him to the residence. But to know the Valkyrie was with him, Silas could have collapsed into a maniacal heap of relief there and then.

A showy flash of light illuminated the person standing not too far ahead, and there could be no doubt it was Bess. A smartly trimmed beard was dark against skin powdered white. Jewels glinted, the red of rubies and perhaps a dash of emerald too, earrings for sure, and a tiara would explain the shimmer in the mass of light curls. Harvington Hall's master cradled Charlie in his velvet-cuffed arms.

'Charlie. Are you hurt?'

'The lad is fine... Well, he will be.' Bess coughed. 'A little bump to the head. My fault I'm afraid. I'm not one for sports. Caught him and then managed to whack his head against the wall while I did so. He'll come around before long though, I'm sure.'

'And Pitch?'

'He's here too. Out cold as well. Be sure to let him know when he comes to that it was the column he landed against to blame for his headache, not me or Mr Ahari. I don't want that one mad at me.'

'It wasn't the column,' Silas said, tension making his shoulders stiff, his throat tight. 'It was the flame...the Sanctuary... He has done too much.'

Silas quickened his pace and was so focused on getting to Bess that he almost collided with the figure that stepped out of the shadows. 'Oh shit.' A quick step and a hop saved him from a collision with the woman whose skin was barely any lighter than the shadows, her cropped short head of hair a layer of tight white curls that were luminous in the stormy atmosphere. 'Sybilla. My god, it is good to see you.'

'You very nearly didn't, Silas. What the fuck did you think you were doing, coming alone like this? Telling no one?' The Valkyrie glowered almost as well as Pitch was capable. The whites of her eyes seemed to glow. Her coat was full length and creaked as she moved, a stiff leather that blended her into the shadows even more fully. 'The Morrigan's seal has taken me near on an hour just to cast a fist-sized hole through. Whoever cast that magick for you from the inside saved your damn hides. Mine was not enough.'

Bess sighed. 'My sister Palatyne has been formidable here. I did not think my youngest sister quite so talented, I'll admit.'

'Without that magick guiding me, we would not have gotten you out in time before the Sanctuary swallowed you whole. Who did that, Silas?' Sybilla demanded between pressed teeth. 'Where did that magick come from?'

'Now perhaps is not the best time for this, Syb,' Bess said gently. 'They aren't safe yet.'

The angel rubbed at her arms, holding the glare for another breath before she shouldered her way past Silas. There was a weariness to her that could not be missed, even in a room that was only lit sporadically by the crazed tempo of lightning outside.

'Now move quickly, my dear. It's best not to hang about.' Bess took control with his familiar amiable manner. 'All that nonsense down below has things rather less than sturdy up here. Mr Ahari has gone to collect our carriage, once he's re-dressed of course. Nobody needs to see a naked elderly gent at the reins. Heavens, that would be the end of some of those poor wretches out there.' He tutted. 'This place is shamefully over-crowded. Small wonder those Morrigan vipers enjoyed hiding amongst all the misery and chaos. No one would notice a few more bad eggs about.'

Sybilla pushed aside some divider curtains that would have been a paltry barrier between patients in their beds, rusted rings squealing as they moved. She kept rubbing at her arm, enough so that Silas wondered if she had received an injury as she worked to free them. 'And what the bloody hell is this all about, Mercer?' She flung her hands towards hulking shadows upon the ground. Four, in fact.

The teratisms were coming too, drawing in ragged breaths suited to someone upon their deathbed. Which, in truth, the teratisms were.

'They will not harm you.' He yelled it, to ensure the Valkyrie heard him. She seemed in the mood for a sudden strike.

'I hope that is reciprocal?' Bess said, adjusting his hold on Charlie, who muttered but stayed with eyes closed.

'Of course. They will heed me.' Silas moved closer to the teratisms, who appeared as dazed as he. The one with the crooked limbs was doing something unsightly with their arm, as though trying to snap it back to where it ought to be without much success. All of them looked to him as he approached. 'Easy, easy now. You've done so very well.'

'It seems you have much to tell us of your adventures in my sister's labyrinth. She always did enjoy a maze, that one,' Old Bess said, almost too quietly to be heard above the thunder and the shudder of brickwork around them.

'If Satine ever lets them out of the bloody Village again,' Sybilla retort-ed. She crouched down to the ground, near to where another window had been shattered of most of its glass, a few triangular shards clinging to the rim.

Silas peered into the shadows, searching for sign of the daemon. 'Where is Pitch? I don't see him.' He stifled the curl of panic that came with saying it.

'He's all right, Silas,' Bess soothed, jewels sparking like the luminous sprays on Edward's miniature river. 'Down to your right, the last column there, that dark lump is your daemon. He must have been lighter than Mr Ahari catered for, as he went the furthest. But he's breathing. Lucid enough to grumble when I touched him.'

Silas balled his fists and headed in the direction given, not caring much that he stubbed his toes within a few paces on a length of chain of all things, a discarded restraint.

A hiss came from the huddled form of the Valkyrie.

'Syb?' Bess called.

The angel grunted and rose to her feet, this time with a bundle in her arms. Edward's head rested against her chest, one arm hanging limp at his side. 'This is the man you came for.'

The oddest tone gripped her words, and Silas could not decide if it was a touch of fear or reverence. The Valkyrie did not seem the sort for either thing.

'It is.'

Sybilla stared down at the lieutenant, and Silas wished he could read her expression more clearly. 'I see.'

Two simple words weighted with far more weight than they should carry. But Silas was too impatient to get to Pitch to bother with pressing her on it. He should have been at the daemon's side the moment he was on his feet.

He broke into a jog, headed for the column that was the last before a set of swinging doors that would lead them out of this ward and this asylum at last.

And at the base of the column was Pitch, sitting as though he had placed himself there to rest a moment. His head hung forward, hands in his lap, slender legs splayed wide. His back rested against the column, and Silas drew a sharp breath. The amuletum could not have endured after the prince's expansive use of the flame. Being pressed up against anything like that would cause the daemon no end of misery when he came to.

Silas was at his side in three giant strides. 'Pitch?'

He tilted the prince's grime-stained chin, searching for signs of life. But there was nothing. 'Pitch, can you hear me?' He held the back of his hand against the daemon's mouth, and some of the knots he'd wound himself up in loosened. 'He's breathing.'

'I did say so.' Bess had come to stand right behind him, Charlie muttering in his arms. The lad's eyes were still closed, but he'd lifted his arm to cradle it against his chest, looking so terribly young in that moment.

'Pick him up, for Christ's sake, Mercer.' Sybilla was not so careful with holding Edward, the lieutenant slung over her shoulder like a stole. 'We need to go.'

The rumbling of the storm mingled with another, less pleasing vibration, coming from below, making the floorboards grind against one another.

'I'd say we have overstayed our welcome considerably.' Bess's heeled shoes rapped the wooden floor as he carried Charlie towards the door. 'Let us vacate this miserable place.'

Silas gathered Pitch's legs together, slipping one arm beneath his knees, the other easing him away from the column and wrapping about his back. He braced for the feel of rough skin, burns reemerging after the strain the Sanctuary had put upon the prince. The amuletum could not have survived that onslaught. But if the halo's wound showed once more, it was hidden beneath the prince's ruinous corset. The prince the Morrigan now knew lived and breathed, thanks to Silas's recklessly loose tongue.

Christ, he despised himself for that moment of madness.

He exhaled and embraced Pitch tightly. The daemon was warm, certainly, but not concernedly so. The flame did not plague him within. Silas had seen the shock on Pitch's face when Edward had reached into the inferno and touched him.

None of them would leave this asylum the same as when they had arrived, but the lieutenant most especially so. There was no denying he was part of Seraphiel's design.

Silas pressed his mouth against Pitch's hair. 'Pitch, we are free,' he whispered. Bess and Sybilla were already making their way through the swinging doors. 'The Order found Edward's light, they found *us*. And it was your sacrifice that made it so. You kept us alive. Now, we are all safe.' He kissed gritty strands, relishing the feel of Pitch's ribs against his hand, the shallow but rhythmic rise and fall as the prince breathed. 'Truly you are a marvel. How could you ever imagine yourself a monster, my darling?'

Silas stilled. That last should not have been said out loud. But if Pitch had heard him, he showed no sign. And good god would he not have made a song and dance out of Silas's sentimental slip of the tongue if he had heard?

With a smile, and great care, Silas rose to his feet. He did not need to turn to know that the teratisms flanked him. Their presence was like an extra layer of clothing upon his back.

No longer slaves to the Blight, they followed a new master.

He thought on George Brewster, the chimney sweep who'd stopped a daemon in his tracks long enough for Silas to arrive. He hoped somehow the ghost had found his way free of the Sanctuary and there would be a chance to thank him one day.

Silas shivered, from the damp or the weight of what it was to discover his power, he did not know. He carried Pitch out of the ward, nodding a thanks to Sybilla, who held a door open for him.

The waft of smoke hit him first, rich enough to make him wince. The corridors were dimmed by a smoky haze. 'The asylum's on fire?' he cried.

'Best way to get everyone out in a hurry,' Sybilla replied. 'Isaac has it under control though. The place won't burn down.'

Silas nodded, knowing just how convenient a well-placed fire could be. Isaac's quick thinking at the Charters' residence had seen Silas and Pitch make a smooth exit from the soirée.

'Quick steps everyone.' Bess sounded almost cheerful as he led the strange group down the smoky corridor. 'The Fulbourn might not burn down, but that's not to say it won't *fall* down. I'll be happier when we are in a carriage.'

Never had Silas agreed more with a sentiment, but it also struck him that there were certain members of this party who might not be welcome in that carriage.

The ones who had just shouldered their way through the swinging doors so violently one side flew off its hinges, the other slammed so hard into the wall there was bound to be cracking in the plasterwork.

DK GIRL

The teratisms did not follow along meekly. They raked their impossibly long nails along the walls and butted at one another like unhappy wolves in a pack.

But before Silas could wonder at what to do with his merry band of miscreants, Bess was kicking at a white wooden door, landing her foot so hard there was barely a protest before the lock snapped and the door swung wide open.

Yellow light, the colour of a field of dandelions, spilled into the corridor. Mixing with the smoke came the damp, crisp relief of fresh air.

They were leaving the Fulbourn at last.

Silas sucked in the air. Christ almighty, it was an absolute joy to breathe in, even with the sooty harshness raking at his nostrils. It was evening, deep into it he would guess. The storm-flushed sky was heavy, the cloud cover pressing down so low there were no tops to the trees. It was pouring with rain, a curious contrast to the fire that gripped sections of the Fulbourn, but Silas thought he'd never seen a sight so beautiful.

Nor chaotic.

There were alarm bells ringing, and he glimpsed a fire truck racing along, pulled by a team of heavy horses making great splashes in the puddles that soaked the ground. Beyond them, lit by bobbing torches and held lanterns, he spotted a group of frightened patients being ushered towards several omnibuses that lined the road leading out of the Fulbourn. Hardly sufficient numbers of vehicles since the place was overcrowded to buggery. He swallowed down a swell of guilt, seeing all the damage done since their arrival.

Bess left first with Charlie. She had cleared the doorway, and Sybilla was about to follow when she jerked back, cursing, swinging around to shield the man she carried.

'Sybilla?' Silas frowned.

'Too much tongue,' she snapped. 'I can't abide it.'

What the blazes was she on about?

An enormous hound bounded through the open doorway. Shaggy, dripping, one eye a red glowing ember, the other like the sliver of a candy apple.

'Forneus!' he cried.

The beast nuzzled at Sybilla's leg and was shouted at before bounding towards Silas.

The skriker bared its teeth all the way to the very last molar. He shrank his head low between his shoulder and growled as he approached.

'Forneus? It's me...Silas...' He clutched Pitch closer to him. The creature had not been overly fond of the daemon to begin with, but Pitch had told him what Forneus had done at Gidleigh House. Surely this aggressive greeting was not aimed at the daemon?

The skriker growled.

And the teratisms released shudder-inducing howls in return.

Forneus barked, a whopping sound not unlike anything the storm was releasing.

The teratisms quietened. The hound dashed past Silas, snapping his jaws.

'No, Forneus, they are not our foe.'

The skriker took heed at once, closing black lips and letting a growl rumble softly, but he nudged his snout forward, tossing his head. The teratisms backed up in one swaying mass of unsightliness, huddling like sheep against one another. The skriker barked again, this time sharper, and the teratisms lowered their heads, bunching in closer.

Silas's laugh popped from him. The hound was keeping them in order, like a farmer's dog handling a flock.

'Silas,' Sybilla urged. 'Can we save the show for later?'

'When did the skriker arrive?'

'Before us. He is the reason we found you. Well, he and the girl.' Silas frowned, but Sybilla shook her head. 'Later, I'll explain. Come on, Silas, get in the carriage.'

'But they can't. Get in the carriage I mean.' Silas was bright with an idea. He turned to the hound. 'Can you keep them safe, Forneus? I may have need of them.'

The hound cocked his head, eyeing Silas. He whined and Silas thought he detected agreement.

'Good.' He looked to the teratisms, a huddled mass of distorted flesh and wronged matter who had been saved by a whistle.

His whistle.

A few notes that had ended the ceaseless attack at the monopteros. Desperation had brought the brief tune to him there. Now he was only anxious that Pitch be tended and have a roof over his head that did not threaten to cave in.

Would that suffice?

Silas drew in a breath and let go of all but his need to convey a message to these creatures. *His* creatures. He pursed his lips and did not think too hard on what might come. He whistled, a wandering, airy melody, the type of tune that might be sung as one lay upon a hill in the warming breeze of a summer eve. Silas wished for the teratisms to calm, to know an iota of peace, and his wants were there in the melody that left him.

Wait for me. Be at rest.

The drawling cry that left the faceless teratism could have peeled the paint from the walls. But he *felt* the creature's accord. An acknowledgement of his will. The others joined in, the creature that resembled Black Annis the loudest of all. The cacophony was rough and fraught with keen edges, a terror on the ears really, but so very welcome.

'Go now, they will follow,' he said softly, nodding at the skriker. The hound snapped at the air, but his next move was far more disconcerting. Forneus lowered his damp nose all the way to the ground, splaying his front legs in what looked uncomfortably like a canine version of a bow.

'Enough of that.' Silas's cheeks warmed, and he waved the hound on. 'Off you go.'

Forneus righted himself and set straight to the task, shepherding the teratisms back down the corridor, nipping the air at their heels to urge them on.

Not wishing to test Sybilla's patience any longer, Silas pulled his gaze away from his curious band. He cradled Pitch close, racing out into the rain and the carriage that awaited. Mr Ahari sat in the driver's seat, calm as you like as though he'd not just been a giant fox and dragged them all out of hell. Silas nodded, the kitsune gave him a grim smile, and then there was much to occupy Silas as he negotiated bundling the unconscious daemon into the carriage. A task he was becoming quite adept at now.

Silas clambered in with some grunting and fuss, grateful for the carriage's double doors that gave him less need to relinquish Pitch fully to Sybilla, who sought to aid him. Silas slumped onto the seat beside the Valkyrie. She in turn had settled Edward into the seat opposite her. She muttered and pushed at Pitch's dirty bare foot, which had come to rest on her coat. Bess sat opposite Silas, Charlie on his lap, the lad's feet resting on the lieutenant's thighs.

'The fog now, if you will please, Matilda,' Mr Ahari called out to the water elemental, and they were away.

The carriage picked up speed, drawing them away from the Fulbourn. There was something reminiscent in the journey, fleeing with Matilda's storm raging about them, only this time they were doing so on the ground, not carried away by sirin. Silas sat facing the back of the carriage, watching the swirls of a thickening mist descend, capturing the grey of the smoke in its sweep. They were not yet encased in the concealing fog when the asylum's collapse began. Silas had a perfect view of it through the narrow back window.

He touched his lips absently to Pitch's hair, hugging the daemon in closer. The wing they had just fled collapsed at the middle, the two halves tilting in towards one another as a great rent, like a knife drawn through a cake, tore down the middle. Chimney pots toppled, and windows burst as the storeys came down upon one another, their weight forcing the one beneath to crumble. A huge plume of dust and debris defied the heavy rain to rise upwards. There were distant screams, and the throngs scattered, their garb made brilliant white as a blast of lightning came to highlight the Fulbourn as it fell apart.

'Oh god, do you think everyone was out?' Silas whispered.

'I'm sure they were.' Bess leaned forward to pat his knee. 'The Lady will have seen to it.'

He glanced at Sybilla, hoping to see the Valkyrie nod. The angel stared grimly ahead, watching the destruction.

'It is always the weak who suffer when the strong make mistakes, Silas,' she said. 'You'd do well to remember that.'

CHAPTER 36

P itch knew himself to be dreaming, a sublime imagining where he teased his tongue at Silas's lips, darting it between them but nipping away before the ankou got the deeper kiss he was begging for. Pitch was laughing, giggling if he were honest, like a bloody maiden with her beau, all manner of happy silliness filling him. They were laid out on a soft patch of grass, surrounded by an array of flowers, all shades of the rainbow, bobbing grasses rustling with the touch of a clement breeze. They were very much naked, and both hard as headstones, cocks glancing against one another like hesitant lovers.

Silas slid a hand between Pitch's legs, encouraging his knees to part, a move that needed little encouragement and stirred him so hard the dream wavered.

Pitch tried to grasp at the frail edges, but he was dragged from the depths of slumber.

Awake.

Pitch opened his eyes.

He was curled up on a window seat, laid on tapestry cushions that surrounded him in a low fortress of softness. His cock hard up against his belly. Blankets had been laid over him, smelling faintly of lemon and divinely velvet against his skin. The seat filled the deep recess of a bay window, broad enough that he could have shared it with Silas if the ankou were not outside. With Charlie.

Pitch luxuriated in the gentle stupor of being only half-awake, eyes heavy-lidded as he watched them. The ankou and the purebred sat a little too close, if he was being particular, but he knew the joy that must be Silas's right now. He would be beside himself with relief to have found that odd little creature.

And if Pitch closed one eye and tilted his head just so, he could block Charlie from his view anyway.

The pair sat on a garden bench in feeble wintery sunshine. They were in the midst of a garden that looked not to have seen a gardener's hand in some time. The bare-boned apple trees beyond where they sat were swamped by tall grasses that were making ground on much of the rest of the garden. He thought he spied a few garden beds, a few naked, crooked rose bushes, all stripped back and burying their beauty until spring came calling again, but he cared little for the landscape.

The lad held out his arm and pushed up his shirtsleeve. Ottelie's bracelet was still on his wrist, though Pitch could make out little detail. Silas stared down at it in some awe. That much Pitch *could* discern, for the ankou's hair was yet to return to its longer lengths and was slicked back against the sides of his head. He held Charlie's hand with his fingertips, turning it to and fro, saying something to the vagabond that caused him to smile and shake his head.

'I bet he's asking if it hurts,' Pitch muttered.

Silas did not like those he cared for to be in any pain at all. He was inexorable in that.

Pitch exhaled, relaxing into the view. Silas would be pleased to know how little Pitch's back bothered him. He glanced at his arm. The gouge he had made to conceal the watch had knitted so well as to be hardly visible at all, but seeing the faint scar brought reality swooping in with a nasty rush.

The Fulbourn had been a nightmare.

He had come very near to losing the ankou...to losing himself.

But he'd *found* Edward.

Gods. Pitch shifted, no longer so comfortable.

Even though he had watched the lieutenant cast divine magick, had seen the glint of angelfire in his eyes and heard that all-too-familiar command in his voice, Pitch *still* could not believe that the Seraph had truly returned.

Pitch had languished in an abaddon, had nearly turned himself inside out with grief and guilt, and had been cast from Arcadia believing himself a murderous, senseless creature.

And Seraphiel had lived.

He scowled.

The angel was capable of being a huge arsehole, that was no revelation. But would he go so far as to stage his own demise? He was clearly obsessed with the cursed halo, willing to try anything to undo the mistake he'd made on the Day of Ruination: hold a Dominion prince hostage and contort him to create a beast of burden for his almighty will.

But what purpose would faking his own death serve?

Pitch curled his toes, feet bare beneath the blankets.

Enoch's rage at Seraphiel's death had been a tangible force, as real as the heat of the creation fire the Lord of Arcadia reigned over. And Lucifer's hatred of Prince Vassago, the one he believed the angel's murderer, was strong enough to curdle a bucket of milk.

Both Enoch and Lucifer were in true mourning.

They believed Seraphiel dead. And there seemed small chance Enoch would not notice a deception if it existed.

Raph had died that day upon the cliff.

So what was Pitch seeing in the lieutenant? A resurrection? A haunting? Had the watch birthed something akin to a tsukumogami? If an object was old enough and handled often enough by the living, it was capable of growing a spirit, an entity that could learn to mimic the living so well it was indistinguishable from them. Maybe this wasn't Edward or Seraphiel at all, but a spirit that knew how to mimic them both.

Pitch clucked his tongue at the idiotic notion. No spirit he'd ever known or heard of was capable of casting divine magick. They certainly weren't capable of sending Pitch's wildness scurrying back into its cage like a petulant bear and removing the burn from the halo's mark with a single touch.

Pitch wriggled deeper into his blankets. He should move his arse off this seat and find the lieutenant, see what state the poor bastard was in.

I must take you there.

I know the way.

Edward's words, spoken as the Fulbourn bore down on them. He was speaking of Seraphiel's Sanctuary. And if it were true that the lieutenant knew the way, then he was the only one who did.

So was this why the watch bade Pitch find Edward? Seraphiel had made him a living map?

Pitch curled in on himself, wishing desperately to return to the dream. Not yet ready for another conversation with Edward...or whatever anomaly he'd become.

As though Silas sensed Pitch's worrying thoughts, he looked up. Their eyes met. The sunshine was paltry, but it was as though the strongest beams found the ankou's face, framing his smile. He spoke hurriedly to Charlie, who looked Pitch's way. The lad smiled broadly, squeezing Silas's arm as they both rose to their feet.

Go. Go. Charlie's words were clear on his lips.

The ankou broke into a run towards the house. Towards Pitch.

He wore a coat of azure blue which fanned around his ankles as he moved, gold buttons fabulous with the touch of the sun. For a moment Pitch thought it the ankou's favourite Inverness coat, but this one was a shade brighter and did not sit quite so perfectly upon his broad shoulders. A fine replica but the other suited him better somehow.

Silas held Pitch's gaze, grinning like the dolt he was, until he was forced to turn with the path that led off to the left and presumably a door that would allow him inside.

Pitch sat up, fluttering his fingers as Charlie gave him a wave. The lad turned suddenly and waved again. Old Bess sauntered into view, a grey cloak covering whatever extravagance was undoubtedly beneath. He offered Charlie his arm, but Pitch did not bother to watch the pair any longer.

Silas would be here very shortly.

A stirring in his belly, like a plethora of moths had been set loose, had him running his hands across his stomach. For once it was not the wildness to blame. That tempestuous creature had not stirred since

Edward's touch. But, foolishly, Pitch would almost have preferred to feel its movements. Anything was better than this silly, nervous excitement.

He let the blankets fall into his lap. He wore a nightshirt, clean and scented with a hint of lavender. He was naked beneath it. The notion that it was likely Silas who had stripped him down and tended to him reawakened the arousal of the dream. Pitch touched at his hair, judging its state, finding it mussed and tangled, rough with horrid things still. A bath was in order. But at least his limbs seemed to have been washed down, and his face, caught in the reflection in the glass, appeared wiped clean of the Sanctuary's smears.

Pitch swung his legs over the edge of the window seat, pleased with how easy it was to do so. He could feel nothing of the tightness of the amuletum at his back. It had not been replenished, and yet no angry aches and pains plagued him.

So far.

The sitting room he was in was a cosy affair, with a wall of books and a couple of armchairs resting before a healthy fire, and there was a faint waft of something baking beyond the closed doors.

His bare feet searched for the ground and touched instead on something cool and hard and rounded. He'd almost trodden on a pile of tangled necklaces, pearls mostly, along with a hairbrush, a mahogany comb and a hand mirror with a soft embroidered back needled with a posy of violets.

As he scowled down at the collection, the doors to the sitting room opened in a rush. Pitch raised his head, the ankou's name on his lips.

But it was not Silas at all.

'Fire man.'

The squeal might have annoyed him far more if all his attention were not stolen by the sight. The irritating child from the Crimson Bow entered the room in a peculiar fashion. Tilly sat perched atop the skriker like a tiny jockey. Fat little hands stuck into coarse black fur, her chubby legs clad in yellow knickerbockers, a white linen blouse covering the rest. Her fair hair, near to snow in colour, was caught up in all manner of clips and bows that sparkled as Silas's hound lumbered across the rug, baleful eyes set on Pitch as it went.

'Fire man,' the child said again, those distinctive olive-green eyes with their rim of amber were wide with delight. A dreadful smear of claret marred her lips. She had evidently decided to play with someone's rouge with disastrous results.

Pitch drew his legs back up onto the window seat. 'Shoo.' He flicked his fingers. 'Go away. Both of you.'

Forneus heaved a sigh and plonked himself down just shy of the gathering of trinkets on the floor. Tilly dismounted with all the grace of a lush arriving home after a night of swizzling. She thumped on the ground. Momentum rolled her onto her side, but she managed to keep ahold of the article she clutched in one bunched fist. A flash of blue and white came from it as she got to her feet and toddled towards him.

'Oh shit, go away...Silas!' How long did it take the blasted ankou to negotiate a few rooms? 'Silas, for fu–' He caught himself. 'Where the blazes are you?'

'You safe.' Tilly was a determined little changeling, no doubt about it. Forneus trotted off to lump himself in front of the fire, no use at all. 'You safe now, fire man.'

She reached out, uncurling her stubby little fingers. She held the pair to the amber earring she'd given him, the one with a tiny flower embedded in the rock and a gold leaf forming the clasp. Pitch had handed the one he'd had over to the itchy, bloodied man in Fulbourn.

'I don't want your earring.'

Tilly was not taking no for an answer. She grabbed at the blankets, meaning to hoist herself up.

Footsteps thumped into the room. And finally, there he was. Pink-cheeked, slightly wild-eyed, his jawline shaded dark with the creeping return of his beard giving him an unkempt, deliciously brutish look.

'What's wrong?' Silas scanned the room.

'This.' Pitch jabbed his finger at the child, who leaned over the edge of the seat, legs dangling, trying to draw herself up by using the blanket as a climbing rope. 'What is it doing here?'

'Damn it, don't frighten me like that.' Silas exhaled. 'It was not safe to leave Tilly and her mothers behind. Likely Old Bess will harbour them at Harvington Hall once arrangements have been made.'

'And we are where?'

'It belongs to a benefactor of Ada and Nancy's who went abroad years ago and decided not to return. He'd always extended an invitation to them to use it when they saw fit...' Silas lifted his arms. 'And well, they saw fit. We are a decent way from Cambridge, a few hours northeast. The Fulbourn is far behind us.'

Pitch could not help his shudder. 'Why were we not taken back to the Village? To London?'

Silas made his way across the room, glancing at Forneus by the fire. 'There are some concerns that it is not so secure as we may like. I told Satine of how the sorceress seemed to know you'd been ill for days with the Gu, of how they seemed to know of your phone call to Kaneko too, plus the places that appeared in the Sanctuary, like the hallway from The Atlas. She did not take it well.'

'Have them start with Kaneko if they are looking for a traitor.'

'Any reason?' Silas leaned against the wall beside the window. 'Or just because he does not fill your glasses as full as you'd like at The Atlas?'

Pitch's scowl veered too close to a smile. There was something oddly pleasant in being known so well. 'He was at the soirée. He might have noticed me and alerted them. Did Macha not say there was a tsukumogami at the marquess's ball they used to watch you tread on people's feet?'

'She did, but is that to say every single tsukumogami is a spy? Could not the phone at The Atlas be rigged somehow? Besides, at the soirée the elixir was still working well. Kaneko didn't know you were there. And Macha said Mr Fothergill was their peeping Tom there.'

'Regardless.' Pitch huffed at the common sense. 'Kaneko is a terrible barkeep.'

Silas's placating smile should have been very annoying, but clearly Pitch was not himself, for he thought it rather charming.

'Well,' the ankou said. 'If not for your call to Kaneko, the Order might never have found us. When you rang, he recalled hearing a lot of goings-on in the background and thought he might have heard the name of the venue but couldn't bring it to mind. He agreed to let the Lady and Mr Ahari try and find the memory and delve into it. He even brought the umbrella that birthed him out of hiding so they might use it to delve deeper. That does not sound to me like someone who is a traitor.' No. It certainly did not. The object that birthed a tsukumogami was fiercely guarded, for it was the heart of the spirit. Without it, they ceased to exist. But Pitch made a nonchalant sound, not committing an opinion either way, and Silas continued, 'Once they had the name, it took time to realise the Crimson Bow was not in London at all. Apparently, it was quite the task. We certainly did not make it easy to be rescued.'

'How were we to know we'd need to be so?' Pitch raised a languid shrug. 'Anyway, that hardly venerates Kaneko. His memory loss could still have been a ploy. One which gave the Morrigan plenty of time to bury us deep.'

Silas sighed. 'My dear, I fear we gave them plenty of that ourselves.'

The words weren't meant to be unkind, for the ankou rarely was, but Pitch flinched nonetheless. The blame for the entire cock-up could be laid squarely at Pitch's feet. 'Is Mr Ahari still here?' he asked. 'Perhaps we should speak with him now.' He edged his foot under the blanket so he could poke at the child, who was making some headway on her attempt to scale the seat.

'No.' Silas shook his head. 'He's called some conference of the kitsunes of London together, trying to find trace of Ernest Weatherby. I think they believe him a weak link in the scheme of things. Isaac and Matilda went with him, and it's been agreed that any rumours of our demise will not be refuted. There's a chance the Morrigan may believe we did not escape. The seal was opened a mere crack to free us, I'm told. At the very least they may believe not *all* of us survived. Lady Satine has gone to organise Sanu and Lalassu to be brought to us. She will be back within a day or two.'

Pitch's mood dipped a little lower. 'Edward told her, then? About where we are to go next?'

Silas's face shadowed. 'No...but did he tell you?'

'He did.' Pitch glanced at Tilly. 'A place only he can lead us.'

Silas looked pained. 'Edward is not well, Pitch. Sybilla is with him now, but he has a terrible fever and isn't lucid. I've only just managed to get Charlie out of his sickroom this hour, out into the fresh air. He's barely left the lieutenant's side.'

But Pitch was not interested in the lad playing nurse. 'Sybilla? The Valkyrie is here?'

Silas nodded. 'It was she who was able to pierce the Morrigan's seal and free us. Well, her magick...and whatever it was Edward did. I'm afraid it has cost him rather dearly, Pitch. He's awfully weak. Where is it we must go? What did he say?' Silas crouched down beside Tilly.

'The angel's Sanctuary. That's where we are to go.' Pitch rushed the words before they choked him. He'd have preferred to learn he was to go straight to Blood Lake rather than wander those halls again, now made all the worse for knowing how used there he'd been.

Silas drew in a breath, and his expression veered dangerously close to pity. 'Oh, Pitch...'

'For the gods' sake, Mercer, don't look at me like that. A trip down memory lane is hardly the worst of my worries.'

Silas's hands twitched. Damn him, he seemed to be considering one of his hugs. So Pitch did the most sensible thing. He gave Tilly's shoulder a hard nudge and toppled the child off its summit. It fell with a thump on its backside on the floorboards. The child's bottom lip did very strange things, wriggling about like a lizard's cut tail.

'Blast it, Pitch.' Silas scooped up the child a moment before it released the most god-awful racket. 'Be gentle, she is just a babe.'

He bounced the mewling brat in his arms, pacing over to where Forneus had lifted his broad head, ears flattened back as he glared at Pitch.

'There, there,' Silas soothed.

Pitch did not like the brush of guilt he felt at having dispensed with the child so roughly. So what if the ankou might think less of him? With an indignant huff, Pitch gathered up his blankets and got to his feet. The earring flashed golden as it fell from the folds and hit the floor, skidding to the edge of the rug. He had been preparing to march off in a huff, but he felt inclined to gather up the changeling's gift.

The child's tears turned to quieter sniffs, Silas still muttering consoling nonsense. He set her down next to the skriker, patted the hound's head, and ruffled the girl's snowy strands before he straightened. By the time he was upright, the child was busy removing one of her hair clips to tie it to the hound's fur, only the dampness on her face showing any sign she'd been upset to begin with.

Pitch stared down at the earring as Silas approached. He could not bring himself to look at the ankou, fearing he'd see disapproval there and knowing it was rightly deserved.

'She is fast to recover,' Silas said quietly, stepping behind him. 'But perhaps you could be kinder next time she wishes to sit with you?'

The ankou wrapped his arms about Pitch's middle, bringing with him that sense of impermeability that Pitch craved so much.

'I suppose so.'

Silas touched his lips to Pitch's cheek. 'How are you feeling?' he whispered. The heat of his breath sent shivers down Pitch's neck. 'Does your back pain you? Be honest now.'

'Honestly, it does not. I feel...' Pitch frowned. 'I feel quite well, all told. Surprisingly so.'

'I am very glad.' Another soft kiss, this one to the lobe of Pitch's ear. 'You slept so soundly overnight, not a single nightmare. You barely stirred. I poked you once just to ensure you hadn't left me.' He nuzzled his lips in behind Pitch's ear, kissing the thin skin there. 'Forgive me but I didn't have the heart to replenish the amuletum... You looked so very peaceful, and did not seem in any pain.'

'Have you been watching me sleep, Mr Mercer?'

'Would it bother you if I had, Mr Astaroth?'

Pitch did not pause. 'Not at all.' He felt Silas's smile, felt the roughness of the ankou's returning stubble against his cheek.

'I am so very pleased you are not in any discomfort.' Silas's mouth rested near Pitch's temple, his bulk pressed in tight. 'After all you did...' He ran his fingers beneath the arm of the nightshirt, whispering his touch against Pitch's skin. 'I saw how close Edward went to the flame. I saw him touch you...right where the mark lies. I saw him...cast magick.' Silas kissed him again and held his lips against Pitch's hair. They stood that way a long while before Silas spoke again. 'You are not the only one the angel has meddled with, are you, my dear?'

Pitch sighed and tilted his head, resting against Silas's shoulder. 'No. I am not.'

The ankou's embrace firmed, taking Pitch's weight so his feet barely needed to touch the floor at all. 'When you are ready to speak of it...I will listen.'

Pitch pressed into the contours of Silas's body, needing those far more than he did the ankou's ears. 'And you? Are you wounds from the Dullahan gone?'

The headless bastard with Pitch's flesh upon his tongue. The Erlking was a fool if he thought there was any chance of claiming his prize, but if that creature laid a hand upon Silas again, the Unseelie Court would know wrath.

'They are. And not a scar remains from your flame... Is it terrible I'm rather disappointed with that? I wouldn't have minded a souvenir of your handiwork.'

Pitch nudged his backside against Silas's thigh. 'Did you expect anything less than perfection from me, Mr Mercer?'

Silas laughed against the nape of Pitch's neck. 'Certainly not.'

They swayed where they stood, and it was lovelier than the finest dance.

'Tell me, how is Charlie?' Pitch said, closing his eyes as he sank into the ankou.

'Remarkably well, though he says he has something he wishes to speak to me about, but seems reticent to do so. I was trying to press it out of him when we saw that you had awoken.'

'Likely he's just going to tell you he fancies Edward. I hope you shall not be too heartbroken, my dear oaf, but it seems the pair of them formed quite a bond in the madhouse.'

Silas laughed, and Pitch savoured every morsel of the sound.

'Apparently so. I'm glad for them both, I must say.' If Pitch searched for sign of any jealousy on the ankou's part, he saw none of it whatsoever. 'Though I'll be happiest when Charlie is away from all this once more.'

Pitch stayed silent, quite certain that day was far from near.

'Our room is lovely,' Silas continued. 'The bed is ridiculously large. I feared I'd lost you in it a couple of times.' Another kiss, another stroke of the hand. 'But after twelve hours, I was done with sleeping. I hope you don't mind that I brought you down here. I wanted to be near when you woke, and I thought you'd appreciate the sunlight.' His other hand traced Pitch's hip as he spoke. 'It has been quite the couple of days, has it not?'

Pitch nodded. Silas lifted a hand to touch at the earring.

'She found us, you know,' he said.

'What?'

Silas turned them around so they were facing the fireplace, and the hound and child before it.

'Adamaris told me that the afternoon we left for Fulbourn, Tilly was inconsolable, demanding to be taken to her fire man. She wouldn't let go of the twin to the earring she'd given you.'

'She'd forced on me...'

Silas nuzzled again behind Pitch's ear, breathing him in. 'Forneus turned up at the Crimson Bow several hours after we left. Can you imagine? You'd think they would have slammed the door in his face, I think Nancy would like to even now, but Adamaris I suspect understands something of what Tilly is. She said the child's uniqueness is unearthly at times.' Silas smiled. 'So, when Tilly wanted the skriker allowed in, threw a tantrum until it was done, she relented.' Silas cleared his throat. 'He went straight to the private box apparently.'

'Well, more the fool him,' Pitch declared. 'He would have copped a snout full of scents there.'

Silas chuckled, slipping his fingers between the buttons of Pitch's nightshirt. 'Very true.'

'What then?' Pitch prodded.

'Then we found ourselves readying a carriage and taking our four-year-old daughter and an enormous wolfhound to an asylum because she would not stop crying for it.' Adamaris stood in the doorway, far less jubilant than when Pitch had seen her last. Tugging at the black shawl around her shoulders, she let her gaze settle on Tilly, who still insisted on giving Forneus a finer hairdo.

Silas pulled back but not away and kept his arms about Pitch's waist.

'She has always had an affinity with nature,' Adamaris went on. 'She likes to sneak out in a rainstorm and sit in the puddles, climbs the highest tree in the blink of an eye and gives us heart attacks. Put an ailing plant in her room and within a day or two it would set itself right. There were always butterflies at her window. Birds used to settle on her perambulator when she was a baby.'

She inhaled and breathed out slowly. Pitch was curious as to how a dryad fae had ended up in the women's care. Dryads were not unheard of as changelings but rare. It was a question for another time though.

'Nancy will need time to come to grips with all this... Hell, I will too, but I think I saw it before now, that Tilly was special. She wanted to get out of the carriage as soon as we were through the gates at Fulbourn, said the trees were calling her. She opened the door and slipped out before I could stop her, with your dog in tow. I thought I'd never find her. Never felt so sick in my life. Nancy didn't even know I'd taken her there, how was I going to explain that I'd lost our daughter on the grounds of a lunatic asylum with a stray dog?'

Her laughter bordered on hysterical. Pitch and Silas waited for her to continue.

'I found her after half an hour of searching...sitting up in an oak tree's branches, crying, saying that the trees said bad things were happening in the earth. A nurse who was out escorting a patient was trying to coax her down. The patient had the earring on him apparently. Tilly's earring. They were the only thing she had on her when she was found abandoned, no clothes, just a blanket and that pair of amber earrings pinned to it. I would know them anywhere. But this fellow insisted it had been given to him...by an angel.' Pitch stiffened at the poor analogy. 'He handed it over quick smart when your dog started snarling.' Adamaris looked to them. 'I asked after you both, but the secretary I spoke to denied anyone of your description had visited the Fulbourn that day. Tilly cried herself to sleep on the way home and wouldn't let go of the earring. Liars, she said, bad place. The trees told her that you were there, she said. But she's happy now, very happy. I can tell because there are asters blooming outside her window today.' Adamaris's sigh was heavy, in the way that those who are beyond bamboozled can manage. 'The flowerbox only had old soil in it yesterday...not to mention it is winter.'

Pitch stared at the frost-haired child humming alongside the skriker. Well, he'd not been expecting that tall tale. He supposed he might as well keep the earring awhile, then.

'Sybilla believes that the Morrigan placed some type of deflection hex on the Fulbourn,' Silas said, moving to one side but keeping an arm about Pitch. 'And that is why Forneus could only trace me as far as the Crimson Bow. He had no sense of me elsewhere. Sybilla had been in Oxford on the search and was closest to reach us when word came in of the theatre. But she said she too would have moved on were Tilly and Forneus not so insistent we were to be found there. There was no inkling of magick, no trace of us at all. The Morrigan had concealed their nest well. The child and her family played a big part in our rescue.'

'And I'm not sure that family shall ever be the same,' Adamaris said quietly. She moved to gather up her daughter. 'Time for your afternoon nap, my sweetheart.' The child only protested a little at being removed. Forneus breathed a hefty exhale and lay his head upon his front paws, watching the dryad child as her mother carried her to the doorway. Adamaris paused, turning back.

'Those strawberry tarts you asked for are coming out of the oven shortly, Silas. And the bathwater has just been drawn. It may be too warm yet, but I've had the tub set up in your room as you requested.'

'Thank you Adamaris, for everything. I'm sorry you have been thrown into all this. I hope you understand the Order's need to keep your family protected.' Silas inclined his head towards the little girl, who rested, thumb in mouth, head heavy on her mother's shoulder. Adamaris nodded, a fierce set to her features. She turned and headed out of the room.

'Sleep well, Tilly,' Silas called.

The child wiggled her tiny fingers, eyes already closing as she was carried away.

'Please, by all the gods, tell me those tarts are for me?' Pitch fairly drooled.

'I wouldn't dream of eating them without you.' Silas gathered Pitch to him and leaned in to steal a kiss. A full press of lips with a quick dart of searching tongue. He pulled away, leaving Pitch open-mouthed and leaning in for more. 'And I know you are fond of a hot bath. I figured one was in order. I tried to clean you up best as I could, but I didn't wish to wake you.'

Pitch melted against him, setting aside all thoughts of headless horsemen and Sanctuaries, cursed halos and the lieutenant. Sybilla was with Edward, so he was in good hands. Safe hands. Their meeting could wait.

'Well, I'm awake now,' he said. 'But I am feeling rather faint.'

Silas raised his brows. 'Is that so?'

'Terribly so. I dare say I shan't trust myself to bathe in this state.' Pitch angled his hips, teasing at the stiffness in Silas's trousers. 'I'll need a good scrub to remove all this nasty dirt.' He pressed onto his toes, his full weight against Silas, who didn't waver in the slightest. Pitch leaned close to his ear. 'Would you bathe with me perhaps?'

'I...bathe...with you...' Silas's hold tightened, and a hushed breath escaped him. 'Do you think the tub could take us both?'

Pitch had been certain the ankou would decline. Now his mind was afire with thought of Silas settled behind him in the bath, rubbing him down with a firm hand and decent piece of soap.

'I shall make certain we both fit,' Pitch rushed. 'We'll find a way, if you would like to try.'

'I would.' Silas released Pitch from his embrace and took his hand. The ankou was trembling. 'I would like to try it, very much. With you. Only with you. For I trust you most of all.'

Gods, there was every chance Pitch's heart was going to thump itself onto the floor between them. The fire popped, and Pitch nearly flew out of his skin.

'Trust me? After all I've put us through? Perhaps the heat of my flame melted what remained of your good sense.'

'Or made the truth burn brighter.' Silas tugged at his hand, a gentle urging for Pitch to follow. 'I trust you *because* of all that we have been through, not despite it. The Fulbourn was a mistake, but it was *our* mistake, Pitch. There is much to speak of, I know, but we shall do so when you are clean and warm and dressed. I've asked Bess to have a selection of corsets brought from Harvington Hall. You should see this marvellous chest he has in his room. It's been bringing all manner of things to us from the hall. Fae magick, I'm told, but nothing so dreadful as we've encountered so far.' He brushed a hand against his coat. 'Bess arranged to have this delivered for me. It fits wonderfully.'

'Lovely, but the original is a better shade of blue for your complexion.'

'Do you think so?' Silas seemed pleased Pitch had noticed such a detail.

'I do. You are very handsome in the Inverness.'

The duck of the ankou's head was achingly sweet. 'You think me handsome?'

'*Very* handsome.' Pitch smiled at the scarlet patches creeping up Silas's neck. 'The tarts, the bath...the corsets from the hall...you've done all that...for me?'

Was the air thin in this room? Pitch was light-headed, a little dizzy.

'Of course. And I would do so much more.' But Silas's bright smile wavered. 'You mustn't feel obliged, though. If you want none of it –'

Pitch touched his fingertips to the ankou's lips. 'I want it all, Sickle.'

'Then, Mr Astaroth,' he kissed Pitch's fingers, 'will you allow me to take you upstairs and see to all your needs?'

'I should like that very much, Mr Mercer.' Pitch's bare feet seemed to float an inch above the floor. 'Very much indeed.'

Danielle K Girl is an Aussie who lives in stunning Tasmania with her three furkids, cats Luffy, Sweetie and Ren.

Her idea of heaven would be owning a farm full of rescue animals and a vegie garden that sprouted peanut M&M's and chocolate wheaten biscuits, with a never-ending supply of K-dramas on her big-screen TV.

Join the newsletter - Get a **FREE** D K Girl novella!

If you'd like to receive DK's monthly newsletter AND a FREE Dystopian novella as a thank you, then head to....

https://daniellekgirl.com/subscribe/

Find D K Girl online:

https://daniellekgirl.com/

https://www.instagram.com/daniellekgirl/

www.ingramcontent.com/pod-product-compliance
Lightning Source LLC
Chambersburg PA
CBHW050114120726
47904CB00004B/1349

* 9 7 8 0 6 4 5 3 2 7 4 6 5 *